MISS HAWTHORNE'S UNLIKELY HUSBAND

The Troublemakers Trilogy
Book 3

by

Addy Du Lac

ARE YOU SIGNED UP FOR DRAGONBLADE'S BLOG?

You'll get the latest news and information on exclusive giveaways, exclusive excerpts, coming releases, sales, free books, cover reveals and more.

Check out our complete list of authors, too!

No spam, no junk. That's a promise!

Sign Up Here

www.dragonbladepublishing.com

Dearest Reader;

Thank you for your support of a small press. At Dragonblade Publishing, we strive to bring you the highest quality Historical Romance from some of the best authors in the business. Without your support, there is no 'us', so we sincerely hope you adore these stories and find some new favorite authors along the way.

Happy Reading!

CEO, Dragonblade Publishing

**Additional Dragonblade books by
Author Addy Du Lac**

The Troublemakers Trilogy
Miss Thornfield's Daring Bargain (Book 1)
Miss Mason's Secret Baron (Book 2)
Miss Hawthorne's Unlikely Husband (Book 3)

Dedication

To Mom for allowing me to get a degree in creative writing.

To Dad and Auntie Joyce for starting me on my professional path.

To my siblings for always supporting my writing.

To my village, thank you for always giving me insight, listening to my rambling, having my back and loving me through all disappearances and anti-social behaviors.

For Ashley, my water goddess, here's our man!

PROLOGUE

Miss Pollitt's School for Young Ladies
Hertfordshire, June 1846

T HEY HAD STOLEN the boat again. In Elodia's opinion, 'stolen' was too strong a word, even if it was the one most commonly used when she and her friends wanted to spend time on the lake. After all, the boat in question never left the premises and they always returned it.

There was nothing Elodia loved more than open water. She loved visiting any beach and swimming in the ocean. She had even enjoyed the months long journey from Trinidad to England via France she'd taken last year. If she had been home, her father would have taken her out on his sailboat. As it was, she had to make do with dangling her bare feet in the cool but murky lake waters on the grounds of Miss Pollitt's.

It was early summer, soon they would all return to their family homes for the summer break and then again, for the autumn break in September. Maybe she would be able to persuade Ada and Regina to spend time with her over the break at her father's estate. She didn't want to have to return to being alone. For Elodia, despite her status as the daughter of a viscount, finding companionship had still been an issue. She loved her father but she had never felt out of place as his daughter or lonely until he'd moved them to England. It was a strange existence, knowing that her social status was higher than most and yet her acceptance in the ton was always an unspoken question with no real answer so far. At Miss Pollitt's, she at least had people who liked her as she was, and didn't see her nature as something to be fixed or endured.

"Ellie, are you engaged already?" Regina asked. All three of them were laying on their backs in the small rowboat, staring up at the sky, counting clouds, or dreading prospective marriage arrangements.

Marriage was the furthest thing from Elodia's mind. She wanted to be a fine lady, like her Aunt Theo was, for her own sake, not to attract some milksop gentleman to accuse her of his own inadequacies. "No, are you?" Was that strange? Should she be?

"Since I was fourteen. I'm only here as part of my preparation for it."

Elodia wasn't certain she'd like Regina's parents at all. What on earth were they thinking contracting her into a marriage at such a young age? "Do you know who he is?"

"I know I am to be the Baroness Starkley. Other than that, I know nothing."

"Is that usual?"

"I think so," Ada said. "Engagements can happen at any time, honestly. It's the wedding that usually happens later."

"The later the better, I say," Regina grumbled.

Elodia heartily agreed. "Are you engaged, Ada?"

Ada shook her head. "My brother hasn't mentioned it to me either. If I was, I think he'd let me know. But your father is a viscount, Ellie," Ada continued. "How soon do you think you'll have to marry once you are out?"

Elodia hardly knew the answer to that question. By most measures she was accomplished enough. True, she had been raised in the British colony of Trinidad, but her education had been no less thorough. She already knew her languages and played the piano to perfection. She knew all the popular and expected dances, sketched, rode and could match anyone in needlework. Well, that may have been an exaggeration. Her needlework could be better, and her watercolors were recognizable at best.

What had reportedly worried her father the most was her lack of socialization. Perhaps she didn't need to rely on accomplishments as much as others had claimed. She had made two new friends so far, and neither had required any knowledge of social graces. All she had used was what her parents had modeled and instilled in her since birth. Integrity, uncompromising moral courage and a touch of violence. It hadn't mattered to her earlier that year, what the Chinese girl she'd defended from bullies did afterwards, or if she would be in trouble for using violence. All that had mattered to Elodia in the moment was ensuring the blonde witch understood that she, Elodia Hawthorne, wouldn't tolerate her behavior.

The more she thought about it, the more the idea of the marriage mart filled Elodia with anxiety. From what she had been told, marriage would be tricky if she wasn't seen as capable of blending in or partaking in society, and at sixteen, the social niceties were still beyond her. She still didn't understand why they would be so important in finding a husband. Surely marriage was based on more important things than musical ability, politesse and linguistics.

But all of that was nothing compared to what she saw as her worst feature. Elodia knew she was pretty enough from the neck up. She had been blessed with high cheekbones, wide, beautifully shaped eyes, long lashes, and a well-formed if overly full mouth. But that was where the blessings had ended because her figure was nonexistent. A flat chest, and a shape like a loaf of bread according to her nanny. Nothing to entice or draw the eye of anyone.

She didn't know who was to blame, her mother, her father or the good Lord Almighty, but either way, she had complaints about it. As a child her nurse had called it a blessing, a way to avoid unwanted attention from lusty men who preyed on young girls, especially young black ones like her. But now she was approaching the age where she'd need to attract interest, it was a point of concern, most particularly because it meant that the man she married, more than likely wouldn't be attracted to her.

"I don't think he wants me to marry too soon. He doesn't really speak of it to me at all."

"Do you think he wants to marry?" Regina asked.

"I imagine he'll have to at some point. He needs an heir after all." Although truth be told, she didn't know what she would do when that happened. Her mother died trying to give him one.

She blinked back hot tears and took a deep breath, trying to push past the painful ache that always sprung up whenever she thought of her mother. Giselle Hawthorne, Elodia's late mother, had been dead for two years, but the pain had barely subsided. Her death had been swift and unexpected. Elodia's nanny had taken her to church to pray for her mother's safety and then to the beach while her mother gave birth to what would have been Elodia's little brother and her father's heir. In the morning, Ellie was expecting a new sibling, and by nightfall, her mother was gone along with her baby brother.

Elodia still remembered her mother clearly from her wide smile and gentle voice, to her favorite earrings and her scent of lilies and cloves. She still missed her terribly, especially on sunny days like this one, missed the way she always hugged her a little too tightly whenever they swam in the ocean, her sweet voice whenever she sang to herself, and her steely insistence whenever she encouraged Elodia to ask questions.

She couldn't imagine her father with a woman who wasn't her mother. Her father had defied convention and every social expectation when he'd married her mother, a freed slave. They'd kept the particulars from her, but there were two things Elodia knew for sure. Their courtship and married life had come with extreme adversity and her parents had loved each other enormously.

Would Elodia be so lucky? She doubted it. But she was lucky enough that while her wish was to marry a good man and have a family, her happiness and livelihood wouldn't depend on it. A hefty dowry and inheritance made certain of that. Perhaps she could stay a merry spinster and spend her life pleasing herself and traveling the world.

"You're so lucky to have your father, Ellie. You hear such horror stories of fathers not caring about their daughters when their mothers pass on."

"He's a good egg." She wondered if it had ever occurred to him to send her away after her mother had passed so unexpectedly in childbirth. In response, Elodia's father had chosen instead to pull her even closer, electing to stay with her at their home until his father died, finally forcing him to return to his homeland. Elodia had never met her grandfather, but from what she'd heard, she was glad he had stayed a stranger.

Her father had been determined to keep him as far away from Elodia and her mother as long as possible. Her father had never really spoken warmly of England, but when he'd announced his intention to return, there had been no hesitation. He would not spend months away from his child; Elodia was coming with him. She wasn't sure she could thank him for that. She was sure England had its advantages but she hadn't seen them so far. Left to her own devices, she would much rather have stayed in Trinidad, with its beaches, delicious food, ready sunshine and warm people.

"Do you think we should bring the boat back now?" Regina asked. "Based on the position of the sun, it's nearly two in the afternoon."

Elodia glanced at her in bewilderment, the ache in her throat finally subsiding. "How do you do that?"

Regina was full of surprises. True, they hadn't been friends very long, but the sheer range of her abilities from dance and military tactics to tracking and navigation was uncanny.

Regina merely shrugged. "It's like a sundial," she replied.

Elodia glanced at Ada who was also staring at her with wide, mystified eyes.

Regina rolled her eyes. "My father taught me. It's not always exact but I can manage a decent approximation."

Elodia shook her head, "Just take an oar and row."

It was things like this that made Regina and Ada indispensable. How could she focus on the gaping hole her mother had left behind when she was trying to figure out why her new friend had the practical skills of a scout? In a matter of minutes they were back at the dock. Faintly Elodia heard a bell ringing. "Oh, blast, we're late for tea," Regina grumbled.

"It's only the third time, it can't be too much of an issue," Ada said.

"Says you," Regina fretted, clambering to her feet, "if they write to my mother about this, she'll pull me out of school and I'll be stuck in a room with nothing but dry old tutors until they ship me off to Lord Pecksniffian the Third of the Cheshire Prigs."

Elodia snorted a laugh and scrambled up onto the dock first while Ada threw the rope for her to tie it off. Just as she finished the knot, a shadow fell over her. Tentatively, she glanced over her shoulder, ready to face a livid teacher or groundskeeper and was met with the sight of the most gorgeous man she'd ever seen. He was frowning playfully, his dark, silky hair falling into his shining dark eyes, and a slight beard covered his sharp jaw. He was tall, broad shouldered and almost impeccably dressed. Everything about him was just an inch shy of correct, from the length of his hair to the cut of his suit, as if he'd lost weight and missed his barber.

"Xiao, mèimei?" he said, drawing Elodia's gaze to his full lips. Where on earth had he come from?

"Gēgē!" Ada shrieked from over Elodia's shoulder, and then she was scrabbling past her onto the dock and launching herself into the outstretched arms of the now laughing stranger. He picked her up and spun her around, sending her bare feet swinging in a circle, her friend's laughter echoing across the water.

In an instant, her brain made the connection. This had to be Richard, Ada's brother. The one who had written to Ada, the writer of the letter which had brought them all together. She had been staring like a simpleton, slack jawed and starry eyed at Ada's brother who was still spinning his sister in a giddy circle while she giggled.

Elodia turned to Regina to help her onto the dock and then waited for Ada to introduce them. She had to get herself in hand because she couldn't imagine anything worse than making a fool of herself in front of him. Ada had spoken of a trickster, someone who loved to tease and aggravate as much as he protected and doted on her. Elodia had felt her loneliness when she described crawling into his bed when they'd heard of their parents' deaths, the way he'd gone out of his way to carry on certain traditions their mother had maintained. Making her 'longevity noodle' soup for her birthday and 'moon cakes' for the autumn equinox. Elodia had imagined a round faced man with merry pink cheeks, not this tall, amber skinned work of art with a merry laugh.

By the time they had collected their discarded shoes and joined them on the dock, Ada's brother had finally placed her on her feet, and appeared ready to make a detailed study of her.

He pulled back from her, taking her shoulders into his hands. "What on earth are you doing out here? I came to have tea with you and you were nowhere to be found."

"We were getting some sun," she replied, clinging to his hands.

"I thought ladies were meant to avoid the sun," he commented wryly.

"Well, I'm not a lady yet," Ada said. It was strange seeing her like this, the irreverent little sister basking in her brother's attention even as she grew annoyed with his critiques.

"Look at the state of your hair," he said, running a hand gently over Ada's loosened dark hair. His dark eyes flicked down. "Where are your shoes?"

Ada half turned and her eyes dropped to the pile on the dock. "Just there," she replied.

Oh Lord... she wasn't wearing shoes. Elodia had never believed she cared much for convention until now when a perfect stranger was about to see her bare feet. A handsome, debonair, eligible stranger with the most delightfully deep and smooth tenor of a voice.

"Why are they not on your feet, mèimei?" he asked, shaking his head.

"Oh… the water is lovely, how would we be able to feel it with our shoes on?"

He blinked at her for a moment and then nodded. "Ah, fair point, perhaps I shall join you," he replied, beginning to crouch down himself, and Elodia didn't know where to look. Was he truly going to just begin undressing in front of them? In broad daylight?

"Gēgē!" Ada cried, yanking him back upright by his arm.

He stood up and stared at her with his eyebrows raised. "Ah, so you understand why running about shoeless was perhaps not the most appropriate idea."

"It's only improper in mixed company," Ada insisted grumpily. "Until you arrived, we were perfectly fine and we didn't expect you to show up out of nowhere. Unshaven, I might add."

"Well, I was eager to see you after months abroad, especially as I had a surprise for you. Next time I will take myself home and save myself the exhaustion, seeing as you are so ungrateful." He proffered the lacquered wooden box he had been holding in one hand the whole time. "And I'll eat these myself."

Quick as a hare, Ada snatched it from his hands and slid open the top to reveal dark orange squashed sort of fruit, dusted with white powder. They looked strange to Elodia, but Ada's face lit up with delight once more.

"The persimmons!"

He smiled at her glee and patted her head. "Yes, you greedy little thing, they arrived at Lodge Hall just before I did. I brought you a small taste since you'll have to wait a bit longer to enjoy them this year."

Ada bounced on her toes in excitement before glaring up at

him teasingly. "Don't eat all of them, gēgē."

His mouth dropped open in outrage. "How dare you? You are the one who gobbles them up within a month. As it is, I made sure to request your own barrel this time from Grandmother."

"Truly?"

He winked in reply. "Share those, mèimei, or you'll grow as round as the barrel they came in."

Ada wrinkled her nose and slapped his arm, and he pulled a face before shifting his attention to Elodia and Regina.

"And speaking of sharing, who are these young ladies you've been leading astray?" he asked.

"These are my friends, the ones I wrote to you about." She turned to Elodia and Regina with a bright smile. "Gēgē, I'd like to introduce you to Gigi and Ellie. Ladies, this is my brother, Richard."

He rolled his eyes at Ada and shook his head before stepping forward to greet them. "Miss Gigi, I'm sure that is not your full name."

"No," Regina replied with a laugh, "I am Miss Regina Mason."

"Lovely, and you," his gaze shifted to Elodia and she felt her mouth go dry. "Miss Ellie, is it?"

Was that good? "I...I'm Miss Elodia Hawthorne." Her voice had gone up at the end for some reason.

He frowned and looked at her askance. "Are you sure?"

She nodded and tried to smile while her heart thudded in her chest.

He sighed and tilted his head. "Well, if you say so. I am Mr. Richard Thornfield. My sister tells me you have both been good to her, so I am at your service, no matter what."

"Thank you," Regina replied, dipping into a curtsey.

"Remind me, mèimei, which one is the fighter?" he asked, and Ada giggled before pointing to Elodia.

For a horrible moment, Elodia thought he would give her a scolding, but instead, something like appreciation showed on his face. "Thank you for protecting my sister."

"It was my pleasure," she said, and he smiled and shook his head slowly. She'd never been smiled at like that, as if her very presence was being appreciated, even admired. Did he smile at everyone like that? It couldn't be safe for him.

"I'll bet it was," he finally replied. "Far too many people deserve a good thumping and never get it, don't you agree?"

Ada and Regina laughed but she couldn't do much more than smile up at him. He'd seen her. He'd looked into her, past the bad behavior, windblown hair and the bare feet, into who she was and saw it as something praiseworthy. He'd heard what she'd done and seen a protector instead of a ruffian. In an instant, all her shame and anxiety melted away, leaving behind a steady glow in the center of her chest and so it was, on an otherwise ordinary summer day in England, Elodia Hawthorne lost her heart to Richard Thornfield.

CHAPTER ONE

Landel House, Cheshire
April, 1853

"ARE YOU PLANNING on marrying, boy?" Aunt Theo barked from her chair near the fireplace. Elodia glanced up from her seat on the sofa to watch her father roll his eyes at what had to be the twentieth marital inquiry from his great aunt since their arrival a fortnight ago. He didn't look up from the letter he was writing, however. They'd decided to spend some time with Aunt Theo before returning to London for the season, especially as Isolde was accompanying Elodia this year. A decision Elodia was almost positive her father was regretting.

Beside her, her aunt's guest, Miss Walsh, or Isolde as she insisted on being called by Elodia and her aunt, pressed her lips together as if hiding a smile. She had become a firm fixture at her aunt's house lately. She didn't know why but it seemed as though the woman had all but adopted her after last year. Elodia couldn't pretend it wasn't a relief to have female companionship that wasn't either a servant or nearly one hundred years old.

With Ada and now Regina married and settled, she was finding herself increasingly on her own. Elodia loved her father, but after having Regina and Ada, it was difficult to go back to having only him for company. She didn't judge them for it. It made sense that they would spend more time with their beloved husbands. Regina and Leo had gone to the continent for their honeymoon after Parliament closed the previous year, and Ada had gone into her confinement to give birth to her daughter and son. Thankfully, they were all healthy and happy in the aftermath.

"A pound says he'll answer this time," Isolde murmured, and Elodia fought back a chuckle of her own. They'd taken up this particular bet on the third night with the agreement to settle scores before she and her father left for London and the season. So far they'd broken even, but this one could be the decider.

"A pound he'll avoid it like the plague," Elodia replied. They pressed their palms together for a moment, their version of a handshake, then watched and waited.

"You seem inordinately curious about that subject, madame," her father replied, his tone even.

Elodia winked at Isolde who narrowed her eyes playfully, "Best of three."

"Only curious," Aunt Theo continued. "The season is approaching after all, and I am in the twilight of my life. I want all my chickens sorted."

"Why me so damned particularly?" he groused, aggressively dipping his quill in the crystal ink well. Aunt Theo let out a wheeze that could have been a laugh. Her father was a man of experience with a formidable reputation. He was tall, handsome, and considered to be in his prime. A peer of the realm. And yet he was always 'Cuddy' to Aunt Theo. Always her great nephew, never Lord Melbroke.

"You are already five and forty years of age, Cuddy, with no heir in sight. You inherited your father's title easily enough but his will stipulates a wife for a reason, unless I'm very much mistaken."

He let out a short breath and finally looked up at her, his bright blue eyes annoyed behind his reading glasses. "It does. And to answer your very nosy question, yes, I am."

The sinking feeling in Ellie's stomach had little to do with the loss of a pound. It was happening. Her father was going to remarry. But what was the stipulation they had mentioned?

"What stipulation?" she asked.

Lord Melbroke pursed his lips, glaring at Aunt Theo for a

moment before turning to Elodia. "I really didn't want to get into this at all. It's nothing to concern you, sweeting."

"If it has to do with you then it concerns me."

He closed his eyes for a moment and nodded before meeting her eyes. "It's to do with the balance of my inheritance. There is a deadline for me to remarry in order to receive the rest of my father's fortune."

"When is the deadline?"

"The end of this year," he replied.

"Oh." She didn't know how to feel about it. Her mother had been dead for some time, almost a decade. She couldn't pretend he hadn't mourned her or respected her memory.

"I was hoping to have you settled first, Ellie, before bringing another woman into our home. You have been and will always be my first priority."

"The girl is three and twenty." Aunt Theo grumbled, "You've hardly been pushing the matter."

"Because I'm not disposing of unwanted property, it cannot simply be anyone who asks. Elodia is special in more ways than one. Her husband must be at the very least equally remarkable with sensibility, intelligence and his own degree of accomplishment or she would never be happy. To say nothing of his social status and background."

"Those must be very thin on the ground," Isolde commented.

Elodia shot her a look. "Practically extinct."

He spared her a glance, "Yes. But thanks to the law of the land, she only needs one."

"Have you been looking for your unlikely and elusive match in the wilds of England, Elodia?" Aunt Theo asked.

An image of Richard swam before her eyes, complete with the twinkling eyes and mischievous grin. Her heart fluttered and her cheeks prickled with heat. "I have been, in fact."

The three adults turned to her with interest. "And?"

"There have been a couple of promising candidates but nothing concrete so far." Namely because the man she decided on when she was fifteen had no idea how she felt.

"Who?" Lord Melbroke asked.

"I will tell you when there is something to tell, Papa," she replied. No doubt her father would beat down the man's door and demand his compliance if he knew the truth. Elodia wanted Richard to love her freely before she sought and attained her father's blessing. She'd watched the way he loved his sister, Ada. He was a passionate man, thoughtful and unapologetically caring when it came to those precious to him. How much more would he love his wife and children? The woman who married him would never want for anything or anyone else. Elodia had dreamt of being the recipient of that love, of being the one to return it fully the way he deserved. For that to happen, he couldn't be pressured by her father or anyone else.

"What about you, Isolde?" Aunt Theo asked.

Isolde's head swung in her Aunt's direction with comical swiftness. "Me? What have I done?"

"You would do well to marry yourself."

Clearly her aunt also considered the woman to be one of her 'chickens'. Ellie had often wondered what it would be like to reach Isolde's age with no marital prospects. The older woman was wonderful in every way but had no permanent home. And yet she seemed entirely unfazed by it. Perhaps she had some wisdom to teach in that respect.

"I have no interest in that prospect, ma'am. You would do better to lend your force to your nephew and your great niece."

Aunt Theo dismissed her statement with a wave of her hand. "Nonsense, I have energy to spare. You are far too young and pretty to spend your life alone."

Isolde chuckled lightly and smiled at the old woman with what seemed like effortless patience. "I am thirty-eight years old, ma'am. I may be young compared to yourself, but too young is a bit of an exaggeration. Besides which, I will not be alone as you say. I have a wonderful circle of friends, the means to secure and maintain a living, and your good self for company at the moment."

Aunt Theo grumbled but left the matter alone.

Elodia watched her father's gaze bounce between his aunt and Isolde in shock. "Is that all?" he asked.

"For now," Aunt Theo replied.

"Why didn't I think of that answer?" Lord Melbroke mumbled.

"Maybe you're not so opposed to your fate after all," Isolde replied with a cheeky smile. Her father gave her a deeply disingenuous smile before returning to his letter. The room settled back into a companionable silence once again but Elodia couldn't help but be ill at ease.

Was Isolde right? Elodia felt odd thinking about it. It had never occurred to her that her father had been waiting for her sake all this time. That he'd been lonely without a companion. Had she been selfish waiting for so long? Should she have been practical from the beginning instead of waiting for a dream match with Richard Thornfield? Over the years, he had always been kind and considerate, even attentive.

She still carried Richard's father's pocket watch from the time she'd found it at a pawn shop, just before she and Ada had been kidnapped nearly two years ago. The minute she'd seen it in the window, she'd recognized it as his from the two silver cranes against a gold background to the mother of pearl moon. She'd spent every farthing she had on hand in order to get it back that day, in lieu of buying new dresses with Ada.

But then Mr. Trent had struck and in all that danger, the glass face had been cracked. Elodia had used her pin money to have it fixed and cleaned. Her plan was to present it to Richard as a gift and confess her feelings. It was a bit improper as he was an eligible gentleman and she was an unmarried woman, but it was his property after all, and while they had never been truly inappropriate, nothing about their relationship was strictly obedient to societal doctrines. But then Ada had gone on her honeymoon and Richard had all but disappeared between renovating Ada's houses in town and the countryside.

If Ada wasn't there, then Elodia had no real opportunity to give Richard his gift. Now it was nearly two years later and she still had it. The longer it took, the more likely he would be upset that she had kept something so precious to him for so long. What if he thought she was cruel and selfish instead of recognizing her true intentions? Perhaps it was better to simply get it over with and damn the consequences. If he was angry, she'd wait. If he was appreciative, she'd press her advantage.

"Ellie, dear," her father called, and she looked up at him with wide eyes.

"Yes, Papa?" He was staring at her expectantly. As if he'd been calling her for some time.

"Are you well, sweeting?" he asked, his brow creasing in concern.

"Yes."

He stared at her for a moment, unmoving and unflinching, then he put down his quill. "I've a mind to take a turn in the garden, will you accompany me?"

"What, now?" It was nearly ten at night.

"Yes, I think so," he replied, rising to his feet and tugging his jacket and waistcoat into place.

"There's nothing better than a garden at night," Isolde commented, snatching Elodia's book from her hands.

She looked back to her father who was now somewhat amused at her reticence. "Of course, Papa,"

She stood and followed him out the door, down the staircase and out the back door to the grounds. Isolde was correct, of course, even if it was still a bit chilly at night. She folded her arms around her torso, waiting for her father to speak. Was he upset with her? He didn't seem angry or annoyed, and typically he was straightforward with that sort of thing.

Then his arm slid around her shoulders, pulling her against his side, keeping her warm. They went through the grass like that, her head leaning against his chest, his hand rubbing her arm.

"Is there anything you'd like to say, sweeting?" he asked.

"What do you mean?"

"Don't play that game with me, Miss Hawthorne," he grumbled, giving her an affectionate squeeze. It was his first warning when he suspected she was up to something.

"Are you really going to marry this year?" she asked.

He sighed and kissed her hair. "I'm afraid I have to, sweeting. Your grandfather's stipulation affects your dowry."

"Oh." She'd never liked the old man. Even in his grave he was a menace. "Do you know who?"

"No, but his requirements will make it difficult to find someone who will treat you in the way you deserve. I don't want to subject you to that, so I thought it better to wait until you were married."

"But I took too long."

"It's my fault. I should have pushed you harder, or made you aware sooner. But I didn't want to pressure you, especially when you were enjoying your girlhood with your friends. And I didn't want to part with you so soon after—" he broke off sharply and took a deep breath.

"After Mama," she finished, stealing a glance up at him, noting his tight jaw and pursed lips. He nodded but didn't meet her eyes. His pain was always difficult to witness. After her mother's funeral, he'd locked himself away for weeks in their room, unable or unwilling to deal with anything in the aftermath. Elodia had stayed away, missing him but at the same time unwilling to see him so broken. That was until she'd gotten lost coming back from the beach. One evening she'd slipped out to sit on the beach, the only place she could feel close to her mother. A place to grieve without being seen. But on the way back, she'd lost her way.

Those two hours had been truly terrifying. Everything had been pitch black, with only the sounds of the rainforest around her, reminding her that she was not alone and yet still unfound. Then she'd heard the calls of her name. She would never forget the sight of her father, Bearded, his eyes and hair wild, his clothing damp with sweat and blood from scrapes, emerging from the darkness with nothing but a cutlass and a lamp.

That night and every night for the rest of that year, he'd slept in her room, squeezed in behind her on her little bed, holding her tightly. Elodia still didn't know if it was to keep an eye on her, or to comfort the both of them. What she did know, was that her father had never left her side again. She'd believed they would always be that close to each other, but now she understood that it was a childish idea. Viscount's needed heirs and daughters needed husbands.

"So I must marry first,"

"For your own benefit, I believe that would be best."

"What if I cannot find anyone?" she asked.

"You?" he asked in disbelief.

"It's possible." Especially if she was unsuccessful in winning Richard's love.

"We will cross that bridge when we get to it," he said, "but rest assured, I will not abandon you to the English ton."

"I wouldn't have thought you capable of that, Papa,"

"I am glad to hear it."

"I'm sorry if I've made things harder for you. I should have been trying harder during the season, instead of indulging myself with my friends and wasting time."

"Nonsense. You are a gift to me from your mother, a treasure. I have never taken it lightly even before you were born, and I have no intention of doing so now."

"I know."

"Well then, let us say it suited us both to dilly dally and leave it at that."

She smiled and nodded. "Agreed."

"Good. Now, who are these gentlemen who have caught your eye?"

Richard came to mind again. She had truly never met a more perfect man in her life. Tall and strong yet elegant with sharp features and a sinful mouth, with eyes like obsidian that sparkled with laughter and mischief. Every time she thought of him, from his deep voice to his elegant hands, her stomach became infested with butterflies.

There was no one cleverer, more loving and kind or more honorable than him. His consideration and care for Ada while she was at school had been her first insight into the sort of man he was. The stories Ada had told about the big brother who teased her by squeezing her cheeks, but also allowed her to sleep in his bed whenever she had nightmares. Even knowing she wasn't alone, he always sent her letters and thoughtful gifts from the dried persimmons they loved so much to strange molded cakes he had made himself for what Ada called the Mid-Autumn Festival. His love for her was always visible and tangible.

In the years since they met, Richard hadn't kept his thoughtful attentiveness to Ada alone. Elodia had realized years ago that he seemed to favor her, from including her in conversations or claiming a dance at balls. More than once she'd imagined and hoped there was more to all of that than kindness. That perhaps, he saw her as something special and was giving her time to grow into her own person before expressing his interest.

"Ellie?"

She glanced up at her father with wide eyes, her mind scrambling to remember his question. "Yes, Papa?"

"Who are the gentlemen you are interested in? Perhaps I can speak to them or their fathers."

"I will let you know when I am more certain, Papa,"

"More certain of what?"

"Of everything."

"Why are you being so secretive?" He was getting too curious now, so there was only one approach.

"Why are you turning into Aunt Theo?" she asked. He gasped, his eyes wide with outrage, but then the corners of his mouth twitched against a smile.

"The temerity of this young miss," he muttered, shaking his head and looking away from her. "It is the disrespectfulness I cannot seem to manage."

She giggled and pressed her face to his side, squeezing him tightly. He always smelt of old books, lemons and talc and had always been a steadfast source of love and safety. In the coming months and years, she wouldn't be able to spend as much time with her father as she was used to, but for now, for now, she could enjoy his attention and his love.

Lodge Hall, Cumbria
May, 1853

THERE WERE TWO letters in Richard's hands from two of the dearest women in his life. One was from A'wei, his sweet mèimei, or Ada as she was called by everyone else, and the other was from his wài pó, his maternal grandmother who lived in his mother's ancestral home in Wuhan. Every year, his grandmother sent barrels and crates to them at Lodge Hall. The items varied over time: lotus seeds, red beans, soy sauce, wine, ink blocks, new brushes, strings for the guqin, new sheet music, brocade silks, paper or soap, but one thing was always constant. One more thing that he and Ada had always fought over as children.

Persimmons.

Every year, thousands of carefully peeled and packed persimmons arrived dried to chewy, sugar crusted perfection.

He remembered meeting his maternal grandmother twice in his life, once with his parents when he was fifteen and again when he was twenty-three. He had been utterly foreign and confused, but her warmth and humor was something he'd never forgotten. She'd been so excited by his interest in books, music, calligraphy and food preparation. He missed her almost as much as he'd missed his parents. Those fruits were like a hug from her, the last tenuous connection to his mother and her family. His family.

A'wei's letter informed him that she and her small family

would be spending the season with him. He was glad of it. He was all too eager to meet his young niece and nephew again. He wanted to see how much they had grown now that they were a few months older. The second letter from his grandmother heralded a starker new future, informing him that this last shipment would be the last for the foreseeable future, between a rebellion in Taiping and growing tensions between the Qing government and England.

They'd been forced to use ports in the south to send these last barrels. But she'd also sent two saplings he was certain were near death at this point, and a pouch of seeds from the family orchard with instructions for him to begin his own orchard. The hope was that even if she couldn't send him those things ever again, he could still keep that connection as a branch of that family tree. A reminder that he was no longer a son but a patriarch.

He was grateful for her consideration in working so hard to send them this last shipment along with a way to continue the legacy in this home away from home. Indeed, she had sent more of everything. A fact that hadn't gone unnoticed by Richard when he'd first seen the wagons lumbering down the drive. But the idea of this letter being the last he would receive from her was difficult to swallow. Once again, he and A'wei were being cut loose to face a lonely future in a world that was rarely kind or welcoming to them.

Isolation wasn't new to him. He'd faced it a thousand times in a thousand different ways, or so he'd believed. Now he wondered if he'd ever understood what it meant to be on his own because he'd never in his entire life felt like *this*. A'wei, thank God, was taken care of and his two closest friends were married and settled in their own lives with their wives; Basil with A'wei and Leo with Regina Mason. They weren't truly out of touch, but there was an unmistakable distance now. After all, they were in a different stage of their lives.

Now it was only him.

Unless he took a wife and started a family of his own, that is.

The prospect had never been unappealing as a concept for Richard. Having been raised in a close and loving family, he had always wanted to recreate that for himself, especially after losing his parents at such a young age. He'd always liked the idea of laying down his own roots and establishing some stable ground.

There was only one true issue. His choice of bride. The women of England and Europe were fine and well, but while they had just about come to terms with the existence of black men in their countries, they still had little to no idea what to do with a Chinese man like him. He was a novel curiosity at best or a dangerous alien at worst. Sentiments in America were even worse. His father had paved his way as best he could. Everyone knew Edmund Thornfield of Durant Mills, and as his son, Richard was a known entity within the family business before his father passed away. Business was business and money opened doors, especially when it was associated with established pillars of industry like his family.

But as much as marriage was firstly a matter of business to so many, the idea of marrying their daughters to a Chinese lurker somehow seemed a bridge too far. At thirty-four years of age, Richard was rich, landed and possessed of not only several properties in Britain and Europe, but a scrupulously maintained reputation. Yet, he danced and charmed debutantes with a peculiar amount of freedom and ease that few, if any other eligible gentlemen of his ilk could boast for one very simple reason. He wasn't truly pursued by even the most desperate of mamas. Members of the ton had never seen him as a desirable son-in-law.

It had occurred to him to ask his grandmother to arrange a marriage for him with a family in China as his father had done. It would have been easily done as marriage to a European based Chinese merchant would be seen as a rare enough opportunity for the many Han merchant families in China. But that would inevitably leave A'wei on the outside. They would never truly accept her as a member of his family.

The idea of moving to China had occurred as well. He could sign over the bulk of his holdings and the business to A'wei and her children with Basil, shave half his head in the Manchurian style and live out his days with his mother's family. But that would not only leave A'wei ostracized, but he would barely be able to see her. When she died, he would be halfway around the world. By the time he got word of it, she would already be cold in her grave.

The idea left him physically ill.

Richard had always known, even as a child, that his bottom line was and would always be his family. The death of his parents had only reinforced that sentiment and focused it squarely on his sister. The idea of leaving her or making a choice that separated them was impossible. So that left him in England where the best he could hope for was a polite marriage to a woman who tolerated him but in some way would always be ashamed of him.

He'd spent his entire life fighting against the stereotype of being weak, effeminate and strange regardless of the fact that very little about his body was visibly dissimilar to any other men in England. In fact, he was taller than most of them at six foot two with a build to match. The most stark difference was perhaps his face, the 'phoenix eyes' his mother had given him and the olive tone of his skin.

He'd gotten into the habit of keeping his body strong and healthy because he'd learned to stay prepared between Eton and Cambridge. Those pale little round eyed boys loved nothing better than to pick on the lone skinny Chinese student in their midst. Those attacks became less frequent when they realized that diffidence wasn't in Richard's nature, and of course having good friends like Leo and Basil had certainly helped. Now the attacks were less obvious. They came in substandard business proposals, the occasional lost invitation, generalized insolence or the occasional kidnapping.

He didn't like thinking about it, but that experience had shaken him to his core. The fact that it had happened, that Trent could have smiled and played the part and then done that to him when embezzlement didn't work out. The fact that his uncle could hate him enough to make him disappear. He'd never fully confronted his uncle about his role in that, mostly because he couldn't trust himself to keep a level head around the man. Richard had managed to regain his freedom in relatively short order, but even two years later, he still had the occasional nightmare about the clank of steel manacles and dark stinking rooms with no way out.

The things he found himself unable to move past in the aftermath were the two things that were irreplaceable to him: the pocket watch his father had passed to him before he died, and the experience of giving A'wei away at her wedding. The rest didn't matter as much. It still bothered him that he couldn't find his father's pocket watch no matter where he looked.

A'wei, at least, was deliriously happy, reveling in her loving marriage and her brand new adorable children. He could take some comfort in that even though he hated that he hadn't been there to do his duty as her brother. The replacement pocket watch he'd purchased over a year ago, however, only served as a reminder of what he'd lost. Every time he looked at it, a dull rage began to boil in his blood.

Any enjoyment Richard got from society at this point was petty and grim. There was an ugly satisfaction in the fact that his uncle lived off an allowance controlled by Richard and if he wanted to, he could destroy that man's life on a whim. The only thing that held him back was his mother's lessons and the love his father had still harbored for his little brother even after years of arguing.

Richard was honest enough to admit that he took up space in every public area he could simply to watch the ton squirm. He knew that most of them felt the same way as his uncle, that they would rather he disappeared instead of forcing them to witness his existence, his success, his growing prominence in their sacred circles thanks to Leo and Ada. They would never make him bow, hide or defer to them. He would claim every inch of ground he was entitled to as his father's son regardless of the cost.

All that was what he faced outside his home, however. The home his parents had made was still a source of comfort to him, a true blend of his two parents from the lotus pond in the garden to the architecture of the dwelling. Did he really want to let someone who couldn't value those things into his only place of refuge for the sake of children? Before today, the answer was no, but now with the letter before him in his grandmother's neat Mandarin characters, he was beginning to wonder. He'd never wanted to be alone, but the idea had never left him feeling lonely before.

Would marriage fix that?

He sighed and set the letter down on the desk, rubbing his hands roughly over his face. He needed to get out of this room and do something with himself. He stood and snatched up his jacket before striding out the study door. Exercise was what he needed. Should he go for a ride or simply a walk? Or maybe he needed something more visceral, something to get him out of his morose thoughts for the rest of the day and likely the night.

His butler, a tall, reedy man with a hard face and a soft heart, stopped him at the stairs. "Are you going out, sir?" he asked.

"I am. Do you need me, Evers?"

"Yes, sir. Did you have any plans for this particular shipment?"

Richard spared him an unamused look as he continued down the stairs. "You've been dealing with this since before I've been in this house, Evers. Do you still need direction?"

"Yes, sir, only there seems to be a good deal more than usual this time."

Richard ran over the list in his mind. He hadn't seen anything out of the usual. "What do you mean?"

"I'd rather not say, sir, but it is far more than food and the odd scholarly items."

What else had she put in those damn crates? "Put the food

stuff in the cellar, the two plants on my desk in the greenhouse and the rest in the study on the first floor. I will handle it when I return."

"All of the rest, sir? Those alone are nearly forty crates, sir."

Richard let out a breath. Forty crates. Only forty to last the rest of his life. "Yes. All of them."

"Very good, sir. Will you be back for dinner?"

"No, but I should be back tonight."

Should he go to Rachel? She wasn't a pleasant woman, his mistress of thirteen years, but it hadn't stopped him from taking her as a lover. Last year, he'd been busy with Ada's residences and fixing the damage Trent had done to his family business, leaving little time for such pleasures. She, in turn, had taken her pleasures elsewhere on the continent. He knew she must have returned home from her time abroad in Italy, and she didn't live too far from Lodge Hall. Lady Rachel Tremaine never missed the London season or a chance at sex. Perhaps a solid fuck was what he needed to reset his head and decide what it was he truly wanted.

CHAPTER TWO

Thornfield House, London
Late May, 1853

ELODIA HAD NEVER had much experience with babies, being the only child of an only child. She couldn't say with much certainty if she liked them in general or if Ada's children were objectively the most adorable little cherubs ever birthed in the history of mankind. But as she stared into the wide, black eyes in the soft, round little face of Ada's daughter, she was beginning to think she had the right of it.

Ada herself was feeding her son while her husband, Basil Thompson, sat vigil, watching them closely. She seemed tired. Her hair was a bit more unkempt, and her clothing far more relaxed than usual, but Elodia had to assume she was happy based on the smile that perpetually lingered on her face. Twins. Two children at once. It boggled the mind how she'd managed to fit two babies inside her.

"She is the most precious thing, Ada," she whispered, cradling the light, chubby bundle in her arms as the little girl observed her closely with little to no expression.

"She's the greediest thing," Ada grumbled, passing her son to Basil, so she could finish fastening her blouse. Basil took his son easily, allowing the boy to lay face down on one arm, while he gently patted his small back.

"She should be. She should eat well and sleep well," Elodia said, running one fingertip over the baby girl's cheek.

"Mmmm, well, they are both managing that well enough,"

Basil replied, fighting back a yawn.

"What is her name?" she asked as the little girl yawned widely and closed her eyes, ready to go to sleep now that her belly was full.

"She will be Eleanor Matilda, but we will be calling her Ellie."

"Probably 'Young Ellie', to differentiate," Basil added.

Elodia looked up at Ada as tears stung her eyes. "Truly?"

"Yes, after her godmother?"

"Oh," the word left her mouth on an exhale. It had never occurred to her that Ada would want her to be godmother to her child. "Ada, are you sure?"

"Of course I am."

"But what about Lady Sterling?"

Basil scoffed, "Are you mad? She is their grandmother; she is close enough."

Ada laughed and shook her head. "Basil, you are too bad."

"I'm correct," he replied with a sardonic glance in her direction. "The less influence they have, the better."

"What about the little gentleman over there?" Elodia asked, nodding at Ada's son. "What will he be named?"

"He will be Thomas after my father," Ada replied, "and his middle name will be Lewis after Basil."

"Oh, how lovely,"

"Yes, I wanted to name him Basil but someone put his foot down about that." Ada sent a halfhearted glare towards her husband, who met her gaze evenly and unapologetically.

"And his foot will remain down. No child should be named after an herb."

Ada rolled her eyes and shook her head. "You are not named for a herb, my love. It is a noble, kingly name of Greek origin."

"Surely there are worse names for a boy," Elodia said.

"I dare you to name three," he replied, raising one eyebrow.

Elodia glanced up at the ceiling as she searched her mind. "Peregrine, Adolphus and perhaps Bartholomew."

Basil stared at her in stunned silence. "I stand corrected."

It seemed an innocent moment to bring up Richard, especially as he wasn't there and they were in his home. "How is your brother enjoying being an uncle?"

Ada rolled her eyes but her smile grew wider. "Oh, he—"

"He is doing very well," his voice came over her shoulder as if summoned. Elodia's breath caught in her throat at the sight of him, her mouth going dry with nerves. He strode in none the wiser, the very image of virility and elegance in his riding clothes, his inky, silken hair still wind swept.

"Gēgē, you're back, I didn't hear you." Ada smiled up at him widely.

Richard pressed a kiss to the top of Ada's head and then turned his attention to Basil. "Give me my nephew," he said, shoving his riding gloves into his pocket.

"Absolutely not, go bathe first."

"Spoil sport," he grumbled before his eyes fell on Elodia and his niece. He smiled, his eyes warming with what she hoped was fondness. "Hello you," he greeted her.

"Hello yourself." It was how they always greeted each other. No formality or insipid politesse.

"I didn't know you were coming today," he braced one hand against the back of her chair, smiling down at her.

"Would you have been here to greet me if you did?" she asked, glancing over at him.

"Such an illustrious personage deserves a warm welcome after all."

She squinted at him. She was familiar enough with him to see when he was plotting, and his eyes kept shifting down to the chubby prize in her arms. "Are you coming for your niece?"

"I might be," his gaze fell to the sleepy cherub and stayed there, giving up all pretense.

Not exactly what she wanted but it was too endearing to hold against him. "You'll have to wait, I've only just gotten my hands on her."

"Are you open to a bribe?" he asked, crouching down beside

Elodia and brushing his fingers over the top of Young Ellie's head.

"I am not," Elodia replied. She caught his scent, amber, sage and cloves. It was different than usual, warmer or deeper from the heat of his body and his morning exercise.

"How was the park, gēgē?" Ada asked.

"Green." His eyes stayed focused on Young Ellie.

"How descriptive," she grumbled.

"Can you not see that I am in very important negotiations, mèimei?" he replied, wiggling his fingers at Young Ellie until Elodia snapped her teeth at them.

"She's mine, sir. Go perform your ablutions and we will discuss this later."

His eyes went wide and an amused smile curved his mouth. "The temerity. In my own home, no less," he marveled, nodding at her, and Elodia giggled. "That is *my* niece, young lady."

"And she is my goddaughter," she replied.

At the announcement, his fake outrage melted into a true smile. "She is indeed. There isn't a finer choice in England."

She forced breath back into her lungs and turned her gaze back to the bundle in her lap. "Thank you," It was always like this with him. Admiration that could easily be confused with affection or even something more.

"Well, I will cede this round to you, Miss Elodia, but make no mistake, I will return," he said with mock severity.

"As you said, it is your house," she teased. He winked and looked down at his niece, running a gentle hand over the sparse dark hair on her little head.

He murmured something in Mandarin that Elodia didn't understand, then stood and left the room. She couldn't deny herself the pleasure of watching him walk away before returning her attention to Ada and Basil who were watching her with interest. Had she done something obvious? "He is very merry," she said, hoping they didn't try to probe.

"*Very* merry," Basil replied.

There was something in his tone that had her stomach

squirming. Had they noticed? Did they also think Richard was paying her special notice? "He probably missed having company while you were both away."

"Yes," Ada said, shooting a quick warning glance at her husband. "I don't think he's ever lived alone before."

"Oh," she kept her gaze on Young Ellie and asked the next question as innocently as she could manage.

"Have you chosen the godfather for her?"

"Yes,"

"It's Richard."

"Oh." She and Richard were godparents to their daughter. "That's going to make fighting him for Young Ellie more difficult."

Ada laughed at that and tickled her son's foot.

"Do you think he'll marry this year?" Elodia asked.

"Why do you ask?" Basil asked.

"Well, if he is, then he'll be distracted."

"True." Ada and Basil shared a glance. "I suppose it depends on how long he holds out," Ada said.

"Or if a more tempting offer than being a bachelor makes itself apparent," Basil added, his tone careful.

So nothing had been definitively said as yet. Was it a good sign that he hadn't found anyone yet? Or a warning sign that he had no interest in the prospect. She needed more information from him before she put herself forward. She'd waited this long; she could wait a little longer.

Sterling House, London, 1853
One Week later

RICHARD HAD NEVER had cause to complain about attending social gatherings like his contemporaries. Finding dance partners if he was of a mind to dance wasn't difficult. He was handsome enough, he knew, and an accomplished dancer. He made small talk, smiled and moved along. He never danced with the same girl twice at a ball and he was never pursued.

That had been fine when he wasn't interested in marriage, but now it was a problem. Somehow he had to find a way to make himself more of a prospect. The only thing really standing in his way was his social status. He'd have to begin leveraging his social circle to get him into more dinners and soirees with impoverished gentility looking for a bank account to plunder. Surely if his sister was good enough for the Viscount Sterling's son, then he would suit for a poor baron's third daughter.

It was the entire reason he'd agreed to attend this ball hosted by the Viscountess Sterling. The woman was civil enough, and more kind than the average white peer in England, especially toward Leo and Regina or A'wei. If he was honest, however, he still remembered how anxious Basil had been to accept A'wei as his wife because of the behavior of his family. Richard would never be able to fully trust the woman or her husband as long as he lived, but his entire family couldn't avoid her invitations. Especially when those invitations were so sought after among the ton.

He only needed to find a man or woman that he'd already been introduced to so he could find an entrée to other introductions. The viscount and viscountess were busy with their guests. His eyes scanned the rooms as he made his way to the ballroom. There were stares, as always. People wondering at his existence among such rarified company. He ignored them all and stood at the edge of the ballroom with aimless roving eyes until a flash of color caught his attention. Robin blue shot silk with hints of orange, elegant styling, minimal lace, brown skin... his eyes flicked up to the woman's face and his shoulders relaxed a little.

Elodia Hawthorne.

It was the strangest thing how his eyes always managed to find her in a crowded room. The pretty, warm hearted, clear headed, brave girl he'd met years before had grown into an elegant, accomplished and beautiful woman from the shape of her eyes to the curve of her full lips. These days she was always the picture of feminine elegance, especially on nights like tonight in her kid skin gloves, with diamonds twinkling at her wrists and earlobes. Her strong slender shoulders and graceful neck were bare, her brown skin gleaming under the candlelight.

There was nothing more entertaining than a conversation with her. She had the most mischievous and designing mind, the most welcoming smile and an alluring scent he was almost ashamed to have noticed. Like her, it was bold and unapologetically unique; sandalwood, ginger and cloves. No perfunctory florals for Miss Elodia Hawthorne. With such inducement, he told himself, it was a perfectly natural thing for him to seek out her company whenever it was available.

But tonight she looked nervous for some reason. Her smile didn't quite reach her eyes and she kept fiddling with her bracelet and glancing about the room nervously. It was, after all, the first time since she'd been out that she was in a ballroom without her friends. Lord and Lady Starkley had yet to return from abroad, and A'wei and Basil had opted against attending this ball.

Without her faithful companions, Elodia seemed smaller, more vulnerable. Where was her father? There was no way the Viscount Melbroke had allowed her to attend such an event on her own. She was a feisty little thing to be sure, but she was still a well-bred young lady, and her brown skin stood out among the crowd of white faces. Even at an event such as this one, there would be scoundrels looking to seduce an heiress such as her. Richard made one more sweep of the ballroom for a sign of her father, then started towards her. She noticed him halfway and her face lit up, as she waved, heedless of the glances sent her way. She always had a smile for him. Not a polite or shy one, an exuberant and entirely undignified one that never failed to pull one out of him in return.

Adorable.

"Hello you," he greeted her with a slight bow, and she smiled brightly at him, dipping into a curtsey. She always did.

"Hello to you," she replied. He was gratified to notice that she had stopped fiddling with her bracelet.

"Missing your posse?" he asked.

She rolled her eyes at him, "What gave me away?"

"You have the look of a cornered fawn. All twitches and wide eyes."

She looked away, her lips twitching. "How flattering. Have you been making a study of me?"

"Only a little." She pursed her lips but the corner of her mouth kept twitching against a smile. He wondered how long it would take for her to give in.

"How long have you been here?" she finally asked, meeting his eyes.

"An hour or so."

"And have you been playing the wallflower the whole time?" she asked.

Cheeky little thing. "I beg your pardon. I've been surveying my options. Like a falcon."

She hummed in disbelief, shaking her head. "So you say. How will you ever find a wife this way?"

He glanced down at her. The naughty little sprite knew something. "You've been speaking with my sister?"

She smiled. "And her husband."

"Tedious little busy bodies," he grumbled.

"You'd better marry soon then, so they leave you well enough alone."

He chuckled and shook his head. "It is a thought, isn't it? But they'll take my nephew and niece with them."

"That is true. Perhaps it's not worth it."

"At least I'll have you for company. Speaking of, how is your dance card looking this evening?" She was a good dancer, too good for the number of offers that came her way.

"Oh, it is alright." She looked away from him with a tight smile.

"Room for one more?"

She seemed uncertain for a moment, but then she unhooked her dance card and handed it to him. He opened his mouth to say she could have done it herself, but in the end, he decided against it. The music for the next dance began and he saw she was free for it. She was free for most of her dances. Was this what she was nervous about? Was she embarrassed about her lack of prospects? He knew what it was like to feel like the only unwanted person in the room. He refused to allow her to feel that hollow any further. She only needed one partner and the others would follow. Deftly, he fastened the thin golden bracelet holding her dance card around her gloved wrist.

"I'm taking you for this one," he announced.

She blinked up at him. "I beg your pardon?"

Maybe he could have worded that differently. "Are you dancing this evening?"

"Well, yes—"

"Then come along, Miss Elodia." He offered his arm and she took it with a bewildered smile. They made it to the dance floor just in time for the waltz to begin. "Am I correct in thinking that you are here with your father?"

"Yes, and Miss Walsh. You remember her from Lady Starkley's wedding?"

"I remember her from all Ada's years of education at Miss Pollitt's."

"Oh yes, that is true. I wasn't sure how familiar you were with her."

"With your antics? We are practically best friends."

She frowned in confusion. "I never knew you were there to see her so often."

"I will refer you to my previous statement."

"What I mean is, we never heard of you being there."

"I made sure of that. Ada was a target as much as the rest of you. Every time there was a fight or a dispute and you all ended up in trouble, the parents were called to plead the case as to why you all should be allowed to remain at school with your racial betters."

"Was my father always there?"

"Oh yes. He and I tended to be of a mind more or less when it came to all of you. I found it ridiculous that you all should be expected to roll over and show your belly because it was ladylike. No one ever seemed of a mind to remind those bullies that good manners were free and incidentally, also a sign of good breeding."

"What did they used to say?"

"I reminded them that fighting against injustice was a most English virtue. If their daughters couldn't handle a fight then they shouldn't be in the habit of starting them. I believe at one time I invoked Charles the First and his grandson James."

"My goodness."

"Miss Walsh, as she is now, always seemed to appreciate my candor on the subject."

"Your defense of us served us well, it seems."

"The evidence does lean that way. What about you, are you finally of a mind to take a husband?" he asked.

Her eyes widened slightly. "I beg your pardon, sir. Women do not take husbands. As a rule. Men take wives."

As if she would ever consider being 'taken' by anyone. "If I was speaking to anyone else, I would agree with that sentiment."

"I am not quite that shameless," she replied with a sniff worthy of her Aunt Theo.

"There is no shame in honesty, Miss Hawthorne." He led her in a turn, "Any man would be lucky to be claimed by you."

If he didn't know her well enough, he'd assume she was blushing based on the way she refused to meet his gaze. "I don't think you would wish to be 'taken' as you say," she finally said.

"Depends on the woman," he replied with a grin as the dance came to an end. He glanced around and saw that her father and Miss Walsh had finally entered the room. "I'll return you to your father now."

"What?" She turned around. "Oh."

He offered his arm again and she took it, allowing him to lead her back to her party.

"Good evening, Mr. Thornfield," Lord Melbroke greeted him.

"Good evening, my lord. Good evening, Miss Walsh." He gave them both a bow. "I am returning your pride and joy to you."

"Yes, I can see that," the viscount glanced at her.

"Miss Hawthorne was gracious enough to gift me a dance this evening," Richard clarified.

"Thank you," Elodia said with her characteristically sunny smile.

"Not at all, it was my pleasure. Enjoy the rest of your evening." He bowed to her, kissed the back of her hand and walked back to his spot on the other side of the ballroom. He watched as two other young gentlemen approached her for dances. They were too green by half, likely careless and opportunistic, but the more dances she took, the more she'd be offered.

"She's pretty," a husky familiar voice came from his side. Then the scent of orange blossoms. Rachel.

He turned in her direction and made a show of bowing to his mistress of nearly a decade. She was an attractive woman with a statuesque build, at once slender and strong with golden hair, dark eyes and even darker tastes. She'd married young and unhappily from all accounts, but her husband had done her the courtesy of dying early, leaving her with a generous provision and a lifetime to enjoy it with. She had a son, although how close she was to that son, he couldn't say.

"Lady Tremaine," he greeted her, turning his attention back to the dance floor. She'd wrapped her curvaceous body in silver silk. It was certainly elegant and sophisticated, but it lacked something. Or perhaps it wasn't eliciting the same response for some reason. He wasn't sure why; she had been just fine a week or so ago when he visited her.

"Mr. Thornfield. I didn't know you were attending tonight."

"Nor did I in truth."

"You should have told me," she murmured behind her fan.

"It was a bit last minute," he replied, wondering if he was imagining the pressure sliding up his back. Was that her hand? There was a time it would have given him a dark thrill knowing she couldn't wait. Knowing that this was going on right under the ton's snobbish noses.

"I suppose I must reacquaint myself with your circle. You've been widening your horizons lately."

There was a strange edge to her voice. "Have I?"

"Your sister married the second son of Lord Sterling, did she not?"

"She did." Although the particulars were not common knowledge. The last thing he needed was his name in the papers associated with scandal, financial or otherwise. He had no interest in being a cautionary tale.

"And that policeman friend of yours is now a Baron, heaven forbid."

Close enough. "So he is."

"And now you are dancing with Melbroke's... what is she exactly?"

"His daughter," he replied even as his hand curled into a fist at his side. Everything inside him was rejecting the idea of allowing this woman to speak disparagingly of Elodia. She floated and spun, her skill and grace evident as she smiled at her partners and fellow guests, although never as brightly as when she looked at him.

Rachel was beautiful, but hard, empty and solely focused on her own interests and feelings. He couldn't blame her for it, but in the end, she was no different from any other woman of the ton. Self-interested and eager to use what little power they wielded to subjugate others. But Elodia, she was like a rare thousand-year jade, a pristine, perfect black pearl, exquisitely vibrant and dynamic, like an embroidered Su tapestry made from a million stitches of ten thousand single strands of silk.

"I'm not sure she will give you the entrée you are looking for."

"Mmmm," he didn't have a polite response to that statement. Was she more annoying as well? It was odd; there was nothing surprising or unusual about her statement. She had always been that way, her bigotry and insolence so general and flippant that it was hard to take any insult personally. It was one of the main reasons he would never have considered her for a wife. Her opinion of people outside her race was, at best, dismissive and demeaning. At worst, it bordered on vile and almost violent.

"How on earth did that black sheep wander into the fold?"

He clenched his jaw against a response. It was a defect in her he'd always been aware of, so he'd been careful to make sure no one in his circle knew of his arrangement with her. Basil would never have let him live it down but Leo might have seen it as pitiful. Neither of them had his problem. Basil could swing a cat and find a dalliance whenever he wanted. Leo was equally dehumanized by the ton, but his sexual prowess or masculinity were never in question. "The old way, I imagine."

"What way is that?"

"Nonconformity. Someone clearly broke ranks. Not that a lady such as yourself would know anything about that, of course." His tone was only slightly mocking. She'd ride anything so long as she could leave it where she found it.

"I keep my divergence under strict regulation," she replied.

"I'm glad to hear it." It was one of the few things that made them a good match. She didn't see Richard any differently than any person she looked down upon; he was just her favorite bed partner. Perhaps it was a point of pride for him. Most people in the ton didn't think he had much in him, but at least one person knew differently. For Richard, that made her the most convenient option. Easy to pick up and easy to put down. No chance of things getting complicated or indiscreet.

"Is tonight a good one for some divergence?"

Across the ballroom, Elodia stepped out onto the dance floor for a third time. She met his eyes and smiled. He returned the gesture but his stomach churned. He didn't like her watching him when Rachel had her hands on him. It made him feel sordid. He needed to leave.

"Perhaps," he replied, giving Rachel a long side glance. The invitation had been sent and the message was received.

CHAPTER THREE

I T HAD BEEN a successful ball for Elodia, by and large. No less
than six dances with sons of affluent families, and no mishaps
with her shoes or her dress. Now she stood near the door with
her father and Isolde waiting for their carriage to be brought
around so they could leave. If everything went according to plan,
then flowers, calling cards and requests for promenades would
follow. She wasn't overly interested in them, however. There was
only one person who she was interested in and he'd been the first
person to dance with her.

It had been something from a dream, searching for a familiar
face only to look up and see him striding across the room with a
smile and a twinkle in his dark eyes. Richard was always
handsome, his clothing cut to perfection, his color pairings
exquisitely chosen. In evening wear, however, he was breathtaking. The snow-white shirt and cravat against the warm tone of his
skin, all that dark silken hair perfectly styled, his beautiful face
with its high forehead and cheekbones, carved out of amber. Her
heart had been racing from the first glance to the moment he
walked away, with his touch still burning through her dress and
gloves. His scent still in her nostrils.

All her dances with other men had been to draw attention
away from the fact that Richard had spoken to her so long
without her father there and danced a waltz with her. If she had
abstained after that, people would talk and assumptions would be

made. She didn't want any gossip spreading about her or him, especially when there was no cause for it. What she wanted more than anything was his love given freely and openly. Not his compliance to her father's will or social convention.

He was an honorable and decent man. If he suspected that there were rumors about them, if he thought she had been compromised, especially by him, he would offer for her, whether he wanted her or not. She couldn't imagine anything worse than that.

"Mr. Thornfield left early," Isolde said to Elodia as the carriage drove up.

"Did he?" Elodia mused innocently. "I hadn't noticed." It was, of course, a lie. There was nothing she noticed faster than Richard's absence. He'd left half an hour after their dance without taking to the floor with anyone else. Was there some underlying meaning to that?

"Oh, I wonder why," Isolde continued.

"Perhaps he didn't find anything to his taste," Elodia commented.

"Perhaps,"

At least I'll have you for company...

They climbed into the velvet upholstered carriage, Isolde beside Elodia and Lord Melbroke across from both of them. Elodia started removing her gloves, her fingers working at the small pearl buttons at the inside of her wrists.

"Is it so odd? Papa never dances when he attends events."

Isolde nodded. "True, but I was under the impression that the path to affection began with dancing. That is what Miss Austen says."

It made sense that perhaps he hadn't been interested in dancing with anyone there.

Except he had danced with her. She could still see him in front of her, all shining dark eyes and warm smiles. She could still feel his hand on her waist, the way her heart thumped in her chest when he walked over to her, as they danced.

I'm taking you for this one.

Had he attended with the intention of dancing with her alone? It was a romantic idea, if entirely wishful. Or perhaps he had danced before she had arrived. He had said that he'd been there for hours before her. Was that a lie?

"He's an enterprising young man. No doubt he had business to attend to," Lord Melbroke replied. Elodia glanced at her father. His head was leaning against the seat rest, his eyes closed.

It was true enough. Any number of things could have called him away. Was it ridiculous to imagine that he had left because she was dancing with other men? Should she have stopped?

Any man would be lucky to be taken by you.

"Does he usually spend so little time at balls?" Isolde asked.

"No. He never stays until the end but he rarely leaves that early," Elodia's father responded. Then one blue eye opened. "Are you making a study of him, Miss Walsh?"

"No, my lord, he was merely one of the few people I recognized in the room. I hope he isn't ill."

What had he meant by their conversation, saying that any man would be happy to be claimed by her, even him? Was that an invitation or merely encouragement meant to bolster her spirits? Had he been signaling that he wanted her to claim him? So much could be twisted to mean one thing or another.

"Ellie?"

She turned her head to her father. "Yes, Papa?"

"Miss Walsh asked you a question."

"Oh, I'm so sorry." She shook her head and turned to the woman beside her who was staring at her as if she were a strange type of bird.

Any man would be lucky…

"I only wanted to know if you'd enjoyed yourself, dear. You had quite a few partners."

She smiled and gave what she was sure was an appropriate answer. "I did."

"A glowing endorsement indeed," Lord Melbroke teased her.

"I'm sorry, I am a little tired." Her mind was going a thousand miles a minute, wondering if her time had finally come. If Richard had finally returned her feelings. Her heart began to race again.

I'll have you for company.

"Of course you are," Isolde said.

Elodia could barely meet their eyes. "I did enjoy myself. It's a little strange getting used to attending events without Ada and Gigi,"

"I can imagine. I shall try to be a reasonable substitute."

She gave her a quick glance. "You are wonderful. Without you, I'd have hidden in the cloak room." That at least wasn't a lie.

"Thank you very much for that," her father said, shaking his head.

She needed to speak to Richard. She had to know what he'd meant. Why had he singled her out for a dance and then left? She needed an answer or she would go mad. Ada was staying with him. Perhaps it was the universe helping her. Now that Ada was married, Ellie had nearly given up all hope of giving him his pocket watch. There was no way she could visit him without Ada. She would go tomorrow. She would take it to him and offer it along with her heart and hope that her sincerity prompted him to do the same.

…you wouldn't want to be claimed…

It depends on the woman.

HE WAS TIRED. Not physically, not really. Even after how many hours? His pocket watch was too far away to check. He searched the room for a clock. Was that saying one o'clock? Either way, he wasn't physically exhausted. He was sated… in a way, as if the feral energy inside him had been exorcised enough.

Sex was good exercise if done the correct way, and one thing he would say for Rachel was she knew the correct way. But now there was something missing, like he had just discovered an itch he couldn't quite get to. Or champagne gone flat. The way good sex used to give him energy was, it seemed, a thing of the past. Or perhaps the sex wasn't as good? Eyes closed, he ran a brief inventory of his body. No. His heart was pounding, his body covered in sweat, his toes were just a little numb. No, the sex wasn't the issue.

"I'm so glad you decided against staying in the countryside, my dear."

"Mmm." Maybe he truly did want something more than the woman beside him. He'd taken up with her the year his parents died, when the grief and loneliness had proved to be too much to cope with alone. Now it seemed a different kind of loneliness had set in and time with her was only making it worse.

"Last year was so dreary without you, I had to take myself off to Italy."

"I thought it was the dancing instructor," he replied. She slapped his chest lazily from where she lay beside him.

"He was being far more obliging than you were. Not a word of English but—"

"But you got your point across."

"Well, you know me."

"I do." She was a passionate woman, utterly fixated on pleasing herself. Bold and beautiful and selfish enough to not care about the opinions of others. No. No, that wasn't quite it. She simply didn't like being told what to do. Again, after her marriage record, he couldn't fault her for it, but a lack of accountability wasn't something he wanted in a partner.

If she wanted a new necklace, she bought it. If she wanted to spend two years in Italy, she did so. And if she decided to fuck a twenty-year-old Chinese man off and on for over a decade, she did. When all he'd wanted was to be touched by someone, she'd matched appetites well. It was what had kept him here. But now he was tired of being touched by someone who didn't care about him on even the most basic level, someone he was sure barely saw him as fully human. A woman who only saw him as a novel addition to her collection of lovers. He wanted to feel like he was part of something. He wanted his own family and his own roots.

"You're quiet this evening," she commented, propping herself up on her elbow beside him, her pale sumptuous body bare over the sheets.

"Am I? How was your Italian conquest?" he asked.

"Lovely. But I don't imagine I have the energy for the both of you. I'll have to give him up now that you've decided to make an appearance."

"You mean he's here?" So she had brought him back to England? It was bold but not unlike her. No doubt she'd left him at her country house. Jesus, would it be that easy?

"For now."

This was it. Better to cut it off now while she was still sexed up with other lovers on standby. There wouldn't be a finer opportunity to end things on good terms. "Don't give him up."

"What?" she asked, chuckling.

He turned his head towards her. Her pale skin glistened with sweat, a light flush still painting her face and neck. "Don't send him away. I plan on taking a wife this year."

"So?"

He frowned, confused by her question. "So I don't have the energy for you and the marriage mart, and that's before approaching the tastelessness of keeping a mistress while courting a wife."

"A mistress?" she repeated slowly.

He blinked. "What did you think you were?"

"You are my lover."

"Yes, and I am one of many, so let's not get precious about semantics." He sat up and began the hunt for his clothes. He had even less energy to argue over word choice. The sooner he was out of here, the better.

"Are you casting me aside?" she demanded, sitting up, naked

as the day she was born and all her golden hair tumbling around her shoulders.

"I'm saying you don't need to consider me at all anymore when planning for your future because this dalliance has run its course for me. You have a new amusement, so enjoy him."

"Because you want a nice virgin," she sneered.

Somehow it hadn't occurred to him that she would take it badly. They had never been close; they were barely friends. Had he missed something? He paused to take her in, waited for the guilt to settle in. Was he being too terse and unfeeling?

Nothing. It was like looking at a tepid painting.

"I have to say, Rachel, I'm not sure what you are cross about." He pulled on his trousers and pulled his shirt over his head. "Are you upset that I don't want to marry you?"

"As if I'd have you."

He barely stopped himself from rolling his eyes. "Precisely. We've had such a nice evening so far, my dear, let's not argue about this nonsense." Not even her jabs mattered. What was wrong with him?

"If it's such a good evening then why are you leaving so early?"

Was one o'clock in the morning early? "Because I have other business to attend to."

"More important business than me?"

The hell... It had never mattered before what time he left so long as he was discreet. "If you like." Where were his cuff links? A gleam near the fireplace caught his eye. Perfect. He didn't want to leave anything behind. God forbid she try to use it against him.

"I don't like. Who the hell do you think you are?"

There it was. The entitlement which always lurked under the surface. Is that what this was? He was the first to grow tired of her and she was offended? "I'm not sure what you mean." *Socks.* He sat down and pulled them on one foot at a time.

"You think you have the right to cast me aside, you arrogant oriental peasant?"

His jaw clenched against a retort. It had been amusing to catch glimpses of her privileged venom over the years, but this was ugly and exhausting. There was no point in stooping to her level. He slipped on his shoes and began tying the laces. "I believe I asked you to cast *me* aside, actually."

He stood and looked around. *Shoes, cufflinks, shirt, ...* He spotted a sliver of purple under the chaise and started for his waistcoat, snatching it up along with his cravat.

The sheets rustled and he heard footsteps. "You will leave when I am good and ready, and when I am, I will inform you of the fact. You are mine. You belong to me."

"Is that a fact?" he asked, rising to his feet. She'd put on her night robe but hadn't fastened it, offering glimpses of a body he'd desired at least partially only hours ago. Now that attraction was long gone, replaced by apathy and a sort of disgust he'd never fully allowed himself to feel before.

HE'D ALWAYS KNOWN she saw him this way, as a trophy or a toy, but he'd never allowed himself to dwell on it too much. Not while she wasn't making it too much of an issue. Of course it had never crossed her mind that she was getting her way with him because he'd wanted a sexually compatible partner who was free of disease. Or that her unwillingness to reveal her taste in lovers to the public had worked to his advantage as well. How could he possibly be embarrassed to be connected with her? Surely that could only go the other way.

Unfortunately, she took his pause as a chance to win him around. "Don't leave like this. Come back to bed, lover," she crooned, walking up to him and sliding her arms around his waist.

"Step aside, please, Rachel," he replied, unwilling to look at her. Sick of her smell, sick of her touch, sick to death of her. Or perhaps he was sick of himself, sick of who he had allowed himself to be with her. A grasping creature much like she was now, desperate to hold onto something or anyone.

"Make me." Had she always been this embarrassing?

He couldn't think of a polite response to that. Instead, he removed her arms and turned to look for his jacket. There it was on the chair. He snatched it up and shook it out.

"Would you like to play that game instead? You can be the master and make me do what you like."

He almost considered it. He could tie her to the bed and ask her servant to let him out the door before releasing her. It was an idea. No doubt it would take less time than fending off her tentacle-like arms. But it wasn't necessary. He already had his jacket. He could finally get out of this room. "No thank you."

"No—"

He let out a fitful sigh. "I don't want to be your master. I want to go home. I want this little exhibition of yours to be over."

She stared at him in outrage, color turning her face an undignified shade of pink before she launched herself at him with flailing arms and sharp nails. "I cannot believe I allowed you to touch me. As if you could ever deserve me."

He grabbed her wrists and pushed her back with just enough force to send her a few steps backwards. "Keep your hands off me then."

"Do you have any idea how many men would kill to be in my bed?"

"No, but I am all too eager to find out." He started for her bedroom door.

"You bastard!" she shrieked, following him closely, "If you dare walk out of that door, I'll crush you."

He paused long enough to give her a pitying look. "Goodbye, Rachel."

Her pale hand closed around his forearm, her nails digging into his flesh through his clothing. "I mean it, Richard. I will make sure you regret this for the rest of your life."

He met her furious eyes, his jaw tight against words he wouldn't allow himself to throw. He was done lowering himself to her level. Then he let his eyes drop pointedly to her grip on his arm before meeting her gaze again. He didn't speak again, but the meaning was clear enough based on the way her eyes widened slightly.

Remove your hand if you plan on keeping it.

Another breath and she released him. Then he was gone, down the stairs and out the front onto the mostly deserted streets of London. The air was cool if not fully clean. At least it wasn't full of the now nauseating scent of orange blossoms.

How had he let that woman near him? What on earth had he been thinking, allowing that ridiculous affair to continue this long? It was an insult to more than himself, but to his parents and his entire family. She was prettier than his uncle, to be sure, but she was no less vile. On some level he'd always known that. Seeing it so clearly confirmed left him with a bitter taste in his mouth and a sickening sensation in his stomach. How lonely had he been to allow her to be that close to him for so long?

It had been more unpleasant than he'd anticipated but at least the sordid affair was over. He decided to walk off the temper that was under his skin. The journey home was perhaps a ten minute walk and he'd need every second of it to stop his skin from crawling. The last thing he needed was to be around A'wei with this seething irritation roiling inside him.

Never again would he allow himself to be claimed like a thing, or used like a toy to be tossed aside. He was his father's son, his mother's son. Everything about him, from his body, the hair on his head, to the position he held was a gift from them, and he would not allow himself to be treated as a disposable thing ever again. It didn't matter how he felt about the person. He was worth more than that for fucking certain. Love was probably not in the cards, but he could likely manage a modicum of respect. Someone who at least saw him as a person instead of a possession or a literal object. Now all he could do was fight against the sickening feeling of having been tainted by giving someone part of himself that they didn't deserve.

CHAPTER FOUR

Thornfield House, London
The next day

TODAY WAS THE day. She sat on the floor playing with Young Ellie, as the little girl seemed to be discovering her toes. Her brother was content to lay in Isolde's lap while she doted on him. Elodia had made the decision to sit with her back to the door after she found herself staring at the doorway. Her stomach had been in such a disarray that she'd barely been able to choke down anything at breakfast. The longer she sat there, the more she questioned the wisdom of her course of action. She wanted to simply run up the stairs and leave it at his desk. It would have been simple enough, and she wouldn't have to look him in the eye in the event that he was displeased.

There was only one issue with this course of action. He would never know it was her and she wouldn't be able to let him know what she had done. She could give it to Ada, but it lacked the personal touch of delivering it herself. Wouldn't he then assume that she didn't care who delivered it and, by association, that the gesture had less meaning than it did? She should have written a note. Perhaps it was too late for that particular idea. Even now, she couldn't decide what she wanted more, to have it finished or to push for the most ideal outcome.

"Ellie?" She looked up at Ada.

"Yes?"

"I was asking if you had any plans in place for a week from now?"

"No."

"We've decided on a date for the christening. Gigi and Leo will be back from their honeymoon by Saturday, so I thought it would work."

"Yes, that's fine. Whatever you like, Ada."

The front door slammed open and Elodia glanced over to Ada, who pursed her lips, her eyes fixed on the doorway. There were two pairs of heavy footsteps in the entryway. One was even and measured, the other beating out a brisk tattoo on the parquet. He hadn't come in. That wasn't usual for him.

Basil entered the room and pressed a kiss to Ada's head.

"Hello darling," her greeted her, before he plopped down on the floor in front of Elodia. Elodia released the girl and waited for her to crawl to her father. "Miss Elodia, Miss Walsh."

"Good afternoon, Mr. Thompson," Isolde replied. "Was that Mr. Thornfield who came in with you?"

"Yes. He's in a tricky mood at the moment."

Oh God. If he was in a foul temper then she definitely didn't want to face him now. Although Ada had always teased her about her ability to improve his mood, Elodia wasn't ready to put that idea to the test.

"Oh?" Isolde's eyebrows shot up. "I can't imagine him with a temper."

"It's not the sort of thing one would enjoy, believe me. He's not an easy person to anger, but once you've managed it..." Basil shook his head.

Was she being selfish? Perhaps he had been hurt or offended and here she was, only thinking of herself. "Do you know what has angered him?" Elodia asked.

Basil shook his head. "Not a clue. He was like that this morning."

"Did you see him at Lady Sterling's ball, Ellie?" Ada asked.

"Yes, but he left early."

Ada looked at Basil. "Hmmm. By all accounts, he arrived late last night."

"How very mysterious," Isolde commented.

"He only needs a moment to cool off and he'll be back to his typical charming self," Basil assured them.

Elodia wasn't sure if that was true, but what she was certain of was that she couldn't wait and she couldn't face him. If he was bathing and changing his clothes now, then she had time to sneak up there, write a note and then leave it with the gift. If he wanted to address it with her, he could and would, but she would hold the secret no longer. Waiting was becoming torturous and almost silly.

This was the moment. It was perhaps a bit forward of her but there was no time like the present, and no better way to get answers than to ask a question. She'd already waited too long to return it to him, and even if it didn't go the way she'd wanted, he deserved to have his property back.

She stood, excused herself and walked out the door and down the hallway to his study. The dark wooden door was cracked open. She'd seen it a thousand times, but she'd never entered the room before. It had always felt too personal, too close to him. She knocked gently, and when there was no answer, she pushed the door open wide enough for her to slip inside.

Instantly she was consumed by his scent; amber, sage and a spice like pepper or cumin. All of that mixed with leather and fresh paper. There were so many touches that showed it was his, from the guqin resting on a table to the lacquered cherrywood chessboard with white and black stones.

She walked over to his desk and pulled out the package before sitting down to write the letter. A black stick lay against a small stone slab, a row of brushes hung nearby. Did he paint with them? Had she known he painted? Her eyes caught sight of letters and notes in his neat precise handwriting, some in English and some in Chinese characters.

She picked up the silver quill that lay near a crystal ink well. What should she say? She closed her eyes, pen in hand and took a deep breath. This was no time for messing about. She had fifteen minutes at best to speak her mind or carry it in her chest for the rest of her life. She began to write, pouring out every thought, every wish onto the pristine paper in stark black ink.

Finally, when it was done, she folded the sheet and set it along with the package on top of the stack of documents already there, her mouth dry with nerves, her head light with the level of emotion she'd expunged.

Footsteps sounded in the hall and she hurried to her feet, giving his desk one last overview.

"Elodia," his voice came.

Her head snapped up, her eyes wide as her stomach flipped wildly. She couldn't bring herself to speak. Damn. She'd only needed another minute and now he was here, watching her behind his desk, engaging in the most hideous breech of privacy.

"What are you doing here?" There was an edge to his voice she hadn't ever heard before. Was it a sign to leave quickly? She stumbled around his desk, her fingers clutching her skirts as she prayed she didn't trip over her hem. Lord above, what was she supposed to say? "Did Ada send you?"

"No," she replied. He moved further into the room and she backed away until her back was against the book cased wall. She hadn't bothered to come up with anything to say. It was all in the letter. "I'm sorry, I didn't mean to—"

"What is that?" he asked, staring at the package on his desk.

Was he an eagle in another life? "Um… it's for you, I believe."

"Did you leave this here?" His eyes flicked up to hers and her throat clenched down hard on whatever lie was lodged there. Would he know if she did? Had he seen her leave it there? "It's a bit late for a Christmas gift," he continued, "and far too early for my birthday."

"Yes, but—" she swallowed past her nerves. Why couldn't she say it? Why couldn't she simply admit that it was his pocket watch? "I saw it and I thought of you and I wanted you to have it." All of a sudden, she was horribly embarrassed that she'd held onto it for so long.

He closed his eyes and sighed. "Elodia." She watched the muscle in his jaw clench and knew she was running out of time. Better to let it out now, even if it came out a jumbled mess.

"I think of you often. You have always been special in my heart, Richard, and when you said you were going to marry—"

"No."

"No, what?" she asked as her stomach lurched sharply.

"You should stop speaking now, and leave."

It was like falling into a frozen lake. A breathtaking wave of cold and then... nothing. Her brain couldn't understand what he'd said. That he'd said it to *her*. He wanted her to leave. He wanted her to be silent? "Will you not even consider me?" she asked.

"I will not." He seemed almost annoyed. "You are perfectly lovely, but you are a young woman, far too young for me."

Too young? What reasoning was that? Her eyes stung. If he was going to reject her, he could at least say the truth instead of insulting her with such nonsense. "Regina wasn't too young for Mr. Kingston."

He shook his head. "That is different."

"Ada wasn't too young for Mr. Thompson."

He looked up at her. "Those were extenuating circumstances. You think you want this but you would be better served by someone else."

He'd never spoken to her like this, spoken down to her as if she was a child. "You think I am too simple to know my own mind."

"I never said that."

That frustration gave her just enough courage to stand her ground. "I love you. I've loved you since the first moment I saw you. I was... I've been waiting—"

The look on his face cut her words short. He was shocked but there was no delight. *Oh God.*

"I'm glad you spoke then, so I could put an end to this." He closed his eyes again and rubbed his forehead. "I've always admired you, Elodia, I won't pretend otherwise, but not in the way you speak of."

"You do not share my feelings?"

"I am flattered by your regard—"

"Regard—" she choked out.

"But no, I cannot accept your feelings anymore than I can accept that gift." He pointed to the brown paper wrapped package, and she looked at it but stayed where she was. She would sooner cut off her hands than take it back.

"But you…" Her mouth was trembling against tears and her chest felt like it was caving in on itself. "I thought you cared for me."

He sighed forcefully. Was that frustration? "Of course I care for you, you are my sister's friend."

A friend? Ada's friend? "Is that all I am to you?"

He didn't respond, just stared at her with that vexed expression. Was that all it was? Her head was spinning ruthlessly. Every kind word, every dance, every look whether Ada was there or not, was that all him being kind for her sake? She couldn't trust herself to speak.

"You have been a good friend to Ada. From the very first you have always stood between her and danger when it wasn't your duty to do so; it was mine. It is a debt I take seriously."

When her voice came, it was a broken whisper. "A what?" A debt? What on earth was he talking about?

"I believe in repaying kindness."

Was the man trying to kill her? That was even worse. He was simply repaying a *debt?*

Her head was shaking, refusing to acknowledge what was happening as inescapable as it was. "I do not believe that. I… I am more than that, I know I am. I know that you care for me as I am and that you—"

His stare was hard and unmoved, mortifying her into doubtful silence. "Yes?" he prodded, one eyebrow cocked, his arms folded over his chest.

"You danced with me all the time," she finished weakly.

"I enjoyed your company and you are an accomplished dancer."

"But you—" *You only danced with me.* She couldn't say it. It seemed so stupid and obvious with those hard dark eyes staring at her. Did it mean nothing then? "You told me that any man would be lucky to be my husband."

"Yes, I did."

She could barely see him with the tears in her eyes. "You said you wouldn't mind being claimed."

"You were nervous when you entered because Ada and Lady Starkley were absent. I was only trying to encourage you."

She had been a little nervous to be on her own, but— *Kindness.* Was that all it was? Hot tears spilled over her cheeks before she could stop them. She gave herself a moment to catch her breath. It was the only way she could speak past the pressure in her throat and her chest. "I do not want you to only see me as an extension of Ada."

"You have no idea what you are asking for."

His dismissal was almost insulting. She took a step forward, desperate for the insult to shock her into something other than mortified silence. "Yes, I do."

He looked away from her, shifting impatiently on his feet. "Elodia, I have shown you patience today precisely *because* of who you are to her."

He was so mean and implacable. So ruthlessly arrogant. It was almost enough to make her hate him. Or at least want to. "I don't need you to coddle me as if I were a child."

That eyebrow came up again and he tilted his head. "Are you sure about that?"

"Yes, I am a woman in my own right and I want to be seen and treated as such."

He placed his hands on his hips and pinned her with his eyes. "Very well. Then let me make my position as clear as I can. I am sorry you have wasted your time with such delusions. Your behavior today is beneath your rank and breeding and speaks to an immaturity which goes to the very core of why you are not a good match for me. I do not believe that you are acting out of any malicious intent, so I will not demand that you leave my house, but I hope that you have the self-respect to leave my presence and put this fantasy to rest."

She couldn't meet his eyes anymore. She didn't think she would ever be able to do so again. Delusions. It was a harsh word, but an accurate one. She had deluded herself into believing that she meant more to him than she did. How many times had he tolerated her arrogance, her audacity when she'd imagined a rapport? What was she going to do? He wanted her gone. He wanted nothing to do with her now. "I'm sorry to have wasted your time."

"You haven't. Yet."

Yet. The threat was implicit. If she lingered any longer, who knew what he would say or do? She couldn't argue it anymore, couldn't pretend she had allowed herself an inch of dignity to hide behind. There was nothing left but to retreat. She'd asked to be treated as an individual instead of Ada's friend, and he had fulfilled her request.

Without that tenuous thread of connection, they were strangers. He'd said as much. With an agonizingly tight throat and burning eyes, she nodded to herself then turned to walk to the door.

"Elodia," his voice came behind her, terse and sharp. "You need to take this back with you."

She paused and glanced over her shoulder, still unable to look at him. No, she wouldn't take it back; she wouldn't take anything back. It had been the truth of her heart, meant for him alone. It didn't matter that he didn't want it. She'd be damned if she'd gone through all that and broken her heart for nothing. "It's already yours," she replied, unable to keep the sadness from her voice.

Then she slipped from the room, wondering how her legs

could keep moving when she could barely feel them. In the hallway, she leaned against the wall, struggling to breathe.

How had it gone so wrong?

It had been like speaking to a stranger. A cold eyed and stone hearted stranger. And even then she knew he had spared her the worst of his temper. Even now, he was being kind. She'd never known kindness could ache so much.

She would leave; she wouldn't trespass on his goodwill any longer. She returned to the parlor where Ada was playing with her children. When she entered the room, Ada looked up with a smile but a worried frown chased it away the moment she took in the expression on Elodia's face.

"Ellie?"

"I have to go home."

"Is everything alright?" Mr. Thompson asked, his eyes flicking over her shoulder to the empty doorway.

"Yes. I forgot I have a prior engagement with Papa." She forced out a laugh and shook her head. "I have completely lost track of time."

"Do we?" Isolde stood.

"No, you can stay here, Isolde. Don't come with me. Return when you've finished. I will see you all later." *Hurry. Hurry. Get out of there.*

"I'll walk you out," Ada said, rising to her feet.

Elodia shook her head hard. "Don't treat me like a stranger. I know the way." She smiled, turned and left as quickly as she could manage.

She needed to get home as quickly as possible. In the quiet, she'd have to find a way to piece together what was left of her heart and survive.

IT TOOK A'WEI three days to ask.

In hindsight, Richard supposed he should have taken himself

elsewhere. Foolishly, he had imagined her silence was an indication for either ignorance or distraction. She was a new mother after all. But he should never have doubted her ability to multitask or meddle, especially when it came to those she loved, like Elodia or him. She was his sister after all.

Even if he had been entirely justified in his sentiments with respect to Elodia, he regretted allowing his irritation at Rachel to spill over onto her. He was too angry even days later. Too full of shame and venom to be gentle. His skin still crawled with Rachel's belief of her ownership of him, and Elodia's confession, despite its teary and heartfelt delivery, had somehow sounded the same. Another highborn lady believing she had a claim to him and his affection. He hadn't lied to her, but he hadn't been as kind as he knew she deserved.

In the moment, all he'd wanted was for her to leave him alone. To laugh and lie and say she was teasing him. Now every time he saw that damned box on the desk, he remembered the way her face had flooded with incomprehension, and then the stunned shock of hurt and embarrassment. He remembered how thin and soft her voice had been when she'd left. She had always been a bit brazen, stubborn and assured of herself. In truth, he'd enjoyed her forthrightness. But now he was remembering the way she'd fiddled with her bracelet at the ball. How small she'd seemed all by herself until her father appeared. And how quickly he had capitalized on it when it suited his comfort.

Perhaps he'd overestimated her confidence. So much ill humor seemed to bounce off of her as if she were impervious to it. Perhaps he'd never expected it to come in his direction in that way. Or perhaps he was embarrassed to have missed it, especially as Leo and Basil had been proven correct when they pointed out that she seemed sweet on him. If she wasn't arrogant in truth, then was it him? Had he truly treated her differently? Was he to blame for her behavior? Had he strung her along only to crush her in the final moment?

So when the knock came on the door to his study on the third day, he was prepared to face either his sister or her husband.

"Brother," A'wei called, sticking her head around the open door. "May I come in?" He turned to face the door, hoping his expression was more tranquil than he felt.

"This is still your home, A'wei, you don't need permission to be anywhere within it."

She cast her eyes about the room before entering and closing the door behind her.

"What can I do for you, sister?" he asked, sitting down behind his desk.

"I was checking to see if your mood had improved as yet."

Cheeky little busybody. "It has not."

"Ah." She nodded, and took a seat in one of the free chairs.

"Is that all?" he asked.

She fixed an impatient look on him for a few moments before letting out a tolerant sigh. She couldn't know how much she reminded him of their mother at the most inconvenient times. "Did you see Ellie before she left a few days ago?"

"Miss Hawthorne?" The minute the words left his mouth, he knew they were the wrong ones. He only ever called Elodia 'Miss Hawthorne' in mixed company. Ada's head tilted to one side and he knew she was about to take an hour of his life. Their mother used to do the same thing before pinning him down on a lie. One word and she would tilt her head before smiling softly and eviscerating whatever story he'd told with cold, calm precision.

"'Miss Hawthorne'?" she repeated.

"A'wei," He was going to need every ounce of patience for this. Elodia would back down, but his sweet bulldog of a sister never would.

"Something *did* happen, didn't it?" she asked.

He closed his eyes and sighed. The only way out at this point was through. "She did speak to me. I was unable to satisfy her."

"How very mysterious." She leaned forward, glancing down at the box and sealed letter on the desk. He'd left it where Elodia had placed it, untouched. Now he wished he'd hidden it in his drawer.

"What's this?" she asked, reaching over and picking it up.

"I have no idea. Your friend left it here, even though I told her I couldn't accept it." A sudden thought occurred to him. "Would you take it back to her?"

A'wei glanced up at him from the box she held in her hands. "She left it here for you?"

"Yes, but I asked her to take it back."

"And what did she say to that?"

"She said," he paused, wondering if it was better left private. Those words had stayed in his mind. *It's already yours.* Some part of him already imagined she had been speaking about more than whatever was in that box. He didn't want to think about that.

"What did she say?" Ada asked again.

"She said it was 'already mine'."

A'wei blinked for a moment, then lowered her eyes, staring at it with too much interest. "I think you should open it." Her voice was soft but certain.

"A'wei."

She stood and walked around the desk before handing it to him. "If I am correct in my guess, you will regret leaving it here."

He let out an irritated sigh and snatched it from her, pulling impatiently at the twine and brown paper to reveal a small leather covered box. A queer feeling took up residence inside his gut as his throat went dry. Terrifying hope bloomed in his mind.

Was it? Maybe… Somehow, was this *that* thing… that thing he'd spent the better part of a year trying to let go of. He clenched his jaw and opened the lid. Immediately his hand came up to cover his trembling mouth as his eyes began to burn with tears.

There, nestled against the black velvet, as perfect as the day he had been given it over a decade ago, was his father's pocket watch. Somehow *she'd* found it. All the time he'd spent torturing himself with the idea of some asshole throwing it into the Thames, she had been keeping it safe for him. Tears flooded his vision as he removed it from the case, his shaking fingers tracing the golden cranes dancing against the silver background. The mother of pearl moon. He opened it to see his father's initials engraved within. T.A.T. Thomas Alexander Thornfield.

Fùqīn, the word was a broken whisper in his mind. He still remembered the pride and excitement he'd felt the day his father had passed it on to him. It had been the last thing he'd given Richard before he and his mother had left for China. Before the sea had swallowed them both. A shipment of items had returned ahead of them with spices, wine, lotus seeds, ink and brushes, but he had never seen their parents again. His throat was on fire, his chest trapped in a vice-like grip. It was here. After two years of secret despair, of shame, here it was. Returned to him as if by divine intervention. But it wasn't divine at all, unless one could consider the actions of one woman as an act of God.

"Is that—" A'wei didn't finish the question.

He nodded, unable to speak. There was too much inside him fighting to escape. A moment later, he felt her hand on his arm. He wondered if the ache in his chest would ever subside.

"I wondered… She must have found it the day we were kidnapped. She'd seen something in a pawnbroker's window. After she bought it, she refused to say what it was. I never imagined she had found this."

He picked up the letter she'd left behind and flipped it open.

Dearest Richard,

I apologize for returning this to you so late. I didn't mean to keep it from you for so long. I know how precious it is and I wanted to make sure it was mended and perfect for you. After that, I couldn't find an opportunity with Ada leaving town and you leaving yourself. I wanted to give you this and tell you how precious you are to me, how long you've had my heart and all my hopes for my future. You are everywhere, in every step I take. I love you for every smile you've given me, every dance, every kindness. My sincere hope is that you will give me the chance to stay close to you and give you all the love you've kindled in me, and that you will find a space for me in your heart. I will not be angry if you cannot return my feelings, I only couldn't bear to hold onto them any longer. I hope you are not angry with me, and I hope having this keepsake returned to you gives you ease and comfort, as you have given me hope and joy.

Yours forever,
Elodia.

SHE'D DONE IT for him. All this time she'd only been thinking of him, and he had allowed his anger over someone else to hurt her. Whether or not he returned her feelings, they had always been rooted in consideration for him, not arrogance or presumption. It was almost uncomfortable reading those adoring words, seeing them laid out so boldly on the page, his father's pocket watch heavy in his hand as a testament to the truth there in black and white.

Yes, he decided, there was some kind of divinity in her, something perfect and sacred and wonderful that would have driven her to do something like this for him. For her to treasure his father's gift and guard it when he couldn't. And he had nearly given it away a second time because of his refusal to accept her or her gift. The image of her in this same room came to his mind and he saw her again as if for the first time. Her voice soft and halting, her eyes were full of hope and tenderness.

I've loved you since the first moment I saw you.

He couldn't decide which was more embarrassing to him, her candor or his response. No one had ever spoken to him this way or thought of him in such a way, he was sure of it. It was something he had wanted; after all, who didn't want to be loved? But he wasn't exactly happy about it. He didn't feel as he imagined he would. There was no rapture, only unease and a feeling like she had made a mistake giving so much to him. Was that the true source of his discomfort?

Who the hell do you think you are? Rachel's voice appeared suddenly, sneering and all too familiar. He knew he was worth more than she was willing to give, but was he worthy of what Elodia offered so freely? Was it something he could accept and return?

I've been waiting.

Waiting for him. For how many years? Five? Six? Throughout every word they'd spoken, every dance, every game, every smile and jest, she had been loving him quietly and hoping. And what had he been doing? Treating her like a sister and giving his body at the very least to a woman who would have just as easily stepped over it if he was in her way.

It felt wrong somehow to accept her feelings now, like someone had offered him a silk embroidered handkerchief to clean mud off his hands. Surely something so fine had a better use. He'd never seen her as a prospect, knowing somehow in the back of his mind that she was worth far more than him. She was so wonderful and so untainted by the world. There had to be someone better, someone more worthy of her precious feelings. Someone younger, less tainted, less foolish than he was.

He couldn't help disappointing her hopes, but he could at least apologize for his words.

CHAPTER FIVE

Melbroke House, Mayfair, London

AFTER HER BOTCHED confession, Elodia spent the following days trying to think of a way to avoid setting foot outside the house for the rest of the season. Every time she thought about Richard, her eyes filled with tears, so she'd decided to simply stay away from him and anyone who could notice such a thing. Avoiding her father and Isolde had been difficult, but in the end she managed to make enough of an appearance to avoid too much commentary. Sad literary choices had never been more useful.

It had worked until today, the day of the christening for Ada and Basil's children. She couldn't bring Russian literature to the church. When she'd agreed to be godmother to Eleanor, she hadn't anticipated this nightmare of a situation with Richard. As it was, she'd given her word and there was no way she would back out of it. It would be a poor showing as a friend, so to say nothing of the inquisition she would be subjected to by both Ada and Regina.

So after nearly a week at home, lingering in her room as much as possible, Elodia rose early that Wednesday, took a bath and instructed Béa to put out her green and blue shot dupioni silk dress. Béa had questions but she did as she was bid without an inquisition, which was new for her. The tall, dark-skinned woman was around Isolde's age, with deft fingers and a strong body. Her needlework and skill with braids were incomparable but Elodia had no doubt she could also see a man off with a cutlass in short order. She had been Elodia's lady's maid since she had lived in Trinidad, and mercifully had agreed to accompany her when she came to England with her father. In many ways she was more like an older sister to Elodia than a servant, in turns chiding her and encouraging her as she grew into adulthood.

Béa wove Elodia's long curls into braids and twisted them into a crown secured by pearled combs. Then Elodia pulled on her kid gloves and followed her father and Isolde into the carriage. If they noticed anything was wrong, they didn't say anything to her and she was grateful for it. It was all she could do to keep her head up and her eyes dry.

She saw him the moment she entered the church. The very instant. He wore a deep blue velvet coat and buff trousers, a picture of elegance. His pale blue waistcoat was embroidered with white cranes and flowers. Even now their clothing matched as if they had planned it. As if it was fated when it was anything but. She glimpsed the chain under his jacket. Was he wearing his father's pocket watch? Did she have the right to know? It had to be some kind of a curse, this feeling in her chest. The knowledge that someone who meant so much to her saw her as tangential, no better than an acquaintance, was more painful than anything else.

For this morning her marching orders were simple enough. The focus was Eleanor. She would be the perfect gracious guest. She smiled and conversed with whoever was near her, doted on her goddaughter. When the priest gave the blessing to the children, Regina held Thomas and Elodia held Eleanor, focusing all her attention on the cooing baby in her arms and not the man standing behind her, just close enough to tease her with the warmth of his body. If any tears escaped her, she pretended it was happiness at the event.

She did not look at Richard Thornfield outside of what was considered polite. She did not cry or encourage conversation between them. Even at the reception at his house afterwards, she kept her distance, played the piano when asked and drank her tea.

No matter the cost, she would not make their acquaintance any more awkward than it needed to be. It was, however, easier said than done. Every time he spoke, her ear picked up his voice by force of habit. She was constantly aware of where he was, what he was doing.

There would be no way to avoid him, however, not here or in the future. Her only choice was to battle her way through and minimize the scars left. She needed to maintain her dignity, whatever that meant. Right now it meant participating in the marriage mart even if her heart was shattered. She would finish this season, and if her father married before she found a man of her own, she would ask him to help her set up a living elsewhere. Maybe her husband would be willing to establish their living outside of England at least until Richard married.

Ada and Regina hardly needed her anymore. She watched them from her seat across the room. Ada hanging on Basil's arm, now Eleanor had been taken upstairs by the governess to rest. Regina near her husband, the picture of happiness, fully within her role as a baroness. They would have more children and their lives would become even more full.

There were other people of her acquaintance who valued her as she was. Perhaps she would be a companion to Aunt Theo for the years she had left, and then to Isolde. Maybe she and Isolde could take a tour of the continent together. Eventually, when Richard married, Ada would be more assured of his happiness and she would be at her own residence more often. Then Elodia would be able to see Ada more without enduring him. Perhaps when Ada and Regina's children were older they would have more time for their friendship. Perhaps her own marriage and children would lessen the ache in her chest whenever she thought of him.

"Elodia, my dear," Isolde said suddenly, "will you accompany me for a turn about the room?"

"A what?"

"I've been sitting here for some time and I'd like to stretch my legs." Her tone was easy but her stare was too frank and direct. There was no doubt as to her intentions.

"Well, I'll have to check with Ada; she may need me."

"She's already given her approval." She smiled tightly and raised her eyebrows expectantly.

Elodia caught Ada's eye and she gave her a single nod. She was free. "Yes, of course." She took her arm and followed her along the walls of the expansive sitting room at Thornfield House.

"Do you wish to discuss it?" she asked in a low tone meant for Elodia's ear alone.

"No," Elodia replied, smiling at Aunt Theo as she passed.

"Has something gone on between you and Mr. Thornfield?" Isolde continued.

"No," she glanced at her. "What makes you ask that?"

Isolde sighed heavily. "Elodia, you are a brave and resilient girl, but you aren't the best liar." Elodia looked over at her sharply and she smiled back. "Chin up, dear, and speak softly."

"I can't, not here," Elodia begged.

Isolde slid her arm around her waist and guided her out of the room to the corridor leading to the terrace. "Tell me now."

It was strange how much easier it was to breathe knowing he wasn't in the same room. "He hasn't done anything wrong. He has only ever been the kindest and gentlest man to me."

She nodded. "Alright."

"It's my fault, really. I… I thought something, I believed something that wasn't true." Her eyes flooded with tears and she turned away, staring out at the wonderfully manicured lawn. How long had she spent secretly imagining raising her children here? It seemed almost ridiculous now. Who planned a life with a man whose affections hadn't even been expressed to them? No wonder he'd been repulsed by her.

"By that, you mean you confessed your feelings to him?" Isolde continued, her hand rubbing up and down her back.

Elodia nodded. "But he… he doesn't like me. He said that he

had only ever seen me as Ada's friend, nothing more."

"That is a reasonable position for him to take, my dear," Isolde replied.

Elodia nodded forcefully, as if the action would convince her and make everything hurt less. "I know that. I do not blame him. I just thought he cared for me as well. I was waiting for him. I was waiting for him and now I feel so foolish I can barely look anyone in the eye."

"Sweet girl." Isolde brushed her hair back from her brow, and for a moment, Elodia missed her mother so much it felt like her chest was caving in. "If he has made you think he lo—"

"He hasn't. He had no idea what I was on about. He was shocked and embarrassed, and I just kept talking." She'd relived that nightmare so many times. She could still see the way his expression went from annoyance to shock and discomfort to that hard, implacable mask which was so foreign to her. She had shown her heart so fully that there was nowhere left to hide.

"I'm sorry to hear that."

"He asked me to maintain my dignity and give up my feelings, and I am determined to do it. I will leave him alone and treat him as I should have from the beginning. With respect and distance." It would be the hardest thing she'd ever done, but in the end, it was the best for both of them. She would not force him or make him uncomfortable, and she would learn to be more discerning with her feelings.

Isolde hugged her, rubbing her arm briskly. "I am glad to hear that you have decided to move forward from this. It is very good of you."

It would have been better for her not to engage in the behavior to begin with. Now she was hiding from him in his house and he was staying as far away from her as possible. She'd made his house a source of unease for both of them because of her presence. And her presumption. Why would she think he was in love with her or that he would see her as anything more than Ada's friend? It was the exact sort of thing women tried to avoid, a smile and a kind word being taken for romantic interest. How had she managed to engage in that behavior herself? How had she managed to break her own heart?

"I will not burden him with my feelings any more than I already have; he doesn't deserve that. He's a good man, he was being kind to me, and in my wishful arrogance, I assumed it meant more. I just need to get through this season."

Sterling House, London
Three days later

IF RICHARD HAD known Elodia would have been at the Viscountess Sterling's ball, he would have begged off, no matter how much Ada pleaded. After the christening ceremony and the reception, he didn't have the stomach to stand to one side and witness Elodia's misery. Not that she was being melodramatic about the whole affair, which was somehow making it worse.

She was as lovely as ever in her bright blue silk, with orchids in her hair, and her demeanor was still graceful and charming. It would have taken a trained eye to notice the unusual reticence in her now. The natural joie de vivre that allowed her to float from room to room was gone and he knew, he fucking *knew* it was his fault. He wanted to believe that no matter what he had done or said, anything other than acceptance would have resulted in this for her, but he couldn't. Because he had done more than reject her, he had told her that she essentially meant nothing to him personally. A callous lie that he couldn't take back now without confusing her and making things worse.

Her interaction with him now was virtually non-existent. It was the most jarring change. Again, it wasn't anything glaringly obvious to others; she wasn't sitting to one side and glaring at him or making anything awkward. But at the christening, when he'd received his first taste of what it would be like around Elodia, he realized that he'd never not spoken to her when she was around. He'd never realized how many of their interactions she initiated, or, more importantly, how central they were to his natural rhythm at social events.

This was the second time since meeting Elodia that Richard hadn't greeted her almost immediately after entering a room with her in it. Missing that step was more than awkward, it was disorienting. He couldn't tell if she was rightfully angry with him or if it was her way of honoring his feelings. He'd told her to maintain a distance and he'd meant it, but he never expected to feel this bereft as a result.

If this was the new normal, Richard was not enthused about it. Denying himself her company and her affection was painful and he didn't know what that meant. How much of his life had he structured around her without realizing it? How much had he come to rely on her smiles and her bright eyes? It only seemed to confirm what Leo and Basil had suggested, that somehow Richard's feelings for Elodia had evolved past friendship. Richard wasn't convinced though. She was sweet and sincere, but part of him couldn't shake the fact that she was the same age as his little sister. The little sister who used to crawl into his bed when she was afraid, and ran to him whenever she scraped her knee.

He felt a responsibility towards Elodia, and an instinct to protect her, from her smile to every dark, curling hair on her head. He regretted hurting her feelings and despised seeing her upset, but that wasn't the same thing as love, was it? And all of this didn't even begin to touch her father. Even if Richard had thought to return those feelings, there wasn't a chance in hell the viscount would allow his precious child to marry a mixed-race merchant, regardless of how rich the merchant was, or how often he'd been to dinner at his house. The viscount was a tolerant man, but even that seemed to be a bridge too far.

No matter how disappointed she was now, she would recover with time. She would realize that she wanted someone who could give her more. She would thank him for keeping his head and allowing her the time to discover the truth of her heart and keep her father. Once she let go of her naïve feelings, things would resolve themselves naturally. He just had to wait it out. But he couldn't shake the feeling that he was losing something more precious than he even knew, and the cost was something he would never be able to recover from.

Orange blossoms filled his nostrils and his jaw tightened.

"Lover."

He should have known she would be here as well. "Rachel."

"I've missed you."

"What do you want with me?"

"To apologize, of course. I wasn't on my best behavior the last time we were together."

"Mmmm, but perhaps more yourself."

"I wanted an opportunity to make it up to you."

"You can do that by leaving me alone."

"Don't be like that, darling. We've had such a good run. There's no need for it to end on a sour note."

"As long as it ends."

"One more night," she purred. "I promise I'll behave, you can do whatever you want, I'll be whatever you want…"

"No thank you." He began to walk away but she followed him, gripping the arm of his jacket.

"Why not? You aren't married yet."

"I don't owe you a reason. Thank you for the offer but I am not interested."

"You are being very disagreeable," she grumbled.

"That is your opinion." He took a small step back, removing her hand from his person and bowed to her. "Good evening, Lady Tremaine." There was no way for her to follow him now without bringing attention to herself. He turned and walked to the refreshments table.

He poured himself a glass of madeira and choked down the sweet wine. He hated that he had allowed her to be so close to him. Why did it matter so much that he wasn't interested? There was no clout to maintain with anyone, because no one knew. There was no reason to cling to him so damned particularly because they both knew she had other lovers.

It had been annoying before, but now it was getting unsettling. How long did she mean to persist with this?

"Goodness, are you here?" his uncle's snarling voice came from over his shoulder and Richard's back tensed instantly, his jaw locking against a curse. Christ alive, had he been invited as well?

He hadn't heard or seen his uncle in years, but if he never did again in his life, it would be too soon. He didn't turn to face him, merely waited for him to step forward.

"I thought you'd removed yourself last year," he continued.

"How silly of you," Richard replied, consciously relaxing his grip on his glass.

"I hear that girl managed a most advantageous match indeed."

That girl. There were so many ways he could refer to her. His niece. His brother's daughter. Adelaide. Ada. A'wei. *That girl.* "Yes. Thank you for that."

Simon frowned in confusion. If Richard didn't know what he knew, he would almost have believed it. "You flatter me, nephew, I am not acquainted with the Viscount Sterling."

"Mmm, but you are well enough acquainted with others." The words came out before he could stop them.

His frown deepened. "I don't know—"

"What you know or don't know is your first problem." No, he wasn't going to play that game. He could pretend he was innocent, but Richard wasn't about to play along with the farce. "I know *you*, and your limits. That is your second."

"Are you threatening me, boy?"

"Do I need to?" Richard gave him a scathing sidelong glance, taking in his brown hair and eyes, his weak chin, the thin moustache above equally thin lips. He had always been a perfectly average man, eaten up with bitterness over his own mediocrity.

"This conversation is growing tiresome," Simon said, rolling his eyes.

"Feel free to remove yourself from my presence, by all means." It's not as if Richard had sought out the man's company.

"It is not for me to be driven away by the likes of you," he sneered.

"That remains to be seen. You see those you deem beneath you as resources to be plundered or obstacles to be removed, but I shall take this unpleasant moment to remind you that no one is invulnerable. Least of all you."

"Is this an appeal to familial sentiment?" Simon asked with a haughty eyebrow lifted.

Richard's smile was almost feral, the desire to beat him bloody almost overwhelming. "That is amusing. Incidentally, my father's memory is the only thing keeping food in your mouth and a roof over your head. If you want to keep living the life you have then stay away from me and mine."

The mask slipped and his beady little eyes narrowed. "You think because your sister managed to seduce the son of a viscount you can make threats to me?"

"This is your last warning, Simon. You know your nephew but you haven't met *me* yet. Test my patience further and I'll let you spend your last days in that debtor's prison you had arranged for me."

"You little—"

"Mr. Thornfield, and Mr. Thornfield." A light female voice cut his uncle off and Richard turned with a smile he didn't feel to see A'wei approaching with her mother-in-law, the Viscountess Sterling.

He smiled and bowed to her, before brushing a light kiss to A'wei's cheek.

"My lady, sister."

"Brother," A'wei replied evenly before greeting their uncle.

Her sweet face was hardened into something entirely alien to Richard. "Uncle Simon,"

"Adelaide." He turned to their hostess and smiled graciously. "Lady Sterling."

"I do hope you two gentlemen are enjoying yourselves." Her eyes drifted between the both of them. If she sensed the tension, he couldn't tell.

"Perpetually," Richard replied evenly.

"I am glad to hear it." She turned to his uncle, "Mr. Thornfield, there is a person I've been meaning to introduce you to, if you'll come with me."

Then she led him away, all polite condescension and smiles. Was she not a fan of him either? That was interesting. He wondered if that was a recent development due to Ada's influence or whether his grubby little self was simply that disagreeable to everyone.

"That was neatly done," Richard mused.

"What on earth did he want with you, brother?" Ada asked, grabbing his arm. She still had the habit of putting her hands on people without a second thought.

"To annoy me. Was that your version of a rescue?" he asked, patting her hand.

"I thought you were going to hit him," she replied, glancing over to where he now stood with another gentleman.

"I'd considered it."

She began walking with him, leaning her head lightly against his arm. "I'm sorry he is here. I had no idea she would invite him."

"Socially, it makes sense for her to invite him." Even if it was a nasty surprise.

"I know that we generally do not advertise our dislike of him, but if she is unaware, I cannot promise this won't happen again."

"You want to tell her?" he asked, turning to her. His mèimei was becoming even fiercer and bolder.

"He didn't have me taken hostage or try to have me killed.

I've only kept silent because you have, but if you prefer to expose him, I will ask her not to invite him to any events she invites us to."

"Mmmm." It was certainly a thought. Did he want to begin that trouble so early?

"I know Lord and Lady Starkley would support it," Ada continued.

He'd forgotten about them. Leo wouldn't have needed to be told, as he had been the one to investigate and uncover Uncle Simon's involvement in Richard's abduction. If he began that call, others would undoubtedly follow. Lord Melbroke and Lady Sterling would believe him. But despite that knowledge, Richard had always been leery of striking out against his uncle. His fortunes so far were linked to his wife and daughters. They were not close, but Richard bore them no ill will. Having Uncle Simon as a husband or father had to be penance enough. Whatever path he took would need to leave them out of the path of fire. For now.

"Oh, Ellie,"

His head snapped up to see Elodia's eyes darting between him and A'wei like a cornered animal. Fuck. He glanced at Ada and saw her watching Elodia with an expression that was just a little too innocent. *The meddling little…*

"Miss Hawthorne," he greeted Elodia and bowed to her, unsure of what to say.

"Ada, I… I hadn't seen you there." She dipped into a curtsey, "Mr. Thornfield."

"How have you been, Ellie?" A'wei took her gloved hand. "I haven't seen you in over a week."

She smiled softly at Ada and glanced down at their clasped hands. She wouldn't look at him for love or money. He could hardly blame her. He turned his attention to the dance floor where the waltz was drawing to an end.

"Oh, I've been well enough, keeping busy with papa."

"Truly?" A'wei prodded. Richard fought the urge to glare at

her. She could be such a busybody when she was in the mood to be, but this bordered on cruel. What was her intention here? She already knew what had happened, so why couldn't she just leave the poor girl alone?

Elodia gave another thin smile, keeping her eyes on A'wei. "Yes, he is remarrying as I told you, and I am trying my own hand at the marriage mart."

His head swung back in her direction. "Are you?" The words spilled past his lips before he could stop them.

Her grip on her fingers tightened before she met his eyes evenly. "I am. No point in dwelling on the past."

Good girl. It should have been a relief to hear those words. Instead, they filled him with something like sadness and pride. He had lost something costly and irreplaceable, and in doing so he had hurt her, but she still stood here looking him in the eye unflinchingly. He couldn't help but admire her fortitude. There was barely a trace of that shattered young woman who'd stood in his office and pleaded with him for feelings he still didn't believe he could or should return.

"How true," A'wei said. "Are there any gentlemen here in particular that you fancy? I'm a matron now, I can make introductions or bother Basil to do so."

"Not so far," Eloida replied, returning her attention to A'wei.

"Hmmm, well then, I imagine Gigi would suggest we chum the water and attract some interest,"

"Chumming how?" Richard asked. Ada turned to him and smiled in a way that told him that he should have retreated when he had the chance. Was this what he was like? Was this what Basil and Leo dealt with for over a decade? Christ, it was insufferable.

"Dancing."

He started to shake his head. "Mèimei—"

"Don't you want to help her, gēgē?"

"I—"

"If an eligible bachelor such as yourself seeks her out then others will follow." Her eyes were so wide and earnest but he knew all too well she was cackling inside.

He couldn't argue with her logic for two reasons. One, she was correct, and secondly, it would embarrass Elodia past all bearing. He'd harmed her enough. For some reason, the idea of dancing with Elodia, of holding her close even for the space of a song, was terrifying. He didn't want to do it when he was so unsure about his own feelings. He leaned into her and murmured, "I am sure there are more suitable candidates for that office."

"It's hardly a lifetime appointment, gēgē." She replied loud enough for Elodia to hear and he had to fight back the urge to hiss at her, or grab her face between his hands as he used to do. Anything to make her stop. "Just make sure she is dancing tonight and then you can pursue your own candidates. It is as much to your benefit as it is to hers."

"Perhaps you can introduce Ada to some eligible suitors she can send my way, since you are otherwise inclined," Elodia said. Her eyes were dry but there was an awkward desolation on her face. She could barely meet his gaze.

Fuck, now she thought he didn't want to dance with her. "I didn't say that."

Ada patted her arm. "Dear Elodia, Richard would be more than willing to help you. Aren't you, Richard?"

He'd never struck a woman, let alone his sister, before. It was, however, also safe to say that before this moment he'd never been tested in that conviction. Why was his sister pushing this so hard? "I am certainly not unwilling. Provided Miss Hawthorne believes it to be best."

The minute the words left his mouth, he wanted to slap himself. Why had he said that? With one sentence, he'd put her in an impossible position.

CHAPTER SIX

ELODIA STARED AT Richard, a thousand responses rising up in her throat. The wording was diabolical. Provided *she* believed it was best? What on earth was she meant to say? How could she reject him without leaving herself open to a thousand humiliating questions? If she accepted, then he would blame her for subjecting them both to the ensuing debacle, or worse, he would think she was taking advantage of Ada's ignorance when she knew he didn't really want to dance with her.

She glanced to her left and noticed the glances in their direction. If she turned him down, there would be gossip and he would have difficulty explaining or recovering. Unless, of course, she simply didn't dance at all that evening. It would be excruciating, but it was probably the last time she would get to dance with him in this lifetime. Five minutes, ten at most and it would be done.

The opening music began. She met his eyes and gave the closest approximation of a smile she could manage. "Then I accept."

He blinked, as if in surprise, then nodded and offered his arm to her. She took it and allowed him to lead her out to the dance floor. She smiled at the guests who stared, to all appearances, proud and delighted of her partner and her circumstances. Not at all nervous or heartbroken about dancing with a man who had left her in no doubt of his feelings for her. Or the lack thereof.

They took their places for the country dance and Elodia focused her gaze on the space between his eyes. It was just high enough to give the impression that she was staring into his eyes without actually having to do it. It was a slow dance, of course it would be. As if there were no other dances available. At least a quicker tempo would offer more moments of respite.

The dance began with him across from her, and then, all too soon her hand was perched lightly in his, his hand rested on her waist as they walked forward. It felt like it had been an age since they last danced, and yet she knew a lifetime wouldn't be long enough to numb her into insensibility. Not when every one of her senses was greedy for him; from the touch of his hand to the hard muscle of his arm and that hypnotic scent.

"How are you?" he asked softly. At the sound of his voice, she instinctively met his eyes. The concern she saw there left hers stinging. Bad idea.

"I am well enough, as I said earlier." She dropped her gaze down to his chin. Much safer territory. "I apologize for this. I didn't know how to avoid it without prompting more questions from Ada."

"You have nothing to apologize for."

"I know you would rather be doing anything else."

Finally, they were separated for a moment, she smiled at her second partner, trying to maintain the social mask. She'd never truly needed it before with Richard. Now it took far too much effort to maintain it in such close quarters. Too soon she was back at his side, and his hand was at her waist again. It took everything in her not to lean back into his body.

His breath wafted over her bare shoulder as he led her in a turn to face him before moving them both in a slow circle, his arm half around her waist. "Thank you for returning my father's watch to me."

So he had received it. She shook her head. "It is no matter. I meant to do so earlier but the glass on the face was shattered, and I wanted to replace it. After that, it took some time to find an opportunity that wouldn't draw notice."

"Understood."

"I… I wasn't keeping it to be cruel." She had to say it. He hadn't accused her of anything, but she wouldn't take anything for granted again. Not with him.

He turned her away from him and moved them forward, his arm behind her back. "I wouldn't think that of you, Ellie."

The shock of hearing his voice say that name had her meeting his eyes over her shoulder for a moment. Only his face was much closer than she'd anticipated. The cold censure from a week ago was gone, but whatever emotion had escaped his mask was indecipherable to her. It hadn't been like this before, or if it had been, she'd remained blissfully aware. Her heart racing, she turned her head to face forward. "Mr. Thornfield, I do not believe we are on such terms by your own declaration."

"I apologize."

"It is no matter." Did he sound disappointed? Let him be disappointed; he couldn't be more so than she was.

"No, I," he paused and then took a breath, but by that time she was back with her second partner, smiling like a doll with burning eyes. How much longer was this cursed dance supposed to last? She'd been ready to enjoy it in silence after a few pleasantries, but Richard clearly had other ideas. The moment she was beside Richard again, he began to speak.

"I have been meaning to apologize to you for what I said."

Apologize? More kindness to make her feel comfortable. Kindness he didn't owe her. "I do not accept your apology," she replied lightly, "The sentiments you related were natural and just."

"They were also cruel."

Hard. Uncompromising, but she couldn't quite call them cruel. "No, only disappointing. I am allowed my disappointment just as you are allowed your honesty."

"I don't want to be on bad terms, El—" he cut himself off. "Miss Hawthorne."

She wouldn't look at him, she couldn't, not with her name half spoken between them. She believed his apology and that he felt the necessity for it, but she didn't want to go back to what they had been before. It would be torture and she couldn't trust herself to respect his boundaries. This way, she could protect them both. It was painful, but at least the pain was something she could bear.

Mercifully, the dance came to an end at last. She drew away from him and clasped her hands at her waist, nearly breaking her fingers with her grip as she met his eyes for what she told herself would be the last time. "We are not on bad terms. They are merely different."

Was that sadness on his face? Disappointment? Guilt? She couldn't tell anymore.

He nodded finally and gave her a small smile. "I wish you every happiness."

She nodded. "Thank you. I wish the same for you. If I may infringe upon you once more, would you return me to Miss Walsh? She is acting as a sort of chaperone for me in place of my father this evening."

He nodded and led her through the crowd to Isolde who was watching her with a serious expression. She would finish as she began. She kept her back straight and managed a small smile.

"Thank you, Mr. Thornfield,"

He shook his head. "Not at all. It was my honor."

They lingered there for a moment, staring at each other, unsure or unwilling to end the moment, knowing it was an end to more than a dance. She took the moment to take him in this last time, his broad shoulders, his dark eyes, his softly curving mouth. This would be the last time she allowed herself to take him in. After this moment, in her mind, he would be someone else's.

He bowed and Elodia sank into a deep curtsey, keeping her burning eyes on the marble floor until he walked away. It was all over. They'd said everything that they needed to and they could both move on without bitterness. It should have been a relief. She wanted to disappear into a dark room and sob until there wasn't an ounce of water left inside her.

"Elodia," She heard Isolde's voice. "Ellie, are you well?"

"I need a moment outside." Her voice sounded like a broken whimper. A hand gripped her arm firmly and she felt herself being pulled from the room.

"Breathe, Ellie," she murmured, running her hand up and down Elodia's back as she led her out a door to a balcony. It must have been a balcony. She could feel the night air on her skin. It took a few minutes for Elodia to catch her breath.

"I'm alright." But she would be damned if she met anyone's eyes.

"You are second away from bursting into tears."

Elodia felt her mouth tremble almost on cue. *Blast* "I'm sorry."

"Don't apologize, my dear, just breathe."

"Is it obvious?"

"Your discomfiture is obvious, but the cause is less so," she replied.

Ellie pressed her palm to her forehead and paced back and forth as she struggled to maintain her grip on the worst of her emotions. She couldn't lose herself now, not now with so many people close by.

"If you felt this strongly then why on earth did you dance with him?"

"Because Ada insisted it would encourage more suitors to see me dancing with an eligible gentleman."

Isolde stood against the railing, watching her stride back and forth. "And you couldn't find a way out."

"Not a clean one. He was so worried about me, worried about my feelings and my state of mind."

"You said he hadn't been cruel."

Elodia stopped short in her pacing and looked at her. "He wasn't. Or at least not as cruel as he could have been. More than anything, he was firm. His face was so cold. It was like talking to a stranger." A stranger who had found an acquaintance invading his privacy. In a way, it was what she had asked for, but only if he didn't care for her at all outside of Ada.

"How terrifying."

"I would hold it against him, but you know how I am. I'm stubborn. Papa always calls me a bully."

"Oh," Isolde's voice broke off and Elodia looked up to see the older woman's lips twitching against a smile. "Well, not in a bad sort of way."

Elodia leaned against the stone banister beside Isolde and took a deep breath. "Yes, but I don't take 'no' as a response easily."

"Yes, let's call it that." She slipped an arm around Elodia's shoulders and gave her a brisk hug.

"I thought it was this grand romance," she said with a rueful smirk. "I had it all planned out. How arrogant."

"No."

"I was. I was too certain and now I have nowhere to hide from him. He's everywhere and he knows the truth. Every time he sees me looking at him, he'll know what I'm thinking. It was easier when he had no idea."

"You owed it to yourself to check, to know for certain how you both felt."

"You think so?" Elodia asked, looking at her.

"Absolutely." Isolde ran her hand over Elodia's back in a smooth, comforting stroke. "What if he did feel the same way and neither of you ever spoke? Wouldn't that be a waste?"

"I suppose." It didn't feel very brave at the moment. It felt like she had disrespected him and paid the price.

"Chin up, my dear. You were brave, but bravery comes with a price. What now?"

"I will have to get through this season. When Papa marries, I will move to stay with Aunt Theo, and then I will set up my own establishment somewhere. In time, I will marry someone sensible and kind."

"Is that all?"

"What do you mean?"

"What about the rest of the season? Will you hide yourself away?"

"I don't know. Do you think I should try to marry someone else this year?"

"Whyever not? There could be someone right under your nose who has been waiting for your notice just as you waited for Mr. Thornfield's."

It was possible. Perhaps all she needed to do was give it an honest shot. Richard had said any man would be lucky to be chosen by her. It wouldn't be a fairytale, but that didn't mean it couldn't be good, or even wonderful. "I do not believe that I will love anyone else as much as I love Richard, but that doesn't mean I need to stop trying. You are right, I'll keep looking this year. Why should I be the only one unmarried?"

"Very good. You know, your Aunt Theo had a similar story. She says happiness isn't about getting what you want but learning to appreciate what you have. It is a life skill."

"Yes. I will master it in time. But for now, I'd like to stay out here where it's quiet."

Elodia knew time and distance would take the worst of the sting of his rejection away. But she didn't know how to fix the humiliation she felt due to spending nearly a decade pining for him. Maybe it would have been easier if Richard didn't know that particular detail, but in her desperation she had told it all. Maybe she'd hoped that he would take pity on her and give her a chance, but she knew that would have been worse.

Now there was no way to return to any kind of normality with that hanging between them. Every conversation, glance or touch would be weighed down with the knowledge that she had wanted and always would want more from him than he could give. That every interaction between them would leave her sick with a longing that she could never fulfill.

If only there was a way to close the chapter for both of them, a way to even the playing field for them, to move forward at last. It wouldn't fix everything but at least it would be more bearable. Was there a way for her to regain her dignity? She couldn't think of anything at the moment outside of marriage. But she didn't want to marry to prove to Richard she was safe to be around. Perhaps time would provide that answer as well.

CHAPTER SEVEN

I T WAS TOO ridiculous. Rachel watched from her vantage point at the ballroom as Richard danced with that slave girl. That base born cub of a trollop masquerading as a lady. Lady Sterling may have been alright with that thing being paraded around her house because Lord Melbroke was her father, but Rachel saw it for what it was. A disgusting mockery of what blood and breeding should mean. Any person could learn to dance, did that make them a lady? It was insulting.

And Richard. *Her* Richard, dancing with that … girl for all the world to see the way he'd never once danced with her. Not that she would have publicly accepted a dance from a tradesman, let alone one of his background, but still. He'd had the audacity to leave *her*. To leave her behind without so much as a 'by your leave'. As if he could take her or leave her even after ten years. As if he could do without her. As if they were equals. No, not equals. As if he was far her superior. Every time she thought about it, she was left shaking with rage. How dare he treat her as an inconvenience when he should have been grateful she ever deigned to look in his direction.

And now to see him with that girl as if they were already a couple, as if he was more interested in being with her than a born and bred lady. A true English Rose. Was he going to court her? Did he think he was worthy of a viscount's daughter? It was galling to see them together, his hands resting on her as if they belonged there, his eyes warm with affection. As if he cared for her. As if that swine in a dress was more worthy of him than a true lady of the peerage. A woman of substance and breeding, a true woman.

Perhaps the little slut had already given him something to lure him away. She presented herself as quite the little lady, all wide eyes and pristine pearls, staying close to her chaperone. All delicate airs leaving the room after one dance. No doubt her mother had tried one of those tricks with Lord Melbroke, playing the delicate flower when they were nothing more than base born ilk. And Richard was watching her, as if he wanted to go to her. To *her*.

Not Rachel. Not to a woman who would lift him from the oriental gutter he'd crawled out of. No doubt he wanted Melbroke's little island miss for her supposed purity. As if women like that were ever pure. Men were depressingly predictable. That little slut would show her true nature soon enough; they were always all too eager to get on their backs to get ahead. No doubt her mother had the same idea to lure Melbrooke away from good sense. In a way, Miss Hawthorne was doing the nobility a favor by removing herself from it entirely, but the idea of letting her win, of allowing her to take what was *hers*, was intolerable.

Richard Thornfield belonged to her. He was hers, goddamnit. Her hands curled into trembling fists. How *dare* he think he had the right to leave her behind.

His heart was dark and cold like hers, and he loved a good fuck just as she did. She would die before she admitted he was the best lover she'd ever had, at once masterful and sensual with a body that never seemed to tire. No time wasted on sentimentality. Was she meant to give that up to a slip of a girl who was nothing compared to her? What could she possibly give him that she could not?

She would show him. *She* did the leaving. No one left her without her permission. She got what she wanted at all costs.

She would bring him back to heel by force if seduction didn't work, and then she would break him for presuming to think himself better than her.

"Lady Tremaine," she turned to face her hostess with an angelic smile she'd practised a million times.

"Lady Sterling, you have outdone yourself again." She glanced at the stuffy little man beside her, waiting for an introduction. He'd been speaking to Richard earlier, and from all appearances, they weren't on good terms.

"Nonsense, although I am pleased with how it turned out." Lady Sterling finally gestured to the man beside her. "Have you met Mr. Simon Thornfield?"

"Any relation to Mr. Richard Thornfield, the manufacturer?" she asked.

"He is my nephew." His smile was tight. How very interesting.

"I am pleased to meet you, Mr. Thornfield." *Very pleased indeed.*

CHAPTER EIGHT

Thornfield House, London

RICHARD KNEW SHE was here. He'd watched Elodia arrive hours before from above stairs. She'd smiled at Ada and Lady Starkley, that open bright smile that he remembered. He hadn't seen that smile in what felt like forever. Not since that day in his office. She still smiled, of course, but it wasn't the same. Now he knew it was his presence in particular that was dimming her light. So he elected to leave her to his sister and her guests rather than go down there and make her uncomfortable.

It was tea time. If he wanted to, he could ring for the servants to send him a separate tray. His appetite had been shot for the last few days but tea was light enough for him to manage. That dance at Lady Sterling's ball had been torturously awkward but it had brought to bear one key point for Richard in a way he hadn't anticipated before.

He absolutely *hated* the distance between him and Elodia.

Anger from her would have been better, anything but this submission, this meek acceptance of his judgement and what he had said. The fact that she wouldn't even consider the idea that he could be wrong was disturbing. He was used to her needling and forcing her will; he was used to a fight. He'd half expected her to glare at him from across the room, send him snide comments, try to stomp on his foot. He wanted more. He wanted *his* Ellie back, the one with the sharp tongue and the sparkling eyes, the one who smiled widely and showed her feelings boldly.

And *no*, he didn't want to dwell on the fact that he saw her in some way as 'his'.

He knew it was selfish. He understood that technically, she was treating him no differently than Lady Starkley always had in theory. Richard had never disliked Leo's wife. In fact, he could safely say she was an admirable and impressive young woman. But there was more to his relationship with Elodia. They saw and understood each other in a unique way, and the camaraderie they shared had never been equaled with any other woman for him.

Now all that was gone. She was cordial and respectful as befitted their respective positions, so he had no cause for true complaint unless he wanted to be a hypocrite. But he couldn't help but miss the warmth and familiarity she had taken back, a quality he hadn't realized he needed until now.

There was a light in her eyes he missed and was desperate to see again. A light she'd bestowed freely at one time but now she kept behind a cracked mask of politesse. At first he'd thought she was offended by him, that perhaps she was insulted by his rejection. It would have explained her silence, her refusal to engage with him outside of what would be polite in mixed company. But during the dance, one thing was made achingly clear.

She believed that *he* was offended by her and the sentiments she'd communicated.

Everything he now missed had been an expression of her love for him and her reticence was now meant to honor his rejection. Every smile, every teasing word, every private joke, every sidelong glance that made him feel less lonely was an expression of her devotion. How on earth was he supposed to know something like that? Was he clairvoyant?

She wanted him to be more comfortable, and the only way she could think to make that happen was to pull back to a safer distance. The logic was sound and, frankly, an even more potent sign of her affection and regard for him. But how on earth was he meant to explain to her that he didn't want their dynamic to change at all? It would be hideously unfair. He felt more foolish than he could say.

How could he demand that she keep giving him what she'd given him before while pushing her away? It would leave her in a liminal space that would drain her joy over time. He couldn't make her destroy herself for his own convenience. Until he knew how he wanted them to be, he needed to stay away from her for both their sakes. Which left him in the library. He'd taken a seat near the window with a copy of Candide, hoping the humorous satire would lift his spirits.

The door to the study opened abruptly and the object of his thoughts floated through in her morning gown of sheer silk gauze dyed a delicate sea foam green. He watched as she closed the door behind her and let out a weary sigh, the corners of her full mouth curved downwards. His fault. She couldn't even enjoy the company of her friends because of his careless words.

She took a few quiet breaths, then opened her eyes and walked toward the bookshelf furthest away from him.

He didn't even want to breathe lest she turn and see him. He didn't like how tired and sad she appeared, but he couldn't help but enjoy seeing her so unguarded. At least this was really her. From the moment she'd walked out the door after that horrible day, Elodia had only shown her public face to him. The Viscount's daughter, always charming and perfectly poised. The moment she saw him, that mask would return.

Then again, it was bad form to allow an unmarried woman to be in the room with him, an equally unattached male. It could ruin her if others found out. The last thing he ever wanted was to compound the harm he'd caused by taking advantage of her. Bracing himself for the change in her expression, he cleared his throat softly. Her head snapped in his direction and her eyes widened.

"Oh, R—" she pressed her lips together and swallowed back his name. He'd never wanted to hear it more. "Mr. Thornfield. I didn't realize you were here. I thought you were out."

"I was only reading," he replied, proffering the volume in his hand. Her eyes fell to it and she blinked.

She took a step backward as if she was about to escape the room. "I… I was hoping for a moment of quiet."

He nodded. "Understandable, carry on then, don't mind me."

"Thank you," she murmured, giving him a lukewarm smile and returning her attention to the shelf. A small victory. A few days ago, she would have left without another word, he was certain of it. For now, he stayed in his window seat and watched her while pretending to read his book. He'd never appreciated before how the sunlight seemed to enhance the color of her skin. As if it absorbed the light, as if she was herself made of it.

What the hell was he even thinking?

"Looking for anything in particular?" he asked, wondering how long he could tempt her into another dialogue.

She paused and glanced over at him, her full lips parted in surprise. "No. Do you have any recommendations?"

"Not exactly, but I'm familiar with the sections. If there was a subject you were interested in, I would have you directed there."

"Oh, thank you." She continued to search the shelves but said nothing further.

Damn. He looked down at his hands, disappointment swirling with embarrassment. Why was he so desperate to speak to her? Did it really matter? Didn't he have more important things to do?

Then she glanced over at him tentatively, her lips parted, ready to speak. "H… how are you enjoying your niece and nephew?"

The sound of her voice sent his heart racing. Lord, it was pathetic and he couldn't even care. It was a weak attempt at conversation, but he would take it. "They are delightful. I won't deny my niece is my favorite. I've never seen a sweeter looking child."

She nodded, selected a book and turned to face him, clutching it to her chest like armor.

"I… did you," she pressed her lips together again, before

looking down at her shoes. "Are you in here because of me?" she finally asked.

"No." The lie slipped out alarmingly easily.

She glanced up at him, her mouth pursed. She didn't believe him. "You were missed. I don't want you to be uncomfortable because of me. I can stay away if it would make you more comfortable."

"It wouldn't," he said, but she continued heedlessly.

"Ada and Regina can come to me more often, or we can go to Regina's home."

"I don't want you to avoid being here at all," he restated, adding more force to his voice.

She paused, staring at him with wide eyes, her grip on the volume in her hands tightening. "Then you must not hide away either. We cannot avoid each other, Mr. Thornfield."

He nodded. It was an improvement, but he was still *Mr. Thornfield* to her and probably would be the rest of his life. "That is true enough." Did he have the right to ask for anything else? "I was worried for you, in all honesty. You were very upset. I never wanted to hurt you, Miss Hawthorne, no matter what."

She shook her head and smiled weakly. "I was upset. I'd wasted nearly ten years of my life on an arrogant assumption."

"You weren't arrogant."

"Wasn't I?" She gave him a sardonic glance.

He shook his head. "I didn't express myself properly that day. You are more to me than an acquaintance, you are a … friend." It still felt wrong to say but he couldn't allow her to believe the lie any longer.

"A friend," she repeated.

"Yes. I know it is not what you would wish."

"I don't see how that negates my statement."

"You are beautiful, intelligent, accomplished and capable, to say nothing of your wealth and status."

Her eyebrows shot up and the corners of her mouth twitched. "A paragon."

"I meant what I said that night. Any man would be lucky to have you."

"Yes." She smiled softly, but it was still sad. "When you said that, I thought you included yourself in that group."

He shut the book in his hands. "I do include myself there. The truth is, you are entirely outside of my league."

"But you are simply uninterested."

"Mmmm." He couldn't agree or disagree. The noise could be taken whichever way she chose.

She wasn't crying at least. She didn't seem overly upset at all. She shook her head ruefully. "I don't know if that is better or worse." She let out a short laugh and rolled her eyes. "I have half a mind to demand reparations."

That statement shocked a laugh out of him. "And what exactly would you be demanding as payment?"

"A—" that audacity faded away as a thought occurred to her. He could all but see it click in place in her head and settle over her face. He knew what she would ask for before she said it, but he wasn't sure she would ask. "A kiss," she murmured, her eyes fixed on her hands.

"A what?" He didn't know why he was pushing it.

"A kiss," she repeated, lifting her head. There she was. Nervous, shy, but there. "I was saving so much for you, but now it seems a wasted effort."

"Ah." He had no idea what to do with his face.

"It is a small enough concession."

Perhaps, but it was still a damned cheeky thing to ask for. It was, however, too adorably like the old her, he couldn't help but tease her. "Interesting."

"You would be willing to accept the terms?" Her eyes widened in surprise.

"Provided you had the courage to collect," he replied. There was a horrible curiosity in him that wondered how far her courage or boldness would take her.

Her lips parted in outrage. "You think I don't?"

"I think you won't," he corrected, leaning back against the window and tilting his head in consideration. Was it ridiculous that he was enjoying himself? He'd missed her, missed *this* so damned much.

Her eyes narrowed. "What will you give me if I do?"

Greedy little thing. "The kiss is already a payment, you want something else now?"

"That is a separate issue entirely." She took a step forward, her boldness growing by the second.

"How mercenary of you."

"Do you agree?" She asked.

He let out a breath and adjusted his seat by the window. "Are you in earnest?"

"Unless you think you can't handle a little kiss," she teased with a smug smile.

"I'm wondering what on earth you learned in that school." She was dazzling. He still couldn't decide whether to give into her or send her on her way. In a way, if he called it off, she could take it as him being worried about his reaction to her. On the other hand, allowing this madness to continue could prove his point to her, give her what she needed to move on and return them to some semblance of normalcy.

She lifted her eyebrows expectedly and he couldn't keep the smile from his face. One kiss. If it helped her move on, if it gave her back the spark that made her *her*, then it was well worth the momentary awkwardness. Even if it was playing with the worst kind of fire.

"Come along then." He nodded towards her.

She blinked rapidly. "Really?"

"One kiss, one time, as payment for ten years of—"

"—useless waiting," she finished.

He pursed his lips against a smile. "Yes. Those are the terms I agree to. The minute you leave the room, that agreement will be null and void. And we will never revisit this again."

"And if I have the courage, as you say, to collect, what will I get?"

"Respect," he replied flatly.

She pulled a face, almost rolling her eyes, and again he couldn't help his smile. She was enchanting even when she was being a brat. "Agreed."

He nodded. "Well then, you have the room, Miss Hawthorne."

He stayed where he was, at the window, watching as the reality of what she'd said and done sank in. She swallowed hard as her eyes darted around the room.

"Are you just going to sit there?" She finally asked.

He raised his eyebrows. "I'm waiting."

She frowned at him in bewilderment. "I thought you were going to kiss me."

He smiled. "Oh no. If you want your payment then you need to come and claim it yourself, Miss Hawthorne."

"But—" she stopped herself from saying more, then he watched her fiddle with her fingers again.

For a moment he thought he'd won. That he had correctly gauged her. But then she squared her shoulders and walked over to where he sat with halting but ultimately resolute steps. Sitting down as he was, she was just about his height. She was so damned close to him now, closer than they had ever been before. Her spiced perfume was heady and his heart was positively galloping in his chest. He dropped his folded arms and maintained an even stare partly in an attempt to unnerve her, and partly to distract her from the iron grip his hands now had on the edge of the window seat.

He couldn't back down now, even if his stomach was writhing with what he told himself was discomfort, not anticipation. That it was her scent making him lightheaded, not the nervous eagerness in Elodia's dark eyes.

Her fingertips brushed his jaw, and his mouth went dry. Christ, was she really going to do it? Was he proud of her or terrified? Her touch lingered like a cool feather drifting over his cheek to behind his ear. He'd been touched before, but it had never made his throat ache like this. Was it her hesitation? She was too focused on him as if she were waiting for him to stop her as she leaned forward slowly, searching for a sign that he wanted something different. For all her boldness and talk of what she was owed, she didn't truly believe she deserved this. She didn't believe he owed her anything.

She was treating him and his kiss like an unexpected gift and he didn't know how to react to it. He couldn't remember anyone ever touching him like that. The effect was almost painful, like blood rushing back into a numb limb. He couldn't pull away or avoid her even if he wanted to. That was another truth. So much of him was curious as to what it would be like to be kissed by her when her touch made him ache so beautifully. If he was going to truly give her up for good, then he would allow himself to have a taste first.

At the first brush of her plush lips, his grip on the windowsill tightened and he breathed in sharply. She drew away far enough to look at him, wide eyed and anxious. Eager and terrified all at once. When he didn't move, she pressed her lips to his again, this time with a little more certainty. Simple, almost chaste, but it stole the air from his lungs. No matter his determination to keep his hands where they were, he couldn't help leaning into her, parting his lips slightly while she adjusted, moving her focus to his top lip.

If she didn't stop, the wood was going to snap off in his hands at any moment.

He felt the moment she began to pull back, and it took everything in him not to chase after her lips. He wanted to feel them again, to part that soft mouth and taste her, to pull her closer and wrap himself up in that sweet earnest affection until it seeped into his skin. Was this what it felt like to be touched by someone who cared?

It was monstrous to get this feeling as a farewell. What the fuck was he meant to do now? He didn't want to let her go, but he knew better than anyone he had no right to take what she wanted to offer. Her father no doubt had plans for his precious daughter and they would not include a Chinese tradesman as a son-in-law. No one had plans to include him in their family.

Her mouth finally left his, and he opened his eyes to see hers still shut, her face almost rapturous. If he wanted more he could have it, but now that he wanted more, the fact that it wasn't real made her presence as painful as her absence no doubt would be. A kiss under the auspices of payment or settling a score wasn't a basis for anything. She took two breaths then leaned forward again. He couldn't do it. He had to put an end to this. He'd let it go too far already.

He jerked backwards, and her eyes flew open, her hands falling away. "You said one kiss, Miss Hawthorne," he reminded her, even if the words tasted bitter after her mouth.

She gasped softly, her gaze shifting away from his as she fiddled with the flower ring on her index finger. She nodded and took a step back. "So I did. My apologies."

He half expected her to bring up the issue of her reward for winning their challenge. He could mention it. It would give them both what they wanted; to extend this moment a little longer. But it would muddy the water even more.

He'd drawn the line for both their sakes, and the reasons hadn't really changed, even if his feelings had. He was still not an appropriate choice for her. It was better to let the lie stay there rather than allow her to discover a painful truth about the world she lived in.

If he trusted his legs, he would stand up. As it was, he opted to fold his arms. "It's no matter. I believe our business is concluded, Miss Hawthorne."

She took another step backwards and drew a deep breath, pressing her lips together. He wondered if they were still tingling as his were. "Indeed, Mr. Thornfield, thank you for your time. Good day."

He nodded once and watched her leave quickly, her heels clicking sharply on the wood floor.

CHAPTER NINE

Starkley House, Mayfair, London

SMILE, *ELODIA*. IT was a constant reminder lately. It wasn't so much that she wasn't interested in the conversation of the person across from her. Regina knew how to host a party, and tonight was no different. All of the guests were interesting in one way or another, or at the very least capable of maintaining a conversation. Any other time, Elodia would have found herself thoroughly diverted. And Regina, dear Regina was holding court while being visibly pregnant, draped in gold and silks. She reveled in her new position, basking in her authority and her husband's obvious regard.

It was only that Richard was also present and her concentration was still suffering. Despite her determination to ignore his presence as much as possible, she couldn't help but pick out his voice among the hum of chatter and listen for every word. Her one victory for the night was that she had no idea what color waistcoat he was wearing tonight. It was a positively minute victory, but she was clinging to it with both hands. She shifted in her chair, smiled and leaned forward slightly. There, now poor Mr. Lewis would be assured of her attention and interest.

One week. It had been one week since she'd lost her mind and kissed Richard. Or rather, he'd allowed her to kiss him. Once. Lord knew she could never force Richard to do anything he didn't want to do. Now he sat beside a debutante, a Miss Fiest, who was no doubt invited to be a prospect for him. She was pretty, if a bit quiet. Elodia had never imagined he would be interested in someone like that, but perhaps he would enjoy the quiet in his wife. Perhaps he would value someone who was steadier and more sensible. Someone who didn't run around propositioning gentlemen in their studies and libraries. Every time she thought about that day, her face grew hot.

She still didn't know what had possessed her. It could have been curiosity after spending so long wondering, or it could have been pride over his smug confidence that she would back down. It could even have been one last attempt to change his mind. In the end, it had served as a sweet and heady close to a chapter of her life. Unsatisfying, but definite. If he'd wanted to stop her from leaving, he would have. If he'd had a change of heart, she was sure that would have been the moment. He was kind so he'd allowed her a moment of madness set within walls of iron, indulging her without allowing herself to lose herself.

She still remembered his steady controlled voice telling her their business was over. That they were now both free and clear. Reminding her of the terms. At the time, she had been embarrassed and even hurt, but in the days since, she'd come to appreciate his firmness. That kiss had left her floundering, aching for more. If he hadn't forced her to stop, who knows what she would have done. But Richard had proven himself a consummate businessman. He stated the parameters clearly and maintained the original terms ruthlessly. Now it was over, and she still had her dignity and her pride. All that was left was the future.

She would always want him, would always dream of him and ache for what might have been, but now perhaps it would be easier to keep it to herself as she no longer felt so unfulfilled. In the days since she'd spent her time doing what she probably should have been doing since she left Miss Pollitt's. She danced often, smiled widely and charmed anyone in the room. If Richard happened to be there, she still mostly maintained her distance. She wouldn't keep hoping things would change. There was no point.

But after a week of dancing, smiling and flirting, Elodia didn't appear to be any better off prospect wise than when the season began. Now she was wondering if every man in London felt the same as Richard. They danced with her, smiled and chatted with her, but for all her charm, money, social connections, and supposed beauty, she had no callers. Not one. How was that possible?

"Miss Hawthorne?"

She blinked at Mr. Lewis. Blast, had she been ignoring him again? "I'm sorry?"

"They are arranging for some young ladies to entertain us. I wondered if you would be playing for us tonight."

She gave him her most winning smile. "Certainly, Mr. Lewis, if you will turn the pages for me."

"I cannot promise a duet but I can manage that." He turned to Lady Gebling, "I believe we have another, my lady."

Lady Gebling clapped excitedly, "Oh, how lovely, Miss Hawthorne has agreed to play."

"Very kind of her," Richard commented from somewhere in the room. "Miss Hawthorne is a rare talent."

"I agree," Lady Sterling replied.

"Then she must go first," Lady Gebling said.

Elodia smiled and rose to her feet. She strode to the piano, brushing past a chair that smelled suspiciously like Richard, careful not to breathe in his scent. Mr. Lewis followed her eagerly, but she couldn't take much encouragement from it. He was a perfect example of her quandary. A second son of a baron, educated, kind and lively enough if a bit plain looking. He would have made a fine prospect. He'd danced with Elodia no less than three times in the past week, to say nothing of the attention he'd paid her at two other soirees including this one. But that was all. No calls, no flowers, no conversations with her father.

Mr. Lewis handed her three pieces: Mozart's Turkish March, Beethoven's Tempest in D minor and Schubert's Serenade. Typically she preferred Schubert, although his Serenade wasn't her favorite to play. But tonight she wanted something to exorcise her inner confusion and allow her to bang on a few keys. For that, the best candidate was Beethoven.

She began the fiery and complicated piece, making sure to keep her eyes fixed on the pages, instead of allowing them to wander to a certain gentleman. A certain gentleman with an uncanny ear for music and an appreciation equal to her own. Mr. Lewis was a good sort but he couldn't read music worth a damn and she would need to give him the cues. He was attentive, however, never letting his attention waver from her. So she made sure to give him a big smile whenever he turned the page at the right moment.

He always smiled back, perfectly doting, and rather pleased with himself. He was perfectly acceptable if only he would take the next step and propose. The forced passivity had to be the most infuriating part of being a woman. Here she was preening and fawning over a perfectly average man in the hope that if he memorized her teeth, he would pluck up the courage to *do something*. Or perhaps much like Richard, he simply wasn't that interested. Perhaps it was her own arrogance, assuming that any man who smiled at her was surely half in love. It was a fact that no matter how many virtues one possessed, love was another matter, to say nothing of marriage. She was more than pretty enough. Was it her lack of a figure? What else was she meant to do to encourage him?

When she concluded the piece, pounding out the final notes, he clapped so exuberantly she couldn't help but laugh.

"It is always such a delight to listen to you play, Miss Hawthorne," he said, nearly bouncing on his toes.

"Thank you, Mr. Lewis."

He looked over to her father who was watching her with his usual fondness and pride. "I confess I quite envy you, my lord," he continued. "To be able to hear such lovely music at any given moment."

"Indeed, only her husband will share that privilege." Lady Sterling commented.

"Enticement enough, I say, eh Lewis?" Cousin Albert commented.

"Yes, almost," Mr. Lewis replied with a laugh.

Almost? "Meaning?" The word slipped past her lips even as a chill went up her spine.

Mr. Lewis looked down at her, his eyes blinking a mile a minute while he no doubt found a way to save himself. *Almost.* To be rejected by Richard was one thing, but this little boy had no business pretending he could do better.

"Well, musical ability alone is not enough for a sensible man, but alongside a host of other virtues as you have cultivated, Miss Hawthorne, it is a boon indeed."

Her face was on fire, but thankfully, between her complexion and the dim lighting of the room, she could bluff her way out of this situation. "Ah." Of course. In theory it was true enough, but she was certain he was hiding something. A kind liar. How utterly unattractive. If he was going to lie, he might as well pay her the compliment of being at least half competent at it. Did he really think anyone was convinced by his nonsense? Richard may not have been easily persuaded or agreeable, but at least he spoke the truth.

"Surely such talent could hardly count against you," he joked, but no one laughed.

She smiled again and cast her eyes over the room. Everyone was smiling nervously, with a few half-hearted chuckles scattered through the room. Regina looked annoyed, but Richard… his face was carved out of stone, his eyes ready to stare a hole through Mr. Lewis's head. As if it mattered. How perfectly humiliating.

She stood and stared at Regina and gestured to the piano. "This exceptional instrument is now free for your next talent, Lady Starkley."

Regina smiled at her, her eyes bright with sympathy, but Elodia couldn't take comfort in it. Not while her stomach was still squirming like knotted eels. After all these years, and all her effort, she was still an 'almost'. Still, somehow, she was something shameful, as if they wouldn't be lucky to have her.

She returned to her seat and waited until the guests were reasonably engrossed in the young lady currently playing Fur Elise, before removing herself from the room entirely.

"Running away early?" a voice came down the corridor.

She turned to see Leo Kingston, or Lord Starkley as he was now called, watching her with some amusement. "I only needed a moment. I won't go far."

"After that performance, I'd say you earned it." He nodded down the hall. "There is a sitting room back there."

She nodded her thanks and followed his instructions. As promised, the room was unoccupied, and the window was open, allowing a cool breeze from the garden to enter. Almost. It was a word that haunted her. Nothing surprising there. Her father's title didn't fully make up for her skin color, her face didn't fully make up for her figure, or lack thereof. Richard almost saw her as worthy to be a wife. Perhaps she shouldn't have tried to have too much when the nobility was so determined to keep her out. Her nose wasn't pressed up against the glass exactly, but her ear was certainly to the parlor door. Not barred entry entirely but not fully welcome.

Why was she trying so hard to be accepted by them? They didn't have much of anything she wanted. She'd never dreamt of being a countess or a viscountess. She'd only ever dreamt of a marriage like the one her parents had enjoyed. One full of love, passion, kindness, laughter and respect. When had that turned into a marriage the ton would respect? As if they had ever respected her. It could be pride. She'd wanted Richard, but if she couldn't have the man her heart wanted, then the man she settled for shouldn't be beneath her social rank.

Of course, she didn't have to settle at all. She had money and friends. As long as she stayed single, she was her father's daughter and a member of the nobility. But she would be on her own while everyone else was happily paired up with the love of their lives. Ada had already delivered two children, and Regina was about to deliver her own. She sat there in green silk, her full belly brazenly apparent to all, despite social convention, utterly victorious in her new role as the Baroness Starkley.

It seemed only Elodia was destined to be left alone while the man who had her heart went on to marry someone else. And now it was becoming more obvious that her lack of allure was not unique to Richard. Indeed, she could not manage to find any man to consider her on her own. She would have to bring in her father and ask him to make arrangements for her. It was what she had feared since childhood: the notion of a husband who wanted her for everything but herself. When she was younger, she had pitied Regina and her arranged marriage. Now she wasn't sure Captain Mason hadn't been wise to secure her a match when she was so young. At least her future had been certain.

Was that worth it? Surely it was better to be on her own and not even bother with anyone else rather than risk a bad match. What was the point of her advantages if she would throw them away over something so wholly unequal to what she had now? She sighed and rubbed her hand over her forehead. Would it be enough to simply have a husband and children? Would it make it easier to see everyone else with their loved ones while she was with a man her father had forced down the aisle by leveraging his position? Was it a blessing that no one had arrived?

What she was looking for wasn't something they could give, so she would let it go. She would do what she had planned to do before the kiss, namely staying close to Aunt Theo and Isolde. There was no point waiting here anymore. The last thing she needed was someone coming to look for her. It would only lead to more questions she wasn't prepared to answer. She stood, shook out her skirts and started for the door.

"Mama, please," a man said. Was that Mr. Lewis?

"I will not discuss this any further," his mother snapped. "I am not having that bastard girl as my daughter-in-law, I don't care what your father says or who her father is."

Elodia pressed herself against the door frame, listening intently to the conversation. Who on earth were they discussing?

"Her dowry is substantial, and she's a good sort, and even Papa—"

"I forbid it. Honestly, it's bad enough Melbroke insists on inflicting his island dalliance on decent people, but I draw the line at allowing her to take over my home."

Melbroke? Were they talking about her?! The utter cheek of the woman!

Lady Lewis continued, "Enjoy her music when you can, but there will be no more dances, do you hear me? I have already been made a laughingstock enough over this ridiculous fixation."

"I do not think anyone would see us as a laughingstock."

"Do you see anyone else pursuing her? Dancing with her? Have you heard about anyone calling on her?"

A gasp caught in Elodia's throat as her stomach turned. Was this a widespread belief? Did the entire ton think this?

"No," Mr. Lewis admitted quietly.

"Do you imagine it is because they are all too afraid to seize some great prize? No. It is precisely because she is of inferior birth. You are a sweet boy, my dear, but you are not wise to these things. You must consider more than your own wants when choosing who will be the mother of your children."

"Yes, Mama,"

"Any animal can wear a pretty dress and pound out notes on a piano. Breeding is about a good deal more."

Bastard girl...

Elodia stayed frozen where she was by the door, refusing to move until she knew they were both gone. *Melbroke's island dalliance?* Was that how they saw her? She had been called many things in her life, none of them complimentary, but never a bastard.

A bastard? It was impossible. There was no way they all believed that. No way her father would have allowed her reputation to be demeaned, to say nothing of her mother's. There had to be a misunderstanding. Could he allow the woman he loved to be shamed in such a way simply because she was dead? Why bring Elodia to England if he wasn't going to claim her?

She rejoined the party in the salon, taking a chair in the back of the room. Her hands were numb, her stomach ready to retch its contents all over the floor. *Any animal can wear a pretty dress.* Somehow, that wasn't the most hurtful thing Lady Lewis had said. The sentiment was perfectly in keeping with any white member of the ton, let alone the nobility. No doubt she was only here at Regina and Leo's soiree because of their alliance with the Sterlings and her father.

"Ellie?" She glanced up to see her father standing beside her. When had he come over? Those blue eyes which had once been a source of comfort now made her uneasy. This man who had raised her with so much love and care, had he lied to her or to everyone else? What did he mean by his behavior? Did he love and cherish her as he had always claimed to or was he a particularly good liar? Was she not his legitimate child or was he ashamed of his youthful dissension now that he was back in England? "Sweetheart, what is it?"

She opened her mouth to speak but her throat tightened painfully. *Melbroke's island dalliance.* Was that truly what she was or was that what he had made her? Was that how he saw her and her mother? Who was this creature she'd called father for her whole life? Who had her mother died and left her with? Even if she asked him, could she trust his answers at all?

"Are you ill?" he asked. She nodded then allowed herself to be bundled off into their carriage while her father made apologies to Regina and Leo. She couldn't help but notice the stares now, especially from Mr. Lewis and his parents. Were all their compliments truly only due to her father's rank and nothing else? Just fear of his ire. If he was willing to defend her to such an extent, did that mean he truly cared for her? Or was that simply because he saw her as an extension of himself?

She had imagined any coolness she faced among the ton to be over her race and her mother's life as a slave before her freedom.

Now it seemed her dignity hung by an even more precarious thread than she had ever imagined. Not just mixed race but the bastard daughter of a slave? Her body kept shifting from hot to cold as her mind reeled with sickening questions.

She didn't want to look at him or answer any questions, so she leaned against the cool glass window of the carriage and pretended to fall asleep. When they got home, she roused herself enough to get to her bedroom where her lady's maid Béa was awaiting her. When Béa walked away with her dress and undergarments, Elodia caught a glimpse of herself in the mirror, stripped of her jewelry and her silks, her coiled hair falling about her shoulders. No crinoline to hide her nonexistent hips or the grotesque spectacle of her bottom and thighs. No gathers or pleats to amplify her flat chest. Small and dark and unfeminine.

Bastard.

Almost. Almost legitimate. Claimed socially but not legally. Almost good enough. Almost lovable.

How arrogant had she been to think she deserved anything. How naïve to imagine her father was any different to the other white men she was determined to avoid. How blind had she been to miss all the signs.

She turned away from the image and crawled into her bed, buring her wet face in her pillow and pulling the covers over her head as her heart finally shattered. Her sobs echoed in the room unfettered, unabated as loneliness filled her heart. She hadn't known how unfortunate she'd been to lose her mother so soon. Her mother's death had left her an orphan surrounded by luxury and yet more disconsolate and abandoned than ever before.

Had she known? Had she realized that the man she loved was the sort of person who would do something like this? If she had lived, if Elodia's little brother had been born, would her father have done more? Would anything have been different or would her father's betrayal have felt the same?

CHAPTER TEN

Thornfield House

RICHARD WAS ANXIOUS. He was man enough to admit that. Elodia had left a soiree hosted by Regina three days ago, and as far as he was aware, she hadn't been seen since. Anywhere. He'd attended no less than five events either hosted or attended by their circle and she was nowhere to be found.

The only source of comfort was that there was no talk of her either, which meant it was self-imposed. Nothing had driven her into seclusion, or at least nothing that was common knowledge. The only lead he had was currently playing on the floor with her two children, her linen gown spread out on the Persian rug.

His current plan was to stay close to A'wei, hoping she would bring up the subject so he could find out details without arousing her dogged interest. Now they were in the sitting room, her reading a book to her squirmy son, and him pretending to work on his business correspondence.

"Would you allow me to host a ball here, brother?" she asked.

He blinked and looked over at her. That was an unexpected question, but his answer was instinctive. "Absolutely not."

She rolled her eyes half-heartedly. "What about a party instead?"

"To what purpose?" He'd learned to be wary of his sister's plotting.

"I thought you wanted to marry this year," she replied, meeting his stare.

"I did."

"Is that still your intention?"

"It is." Although he could wait if it meant that he'd have to put up with all those strangers in his home. Was that what he would have to do? The idea was entirely unappealing.

"I was thinking we could have a party and invite prospective females for you to charm. We have attended a good deal of soirees and balls this season; it would be polite to throw one and extend the courtesy to those who suit our purpose."

"You think they would come?"

"I don't see why not. Our name and reputation must count for something. And if needed, we can sweeten the pot with Leo and dear Basil. You are not without friends, brother."

He wondered if he could explain how it felt to know that the best thing about him was his connection to someone else. What was the point of saying it? She was only trying to help and she wasn't wrong. "True."

"So?"

"A party is fine," he acquiesced, although he still had his doubts. If he wanted to be taken seriously, he'd have to play the part seriously. Better to have the party here than at Lodge Hall.

"Really?" Her eyes grew brighter, and he nearly took it all back.

"Yes. A small one. Run the particulars by me first, though."

"Of course."

Would she invite Elodia? Would she even come? He didn't know what had happened, but he remembered the expression on her face before Viscount Melbroke had taken her home. She looked as though she had seen a ghost, and it had taken everything in him to leave her to her father and not scoop her up and whisk her away himself.

Not that he had any right to do so, of course. Even if that kiss of hers had left an indelible mark on his mind. He could still feel the slight pressure of her fingers against his skin and her soft mouth against his, imparting what all her words hadn't managed to convey. The tenderness of that touch haunted him. It had triggered an ache in his heart, a wish for something more. It had been easy enough to pretend he could do without before he knew what it would feel like to be touched by someone who cared for him, who loved him.

He didn't regret his choice to stay away. He knew well enough that he wasn't the right man for her. She was too fine, too precious for someone like him. Not that anyone else was putting forth the effort. His blood was still at a low boil after the stunt that Lewis boy pulled. He had all but admitted that he had no intention of courting her no matter how he behaved in public. Not a novel concept considering her birth but then why waste her time and give her hope? Was the idiot trying to get called out by the viscount?

The insult of that alone would have been enough to drive a lesser woman to tears, but unless he missed his guess, Elodia had been more annoyed than desolate when she left the room. When she returned, however, there had been no composure left. She was shattered, holding herself together through sheer force of will. Something had happened out there and whatever it was, it had hurt her far beyond anything else. Did A'wei know what had happened? Had Elodia confided in her?

Did it make sense to keep waiting or should he simply ask, especially while she was distracted by flowers, food and musical arrangements?

"Sister," he began, "Have you seen Miss Hawthorne lately?"

A'wei gave him a dubious look. "You mean Ellie?"

"You know I do."

"Since when do you refer to her as 'Miss Hawthorne'?"

He closed his eyes against an uncharacteristic wave of frustration. He rarely grew frustrated with A'wei. But he was nearly beside himself with worry and the last thing he needed was someone needling him. "You know when," he replied, unwilling to play games at the moment. "We both decided that a bit more structure around our interactions couldn't hurt. In any event, it is the correct way after all."

"I suppose. I haven't heard anything. Regina never mentioned it."

"She was very upset when she departed Lady Starkley's soiree a few days ago."

Ada frowned in concern. "What happened?"

"I don't know. She played a piece and then left the room for some time. When she returned, she looked ill."

"And you haven't seen her since."

"No."

"Would you like me to check on her?"

"If you can be bothered." There must have been an edge to his voice because she froze and stared at him. Even his little nephew looked up at him with wide dark eyes before he began to whimper. Damn. He turned away from the desk and stretched out his arms for him. Wordlessly, A'wei passed him along for him to make amends. Within seconds he settled, laying his head on Richard's shoulder, his tiny hand clutching at his waistcoat.

"You are very concerned for her," A'wei continued.

"Is that unusual or something?" As if his concern was somehow insidious or amusing. As if it was unwarranted.

"Not for you."

Not for him. He hated that he couldn't argue the fact. He wanted to go to Elodia and verify for himself that she was well. Perhaps that was part of his resentment. He was bitter that he had to go through these indirect means, subjecting himself to endless obnoxious comments and inquiries. And he was fucking *fed up* with the knowing looks from too many members of his acquaintance as if they had convinced themselves of a fact that he had yet to confirm for himself. What the hell made them so certain they knew him better than he knew himself? As if he were nothing but a stubborn child.

All he wanted was to hold her hand, look into her eyes and assure himself that she was not upset, assure her that she was loved. It was maddening to sit in this room so far away from her, especially knowing she believed he didn't care about her.

"I'll go tomorrow," A'wei mused.

"That's fine," he replied, reminding himself not to be annoyed with his sister. After all, she had done nothing wrong. If he was Elodia's fiancé, he would be able to call on her openly with no questions asked, but he'd closed that door and bolted it himself.

"Brother," A'wei's voice came.

"Yes," he replied with a tense jaw, stroking the little boy's back, allowing the repetitive motion to comfort them both.

"I wasn't trying to be cruel. If Ellie is unwell then I am also concerned about her. My worry for her simply predates your current concern,"

Presumptuous little baggage. "Understood."

"Is there anything you need to tell me about my friend? You and she were very close before this, as familiar as old friends. Now you barely speak or interact at all, even when we are among our inner circle."

"Miss Hawthorne is seeking a husband. We cannot be so familiar if she is meant to be taken seriously as a prospective wife. I mean to marry myself, as you know, the same rule applies."

"But Ellie."

"What?"

"She cares for you, Richard."

Why was it so painful to hear this time? The reminder was bringing tears to his eyes. "I am aware of that." Too aware.

"I know you rejected her already and I understand your reasons."

"Do you?" He didn't even remember them at the moment. He wanted to fix it but knew better than to wade in and muddy the waters again.

"I believe so. I even understand your reasons for distance in mixed company or in public, but in private—"

"—May we discuss something else?" His chest was growing tight again.

"Perhaps you could be kinder to her—"

"—A'wei." His voice snapped out, low and firm, and she fell silent. He didn't typically call her by her name. She knew what it meant. He was pulling rank as her older brother. "Enough. Please."

She blinked in surprise then nodded and returned her attention to her daughter and the book she was reading. Richard turned to his letters, although he could barely comprehend what he was reading. He just needed to bide enough time until he could make his exit.

ELODIA SPENT ONE day in bed. One day before she decided to find some answers of her own. She still didn't know if she could rely solely on her father's word. The fact that someone so unconnected with her as Lady Lewis had such a pronounced opinion of her could only mean one thing: it was not only widespread, it was settled opinion. The opinion was one matter. People believed whispers, especially when they confirmed their own prejudices.

What concerned Elodia was her father. Had that rumor spread despite him or because of him? Had he allowed the misunderstanding to spread? Had he spread it himself? Or was it simply a truth he'd kept from her all her life? There was one way to answer at least one of those questions. She knew where he kept important documents. There was a safe in his office. If she could guess the password and look inside, no doubt the answers would be there. He would have had documentation drawn up of her birth and his marriage to her mother before leaving Trinidad.

She waited until her father was out and snuck down to his study. No one took notice of her, or if they did, they didn't question her entering his study. It took two tries for her to guess the password. Her birthday, April 18th. Within the iron box she found sketches of her mother, some with shorter hair, some as Elodia remembered her, braids and curls and always a flower.

Some were visibly older than others. Did he still sketch her? She found piles of letters, some wrapped in ribbons and some in twine. Correspondence between her parents, deeds, sketches, and... nothing.

Nothing.

There was nothing there to prove she was legitimate. Nothing to prove her belief that her mother had been his wife. How was that possible? Frantically, she tore through the letters, searching for answers, a mention, anything. They were beautiful and tender, showing their blossoming romance, but nothing of their marriage. The letters stopped three years before her birth.

Was it because they had married? Or was it because she had merely moved into his residence as his mistress? If they had married then why on earth wouldn't he have brought proof of it, knowing that she was dead and couldn't say either way? Why bring Elodia with him to England if he was going to leave the memory of her mother behind? Her eyes began to sting as they fell on the charcoal sketch her father had made of her mother. She looked happy there. She looked loved.

Had he ever really loved her? Had it been a convenience that she had died when she did? "Mama," Elodia whispered, her fingers tracing the lines. What had he done to her? Locking her away in a safe without a shred of dignity. What had he done to both of them? With trembling hands, she rewrapped the letters and put them back into the safe with the sketches. Then, with tears blurring her vision, she closed the door and returned to her room.

How much of it had been lies? How could he seem so sincere and be so callous? How could he take such pains to preserve her mother in that safe but allow others to treat her memory so carelessly? It would have been so easy to correct the assumption and yet he'd never done so. Now that she was thinking of it, his actions had always stopped short of what would have truly legitimized her among the ton. He'd given her his last name, he'd raised her publicly as his daughter but he'd never presented her at court or shown legal proof of her legitimacy. He'd never married, since her mother's death, but he'd never legally registered their marriage either within the estate.

That would have proved that he had done more than betray his race, but his class as well by risking a black heir inheriting his title. A title that used to own people who looked like her. Back in her room, she sank into a chair, suddenly exhausted beyond measure. A bitter laugh escaped her. Her father's love had always been her sanctuary. It had seemed as limitless as the ocean her mother loved so much. Now Elodia knew the truth. That ocean was a lake. Large to be sure but limited. Cruelly limited.

The next few days passed in a blur. She didn't want sunlight, food or to speak to a living soul. Then, when Béa threatened to tell her father she was ill, she agreed to bathe and take a meal, but she still wouldn't go downstairs. This morning, Béa had heavily suggested that she should leave her room. After all, it was a 'perfect day with just the right amount of sun and wind' according to Béa. Who could object to that after all? So she'd dressed in the white linen dress her maid had prepared and taken herself to the garden to lounge on the chaise nearest the oak tree. It was a reasonable compromise.

The idea of having to face her father and pretend that she didn't know what she knew about him was unconscionable. She could not reconcile the white plantation owner who could only love those he deemed lesser if no one important witnessed it with the man who had raised her and seemingly devoted himself to her and her mother. What could she say? How could she react to the affection he was all too likely to give her when she knew it was mixed with shame? What would she do if he threw away that facade and she had to deal with him as she feared he would be? Callous, dismissive and selfish to the core.

Leaving the house seemed equally impossible. How could she face society on her own knowing the person who afforded her her position had only partly claimed her and all of them knew? It was humiliating to think that all the time she'd been leaning on him and trusting him, he had never fully supported her. That they had all been too aware of the limits of his love and her acceptance. Of course, she had only been partly accepted by them; she barely had a claim to their circle as it was. She didn't know what was more insulting, if he'd allowed the ton to believe she was illegitimate or if he had actually refused to marry her mother in all the years they had spent together.

If he had known he was to be a father and had chosen to relegate her to the shame of bastardry rather than go against the expectations of his social position and race then he was a coward, but if she was legitimate and his marriage to her mother was true and legal, then his refusal to admit it was more than cowardly, it was hypocritical and cruel. She was too afraid to ask him for answers when any of them would break her heart and leave her more alone than she'd ever been in her life.

And Ada and Regina… they would normally be her second haven outside of her father. Her dearest friends, the ones who had never treated her with anything but love and acceptance, had only just managed to attain the level of social security Elodia had enjoyed her whole life. For them to associate with her would only bring disgrace now, when before, in her mind at least, it had been an honor. If she told them the truth, they would choose her but at what cost? Could she truly ask them to choose between her and their hard-won happiness? If she was as true a friend as they were then she would simply remove herself and allow time to weaken those bonds before severing them entirely.

If she was going to be alone then she would need to get used to it quickly instead of constantly looking for others to hide behind. Her inheritance would, at the very least, ensure that she did not live in squalor, that was more than most could boast. Her father had, at the very least, afforded her that security. The world was big enough for her even if England was not. They would be cross at first, even hurt, but in the end they would move on from her. And the hole in her heart would heal. It was only a matter of time and opportunity.

She faintly heard someone calling out her name. Ada and Regina. They were here. It had taken more than a few days for them to come, but she couldn't help but wish for more time. She closed her eyes and refused to move. Let them think she was sleeping; with any luck, they would go away.

"Ellie?" A hand touched her shoulder then shook it with some force.

Not a chance of them giving up then. She blinked open her eyes and squinted up at them. "Ada? Gigi, what are you doing here?"

Regina raised one eyebrow and crossed her arms above her burgeoning stomach. "What do you think? You left so upset and it's been days now with nothing."

"I'm fine, I've only been resting. I've been tired lately."

"So you've been resting?" Ada repeated dubiously.

"Yes. Is that allowed?"

There was a silence and she looked away from them to the grass, the tree branches, anything but their hurt expressions. She was turning into a horrible person. They were here out of concern and all she could do was take out her anger on them.

"I'm glad that you were able to get some rest," Ada said, her tone cooler than usual. "We'll leave you to it."

"Ada," Regina hissed, and she heard an indistinguishable exchange behind her. Then, "Ask her."

"No."

"Adelaide Thompson, I did not come here to—"

"What is it?" Elodia turned around to look at them.

"It's no matter," Ada replied, glaring at Regina whose hands were firmly rested on her hips.

"What are you whispering about then?"

"Nothing you need concern yourself with, go back to your 'rest'," Ada replied before turning on her heel to walk away. Regina hooked her arm and pulled her back.

"You stop it this moment," Regina scolded before turning to Elodia. "We wanted to invite you to something, but I don't know if it's a good idea."

"What event?" Lord, that was just what she needed.

"It's an evening thing, Richard is finally allowing me to host something at Thornfield House."

"You've been doing so much for us. If it's too much then we should leave you be for now." Regina smiled at her and she somehow felt worse than before. They didn't deserve this.

She sat up and smiled weakly. "Oh, who will be there?"

"A small circle."

"Smaller than a ball but larger than a dinner party."

"Oh." It wasn't horrible, although the last thing she needed was to be surrounded by people who thought she was a bastard, but at the same time, more people meant more anonymity. It was next to impossible to go missing in a small group.

"Ellie, did something happen between you and Richard?" Ada huffed and flopped down beside Elodia's legs on the chaise.

"Why are you asking me that?" Elodia asked in alarm.

"I'm not blind. I know how much you've always cared for him and I have noticed the change in the both of you."

"What change?" Oh God, had it been obvious to everyone?

Regina sat on the other side of her legs and rested a hand on her knee. "Ellie, I know we have not been as available to you as we normally are and I apologize—"

"—Don't," she blurted out. "Don't apologize for being happy." Elodia already felt like a fraud; the last thing she needed to be was a bitter curmudgeon as well.

"I thought you knew that we were and always would be a friend to you," Regina said. "But now it seems you need to be reminded of the fact."

"What are you talking about?"

Ada huffed. "You are sad about something, and for some reason, you have elected to deny us the opportunity to be there for you."

"After you were there for us on multiple occasions, no less," Regina scolded.

"Indeed."

"That was different," Elodia said, wishing her voice didn't sound so juvenile.

"How exactly?" Ada asked.

"Because it wasn't due to anything you'd done." She was a coward, but if they already believed her behavior was due to Richard, then there was no reason to expend energy to disprove it. It was half true in any event.

"Something we've done?" Regina shared a glance with Ada before they both took her hands in theirs.

"So you did tell him." There wasn't a question in Ada's voice.

"I did. He... he didn't want me."

"Oh, Ellie, I'm so sorry." Regina frowned, sympathy painted all over her face.

"How did you know?" Elodia asked them.

Regina shrugged. "Little things over the years, certain looks,"

"It was the smiles for me," Ada added. "You couldn't know how you smile when he is with you, or when you spoke of him."

"Oh..." She supposed she should be grateful that Ada wasn't upset. Somehow, she only felt silly for believing herself to be discreet.

"Frankly, I'm surprised he didn't know before," Ada added.

"Oh God," Elodia buried her face in her hands.

"I am sorry it didn't go the way you wanted it to. I should have liked nothing better than you as a sister-in-law." Ada rubbed Elodia's arm.

"It's so annoying that Leo doesn't have a cousin," Ada joked.

Elodia couldn't help but laugh at that, lifting her face from her hands. "Indeed. Anyone on your mother's side, Gigi?"

"Would you want to live in India?" she asked.

"Maybe I would." It was far away from Richard and her father. "Perhaps you can visit with Leo, make a family trip out of it. I can try my luck."

"I know you're joking, but I don't hate the idea." It would get her out of England. She could start over and create a good name for herself.

"And that is the reason you've decided to hide away?" Ada said, watching her closely.

For a moment, she considered saying the rest. That she was illegitimate. That her father was a cad and a liar. That she didn't know how to make sense of her childhood. That her entire life felt upended. "Yes." She couldn't do it.

"Truly, Ellie?" Regina asked.

She nodded. "I've been trying to get past it but it just got to be too much, especially seeing as my attempts to marry this season have been met with practically no results."

"Richard told me about that."

"I could skin Mr. Crispin Lewis alive." Regina fumed, shaking her head. "You should have seen him, Ada."

"What did he say?"

"He implied that Elodia was almost good enough to marry. Almost."

"What a jackass."

"Ada!" Elodia blurted in shock before giggling. Between marriage and motherhood, Ada had certainly become more straightforward.

"Well, more fool him," Ada said with a decisive nod.

"Indeed," Regina agreed.

"It was a bit demoralizing," Elodia conceded. "Do you still think I should come to your gala?"

"Yes. But because you hid from us instead of trusting us, you now owe me two performances on the piano before you can hide away from the guests."

Elodia laughed and nodded in agreement before allowing herself to be caught up in a three way hug that almost soothed the ache in her heart. No matter what, near or far, she would always have Ada and Regina. No matter who else fell short, these two friends would always be the ones that would stay close and true. In time, she would tell them the truth and deal with the rest as it came. For them, she could and would do anything, even put up with the ton when she would rather stay at home and lick her wounds.

CHAPTER ELEVEN

I T WAS WITH that particular thought in mind that Elodia dressed herself for Ada's soiree. It didn't matter what the ton thought of her in the end. She had her friends and they were the dearest creatures in the world. If she wanted her to attend anything then she would be at her best, bastard as she was. If her father had taken advantage of her mother then she'd earned the velvets, silks, fine muslin and linen, pearls and diamonds for herself and for Elodia. If she wasn't here to enjoy them, Elodia would wear them to death, in full view.

If they didn't have the courage to say anything to her face then that was their failing. They could choke on their whispers for all she cared.

"That dress was made by the angels for you," Béa commented, shaking out the voluminous silk skirts of the dress.

Elodia met her eyes in the mirror and smiled. It was one of her favorite dresses due to the fabric. The shot silk shifted between deep burnt orange and crimson like a flame and paired perfectly with her deep brown skin. She liked it so much she'd ordered three separate bodices for the skirt, one for travel, one for tea and a third for evenings. The neckline for the evening bodice showed off her shoulders and puffed fashionably at her arms with rows of blonde lace. The pleats added needed volume to her diminutive bosom.

It always made her feel beautiful and powerful. She needed

that now more than ever when she was facing an evening full of people who believed she had no business being among them. When she would have to watch Richard give the attention she wanted so badly to women who likely didn't care for him at all. Or perhaps it was arrogant to imagine she was the only woman who could truly love him. After all, she wasn't so special, was she? She knew that now.

"Which flowers for your hair?" Béa asked, drawing the laces of the bodice.

Flowers. She'd always worn them, partly because Richard had mentioned how much they suited her. There was no point to that now. "No flowers tonight, Béa, use the pearl pins."

"That's different for you."

"I just don't want the bother tonight." Béa had already fashioned Elodia's long hair into a low chignon with a braid wrapped around it, leaving some curls framing her face and temples.

"Is the viscount accompanying you?" she asked. She always called her father that but it had never struck Elodia as meaningful until now.

"No."

"Have you spoken to him as of yet about what you overheard?" she asked, giving Elodia a pointed look in the mirror.

"No,"

The answering heavy sigh spoke volumes. Béa had been only too vocal about her opinion of Lady Lewis' words, namely that the racist busybody had merely spared Elodia the indignity of being her daughter-in-law.

"I will speak to him in my own time, Béa."

"That and God's face on this earth..." she mumbled as she continued tying off her bodice laces and Elodia rolled her eyes. When she was finished, Béa sighed and turned her around to face her before taking Elodia's hands in hers, watching her carefully. "Are you sure you are up for this?"

"What do you mean?"

"You love your friends, and your willingness to go face those fools does you credit, but if it is too soon—"

"—it's not."

"—but if it is, there is no shame in saying so." She stepped back as Elodia seated herself at her vanity to await her final touches on her hair.

"I thought you wanted me to go out."

"I wanted you to get out of bed, not go paint the town unwillingly. They will still be your friends in the morning, child."

"I know that."

"They wouldn't want you to hurt yourself for them."

"That is why I want to do it. Because they would never ask it of me. I can do anything for them because they can and would do the same for me. I can bear up to this because they would never let me bear it alone, because they would never blame me for choosing myself."

"Then why do this?"

"Because the truth is, I will never feel comfortable, but I cannot hide away. The ton would love nothing better than for me to hide away in my room. I cannot allow myself to be pushed out because of their opinion. I cannot bow to them. Do you remember what Mama always said, Béa?"

"To the strongest."

"Yes, it is the strong who survive, Béa. Not the fastest or the fiercest, the strongest. I am still her daughter, and I am strong enough to face them."

Béa nodded, but she still seemed unconvinced. At most, she didn't argue the point further, merely patted her shoulder and began adorning Elodia's hair with her signature baroque pearls. Elodia put on her mother's pearl earbobs and dabbed her perfume at her wrists and behind her ears. It was perhaps a bit more restrained than her typical look but still elegant and complementary. Her skin was glowing at least even if her eyes weren't.

A glance at the clock told her she had about five minutes to leave before risking an unfashionably late arrival. She snatched up her reticule and her gloves before walking down to the front door. Hopefully this way she would be able to avoid any unwanted encounters.

"Ellie," her father's voice rang out. She squeezed her eyes shut for a moment, feeling all of her confidence drain out of her body until she was nothing more than the hurt little girl who hid in her room. She took a deep breath before smiling brightly and turning to face him.

"Hello, Papa," she chirped.

"I see you are finally ready for people again. Béa said you were over tired."

"Yes, I fear the season isn't nearly as diverting without Ada and Gigi."

He watched her for a moment, as if he still didn't quite believe her, but then he nodded. "I suppose that makes sense. You look pretty, where are you off to?" He rested his hand on her shoulder and tears stung her eyes. It was terrifying how well he played the part he'd cast himself as.

"Ada is hosting a party and she asked me to attend."

He blinked in surprise. "Ah, so I'm on my own for dinner."

Damn, she hadn't thought of that. She looked down at her hands as she pulled on her gloves. "Umm, not quite. Isolde isn't coming with me."

"So I am having dinner with Miss Walsh?"

That could be awkward. No doubt there would be rumors about that. "Not necessarily. Perhaps she will take dinner in her room."

He sighed and pinned her down with those blue eyes she used to love so much. "You could have told me yourself sooner."

"Yes, that's true. I suppose I thought someone would have told you." A week ago, she would have felt scolded with just that look. Now she just wanted to get away; she didn't know what she would say if she stayed.

"If I didn't know any better, I would think you were avoiding me entirely."

"I'm sorry, Papa."

He shook his head and closed his eyes as if he was dismissing his temper. "It's no matter. You've been in low spirits lately, so I'm glad that you are feeling better."

"Thank you,"

"And in the future, Miss Hawthorne, do not make a habit of using an intermediary. I am your father, you are my daughter, we do not need to go through others."

Was it only a week ago that those words would have filled her with warmth and affection? "Yes, Papa," *Let me go, let me go, let me go.* At the silence, she glanced up to see him staring at her. He was suspicious. She had been far too amenable. Normally she would tease him or make jokes instead of simply agreeing.

She smiled, lifted her eyebrows and tilted her head. "Am I free to go now?"

He squinted at her playfully before shaking his head and rolling his eyes. "Off with you," he grumbled and walked away, his hands in his pockets. She watched him leave, wondering when she would have the courage to ask the questions that plagued her. Or when the hole in her chest would finally fill in with something other than pain. When she would finally begin to feel like a human again instead of this automaton.

"Miss Hawthorne."

She turned to see a footman staring at her.

"The carriage is ready for you, miss," he said. She nodded and followed him out the door, climbing into the carriage and letting out a deep sigh. It was only a ten-minute drive to Ada's. If she gave into her tears, she would not have enough time to repair the damage. She closed her eyes and leaned her head back against the seat, clinging to the edge of the seat.

It had taken so long to get herself under control long enough to think about leaving her room, and with one conversation she was back to square one. Desperate for answers and desperate for something, someone to show her that she still belonged somewhere. Was it weak to want that? To need it? Was it ungrateful for Ada and Regina to not be quite enough for her to be happy?

What would it take?

The carriage came to a stop, and the door opened. She could hear the music emanating from within the house. The windows were full of light. She didn't want to go in there.

The footman stuck his head in curiously, "Are you coming, Miss Hawthorne?"

She nodded and took his hand, climbing down carefully onto the sidewalk. She gave herself a moment to pull on her gloves and then climbed the stairs to the open front door. One step in and she realized that somehow, after nearly a decade of friendship, she had managed to underestimate Ada.

Elodia had spent a good deal of her friendship with Ada believing that she and Regina were the crafty ones. Surely Ada, with her sweet naivete and easy affectionate nature couldn't indulge in plots.

It was only now, when Elodia had arrived at the London home Ada was currently sharing with Richard, and saw his expression in response to her presence that she understood she had been party to a shenanigan. But between his expression and the collection of what she assumed was heiresses surrounding him, Elodia couldn't imagine who the object of Ada's trickery was. One thing was certain, however: Ada was more like her brother than anyone was prepared for.

"Dear Ellie," Ada said, taking her hands in hers and smiling brightly.

"Dear Ada," she replied, casting her eyes around the room. "What on earth are you up to?"

"I can't imagine what you are referring to."

"It would appear that you intend your brother to find his bride here."

"He said he wanted to marry. I thought what better way to help him than to draw in the eligible females for him to charm."

"And what am I doing here?" Who exactly was Ada intending to torture? Richard or Elodia?

"You are an eligible female, are you not?" Ada replied.

So that was the trap. "Not to him."

"We'll see."

"What if he thinks I enlisted you to help me pin him down?" Elodia hissed into her ear, her grip on Ada's arm tightening. "Oh, Ada, I don't want him to imagine that I don't respect his wishes."

"Of course, but I'm his sister. I don't need to respect his wishes," Ada replied, waving off her concerns. "You can engage with him or ignore him entirely, but it is high time he sees you as you are instead of within the role he's cast you in."

It wasn't going to matter in any event. "Ada,"

"Don't worry about him. You are my friend and you have every right to be here and enjoy this evening."

"I suppose I cannot hide away forever." And surely Richard knew his sister was a little devil even if no one else did.

"Nothing about you should be hidden at all. Per our contract, you owe me two piano pieces; after that, you may do as you wish. Do you remember the jade room?"

"Yes."

"It's ready for you whenever you wish. There are tea and biscuits, sandwiches and every good thing."

"To keep me away from unfriendly eyes?"

"For when you decide to deprive these undeserving people of your presence."

Elodia laughed and nodded, patting Ada's arm. "Understood."

It was a strange sensation, being protected by Ada and Gigi, and Elodia wasn't sure how she felt about it. It was different being among the ton, knowing the truth of how they felt about her. She certainly noticed small things she would have blissfully ignored before. Particularly when it came to how mothers of the ton would speak to her but they rarely pushed their children to do the same. How often she would end up on her own without her father or Regina and Ada.

It was humbling. There was no way to avoid that feeling. For so long, she'd assumed that any snubs she'd received were due to her race, but now it was clear there was more to it than that.

There was clarity in knowing where she stood, however, and who her true friends were. She watched the young ladies flutter around Richard, smiling and chattering away. Most were white and grasping, some were not. Flirting. As if they'd just noticed him now that it was clear he had close ties to influential members of the ton.

He was taking it in his stride, though, smiling and charming them all as was his way. Ada meant well by placing her here. No doubt she believed that by presenting Elodia as a prospect, he would reconsider things between them. It would never occur to her that there simply wasn't anything to ponder. Surely it was better for him to align himself with a girl who was free of all scandal. Someone who could continue to secure his family's position within the ton. If he had decided what they had to offer was more useful to him then who was she to say otherwise?

She played when Ada asked, choosing particularly difficult pieces to show off a little; Beethoven's Waldstein and Shubert's twenty-first sonata in *allegro*. She cast her eyes over her audience a few times, watching the little strumpets squirm with dismay at the prospect of following her. Perhaps it was unkind, but at that moment, she didn't care. Let those girls follow her and pale in comparison. How was their incompetence her problem?

She told herself that the prickling on her skin was the focus of the guests, not Richard, and even if it was him that it didn't matter. He had nothing to offer her and he'd made it clear she had nothing he wanted. If she was proving to be a distraction, then she would remove herself to the sitting room that Ada had prepared for her. She hoped he found a good and simple wife among the company to give him the home he wanted.

At the end, she stood and curtseyed to enthusiastic applause before taking a seat at the back. She waited until the next girl, a blonde, uninspiring little thing in a perfectly tame shade of pink, began to play The Bluebells of Scotland while she warbled along. Her eyes drifted to Richard and noticed the smile curving up his mouth. So he enjoyed it. She fixed her gaze on a spot on the piano forte until the girl was finished. Then, on the next set of applause, she made her way to the hallway and her sanctuary.

She was in the room for perhaps ten minutes, nibbling on sandwiches and scones before she decided that the tea provided was not going to give the comfort it usually did.

She needed alcohol and silence.

In that order.

She began looking through the cabinets one by one until she found what she was looking for. Almost. She wanted sherry, but he only had brandy. *Any port in a storm.*

She didn't question why it was there, in a random sitting room. Richard wasn't, after all, the type to leave liquor around in any room of the house. She picked it up and made her way out to the garden.

As Richard farewelled the last of Ada's guests, he decided it had to be studied, how a five hour party could seemingly last five years. He'd never had so many inane conversations in his life. He couldn't blame the young ladies; they were the products of their upbringing after all. He had known that they were there chasing connections. He knew that their focus was on his family name at best or his connection to the Viscount Sterling or Leo, and again, he couldn't blame them for being tools of their parents. But did they have to be so blatant about it?

Was it unreasonable to expect… not so much dishonesty but tact? It was impossible not to compare them to Elodia. She had been a vision that evening in a gown that suited her to the ground, confident and so skillful it was almost unfair to the young ladies present. She had made them seem small and flavorless, like half steeped tea. He knew he hadn't imagined the small smirk on her face as she played Waldstein. He'd noticed more than a few disheartened looks from the other attendants at the idea of following in her wake.

When she played, it had been impossible to look at anyone else but her, but all too soon it had been over, leaving him scrambling to concentrate on the people around him instead of the woman who was gone like a flash of summer lightning splintering the sky.

"Brother," Ada walked up to him and took his arm. "How did you like it?"

"Will I have to do another anytime soon?" he asked as they walked back to the parlor where the servants were cleaning up the detritus of the evening and Leo and Basil were in the middle of a talk. Richard sat on the chaise with A'wei and leaned his head on his hand.

"That depends," she replied with a delicate shrug. "If the next few balls produce the needed result, then no. If it doesn't, then needs dictate we must host a dinner next."

"That sounds interminable."

"Chin up,"

He rolled his eyes, but patted her hand. "Thank you. It was exquisitely done, A'wei,"

She leaned her head against his arm. "Thank you for allowing me to."

He couldn't help but tease her a little. "I hope you enjoyed it because—"

"—Where is Ellie?" Lady Starkley asked, walking into the room. "Did she leave already?"

Richard couldn't help it. His head came up at the mention of her name.

"I haven't seen her for some time," Basil said.

"Is she not in the jade parlor?" A'wei asked, as Leo walked out the door to the corridor.

"Why would she be there?" Richard asked.

"I set it up for her to stay there if things became too much."

Too much. How stupid of him to assume she was well just because she was a better actress than most. Had she simply removed herself to a quieter place or had something happened to her? With so many people there, so many debutantes with their parents, it was impossible to keep tabs on all of them.

"Her carriage driver is still here," Leo said, sticking his head in the door. "Wherever she is, she didn't leave."

"Search the house," Richard said, rising to his feet. "I will check the grounds."

A'wei nodded and he took off out the back door, hoping she was somewhere obvious. It was a mercy that they were in town. The gardens here were less expansive. Thunder rumbled low in the distance and the wind picked up slightly which meant only one thing. Rain.

His gut began to swirl with fear. How long had she been out there? What if she was hurt? Why had she gone there when she had a place to escape to within the house? Was she that deter-mined to escape him? Had he unwittingly hurt her again? He walked past the small gazebo where his mother used to play the guqin, the roses his father prided himself on keeping alive and the tree swing he used to push Ada on when she was a child.

Where on earth was she?

"Miss Hawthorne," he called out. It still felt unnatural calling such a formal appellation instead of using her given name.

He called for her again, fear curdling his stomach. He wasn't sure what he would do if she was hurt. Could he keep pretending that he saw her as nothing but A'wei's friend?

A pool of orange in the grass caught his attention. That had to be her. His worry that she was ill or hurt sprang up again. Why else would she be laying on the grass wearing a silk evening gown?

"Miss Hawthorne."

She still wasn't moving. He hurried over and knelt down beside her. He touched her cheeks and tried not to focus on how soft her skin was. "Ellie." He gripped her shoulders and shook her gently. "Ellie, wake up."

She sighed and another scent caught his attention. Brandy.

How had she gotten her hands on that, and what on earth had possessed her to wander around the garden soused? Either way, he couldn't leave her there. He lifted her up by her shoulders and leaned her against his chest. Then he slipped his arm under her knees, working his way past yards of silk until he could get a solid grip on both her legs. Then, with one arm around her shoulders, he picked her up and began the slow trek up the slight slope to the house. It was the closest she had ever been to him, with the exception of that mad kiss that still haunted him. Her scent was overwhelming.

It was a short trip back and he found himself slowing his steps, trying to draw out the moment before he had to put her down. Before he couldn't hold her in his arms. Thunder rumbled again, then he felt the first few raindrops land on his head. Wonderful. Almost on cue, she began to stir, moaning softly and squirming in his grasp. She pressed her face into him, nuzzling like a child seeking comfort, and a knot in his chest dissolved like dew under the sun.

He wanted to be the one she turned to for comfort, the one she clung to and trusted above all others. He wanted to be her rock, her shield, her safe haven. He wanted to be the one who carried her to bed when she fell asleep. He wanted to be the one she curled against at night when she had a bad dream. He was sick to death of standing apart from her, exhausted from the effort of being strong for both of them against something they both bloody well wanted.

Her arm slid around his neck and he froze as her warm breath wafted over his skin. Was she waking up?

"Ellie?"

She began moving around again, moving her arms and legs, trying to turn onto her stomach. At first he tried to maintain his grip on her, but the second time he nearly dropped her, and he gave up and stopped by the gazebo. It was raining after all, and if she was going to be so active, she could bloody well walk herself.

He sat down on the stone bench, resting her in his lap for the time being. Until she woke up fully. Who knew if she would be able to support herself if he set her on the bench? It wasn't the most appropriate thing in the world, but he never claimed to be God's strongest soldier. So he sat there in the garden holding the woman he was almost certain he loved while the rain fell, hoping no one did something wildly inconvenient like come out with an umbrella.

She whimpered and he glanced down at her frowning face. "Ellie?"

One dark eyelid lifted. Then she grinned. "Richard."

What was that look? "Yes, it's me."

"Did you carry me?" She was squinting now.

"I did. And it wasn't easy, let me assure you."

She sighed and then closed her eyes again, nuzzling his chest. "I felt myself floating but I wasn't sure. You carried me once before, do you remember?"

"I do."

"I don't." She almost pouted. "I just wanted to know what it was like."

"So I take it you were awake enough to walk?" She nodded with a proud grin, and he shook his head. "Well done."

"Are you cross?" She blinked up at him, her eyes as wide as his little niece's.

It had a similar effect. If he had been annoyed before, he couldn't possibly be now.

"No, but your antics nearly left you with a wet bottom."

She snickered but didn't move, and curse his weakness, but he couldn't bring himself to make her.

"Why are you drunk, Miss Hawthorne?" he asked.

She frowned. "Don't call me that. I hate when you call me that."

"You asked me to call you that," he reminded her.

"Because you have to. We have to. I still don't like it."

He didn't like it either. "It's not appropriate, Ellie." Her name was like nectar on his tongue. It didn't make sense to call her anything else. She was Ellie, and she was his.

"I know." She curled into him and sighed. "I like how you smell."

He moved his arm from behind her knees and immediately regretted it as the complete weight of her full bottom settled on his thigh and his crotch. Damn. He clenched his teeth together and tried not to focus on where she was sitting. "Ellie, why were you drinking?"

"Because I was sad."

"Why were you sad, sweetheart?" The endearment tumbled past his lips and his hand settled on her arm, keeping her as close as possible.

"Because I ended up by myself."

"What do you mean?" he asked.

Her fingers plucked at the buttons of his waistcoat. "Everyone has someone. Everyone had someone who wants them but me."

"Why do you imagine no one wants you?" he asked, his other hand curving around her shoulder.

"No callers. I dance and dance and smile and play and nothing happens. No interest. I didn't think it would be so hard."

"You are a rarity. Not every man will have the courage to pursue you."

She smiled, but he could tell she wasn't convinced. "I miss you," she murmured.

I miss you as well. He very nearly said it. It was true and she was likely too drunk to remember. No harm done. Except he'd told her something else, something she was trying desperately to respect no matter the cost to herself. It wouldn't be fair for him to blur the line now. "I have to take you inside, Ellie. It's too cold and we are both soaked through."

She whimpered a protest and cuddled closer, pressing her face to his neck, her fingers curling into his clothes. "No."

"Darling, I don't want you to catch a chill."

"I'm not cold, I like it here."

"What about me? I'm cold," he lied.

"I'll get closer." She slid her arm under his jacket and around his waist. "Are you warmer now?"

He glanced down and saw her staring up at him, all wide brown eyes, sodden hair and damp skin. A year ago or even two months ago, he would have assumed she was coming to him as a sister. Now he knew better, and the effect was overwhelming. She was plastered to him as it was and all he wanted was to draw her closer, stroke her hair, and show her what a real kiss was instead of the tremulous thing they'd shared before. A kiss that left them both weak, overheated and breathless. He needed to get her out of his lap. "We need to go back in. You've been missed."

She shook her head, laying her head against his shoulder and staring up at him. "A moment longer, please." Her hand came up, soft and cold, and cupped his face hesitantly. "When we go back, I won't be able to look at you anymore."

"Why not?" he asked.

"Because you don't like me. You wouldn't like me looking at you. Not like that."

He didn't know how he stared at her forlorn face without breaking and giving her everything. He wanted to say he didn't mind, that he missed catching her eye across the room in a secret joke. That he wanted nothing more than to keep her hand in his and smile at her openly.

"You're so handsome, did you know that?"

His heart leapt in his chest. He'd assumed she felt that way about him but it was jarring to hear it said so baldly. "I don't think I have an answer for that."

She smiled, but the moonlight was glinting on a wet sheen in her eyes. If she began to cry, he wouldn't be able to hold himself back. "The first time I met you, I thought you were the most breathtaking man I'd ever seen."

His throat was like a vice. "Did you?"

She nodded. "Nothing's changed."

He closed his eyes and tried to breathe past the weight in his chest. He had to stop this. He had to take her inside. He had to stop this gentle torture before she said something else he couldn't unhear. She would already regret all of this in the morning.

"Are you sad?"

His eyes opened to see her frowning.

"A little."

"Because of me?"

He shook his head and encircled her narrow wrist with his fingers, pulling her hand away from his skin. "Not you, àirén. You never make me unhappy."

"We can go in now," she said. "Will you carry me one more time?"

"Are you going to behave?"

She nodded and slid her hand up his chest to hold onto his shoulder while he picked her up and continued the trek in the rain to the house. By the time he reached the pavestones, she was fast asleep, her head heavy against his shoulder, her little hand curled tightly into his lapel. If he held her a little closer or if he leaned his cheek against her head, he told himself it was a goodbye. He walked through the French doors and was greeted by the sight of Lady Starkley and A'wei staring at him with concerned faces.

"Is she alright?"

"A bit soggy and a bit pickled, but other than that, she's right as rain."

"Pickled."

"In brandy, to be exact." He looked at his sister. "Do you know anything about that?"

A'wei's eyes slid away from his. "I didn't direct her towards it or anything. She was sad, gēgē."

He shook his head as Basil watched her in askance. "You didn't."

"You told me where the secret brandy was when I stayed by your parents the first time," she hissed.

"Goodness, we can't send her home like that." Lady Starkley

fretted, resting her jeweled hand on Elodia's knee.

"No, we cannot. I'll take her upstairs, mèimei. Basil, send a note to her father with the driver, let him know she is asleep and will return home tomorrow morning."

Basil nodded and left to complete the task.

Richard started up the stairs. "I'll take her up."

"We don't have a room ready," A'wei argued.

"She can sleep in my room," he said.

"Where will you sleep?"

"I can manage for one night." For once, A'wei didn't argue with him. He didn't have an answer for why he was loath to give up the precious, brandy scented weight in his arms, or why the idea of her sleeping in any room other than his seemed… wrong.

When he entered his bedroom, his valet turned to him with a near comical amount of shock.

"Sir?"

"I won't need you tonight, Morris." He laid Elodia down on his bed, careful not to wake her. She frowned and whimpered, and he ran his hand over her head. She turned her face into his palm and went still again. How could he explain what it felt like for someone like her to see him as everything she wanted, as if he was precious to her? After weeks of people looking to his connections to determine his worth, here she was seeking only his touch, his warmth. Would anyone ever make him feel like this again?

"The young lady is sleeping here?" Morris asked.

"She is. I'm not," Richard replied quietly but firmly. "You can leave Morris."

"I'll get her out of these wet things," A'wei said, coming up behind him.

"Yes." His hand lingered on the smooth, soft skin of her bare brown shoulder, brushing a damp lock of hair from her high forehead, stroking her hand.

"Brother," Ada murmured.

"What?" He didn't want to stop touching her.

"I can't change her unless you leave."

That broke the spell. What was he doing? He jerked his hand away and stepped back, pressing his lips together. He nodded and turned away, refusing to meet Ada's eyes. With numb hands, he grabbed a change of clothes and left the room.

CHAPTER TWELVE

HE WAS THERE. She could feel him holding her hand, his scent surrounding her. She didn't want to wake up and give up his touch, but her body was becoming more aware with each passing second until the voices around her became clearer, and the ache in her head throbbed relentlessly. Oh god, her mouth felt awful. What on earth had she done the night before?

The only source of comfort was Richard. So comforting that she didn't question why the air smelt more of him while the dream slipped further away.

"I know you're awake, Ellie," Regina said. Elodia frowned and turned her face into the pillow. Why was she here?

A hand landed on her shoulder and shook it. "Get up now."

Ada. Why were they always around lately? Elodia grumbled and cracked one eye open. "What is it?"

"Good morning," Ada said, handing her a cup. "Drink this."

Ellie sat up, looking down at her body, which was clad only in her chemise and pantaloons. She took in her surroundings which included Regina sitting in a chair to her right and Ada, sitting on the bed beside her to her left. The room was unfamiliar. The dark wood paneling on the walls was varied with dark wallpaper in dark green, brown and gold. Ada nudged her again, and Elodia accepted the cup and began sipping at the contents.

Hot water, ginger and honey.

"Where am I, Ada?"

"You are in my brother's room."

She nearly spit out her drink. "What?" No wonder the room smelt of him.

Ada nodded. "Mmm, I think he slept in his study."

"But why—" Images swirled in her mind. A garden at night, someone holding her close, carrying her across the grass. "Did something happen?"

"We were rather hoping you would answer that question."

"Although our question is more along the lines of 'What on earth happened?'" Regina clarified.

"Specifically, why did you take a bottle of brandy onto the lawn in the middle of an event which then necessitated my brother having to carry you back to his room because you both were caught in the rain?"

"Oh…"

"Yes. So we will ask one more time, what is the matter?"

"And I swear if you fob us off like last time, I will not be held responsible for my actions." Ada's eyes were steely.

"And if I don't? It's not as if you can keep me hostage."

"I beg to differ. I have your clothes, remember?" she replied, with the same cool look Elodia had seen on Richard's face.

Damn… she had forgotten.

"Why are you treating us like strangers?" Regina asked softly. She wasn't angry like Ada, she was… hurt.

"I am not."

"You *are*, and I cannot account for it. Is it our fault? Is it us?"

"No,"

"Have we made you feel as though you cannot come to us anymore?"

"Of course not, Ada," Elodia said, pushing herself up until she was sitting upright.

"Or is it that you don't trust us because we are married now?" Regina asked.

It was uncomfortably close to the truth but not quite. "It's not that."

"No?"

"It's… I haven't told anyone. It's not as if I am making exceptions for you in that department."

"But you used to." Ada insisted. "You used to make exceptions and tell us everything; we all did. And we found our way through together."

Elodia sighed in defeat and pulled her legs up to her chest, wrapping her arms around them. "The truth is, I don't know *how* to speak of it."

Regina sighed then crawled onto the bed beside her, so she was trapped between them, and then took her hand. "Never mind about the how, just spit it out."

No way out but through. "I heard something said, that people think I'm a bastard."

"A what?" Ada blinked in confusion.

"A bastard. That my parents weren't married." There was a shocked silence. "Have you heard anything about that?"

"I haven't," Ada replied. "Gigi?"

Regina didn't look shocked at all. "No, but I imagine my parents did. My mother never approved of you no matter how Baba and I defended you, but she never told me why."

"Just because people talk doesn't mean it's true, Ellie."

"I checked his study. There is no mention of a wedding. There is no marriage contract, no license, no birth record for me. There were letters from their courtship as well. No mention of a wedding or a proposal."

"When did you hear this rumor, Ellie?" Ada asked.

"At Gigi's soiree. There was a woman berating her son for considering me for a bride."

"Who?" Regina's voice was deceptively calm.

"It doesn't matter. It's not their fault that I'm illegitimate. It's reasonable to want to protect your family from scandal."

"I beg to differ," Ada grumbled.

"Never mind that. My soiree, the one you left early, was over a week ago, Ellie."

"I know."

"We came to you only a few days ago and asked what was wrong and you told us it was about Mr. Thornfield."

"It was about him as well. But I was thinking that it would be reasonable if, bearing this in mind, you wanted to put som—"

"Elodia Hawthorne, I want you to think very carefully about finishing that sentence." Ada's voice had never sounded so sharp.

Regina was staring at her with an expression so stricken that Elodia couldn't bear to look her in the eyes. "Did you think we wouldn't want you around because you couldn't be a social boon to us as you were before?"

"Not exactly."

"I have never been so insulted in my entire life—"

"—Ada,"

"—And that is including my very *charming* brother-in-law and father-in-law."

"I just don't want you to have to—"

"You are going to make me lose my temper in a minute," Ada snapped, and Elodia fell silent. If Ada hadn't lost her temper as yet, it wasn't a good beginning.

"After all we've been through, how could you imagine we would even think of abandoning you because of something like that?" Regina said, her voice low and even. But it was the tears in her eyes that made Elodia want to sink into a hole.

"Not abandoning me, just—"

"Stop speaking. I mean it. I cannot believe you would think we would value the ton more than we value you or our friendship."

"I didn't mean it in that way."

"Then how exactly did you mean it?" Regina asked.

"I was afraid because I thought I knew him, my father. I thought I knew what he was and what my parents were to each other. I remember them together and I believed that they were in love, that he loved her as much as he loves me."

"I'm sure he does," Ada said, pressing close beside her, now that her wave of temper had passed.

"But don't you see? He lied to me and I don't even know what he lied about. He lied and his lie ruined my mother and myself. It demeaned us. And he did it while making me believe he loved me."

"Have you spoken to your father about this?"

"No. I told you I haven't told anyone."

"Ellie, you don't know that he lied to you. You don't know that you are illegitimate."

"It doesn't matter. It doesn't matter if he lied to me about marrying my mother or if he lied to the ton about not having done so. In the end, the result is the same. She died trying to give him a son he didn't deserve. She died loving him and he degraded her. I am all that is left of her in the world and he degraded me as well."

"Did you think that if he could turn his back, so could we?" Ada asked.

"I didn't really believe you would, I only didn't want to test it."

"It must have been quite a shock to hear that. I'm sorry that your father is a blaggard," Regina said, laying her head on Elodia's shoulder.

"We don't know that he's a blaggard. He might be an igno-ramus," Ada said with a shrug.

"I beg your pardon?" Elodia turned her head towards her.

"I married into a family of them. Believe me, one should always leave room for sheer stupidity. It is possible that he is unaware."

"The level of idiocy that would entail is unimaginable," Regina said dryly.

"Not necessarily."

"Would you say that about your Mr. Thompson?" Elodia asked.

"Oh, Basil has had his moments, believe me," she said, shaking her head and rolling her eyes. "Your father is an intimidating man. He has claimed you openly and vociferously which means that to go against you is to go against him. Few people have the stomach for that. And most wouldn't speak of it within his earshot, or yours."

"Even so."

"I'm not saying it is likely to be that, but incompetence can be as cruel as malice."

It was a good point. Somehow it felt even stranger to imagine that her father was dim witted. Even scoundrels could be mighty, and she couldn't imagine her father to be anything so common as *foolish*. Was that more forgivable?

"I still can't believe you said that to us. To *us*." Regina shook her head and glared at Elodia so fiercely that Elodia couldn't help but laugh.

"It's not funny, Ellie," she groused. "Apologize!"

"I'm sorry, Ada and Gigi. I should not have underestimated you both in that way."

"That is correct."

"Do you accept my apology?"

"Yes. Once." She nudged her playfully with her elbow and Elodia almost laughed. She was still upset, but she was glad that the secret at least was out with Regina and Ada. She should never have kept the truth from them.

"May I have my clothes now?"

Starkley House, Mayfair, London

TO SAY THAT Richard found himself in a bit of a quandary would be an understatement. Threading the needle between maintaining the appropriate boundaries with Elodia while not treating her cruelly or attracting attention was difficult enough when he thought her feelings were only an infatuation, but now it was clear it was something else. She loved him. She'd said it, but if he was honest, he'd never believed it fully until that first kiss in the study.

That first touch of her hand had been the proof. He wasn't an amusement, a novelty or a conquest to Elodia. She loved him. Enough to walk away and hold herself apart even when it was painful. Enough to take his side even when it wasn't what she wanted. It made him want to tear apart anyone who made her cry. It made him want to prove himself worthy of it not only to her but to the world. More than any of that, it was eating away at the old forgotten walls around his heart until it was left raw, exposed and eager to return her love as boldly as she had declared herself.

But the moment he did that, he would have taken a position he couldn't back down from. A position he knew better than to take. He understood better than Elodia what the risks were of their union. It seemed so simple to go to her. Too simple. As if he was setting them both up for something that would cost too much.

No one had mentioned the previous night to him as yet, which was suspicious in the extreme, but he had a feeling that his luck there was about to run out.

Lady Starkley was watching him quietly with her cup of tea and had been ever since they retired to the sitting room at Starkley House. He should have known that the invitation to dinner was a trap.

"Is there something you need from me, my lady?" he asked.

"Not at all. I've been meaning to thank you for what you did for Ellie. It was lucky that you found her. She must have gotten far from the house."

"Not exactly, but drunk people can be unpredictable."

"I shall take your word for it," she replied, her mouth curving in a ghost of a smug smile.

"Do you know what upset her?" Leo asked.

"No," he replied evenly, before turning to Leo's wife. "Lady Starkley?"

She was smiling fully now. "No."

She was lying, he would bet anything on it, but he didn't have a way to prove it. She just sat there staring at him with that secret smile that somehow seemed like a threat.

"What?"

"Did I say something?" she asked.

"You know, the longer you are married to him," he gestured to Leo, "The more tiresome you are growing. If you have something to say, which you clearly do, then bloody well spit it out."

She shook with silent laughter that she hid behind her hand and then nodded. "Very well. I was merely curious as to whether you knew you were in love or not."

There was a cough from beside her, and Richard glanced at Leo who was covering his mouth with his fist. "Was that a question?"

"Which part?" she asked.

"All of it."

She tilted her head and blinked as if she was looking at a foolish but amusing child. "Elodia has always been special to you."

"Because she is Ada's friend. She's been with her through hell."

That blasted smile grew wider. "I beg your pardon, Mr. Thornfield, but I am also Ada's friend. We have supported and loved each other as a triumvirate of sorts since girlhood. But you have never treated me as you treated Ellie. The fact that you insist on calling me by my title instead of my name is proof enough of that."

Why did it seem as though she was scolding him? Had she really felt that he had deliberately kept her at arm's length unlike the rest of their circle? She was the wife of his good friend, in theory as familiar to him as Elodia was, but it was impossible to deny that he felt closer to Elodia than she. He could barely remember to address Elodia as 'Miss Hawthorne'. However, while everyone else, including Basil, seemed able to call Leo's wife by her Christian name, or 'Gigi', to his mind she was either 'Leo's wife' or 'Lady Starkley'.

"Not that I needed you to, because I never regarded you as Ellie did. I will not pretend you have been cruel or apathetic towards me—"

"I'll thank you for that," he grumbled.

"—but she has always been of special regard. Why is that?"

He'd never felt the need to bring her closer to himself, although he'd never disliked her at all. He didn't enjoy feeling like a cad, but he positively despised feeling like a fool. He'd been puzzling over his feelings for Elodia and was no closer to an answer. Perhaps, the good lady had a perspective he could use. "I don't know."

Leo let out a low whistle. "Well, that's further than I've gotten. He's not denying it anymore, at least."

"I will not pretend that I felt this way when you all were girls. But why did I treat her differently? I suppose I liked that she was a fighter."

"Gigi fights," Leo began, but his wife shook her head.

"Ellie is a brawler. I duel. It's different."

Yes. That had been the beginning. Over and over again, he'd seen something he prized blatantly displayed in Elodia. That unapologetic need to protect the ones they loved and *to hell* with the consequences, either with words or by drawing first blood. That indefatigable determination to take up space and make demands.

Lady Starkley, by contrast, had always struck him as more careful, safer, always considering the cost over the principle. And perhaps, as a result, he hadn't trusted her as much as instinctively as he had Elodia. He'd seen her as too aligned with the people her family had been so desperate for her to join. "I suppose in that way I saw myself in Miss Hawthorne."

"That makes sense, you always were a scrapper."

"Is he?" She turned to Richard with surprise. "Are you?"

Richard met her eyes and tilted his head. "Shocked?"

Leo shook his head ruefully. "Richard was always fighting someone. Then he got smarter about it thanks to me, so he wasn't in trouble all the bloody time."

Her head swiveled back and forth between her husband and him, still unable to believe what she was hearing. "Goodness."

"He nearly got kicked out of Eton and Cambridge," Leo added with a grin, and Richard gave him a nod of acknowledgement.

"You see, my lady, I never receive the option of peace until they understand what a fight with me costs. That reality has been ubiquitous throughout my life, even among my supposed family. My own uncle thought nothing of having me kidnapped and murdered to take what he wanted from me."

"Your uncle?" She seemed surprised. Apparently, Leo had kept that particular tidbit to himself. He always had been the pinnacle of discretion. "You mean Mr. Trent was—"

"Oh yes." His smile lacked any humor.

"How is that paragon?" Leo asked.

"Quiet for now. I've put him on notice."

"You've tolerated him far longer than I would have," Leo mumbled.

"I don't want to crush him. I want him to either accept me or leave me alone. But I'm prepared for either outcome." He returned his attention to Regina. "Have I astonished you?"

She shook her head. "I don't judge you for being a fighter. I just can't really picture it."

He gave her a thin smile. "Neither can they."

She choked on her sip of tea before snickering behind her hand.

"They get a good enough view from the ground, though," Leo said with a smirk, and her snicker grew into a full bellied laugh. Not for the first time, he was struck by how similar Leo and his wife were.

"Perhaps I've been unfair to you, Regina," Richard said.

"I'm sure you've had your reasons. But I am glad to be on better terms with you."

He raised his glass to her and took a sip of his scotch.

"At the risk of endangering our new camaraderie, are you going to fight for Ellie?"

"Or are you going to be 'a special type of jackass', if you don't mind me borrowing your own words."

The asshole must have waited over a year to use that against him. As annoying as it was, Richard couldn't help but tip his hat by way of a smile.

It was a fair question. A year ago, comfortably on the other side of the fence, it was clear to see why Leo should have taken the title and declared himself to Regina. Especially when the two of them had clear interest and affection for each other.

Two nights ago it made sense for him to hold back, but now, in the cold light of day, he couldn't remember why he kept insisting on pulling back. It would be so easy to go to her and confess himself. She was in love with him after all, and it was useless to pretend he didn't feel the same way. That night she'd fallen asleep in his arms, he had been left nearly sick with longing. His father's pocket watch, that precious object she had retrieved and protected for him when he couldn't, had never felt heavier in his pocket. Every time he saw it, he was reminded of her kindness and her consideration. Of her silent unwavering devotion.

She was everything he'd been afraid to want. A woman of intelligence and refinement who saw him and loved *him* as he was. Someone who respected him as a man and cherished him as a human being. All he had to do was tell her that he returned her feelings and that beautiful sacred creature would throw away her place in society to stand beside him in defiance of every expectation of the ton or ambition of her father. He would spend the rest of his life with her hand in his, keeping that precious light in her eyes.

Was it that simple?

His heart was pounding so hard it was uncomfortable, and his mouth was arid. He took a deep breath and rubbed a hand over his chest. The idea of reaching for her, of potentially being that happy, was terrifying. But he didn't think he could spend the rest of his life watching her from across the room. It was selfish to allow her to diminish herself for his sake.

No doubt others would see him as the definition of the opportunistic tradesman, taking what he had no right to. They would be an example of what every noble parent feared for their daughters. But he didn't see why he had to starve himself to their benefit when he was only a step away from her. When he would defy anyone, even God himself, to love her as much as he did and would.

He would fight, even if he was sick with terror at the prospect of losing her. He would fight for her as she had done and would continue to do for him. And if anyone got in the way, they would deal with them together.

CHAPTER THIRTEEN

Harley House, Mayfair, London

AFTER HER LITTLE display at Thornfield House, Elodia had determined that she needed to stay clear of there for the time being. Everywhere else was still safe, but she wasn't sure she could be there and look anyone who lived or worked there in the eye. Especially Richard. Wisps of memories kept drifting up like smoke, teasing her with humiliating phantoms. Had she crawled into his lap? Had she really told him all those things? He must have thought she was an absolute maniac.

Her father had been suspicious of her when she'd arrived the morning after. She'd claimed exhaustion, but that excuse was wearing thinner by the moment. In the end, she had come to Aunt Theo, where Isolde was now residing since she had inadvertently dined with Elodia's father. It had been an unexpected change but ultimately a convenient one for Elodia at least. It gave her cover to be out of the house far more often than before, and it offered an alternate topic of discussion if she ever wanted to deflect from her own strange behavior.

So now, instead of withstanding strange looks from her father, Isolde or Aunt Theo, she was picking flowers in Aunt Theo's garden. She felt a little less ridiculous picking flowers instead of sitting indoors thinking about what she had done. What she could remember, at any rate. Her recollection wasn't perfect but it was enough to leave her mortified.

She remembered taking the brandy out to the garden, and thinking, after a few gulps that laying down in the cool grass was a marvelous idea. There had been thoughts of her father and the stars, questions about whether her mother could still see her wherever she was, more brandy, then nothing. She remembered waking up to being carried and Richard's scent everywhere. They had spoken about something. Had she told him her father had effectively disowned her to the ton? She couldn't remember that part.

She remembered lamenting being unable to look at him. She'd clung to him shamelessly like an octopus, all arms and legs. Had she tried to kiss him again? More importantly, was he annoyed? Had he been frustrated by her behavior? She couldn't remember his tone or his expression, only his voice rumbling through her. That wonderful tenor giving her comfort even as it ultimately left her unsatisfied. She'd have to apologize to him *again*, both for drinking his brandy and for making a spectacle of herself at his expense.

Honestly, if she had been trying to prove to him that she was a grown woman worthy of his love and respect then she couldn't have done a worse job of going about it. He must have thought she was an absolute ninny; sloppy, juvenile, tactless. Desperate. She didn't know which descriptor was worse. Trying to see out the season wasn't going all too well; perhaps she should escape to Bath and then the country. For the rest of her life. At least then no one else would be subjected to her nonsense.

"You're here," his voice came from over her shoulder and she froze, her hand convulsing on the shears, accidentally snipping the rose too high up.

Oh God, what the hell is he doing here? She wasn't sure she would ever grow accustomed to the instinctive blend of excitement and dread his presence now inspired in her. She turned around with what she hoped was a composed expression. He was perfect as usual. Perfect and perfectly inaccessible.

"Yes. I thought to pick some flowers for Aunt Theo since she hasn't been able to go out much lately."

"That's very kind," he replied, strolling up to her with an easy expression. As if she hadn't gotten drunk on his lawn a few nights before. As if she hadn't molested him while three sheets to the wind.

"Did Aunt Theo need me?" she asked.

"No,"

Then what the devil did he want? Wasn't he tired of her by now? "Were you looking for Cousin Bertie?"

"No, why…" he paused. "I'm here for you."

Me? "Whatever for?" Perhaps he had gotten drunk too and didn't remember.

"You've been out of sorts lately, and there was that inebriated episode the other night."

Well, so much for that theory. "Yes. I apologize for that."

"There is nothing you need to apologize for. You said you wanted us to be friends."

"I… I did say that." Although she hadn't expected him to stick to it so diligently. She would have forgiven him forgetting her entirely at this rate.

"Then, as a friend, I wanted to see if you are well. You said some things that worried me."

Damn. "I do not remember what I said. I was not in my right mind and I—"

"Ellie—"

"Don't," her voice cracked and she turned away as her eyes burned. It was excruciating having him so close, knowing she couldn't reach for him. It took every ounce of will she possessed. "Don't call me that."

"I am worried about you. It is not an accusation."

She hated her weakness for him, her insatiable need to feel his care. "There have been a number of things that occurred outside of my expectations, and it has been difficult to cope with."

"Do you mean with me?"

Yes. "Not really. It was a disappointment to be sure, but upon reflection, I was vain and presumptuous to think you would see me as anything but a friend. I am only sorry that I put you in such an uncomfortable position."

There was a tense silence behind her and she wondered what he was thinking. "I wish you wouldn't say such things," he finally said.

"It's no matter. I am determined to move on with my life and find a more reasonable prospect, but it is proving to be more difficult than I anticipated." She threw an insincere smile over her shoulder at him and turned her attention to the flowers. She had a task to complete. Perhaps if she focused on that task she would be able to get through this conversation. "I will likely have to ask my father to arrange a contract for me."

"That is—"

"Odd?"

"I was going to say unexpected."

She scoffed. It was close enough. "Yes. No one cares about your dowry or who your father is when you are—"

"Black?"

"Illegitimate." The silence beside her was difficult to read. Had he suspected it? Was it a surprise to him as well? She mustered her courage to glance at him and he blinked before looking away. There was no surprise on his face. "So you did know."

"I'd heard the rumors, but I never presumed to know if they were true or not."

She didn't want to ask the next question but not knowing was excruciating. "Was that why?"

He looked up at her. "Why what?"

"It was, wasn't it? You said that being with me was inappropriate, and I thought you meant something else. Even then, you were being kind."

He shook his head. "That wasn't the reason."

"Really? So it really was just *me*." How many times was she going to rip that wound open? Her mouth began to tremble and she covered it with the back of the hand holding the shears before turning away from him.

"I am so sorry that you are facing this." The gentleness in his voice was devastating.

"I've been taking stock of every encounter, every failed relationship, every dead prospect through the frame of this new information. It's been explaining so much, honestly."

"You didn't know?"

"No. I foolishly believed my parents were in love. That their relationship was based in mutual respect and affection."

"You don't know that they weren't in love."

She shook her head in denial. No, she didn't know it for certain, but whose account did she have to verify it? Her father's word couldn't be relied upon, and there was no documentation. If Béa had known then surely she would have said something by now. "I thought he loved me." Why did her voice sound so small and muffled?

"I'm certain that he does. No one would dare take your name with anything other than the utmost respect within earshot of the man because of how fiercely he defends you. He has claimed you and loved you openly."

"Has he?" she demanded, turning to face him. "He didn't love her enough to legitimize her or me. Or if he did, he didn't have the courage to claim us here, where it was necessary. If she was his lawful wife and I his lawful child, then how could the ton believe otherwise?"

His eyes were full of sympathy for her, a frown of concern creasing his forehead. "I don't know."

"Yes, you do. There is only one reasonable answer; in the end, we were not worth it to him. He could play the hero on the plantation, the kind benevolent landowner with his colored wife and child. But in England, where his love could make him a pariah among the nobility, that courage deserted him. And now I am worthless in their eyes."

"You are not worthless." He took a step forward, his hand clenching by his side.

"I am to them. It is why I only have two friends in all the

world and no man of family will come near me. I am, in fact, a viscount's bastard, and when he dies or remarries, I will be at best an inconvenience and at worst a liability."

"I do not believe that."

"Why did you allow Ada to be friends with me? You knew the rumors; you couldn't be ignorant of the implications. It is no doubt why Gigi's mother never fully approved of her friendship with me. And even though you wouldn't admit it, I know it is at least part of the reason you wouldn't marry me, you were disgusted at the idea, I know it." She was so tired of his kindness. She wished he would just speak his mind and tell her the truth no matter how much it hurt.

"That is not—"

"It is true. Even if you were willing to allow Ada to befriend me, how could you possibly benefit from forming an alliance with a mixed-race bastard?"

"I have never thought that of you, Elodia. Never."

"It doesn't matter." She didn't want to hear him deny something so obvious. "I… you wanted to know why I was out of sorts and I answered you."

She started to walk away, but his hand closed around her wrist. Every nerve in her body went haywire as her breath caught in her throat. Did he know it was the first time he'd touched her skin? The first time he'd ever reached out and touched her. His hand was firm and warm even if the surface was smooth.

"Ellie," his voice came soft and deep.

She turned her head further away, knowing she could never look him in the eye when his hand was on her. "I have to finish this bouquet for Aunt Theo. You should go back inside to her. I know she's missed you."

He pulled her closer by her arm, turning her to face him. She turned her face down to stare at the grass, at his shoes, at the hem of her white muslin dress. His hand closed around her shoulder and she closed her eyes tightly.

"Will you listen to me?" he asked.

She'd dreamt of this, but it was all wrong. "Please," the plea drifted past her lips. She didn't know what she was begging him for. To hold her? To prove her wrong? To let her go? Why wouldn't he allow her to leave? Did he feel guilty? "I'm sorry, I'm not angry with you. I don't blame you."

Before she could process what was happening, she found herself pressed gently against his chest, his arms wrapped around her shoulders. Tingles cascaded all over her body, concentrating in her breasts. She moved her hands to his chest, putting some distance between the two of them. She couldn't imagine anything more embarrassing than him realizing the effect his body had on hers while he was trying to comfort her.

She should push herself away. If anyone saw them like this, the scandal would be unimaginable. He would be forced to marry her then, and she would spend the rest of her life withering away in the knowledge that his good heart had ruined his life. But it felt so wonderful to be held, especially by him. His body was so hard and warm, and if she leaned her face forward, her head would fit perfectly under his chin. And it was his choice, wasn't it? She hadn't coerced him into this. How many times had she wanted him to do this? To stroke her head and her back and comfort her as he was doing in this moment.

How long did she have left? Should she pull away first? What if he was waiting for her to end it? What if he thought she was greedy and shameless? Reluctantly, she lifted her head, drawing away from him. His cheek brushed against her temple, but his arms stayed around her. What was he thinking? Was he pitying her?

She tilted her head back slightly to meet his gaze and regretted it immediately. Her stomach clenched in awareness of how close his face was, how little it would take for him to kiss her. His expression was... different. Serious but with an intensity she'd never seen before from anyone. Was he annoyed?

The hand on her hair moved and he was brushing away a smudged, escaped tear with the back of his fingers. She froze, unable to believe what was happening, even as his hand closed around the back of her neck.

He's going to kiss my forehead, she thought frantically as his head lowered. *Don't assume anything again. He's being kind.*

Then his mouth closed over hers and her mind went blank. Over and over, his lips caught hers in a delicious dance that went so far beyond what she'd attempted in his office. His tongue traced her bottom lip and she gasped, her fingers curling reflexively into his jacket.

He was kissing her. Finally, on a summer day, in a blooming garden, Richard Thornfield was kissing her.

HE HAD TO do it. He hadn't intended to kiss her when he got there. Or at least he hadn't meant to do it before proposing. But the more she spoke, convincing herself that she was beneath the notice of everyone and the more she asserted that he had been aiming to protect his family from her the more it became apparent that words were only going to be his enemy. There wasn't a word he'd said she hadn't taken to heart.

When he'd said he didn't want her, she had believed him, so now, with his feelings so clearly the opposite, he would have to show her the truth. He would have to prove to her that he wanted her, that she was even more precious to him now than before. He could never have imagined how much fear and self-doubt she'd harbored inside. He wanted to chase every shadow of skepticism from her eyes and mind.

She was the sweetest thing. It took a moment for her to relax into him then another for her to respond, echoing his actions with first hesitancy and then growing eagerness. He tilted his head to kiss her deeper and she whimpered softly, melting against him like no one else ever had. She had waited for him, not some nebulous man meant to be her husband, but *him*. He couldn't believe someone like her had known from just one look that he was the one she wanted. It made him want to be worthy of her pure, open heart.

Her fingertips brushed against his neck, his jaw, sending goosebumps racing over his skin. He had ached for that touch since the first time he'd felt it. It was painful how much he wanted her hands on his body. The tenuous hold on his reason slipped. His arm tightened around her waist, pulling her up against him until he could feel every inch of her lithe body against him. She gasped loudly, her hand gripping his shoulder. It was enough to bring him back to reality, but not enough to let her go. There wasn't a force on earth that could take her from his arms.

He ripped his mouth away from hers and buried his face desperately into the soft, rose-scented curls of her hair. He could feel her breath through his cravat as she panted, her face pressed against his neck. It was perfect. She was perfect.

"You said you didn't want me in that way," she whispered.

"Yes, well, clearly I'm either an idiot or a liar," he replied. She giggled and something in his heart fluttered. Fluttered. Like he was a green schoolboy all over again with his first crush. This was what it should have been from the first moment. Soft hands, sweet kisses and wonder. He'd never been able to have it before, but by God, he would have it now. He wanted to stay here for the rest of his life, or at least the rest of the day.

"I'll remember that." She tilted her head back again and he was gratified to see the smile on her face, the drowsy pleasure on her face. "Does this mean you'll marry me?"

"Are you asking me?" he asked, as her fingers curled into his jacket.

"Are you saying yes?"

He glared at her playfully, utterly delighted. "This conversation seems to be happening in reverse."

"Well, you already know I want to marry you. You are the only unknown entity."

"And this wasn't enough elucidation?" He asked, giving her

body a slight squeeze.

Her smile faltered for a moment and her eyes dropped down to where her hands were playing with his clothes. Fuck. Too soon. She wasn't ready for teasing yet at least not about that. He would have to be careful with her in the future. "Yes, Ellie. I would very much like to marry you."

She looked up at him again and he watched her smile curve her mouth and light up her eyes from the inside, brightening her face like a swift sunrise. *Stunning.*

"Truly?" she asked, bouncing on her toes.

"Truly," he replied, rubbing her nose with his.

"You'll call on me tomorrow?" Her eyes were shining up at him with love and trust.

"Would you like that?"

"Yes," she replied with a shy, delighted smile and his heart began thumping even more forcefully in his chest, his stomach swirling with giddy anticipation. This was what he'd wanted to feel his entire life.

"Then I shall call upon you at around eleven o'clock if that would suffice, Miss Hawthorne."

She giggled again and laid her head on his chest, wrapping her arms around his waist. "Thank you."

Thank you. Imagine her thanking him for doing something so self-serving as proposing to the woman he wanted and admired above any others. A woman who loved him truly and deeply. A woman who all conventional wisdom dictated he had no business pursuing at all. Speaking of, there was one bit of business he needed clarity on before he moved forward.

He didn't want to ruin the moment, but if they were going to reveal this to her father, it had to be said. "Sweetheart."

She hummed in acknowledgement.

"Have you spoken to your father about this?" he asked.

"About what?"

"About you and me."

She lifted her head and squinted up at him in confusion. "It's only just happened."

"I mean, does he know that you consider me a suitor. Does he know that you wanted to marry me?"

"Does it matter?" She frowned, and he could see her stubborn nature rising to the fore.

Had she truly not wondered if her father would accept him? "It may well matter to him."

"Because you are Chinese?"

"Because I am a merchant. A lowly tradesman without a single drop of noble blood."

Her frown deepened. "I don't care about that."

"I know, sweetheart, but he might." And by that, Richard meant he *definitely* would. If her suspicions were true, and he was the sort of man to hide the fact that he once saw a black woman as worthy of being a viscountess, then he absolutely would object to Richard marrying Elodia. If not for her sake then for the sake of his reputation as a viscount.

She frowned and shook her head. "I do not believe that he will care, but if he does, it still wouldn't matter. He owes me this."

He nodded but didn't say anything further. It was Elodia's nature to resort to brute force, but Richard had spent enough time among the men of the British ton to know that their marriage would be hard fought. The cost was yet unknown to them but the prize was a lifetime with her, in her arms. A lifetime with every single one of her smiles. For that, there wasn't a damn thing he wouldn't do, any price he wouldn't be willing to pay one hundred times over.

CHAPTER FOURTEEN

Melbroke House, London

FOR ALL HER words, Elodia didn't know what she would do if her father didn't approve of her match with Richard. There was a seething resentment inside her that she was still afraid to give voice to. As if speaking it would make it real. If he didn't support the match, she would fight him until he gave in or gave her up. If that happened, she would truly lose her father for good.

She was angry enough to walk away, but even in her anger, she knew she didn't know what it would mean to not be his daughter. She wasn't ready to orphan herself entirely. Perhaps she wasn't ready to lose the happy memories of the life she'd had in Trinidad, joyful and safe with her parents, surrounded by warmth, love and goodwill.

Would it be easier to leave him behind with Richard by her side, or would it still rip the heart from her chest? Yesterday still seemed like a fever dream. She spent the entire morning reminding herself that it had happened. Richard had sought her out and kissed her in broad daylight in the middle of her aunt's garden. She could still remember the feel of his mouth moving against hers, his arms around her holding her close.

It had been better than any dream she could have had and it was only the beginning, she promised herself. She needed to be available, but still, she didn't want to encourage too much conversation between herself and her father. So she decided to wait in the music room and play the piano until Richard arrived. She dressed in a silver day dress with a wide neckline and gathers at her shoulders and added two pink roses to her hair before leaving her bedroom.

She headed straight for the music room, made a few selections to occupy her time and began playing Beethoven's Tempest in D minor. Her fingers bounced and glided over the ivory and ebony keys, all her concentration taken up by the music in front of her instead of the encroaching battle she was about to face.

"Oh, hello, sweeting," her father's voice came.

She looked up to see him standing in the doorway holding a newspaper. "Hello, Papa."

"You're here." He frowned in confusion.

"Is that so surprising?"

"Well, yes, lately. But I suppose it's not too strange considering the timing. We have both been busy with our own affairs this season." He sat down in one of the chairs and crossed his legs.

"Yes."

"Go on with your playing, Ellie, I haven't heard you play for yourself in some time."

She nodded and resumed the piece, trying to ignore the sudden anxiety in her stomach. It was strange how different she felt. He still treated her the same, with the same freedom and easy affection, but nothing within was warmed by it. Instead, Richard's warning was at the forefront of her mind. It was like watching a wolf wondering if and when it would strike. How much of his true self would make an appearance when she was no longer playing by his rules? As she played the last notes, she glanced at the clock in the room. Ten fifty. Ten more minutes and he would be here. She picked up the second piece, Schubert's sonata in B flat Major and began to play.

At ten fifty-five, the bell rang, and despite her apprehension, her heart swelled in her chest. He was here. Punctual and wonderful. She had never doubted him, but it was gratifying nonetheless to be proven correct. Richard had never let her down and never would. He, at least, was a man who stood by his words.

"Was that the door?" her father asked.

"Yes."

A few moments later, there was the murmur of voices, and then Ingsley, the butler, was there.

"A Mr. Thornfield here to see you, my lord."

Her father dropped his newspaper with a bemused look on his face. "Thornfield? I had no expectation of him calling today." He looked at her, "Did you, Ellie?"

She clenched her hands together. In for a penny... "I did actually."

"Oh?"

"Yes. Mr. Thornfield and I are... well, he has asked me to marry him."

The answering silence was as nerve wrecking as the lack of expression as he folded his paper and laid it on the table beside him. "I beg your pardon."

"Shall I turn him away, my lord?" Ingsley asked, looking nervously between the two of them.

"Don't you dare!" Ellie snapped, shooting to her feet. "Ask him to wait, Ingsley, my father will be out to greet him directly."

"Very good, miss." He nodded and left, no doubt grateful to be far from the line of fire.

"Let me make sure I understand this," Lord Melbroke finally said, his blue eyes hard and piercing. "Thornfield, a manufacturer, has expressed his interest in you, a daughter of the nobility."

"Yes, and I have accepted him."

"The devil you have," he grumbled, rising to his feet.

"It is true, Father."

"No. I refuse to believe that my daughter has given herself away to a mere tradesman."

She rounded the piano and came to stand before him. "Why must you refuse to believe it. I love him and he loves me."

"He loves the connection you will give him. I should have thought you were old enough to know that."

Her outrage at his assessment of Richard's character left her breathless. "How dare you."

"How dare I? Adverse to the facts of life, my darling? First it was his sister and now him."

Elodia crossed her arms over her torso, a sneer curling her lip. "Are you implying that he got himself kidnapped so Ada would be forced to marry Mr. Thompson?"

He rolled his eyes in exasperation. "Don't be ridiculous."

"You are managing that very well yourself."

"Elodia, you cannot, you *will not* marry that man."

"Why, sir?" she gritted out.

"Because he is not right for you!" he shouted. "Because he is unworthy."

Her hands curled into fists as her eyes widened. Unworthy? The utter hypocrisy of the man. "He is more worthy than you." Her voice was low and utterly unrecognizable even to her.

He stared at her in stunned silence, his body utterly still. "What did you just say to me?" he whispered.

For a moment she faltered, seeing the hurt she had caused, but then she remembered what he'd done and who she was fighting for. "He loves me and he has never been afraid to claim me and love me openly which is more than I can say for you."

Then the temper came. The temper he had shared with her. "Have you lost your mind, young lady? I have raised you and claimed you as my own flesh and blood since before the day you were bloody well born."

"And?" she cried, taking a challenging step forward. "Am I supposed to congratulate you on having more morals than a stray dog?"

"Have you forgotten me?" he asked, rising slowly to his feet.

She lifted her chin to meet his eyes and squared her shoulders. She wouldn't cower before him no matter what he did. "No, my lord. Although I wonder if *you* remember my mother at all."

He squinted in confusion and shook his head. "What are you talking about now?"

"My mother," she said, taking a step forward even as her

voice cracked, her eyes burning. "I'm talking about the woman you lived with since before I was born but didn't deem worthy enough to marry."

"What nonsense, of course I married your bloody mother," he snapped.

"Then why does the entire ton believe that I am your *bastard?*" she screamed past her tight throat. Her entire body was shaking.

It was the second time she had rendered her father speechless that morning, but his incomprehension only fueled her rage. *Malicious or incompetent.* From the utterly baffled expression on his face, she now had her answer but there was no comfort in it.

"What?" he whispered.

"I believe that you heard me."

"Elodia—"

"She gave her life's blood to give you a child and you allowed them to believe that she was your mistress. No better than a whore, easily discarded." Her voice sounded alien to her ears, low and harsh, full of contempt. "She gave you *me* and your incompetence ruined my reputation. Such incompetence is a sin."

He was shaking his head in denial. "I didn't know. I would never—"

"No, of course not. You were so confident of your own brilliance that you never wondered how you had managed to keep all your clout while parading me around London. You said I was your daughter to anyone who would listen, but the things that would truly legitimize me in the eyes of the ton, you conveniently forgot, like having me introduced to court when you returned to England."

"I didn't think you would want to deal with the bother."

"You didn't even bother to register your marriage to my mother with your lawyer or our parish. There is no proof of my legitimacy anywhere on this cursed island. In all these years, how could you have overlooked that? And now you have the audacity to say that a man of good family and character, a man who loves me, a man with the courage to stand up and do what you would not, is unworthy of me? Are you even qualified to make such a statement?"

Unable to bear another moment in his presence, she strode out of the room. At the top of the stairs, she saw Richard standing near the banister at the foot of the staircase. His arms were folded, a bouquet of flowers in his hand, and he was staring down at the lacquered parquet floor. His face was somber, and far more composed than she was expecting. It wasn't likely that he had been spared a word of their conversation.

She started down the stairs, and at her footsteps, he looked over and up in her direction. He didn't smile, but he didn't seem angry either.

"Did you hear?" she asked, laying her hand on his arm as she reached him.

"It was difficult not to," he replied with a small smile.

"I'm so sorry." She unfolded his arms and embraced him tightly. She didn't care if anyone saw. He tensed for a moment then hugged her back, laying his cheek against her head with a sigh.

"Don't apologize, àirén," he murmured softly. "I expected it."

She lifted her head to meet his gaze. "You did, didn't you?"

He hummed and brushed the hair at her temple with the back of his fingers. "And I couldn't ask for a fiercer champion than you."

"I meant every word of it."

"I know you did." He showed her the flowers. "These are for you."

She took the bouquet, observing his floral choices with a growing smile; fiery tulips, irises and heliotrope. The meaning behind them wasn't lost on Elodia: passion, trust and devotion, respectively. She'd asked him to call on her and he'd done so on time with a bouquet that meant so much more than red roses.

"How did I do?" he asked.

"Very well. Although it's not at all surprising."

He smiled and nodded. "Yes, I would have brought you lilies as I know they are your favorite, but none of them seemed to fit the occasion."

"My favorite are the orange ones."

"I know, but I thought it would be rather bad form to give you a bouquet of flowers which announced 'deep hatred'."

"Very wise of you."

"I'll save that for our anniversary when we've begun to thoroughly vex one another." He winked at her and she couldn't help but giggle. It was good to know Richard wasn't giving up despite her father's clear objections.

"Are you leaving now?" she asked, holding the fragrant bundle to her chest.

"Yes, I think it's best," he replied, resting his hand on her shoulder. He glanced at the upper floor for a moment, a somber expression on his face.

"But you won't stay away."

His eyes flicked back down to hers and he smiled before cupping her face in one hand, his thumb brushing lightly over her cheek. "Not from you, sweetheart."

"I'm going to marry you. Don't give up on me."

He lifted an imperious eyebrow, "You think I'm that easily deterred?"

She shook her head and he pressed a kiss to her brow. She went up on her toes for more, another kiss like he'd given her the day before, but he pressed his forehead to hers instead, keeping her in place and no doubt out of more trouble. It was probably best, even if his breath left her lips tingling.

"I'll see you later," he murmured.

Later. *And soon*, she promised herself.

Thornfield House, London

RICHARD OPTED TO walk back home instead of taking his carriage. It was a short enough distance and he needed the time to sort out his thoughts before he returned home. He was engaged to the most wonderful person. A young woman of beauty, intelligence, passion and integrity who loved him enormously. In choosing him for her husband, however, she had gone in direct opposition to her father.

Melbroke's reaction to Richard's suit was disappointing to be certain, but he couldn't pretend to be surprised. The man had been a viscount for over a decade at this point and there was no way it hadn't had an effect on him. It served as a sobering reminder, one was either a member of the nobility or not. It didn't matter how friendly they were to your face, or how much they praised you or admired you. In the end, if you didn't have a title, you were nothing in their eyes.

Elodia had been unexpectedly fierce. He'd known she wouldn't stay quiet but he'd never fully witnessed how cutting her tongue could be when unleashed. Listening to her defend him had gone a long way to softening the sting of Melbroke's slanderous words but the issue still remained. No matter how angry Elodia was, Melbroke was still her father, a man she loved deeply. Their bond was rare and precious but it could be easily broken. Melbroke was stubborn and fierce and Elodia was nothing if not her father's daughter.

He reached Thornfield house faster than he'd expected, his long legs eating up the distance as he chewed over the current issue. He loved Elodia and he had no intention of letting her go, but he would have to keep her from burning bridges with her father. He entered through the front door and immediately noticed the unusual scent of mint and talc.

Mrs. Theo was here.

"Is that you, Thornfield?" The old woman's voice called out, and he couldn't help the smile it brought to his face. The cantankerous old woman reminded him so much of his grand-mother. Her sharp tongue and warm smile had brought an unexpected comfort over the past year.

"Is that my mistress?" he called out, before walking into the sitting room. His elderly 'mistress', as he called her, was sitting on the sofa while A'wei served her tea. When she saw him, however, there was none of her typical fondness. No, her lined face was stern, almost cold.

A'wei glanced up at him with an anxious expression before standing. "Gēgē, Mrs. Burghley Harrison is here with a question for you."

He had a horrible feeling he was about to be cut loose again. "Alright."

"Are you playing with my niece?" she asked with no preamble.

Was she going to take the same line as her great nephew? That would be harder to stomach. "I beg your pardon?"

"Miss Elodia Hawthorne, my great great niece, are you playing a farce with her?" she repeated, thumping her cane on the parquet floor, every work crisp with temper.

"I am not," he replied.

"A maid said she saw you kissing her in the garden."

"You kissed Ellie?" A'wei gasped, her eyes wide with surprise but not dismay.

"In broad daylight," Aunt Theo added.

He took a seat and met Aunt Theo's eyes squarely. "I did kiss your niece."

She frowned, "Eh, so you admit it?"

"I did kiss your niece, after I asked her to marry me and she accepted me." There was nothing to be ashamed of. He had been perhaps a bit impolitic, but in the end, he regretted nothing.

"You are engaged to Ellie?" A'wei asked, leaning forward eagerly.

He spared her a glance. "I am."

"Does her father know?" Aunt Theo asked. Yes, she would

have focused on that.

"He does now." *For better or worse.*

"And how did that go?" she asked wryly, as if she already knew the answer.

"Not well based on what I heard," he replied, leaning back in the chair and crossing his legs.

"Ah."

"Is that your only reason for coming to see me?" he asked.

"Well, it was. But your sister makes a suspiciously divine cup of tea, so seeing as I don't have to box your ears, I have decided to stay a bit longer."

"I am gratified to hear it." He moved to sit beside her and took one of her gnarled hands in his. "I taught her everything she knows," he told her in a low voice.

"Will you take some tea, gēgē?" A'wei asked.

"Yes," He paused for a moment before continuing his conversation with Aunt Theo. "You don't seem that shocked."

"Because I'm not shocked. I suspected she was sweet on you for some time now. You are the one I was less certain of."

"You appear to be the only one." He accepted the cup A'wei handed him and gave her a small smile.

"How interesting." Her eyebrows shot up.

The conversation wasn't giving him any real indication of how she felt about him as a member of her family, and at this point, he needed to know. Even if it was painful. "I… I take it that you do not object to our marriage."

She nearly spat out her tea before turning towards him. "Why on earth would I object to you marrying my niece?"

"I can think of two reasons," he replied evenly.

"You think I am like my nephew?" she asked with something like offense on her face.

"Not exactly, but I expected some pushback from you."

She sighed and set down her teacup and saucer. "I suppose if I didn't know you as I do, I would have objected more."

"It didn't stop him."

She nodded with a wry smile. "He doesn't know you as well as you imagine he does. Everyone has their blind spots and Elodia is his. He's entitled to that, I suppose; she is his child."

"I don't begrudge him his misgivings."

"Oh, don't stand on ceremony, boy, you can begrudge him a little. He's become a bit more snobbish with age. When he was younger, he wouldn't have batted an eye at you. But now I think he's settled into his role as viscount with all that comes with it. He doesn't see you as his equal but I think a part of him knows it is not an objective opinion, especially when it comes to Elodia."

"Meaning?"

She sighed wearily and Richard took her teacup and set it down for her. "I don't know if I can speak for him, but I believe when her mother died, he… he very nearly followed her. Her passing was so unexpected and happened so quickly that he had no time to prepare himself. It took some time for him to come to terms with staying on without her, and a good amount of that calculation was Ellie. Whether she knows it or not, he survived because of her. She has been his rock instead of the other way around and you have neatly snatched her away with no notice."

He knew that. He'd known it before she said it but it was gratifying to hear it said by someone who knew the viscount well. "I didn't act alone. She had something to do with it."

"I can believe that," she said with a chuckle. "There is another point of concern. Mrs. Thompson here married Sterling's son, but that elevated her position without diminishing his. Irrespective of my regard for you as a person, Thornfield, even I can acknowledge that for all your wealth and many other fine attributes, Elodia could likely face more difficulty as your wife than as her father's daughter. It isn't fair, but it is a fact, and considering who her mother was, it is something Melbroke is keenly aware of."

"You think he's more afraid for her than angry at me?" Richard asked.

She nodded. "I think he's scared stiff."

It was cold comfort but it meant that there was more to his refusal than Richard's race or his social status. It wasn't bigotry so much as a one-sided assessment. He could work with that. More importantly, it meant that there was a way for Elodia to keep her father. "She will not want to give into him."

"Nor should she."

"No, you don't understand. She believes that Melbroke deliberately concealed the truth of his relationship with her mother to protect his reputation. At the expense of her own."

"You mean that nonsense rumor?"

"She knows about it and she knows why it came about."

"His father was determined to hide it, but I know my nephew. He would never take up with a girl like that. If he had a daughter, that meant he had a wife."

"Yes, but there is no legal record of the fact in England. When he migrated, he didn't bring the needed documentation."

She stared at him in shock before shaking her head. "That idiot."

"I agree. But Ellie, she is… she is so hurt by all of this, I worry what she will do. I don't know if you're aware, but my sister and I lost our parents in a similar way to Elodia and her mother, suddenly and far too soon. It's not the same, I know that, but I cannot allow her to give up her father. Not if he loves her as you say he does."

"He does love her. But that doesn't mean he won't do something foolish to get his way."

He couldn't allow that man to ruin everything for himself and his child, to say nothing of the effect of Richard. He didn't want to spend the rest of his life watching Elodia pretend she didn't miss her father like he knew he missed his parents.

"I imagine this means our torrid affair must come to an end." She gave him a forlorn look and he laughed before sliding an arm around her soft shoulders.

"Regrettably so. But I will always hold you in my heart,"

She let out that dry cackle he had grown so fond of, and patted his leg.

"Don't let go of that girl, Thornfield, or I truly will box your ears."

He nodded and leaned his cheek against her temple as he met A'wei's smiling eyes across the room. "I won't."

The doorbell sounded and he frowned at A'wei's sheepish expression. "Who's that?"

"Erm," she set down her teacup.

Within moments, he had his answer when a heavily pregnant Lady Starkley stormed in with Leo trailing behind her. He removed his arm from Aunt Theo, who let out a low whistle.

"Mr. Thornfield," Regina greeted him, her expression thunderous.

Back to honorifics so soon? "Lady Starkley." He rose to his feet, stealing a glance at Leo. He couldn't read his expression at all. "How can I be of assistance?"

"Are you courting Ellie?" she asked.

Ah. "I am."

"You are going to offer for her, aren't you? This isn't some half-baked idea to determine how you feel?"

"We are already engaged, why on earth would I want to give her to someone else?"

"I told you, Rajani," Leo murmured.

Regina turned to glare at him. "He's your friend. How could you possibly be objective?"

"Now that we know she is not in danger of being jilted, will you please sit down?" Leo replied, his mouth twisting with mild annoyance. She batted his assistance away and lowered herself slowly into an armchair. As cumbersome as she was, she was still terrifying. Richard wasn't foolish enough to tease her. "It has been whispered that you were seen kissing her in broad daylight."

"She was ready to call you out," Leo commented with a small smile, leaning on the chair back. "Frankly, I'm surprised the rumor hasn't reached her father."

"Lord Melbroke is aware that we are engaged, even if he is less than pleased about the fact. So if you would be so kind, please be sure to correct the record."

Leo's eyebrows went up. "That is fast work."

"Not fast enough for her reputation to be spared," Regina interrupted, sounding alarmingly like her mother. "They have exchanged intimacies before their wedding and it is known."

"Devika, you can hardly be the one to cast judgement on that front," Leo replied. Regina gasped and then turned away from him, smoothing her skirts frantically. If Richard didn't know better, he'd think she was blushing.

"Oh?" A'wei commented with amused interest.

"When will the banns be posted?" Regina asked, ignoring her friend entirely.

There was a story there, but having just escaped her ire, Richard wasn't interested in having her gunning for him again. "Soon. I should like to come to an agreement with her father first, but I will likely marry her before the season is finished. The sooner the better."

She nodded briskly. "That will do."

"I'm glad you agree," he replied, wondering what on earth she and Leo had done.

"I am sorry to come here uninvited and impose on you."

"I don't think you need an invitation at this point, Regina,"

She sighed and rubbed a jeweled hand over her enormous stomach, golden bracelets clinking against each other. "I was worried. Ellie is special. I couldn't stand by and allow you to play a losing game with her beautiful heart when she is such a dear person and she has loved you for so long."

"I can assure you that I have every intention to make her wait worthwhile. She is no less dear to me than she is to you."

"We shall see about that," she grumbled.

"Would you care for some tea, Gigi?" Ada asked.

"I think this calls for sandwiches and cakes as well," Richard added, crossing to the bell pull and ringing it.

"The time for that was earlier; a good show deserves some refreshments." Aunt Theo said with a cackle.

"Lady Starkley is entirely within her rights to confront me. Clearly, our Elodia is much beloved. I cannot be angry about that."

"When do you go into confinement, girl?" Aunt Theo asked.

"Not before the wedding. I have to be there for her."

"Agreed. Elodia would want that as well. I shall make arrangements accordingly."

"Thank you." She smiled at him, but she looked a bit more tired now. He remembered his mother during her pregnancy with Ada, and Regina was far more mobile than she had been. No doubt her condition was taking its toll, no matter how terrifying she was.

"Were you really going to duel me?" he asked.

"Absolutely," she replied unapologetically, "But for Ada's sake, I'd only wound you."

Chapter Fifteen

Melbroke House, Mayfair, London

T WO DAYS OF tense silence and general avoidance had passed since Elodia and her father had their argument about Richard. He wouldn't take his words back and she refused to even entertain the idea of changing her mind. He stayed in his study or his club, and she stayed in the parlor or music room when she was home.

She was in the middle of practicing her scales on the piano when heavy footsteps sounded in the hallway. She looked up to see her father enter with a somber expression. He didn't have his paper, and he didn't take a seat. He simply stood there with his folded arms, towering over her like a general.

"Ellie," he began, letting out a puff of air.

"Have you come to apologize?" she asked, continuing with her scales.

"I have not."

"Then I don't want to speak to you."

"I don't very much care," he snapped before closing the lid on the piano. "We need to discuss this further."

She snatched back her hands to avoid the lid and glared up at him. "Discuss what exactly?"

"This misunderstanding about your mother."

She tilted her head. "You mean the misunderstanding about her you allowed to prevail?"

His jaw clenched hard and he closed his eyes for a moment, as she watched him fight back a wave of temper. "I don't want to fight you, Ellie." He opened his eyes. "You have to know it was never my intention to allow your reputation, or your mother's, to be besmirched."

She could continue to fight him but she needed true answers, and if he was willing to speak, it didn't make sense to stay at odds. "Why did they think you'd never been married before?" she asked.

He sat down on the chair and rubbed his face roughly with his hands, his signet ring glinting coldly in the sunlight. "I can only imagine my father somehow kept that information private."

"I'm sure he did," she grumbled. He really had been the most hateful person.

"The point is, I did not intentionally mislead anyone about your status. The truth is, I did not think it was something I needed to prove, as I'd been married to your mother for over a decade before she passed."

That was a fair point. The likelihood that no one knew the firstborn son of a viscount had made a freed slave a prospective viscountess was low, even if it had been in the colonies. People talked, and more often than not word got back home. After all, her presence or ethnicity hadn't been a surprise to anyone, from the staff to the ton in general.

"As it is," her father continued, "I will correct the record which will improve your prospects. Therefore—"

"Therefore nothing. I am still marrying Richard."

"Stop calling him that," he gritted out through clenched teeth.

"He is my fiancé," she replied, her anger returning swiftly.

"Elodia, I have done and will do everything in my power to ensure that your position in society is unquestioned. Your position as the legal first-born daughter of a viscount. You do not understand the protection that you are throwing away by quitting the sphere in which you have been raised. If you marry—"

"—when," she corrected.

He glared at her. "*If* you marry him, you will no longer be a member of the nobility. You will be the wife of a merchant. Your children will be the sons and daughters of merchants."

There was no point arguing that fact. Instead, she took a different approach. "Are you saying that you will abandon me and have nothing to do with me if I leave your social sphere?"

"I am saying that your value of life will decrease."

"Because I won't be invited to balls hosted by the nobility?" Did he truly think she valued such things so highly?

"Yes. There are doors open to you now that you will lose access to."

"Have you considered that there is nothing behind those doors that I want more than Richard? He loves and respects me. Don't you want that for me?"

"If you would at least consider—"

She rose to her feet. "I do not need to consider anyone else. It is precisely because I have been observing them for years that I know my choice is the correct one. I have wanted to be his wife for years."

"Elodia, you do not understand what you are doing."

"Yes, I do, and if you force me to choose between a lonely life among the nobility and life at his side, you are going to be disappointed."

He shook his head and turned away from her, looking up at the ceiling, no doubt praying for patience. "Willful, impossible girl," he grumbled.

"Have we finished discussing for today? Only I have an engagement to attend."

"Yes, as it is clear you cannot be reasoned with."

She whirled on him, unwilling to let him have the last word. "I can reason with *reason*. What you are presenting is something else."

He walked away grumbling under his breath and Elodia let out the breath she'd been holding and unclenched her fists. She couldn't say it was enjoyable being at odds with her father, but there was a certain satisfaction that came from having it all out in the open. In the end, perhaps Béa had been correct in her assessment that she needed to speak to her father, not to give him an out but to establish the truth and find a way forward.

He was rapidly becoming the most insufferable man she'd ever had the displeasure of dealing with, but she would be lying if she didn't acknowledge there was still something of the man who raised her there. At the very least, she now knew he was more of a fool, as Ada had suggested. That he had never been ashamed of her and her mother, although that was likely going to change once she married Richard. He would then consider her a traitor to him.

She walked out of the room to the stairs and heard him calling for his carriage. Probably going to his club again. Unless… Richard. Her father wouldn't be able to persuade Richard, could he? The sudden thought sent a chill through her. What if he managed to get Richard to agree with him and leave her behind for what he believed was her best interest? She couldn't let her father ruin her happiness. She rushed to change her shoes, grabbed a shawl and ran out the door.

THE SUMMONS TO Brooks was unnerving. Richard hadn't known what to expect in the days following Melbroke discovering his engagement with Elodia. He'd had every intention of going to the man and discussing it once he was certain of Elodia's interest in him as a husband even though he was almost certain the man wouldn't agree at first.

But now everything had gone off course and Elodia and her father were at each other's throats. Richard was positive that this last-minute summons to Brooks was in response to that fact. He dressed in a dark green frock coat and a waistcoat made of a brown and green cloud brocade his grandmother had sent over from China and set off in his carriage, his gloved hands fiddling with his father's pocket watch.

When he was dropped off at St James's Street, he took a deep bracing breath and glanced at his driver. "Stay here, I don't see this lasting very long."

The driver nodded, the corners of his mouth tightening. "Very good, sir."

Richard walked through the doors and proffered the note from the viscount to the doorman. "The Viscount Melbroke is expecting me."

The man blinked a few times before glancing down at the logbook and the note. "You are…"

"Thornfield. Mr. Richard Thornfield."

He blinked again and looked up at Richard with widened eyes. Richard met his gaze patiently. This was a typical enough experience for him. No one expected to come face to face with a Chinese man after hearing his name.

"Yes, come this way, Mr. Thornfield."

Richard removed his hat and followed him, taking in the pale green walls and dark wood of the interior. For such an exclusive establishment, it wasn't as opulent as he was expecting.

The footman led him past inquisitive and downright astounded glances of the regular patrons to a private study occupied by the Viscount Sterling, and a tea service that Richard imagined was some kind of attempt at civility.

"Mr. Thornfield, Lord Melbroke," the footman announced him, despite the fact that the man could clearly see him.

"Thank you, John," Melbroke said, staying in his seat.

"Very good, my lord," John nodded and left the room, closing the door behind him. Whatever curiosity he had was no match for his training.

Richard waited a beat after the door clicked shut before speaking. "Lord Melbroke, I take it you would like a word with me?"

"I would. Please have a seat."

Richard sat in the plush leather chair, crossed his legs and eyed the teapot on the table between them. He could already smell that it was overstepped. Hopefully the viscount stopped at appearances and wouldn't try to serve him any of it.

"It was recently brought to my attention that you intend to be married to my daughter." The older man said.

That was one way to put it. "Yes. I also had the privilege of hearing your feelings on the matter."

His mouth tightened as he folded his fingers together on his knee. "It is not a personal objection, Mr. Thornfield."

Richard barely suppressed a scoff. Far be it for a peer of the realm to object personally to someone. "Of course not, that would be unreasonable. As I understood it, your objection is rather more generalized."

Melbroke's mouth tightened. "Yes."

"And I imagine you haven't changed your mind recently."

"No." He sat up and leaned forward. "As a man of the world, I'm sure you appreciate my position. Elodia is a member of the nobility; her position is unique on several levels. It has provided a certain level of protection for her that she has never been without."

"That is true."

"She is not prepared for the reality of life without that protection."

"Make your point, sir."

Melbroke leaned forward, his elbows on his knees. "I would like you to convince Elodia to give you up."

There it was. He hadn't gotten through to her so his new plan was to get around her. Through him. So it was to be a negotiation. If there was one thing Richard knew how to do, it was negotiate. "Why would I do that?"

"Because I am asking you, gentleman to gentleman."

How interesting. Richard imagined Melbroke thought he should be flattered by being held to his standard. "By your estimation, I am not in fact a gentleman, Lord Melbroke. I am a lowly merchant."

"Well," Melbroke shifted in his chair. Was he embarrassed? "You must agree that she is far above your reach."

"I do not agree. With respect to suitability, we are very well matched as far as education, sensibility, temperament and intelligence go."

"And what about your utter lack of connection?"

"I am not so lacking in connection anymore, my lord. I have both friends and family in the nobility." Enough to draw attention anyway.

"That is very good for them but you, as you are, are not. You cannot protect her from them."

It was a fair point. "So your solution is to marry her to the very people she would need protecting from?"

"Of course not. But one of them, one like your Mr. Thrompson, yes."

"Even if I were to take your point, which I don't, I do not believe you should be the one to make it, my lord. A saying is coming to mind about living in glass houses."

"Meaning?"

"I mean her late mother—"

"—you mean my late wife?"

Richard tilted his head in consideration. The man had been quick to correct him, complete with flashing eyes, which was good. If he was going to stay in Elodia's life, Richard wanted to know he was worth the trouble. "Ah, so she was your wife."

"Yes, of course she was my wife," Melbroke replied, growing impatient.

"There is no 'of course' about it, my lord. Men like you are not known for marrying former slaves."

Melbroke frowned. "You mean members of the nobility?"

"I mean white men in general," Richard replied evenly. "And white members of the nobility in particular. A fact of which you could not have been ignorant."

"You didn't think Elodia was legitimate?" Melbroke asked.

"No. But I didn't care. I never cared."

"You say that, but I'll bet you still wish for me to make it public."

"Yes, I do. Because the idea that you were a dishonorable man who allowed not only her but her mother to be spoken of with disrespect at will was devastating to her. Her social status may not matter much to me, my lord, but I hold her dignity no less dearly than my own."

Melbroke looked away from him again, silently ceding him the point. "I have already taken steps to amend that misunderstanding," he replied. "I hardly need you to tell me."

"I am glad to hear it. However, your late wife was not considered a suitable match for you either. In certain circles, she was barely considered human when you married her, but you married her nonetheless. I believe you would disagree with the idea that she was a regrettable choice of spouse for you."

Melbroke's head was shaking in rejection before Richard finished his sentence. "That is not the same thing."

Was the man willfully ignorant or simply blinded by paternal love? "That is your opinion."

"My opinion is the one that counts."

There was no point in debating it any further. As Aunt Theo had guessed, Melbroke was not in the frame of mind to consider or even accept an alternate perspective. Richard didn't like it, but it was clear that he and Elodia would have to move forward without her father's blessing for the time being. "No, in point of fact. Elodia's is. She chose me and I will not undermine her agency or our shared feelings by giving her up. She is everything I didn't know I needed. She is everything to me."

Melbroke's eyes flashed with visible temper. "That is very romantic, but she is my daughter."

His daughter. As if she couldn't have a goal, thought or wish of her own without his permission. "Do you know, the way you say 'daughter' is beginning to sound like something else."

The older man bristled, nostrils flaring, his hands tightening on the arms of the chair. "You would dare—"

"I am merely making an observation," Richard said, before the man could lose his temper.

"I could ruin you over this."

"You could indeed, but I don't believe you will."

"You think I'm afraid of you?"

"No, but you wouldn't be able to do it fast enough to stop me from marrying her. And all you would be doing is hurting her by extension which I do not believe is your wish."

Richard rose to his feet, regarding the older gentleman with some sympathy. He knew everything he needed to know about the viscount at this point, so all that was left was to make his position clear.

"As a supposed gentleman, I will offer you two pieces of advice. Firstly, reconsider your position, my lord. Elodia knows her own mind, and she is of age. She is bold and willful but she had not made this choice lightly."

"Don't tell me about my own child."

"She is your child, but she is not *a* child. She is three and twenty. She does not strictly speaking need your permission, and as to her dowry, I do not need your money."

"Your point being?"

"You do not have to like me, but you do not have to lose your daughter. I agree that the closer you hold to her, the safer she will be. She is precious to both of us and we can both protect her. Leave her heart and wellbeing to me, and we will leave the ton to you." He gave him a shallow bow and headed for the door.

"And the second?" Melbroke called.

Richard paused and turned to see the man watching him, still seated in his chair. One thing Richard would say for him is that, for all he resembled his daughter, he was a very controlled man. Richard could admire a man who had mastered himself. He nodded towards the teapot. "Don't drink that tea. It's unpotable at this point."

He turned and left the room without a backwards glance. He couldn't relax until he was back in his carriage and on his way home with a good deal to think about.

CHAPTER SIXTEEN

Thornfield House, Mayfair, London

ELODIA WANTED TO be mature and dignified. She wanted to show Richard that she was grown enough to handle all of this without losing her composure, but more than that, she needed to know what Richard was thinking. She'd torn down the street on foot, determined to speak to him before her father did. She hadn't considered what she would do if Richard was, in fact, not home.

Which was how she ended up in his house accompanying Ada and Basil while she played with her children. She made no mention of Richard, and chose to ignore the sly looks passing between Ada and Basil.

"I'm so glad to see you in better spirits, Ellie," Ada commented.

"Ada, leave her alone."

"I'm curious as to how long she'll wait before saying anything."

"What do you mean?" Ellie asked, looking up at them and batting her eyes.

"Any recent events you'd like to put on the record?" Basil asked, handing his son a wooden block.

"You mean like the fact that I'm going to become your sister-in-law?"

"Or that fact that you kissed my brother in full view of half of London, based on reports," Ada asked.

That was unexpected. "What reports?"

A throw pillow sailed through the air and bounced on her head. "How could you keep that from me?"

"Well, you know it now." Elodia giggled and dodged another pillow, before picking up Young Ellie and holding her to her front to dissuade Ada from sending any more projectiles.

"Yes, because I had to claw it out of you, and don't you think for a moment you are safe from Regina. She nearly shot my brother because she didn't know the two of you were already engaged. Aunt Theo came here ready to tear off a piece of poor Richard's hide."

Elodia stared in shock. That was a good deal more than she had expected. She couldn't imagine anything Ada had just described. Regina pulling a pistol on Richard? Aunt Theo being cross with him? It boggled the mind.

Just then, she heard a familiar low voice. Was it him? She placed Ada's daughter on the floor and sprang to her feet, running out the door. She wanted to be mature. She knew she should wait for him to come to her instead of showing so blatantly how much she had missed him. But then she saw him standing there in the foyer, still wearing his dark green frock coat, his thick dark hair falling over his forehead and into his eyes.

He was handing his gloves to the footman, but looked up as she arrived. His head tilted and his smile, the smile she associated with him the most, spread across his face.

"Hello you," he said, and she ran across the foyer into his open arms. She buried her face into his broad shoulder and allowed herself to revel in the relief he brought. He chuckled against her, his hand smoothing over her back.

"I missed you."

"So I see," he teased, but his arms tightened around her.

"Did you miss me?" she asked, tilting her head back to meet his fond gaze.

"Always." He slid his arm around her shoulders and walked with her up the stairs towards his office. "Not that I'm not delighted to see you, but what are you doing here?"

"I just wanted to see my fiancé. Since I can call you that now."

His smile was almost bashful as he pulled her closer. "Have you spoken to your father since my last visit?"

"Yes, no luck so far. But I've made my position clear."

"Good, so have I."

"When did you speak to him?" she asked, hoping her voice sounded nonchalant.

"Today. He summoned me to Brooks for a conference. It didn't go the way he intended."

So she had been right in her suspicions. Her father had tried to get around her by scaring Richard off. It hadn't worked this time, but there would be others and eventually Richard would run out of patience. She'd only just gotten him, what if he decided that she wasn't worth the trouble? "He won't give up. We'll never get his blessing; we should just marry."

"We shall." He replied, pushing open the door to his office with one hand as they entered.

"No, I mean now. Let's go to Gretna Green,"

That stopped him in his tracks and earned her a puzzled look. "Whatever for?"

Was he joking again? "To marry, of course."

He frowned and his arm slid away from her shoulders. He sat on his desk and turned her to face him, taking her hands in his. "There is no point in going to Gretna Green."

"I disagree, there is no point in waiting for his blessing when he will never give it."

"Àirén, even if he will not give his blessing, there is no need to go to Gretna Green."

"Why not?" she asked.

"Because we can marry in England without his blessing. Legally."

"But—"

"Gretna Green is for those seeking to circumvent the law in some way or another. We have no reason to escape it. You are of age, I am of significant means, your Aunt Theo is on our side. Between her and Regina, we have a place to host the engagement and the wedding breakfast if needed. Let us post the banns and move forward with planning the wedding."

"That will take a long time."

"No longer than if he were to agree to the marriage. In fact, it may take less time this way."

"So much can happen. You think he will just stand by and allow us to do what we wish?"

"He still can't stop it."

"He can delay us. He could do all kinds of nonsense."

"He can try, of course, but I don't think—"

"We do not need all of that, do we? I just want to be your wife, it doesn't matter how." Didn't it bother him? Why wasn't he concerned about this as she was? Did he not care?

"We need it if we wish to avoid the appearance of impropriety. We are breaking enough rules as it is."

"Oh." Somehow she'd never seen him as someone who would care about that sort of thing. He had been happy enough to see her here waiting for him, but perhaps his patience had a limit. It was her nature to push but she didn't want him to grow annoyed with her so quickly. If she insisted, he'd see her as childish and naïve. He hadn't said he loved her yet, but he never would if she was a brat. "I'll leave you to your work."

"Ellie." Suddenly, he was there, pulling her into his arms and holding her tightly. "Where are you going?"

"You probably have work to see to." And she apparently had a whole wedding to plan when they could have been man and wife within three days at the most.

"Did I say that?"

"No, but you brought us into your office. It's a fair assumption."

"I brought you into my office because I didn't want an audience and my room is not an option at the moment."

"That doesn't mean you aren't busy."

He frowned again. "You didn't care about my work five minutes ago."

She looked down at her hands where they lay trapped against his torso. "I hadn't seen it piled on your desk five minutes ago."

His grip on her loosened and then his fingers were at her chin, lifting her face so he could see it. "Don't do that. If there is something bothering you then say it. I won't want you hiding from me."

"Well… I want to marry you as soon as possible but you don't."

"That is not true."

"It feels true. You want to do all that nonsense and risk my father derailing the entire thing instead of taking the easiest, simplest path to getting what we both want. It makes me feel as though you don't want it as much as I do." She met his eyes tentatively to see him watching her with a thoughtful frown. "You said you wanted to marry me. Do you really?"

"Yes, I do."

"It's so easy for you to be calm and reasonable. I cannot tell if I am impatient or if perhaps I was the easiest option for you instead of the only one as you were for me."

"You think I'm marrying you because it's more convenient?"

"Not exactly. More that it makes sense to marry me because I'm obviously willing and we suit. I am obviously happy that you've agreed to marry me, but agreeing doesn't always mean that it is a priority. Men are different, aren't they?"

He stared in silence, his expression unreadable. Was he upset with her? Or was he simply dismayed by her words?

"It would be alright even if it was. You don't have to feel obligated to love me. I know that—" His mouth was on hers, hard and demanding, cutting off her words. She gasped against him and his hand gripped the back of her neck, holding her in place. Emboldened by the memory of what they'd done in the garden that first afternoon, she tilted her head and parted her lips in invitation, hoping he'd take the initiative. He did.

Within moments, his arm was around her, hauling her against him and his other hand spanned from the back of her neck to the base of her head. His sigh brushed against her mouth while his kiss became hungrier than ever before, and his hands firmer as they swept over her body from her back down to her bottom, molding her to him.

She wanted to focus on everything she was feeling, everything he was doing so she could learn more. But just like in the garden, she kept losing her breath and capitulating to the sensations evoked by his hungry mouth and daring hands. Those butterflies in her stomach kept swooping and sliding all over, leaving her giddy and weak as she clutched his shoulders greedily, arching into him, hoping for more.

He picked her up and spun her around, pressing her into a hard surface so she could feel everything from the corded muscles of his thighs to the firm ridge of flesh between them pressing into her stomach insistently. Had she thought he was uninterested? Unwilling? Had he simply been holding back for her sake?

Perhaps she should have stopped him or pushed back. But her limbs felt like water and it felt too perfect to be held and kissed by him like this after days of being apart. She wanted him to keep going, to show her that she wasn't alone in craving him, or counting the days until she never had to let him go again.

Suddenly, he pulled back and took a deep, if unsteady, breath as he pressed his brow against hers. When she opened her eyes, she found his still closed, his nostrils flaring, his bruised lips parted against desperate breaths, a slight flush painting his cheekbones. Had she done that? Her hands moved from his shoulders up to his face, stroking his cheeks gently, and he nuzzled into her touch.

"I love when you do that," he murmured.

"What, this?" she asked, caressing his face.

He nodded before opening his eyes. "No one has ever touched me like you do." He sighed again and drew back, allowing her to slide down until her feet touched the floor. Clearly, he had more faith in her legs than she did at the moment.

"Ellie," he began again, "I want to marry you and believe me, nothing about this is easy."

"Then why can't we—"

"Because I won't have it said that I'm a thief. There is nothing to hide from, there is no reason for us to run. I won't have our marriage made into some cautionary tale about the Chinese merchant who ran away with the viscount's mixed-race daughter."

She opened her mouth to speak and he shook his head.

"It is what they will say. Perhaps it is selfish of me to insist upon it but it matters to me. Whether you see it as important or not, it does mean something. It means something to post the banns and have it shouted for one and all to hear. For you to choose your trousseau and make the wedding dress you want. To stand in front of all of London and stake our claims on each other publicly in front of our family and friends. It matters that they see we have nothing to hide and nothing to be ashamed of." He stroked her cheek.

"I suppose."

"There is the other matter as well. I know you don't want to give in to him now but I don't want you to do anything that you will regret. HE is your father, Elodia and no matter how angry you are with him now, no matter how unreasonable he is being now, you will both regret not having him at your wedding. It is not something that can be fixed later. It is worth it to be a little patient now, not for his sake but for your own."

"I don't care if he's there."

"Do you really not care or is it that you do not want to cede ground to your father?"

"He betrayed me. I'm angry with him, and I don't see why we should have to spend so much effort to wait for his blessing which I know you want."

Richard shook his head and pulled her close, sliding an arm around her waist. "I am not waiting for him. I'm taking my due. I am only going to marry once in this lifetime, and my bride is the most beautiful, accomplished, warm hearted, clever, sweet natured woman in the world. Both of us deserve the full experience from beginning to end. He may be able to deny us his blessing, if that is indeed his choice in the end, but we will not deny you your full wedding. You deserve that and so do I. I will not give that up any more than I will you. I love you, Ellie."

"Do you really?" she asked. "You didn't say before so—"

"—Yes, very much. You are everything I was afraid to want. I'm sorry I didn't say so earlier."

"I'm sorry I doubted you."

"It's not your fault, it was mine. But if you have doubts or desires, you should speak them, Ellie. Don't hide from me. You will be my wife, you should speak your mind."

"Papa always says I'm a bully."

"You are," he agreed with a smile. "But I'm not afraid of you."

She couldn't help but smile at that. "A gentleman would have denied that assertion."

"Well, you're marrying a tradesman, Miss Hawthorne."

She rolled her eyes and laid her head on his chest, squeezing and slipping her arms around his waist. It was just like him to tease her even while whispering sweet nothings. "Post the banns then," she murmured.

"Thank you, àirén."

"Will you write to me?"

"You live ten minutes away."

"Yes, but in a proper courtship, you would call on me." She lifted her head and rested her chin on his chest. "You can't really do that with my father there, so the next best thing is for you to write to me. So I can show the letters to our children when you are old and annoying."

"As you wish," he murmured, rubbing her nose with his. She could see it now, the love shining in his eyes.

"And I want a ball to celebrate our engagement."

"Perhaps a private soiree?"

"Why not a ball?"

"I thought you wanted to get married within the month? A ball takes weeks to plan."

She squinted at him threateningly, even as her heart swelled in her chest at the adoration on his face. "Are you going to be like this for our entire marriage?"

"If you are having second thoughts, àirén, now is the time to have them," he teased with a smile. She dug her fingers into his ribs and he jerked, squirming away from her with a loud laugh.

That was how she realized Richard Thornfield was ticklish. Her eyes went wide at the sight of his body flinching away from her. "Well, now this is interesting."

"Stay away from me." He held up a warning finger. She wiggled her fingers and started forward.

"Ellie." The door opened and Ada entered. At the sight of her alarmed brother, she turned to Ellie. "Is everything alright?" she asked Ellie.

"Yes, of course," Ellie replied, dropping her hands and clasping them behind her back.

"Take your friend mèimei," he replied, retreating to the other side of the desk. "I have very important work to do, apparently." He gave Elodia a pointed look. She stuck out her tongue at him.

"Very well, I'll leave you for now. But I want it noted for the record that I won this round."

He nodded and waved her off before sitting in his chair.

"Well, it is unsporting to say but," Basil shrugged, "we told you so."

Richard rolled his eyes and wagged his finger. "Yes, yes. Move along." They had invited Richard to their club to celebrate his upcoming nuptials. It was strange, considering how little time it had taken for all of them to march down the aisle. But Richard wasn't going to complain about the results.

Leo raised his glass in a toast. "Congratulations, old man, on securing the most terrifying one of them all."

"Indeed, it took you a minute to catch on, but you got there in the end." Basil winked and Richard pulled a face.

"Thank you, although I still maintain you are both cowards."

"You only say that because she likes you," Basil said.

"No, she loves me," he replied, gloating. "You are the ones who have to worry about her, not I."

"Look at him," Leo shook his head, "Look at this smug bastard."

"For once I can't seem to begrudge him."

Leo nudged Basil. "He wasn't this smug when my Gigi nearly pulled her pistol."

Richard's mouth fell open with outrage, as if his little terrorist wasn't something to be afraid of. "Because it's very tricky to defend oneself against a pregnant woman. Especially when she has the aim of a fucking sharpshooter."

Leo laughed but didn't refute the assertion. "My mother is coming for your wedding by the by."

"Is she?" Richard sat up a little straighter. That was a reunion he would look forward to. "I haven't seen her in so long."

"Yes, I've heard as much," Leo replied, shaking his head. "How are things with Lord Melbroke?"

"As expected." He shrugged. "He is currently mulling over his options."

"Will he make things difficult for you?"

"Not as difficult as Elodia will make it for him."

Basil laughed, "She is not easily deterred, that one."

"She's never heard the word 'no',"

"Oh, she hears it but she doesn't really listen," Richard replied with a chuckle. Unless, of course, he was saying it.

Leo's amused expression shifted into something more guarded, and Richard's hands tightened on the armrest of his chair.

"Nephew," Uncle Simon's voice came from behind him.

Fuck. "Uncle." He turned his head and waited, unwilling to stand for him.

He walked around Richard's chair until his shoes were in sight. "I didn't realize you still attended this club. I haven't seen you here in some time."

"I've been busy of late," Richard replied.

"Yes, so I've heard. Could I trouble you for a moment of your time?"

Richard glanced up at his uncle. He seemed almost panicked and unfocused instead of his usual sulking nonsense. This was new. He rose to his feet and turned to face him expectantly. "After you,"

He followed his uncle into a small alcove and waited with folded arms for his uncle to begin.

"I have heard that you have been circulating rumors of a most presumptuous connection."

It was an interesting way to begin a conversation. "Have you?"

"Yes. Is it true?"

"Would you like to be more specific?"

"Lord Melbroke's daughter," he snapped. "It is said that you are to marry her."

So the reports had been fully circulated. He had to credit Regina with the network she had set up. "I am."

"By what right, sir? The man has refuted it."

So Melbroke was simply making his dissent known. Interesting. "That is to be expected."

"You do not have his blessing, then?"

Now Richard was doubly curious as to what his uncle's intention was in pulling him aside. "Were you concerned that I was courting Melbroke's disfavor by marrying his daughter or were you concerned that I was being misled?"

"You cannot marry her if her father does not agree," Simon insisted.

"Yes, I can."

Simon shook his head, his lip curling in disgust, his eyes burning with contempt. "I always knew you would be the ruin of our family."

"Did you? Is that why you attempted to have me disappeared?"

He hissed and glanced over his shoulder to see if anyone else had heard it. "Keep your voice down."

"So you admit it now?" Richard asked more out of curiosity. He had a bet with himself going now, as to how long it would take for Simon to admit to it.

"I admit nothing, *boy*."

Time to go. "Well. I believe you have received more than a moment of my time. I will leave you now, Mr. Thornfield."

"Who the hell do you think you are?" he hissed.

"I am the man Miss Hawthorne loves. I am her choice above all others."

"You think that marrying a Viscount's bastard will give you ties to the nobility?"

Richard froze and took a deep breath, keeping his arms folded. The man had always been good at getting under his skin, but Richard had never been driven to violence quite so quickly before. Especially over someone else. It was as unnerving as it was thrilling to know how much he felt for her. To know that he didn't have to hide how he felt when it came to her. Regardless, if he lost his temper here, he would be thrown out.

"Although I suppose it is the best you can do."

He turned to face his uncle. "And you, dear uncle, couldn't even manage that."

Simon was practically vibrating with rage, "You arrogant little—"

"Incidentally, she isn't a bastard." He didn't have the patience for any more of his vitriol.

Simon blinked at him in shock. "What? Of course she is."

Richard tilted his head and smiled in vicious delight at his uncle's confusion and growing horror.

"That would mean he married a—" He shook his head in revulsion. "No. No nobleman would do such a thing."

"Perhaps you should seek out his lordship and verify the matter for yourself," Richard replied with a smile. His uncle would receive a nasty shock either way; it was all a matter of timing, really.

"You think you're so clever, don't you?" he sneered.

"I shall leave you to your thoughts, uncle." He walked away, whistling, to rejoin Basil and Leo who were watching him warily.

"What did he want?" Leo asked as Richard took his seat and sighed heavily.

"To congratulate me on my marriage," he replied with raised eyebrows.

"Why do I find that hard to believe?"

"Well, he didn't use those exact words," Richard conceded, "but the gist was the same."

"He must be shitting himself." Basil was smiling widely.

"He is indeed. He can't decide what bothers him more, retaliation for my impudence or for his."

"Has he figured out that you are about to be connected to a viscount's daughter?"

"Do you know I'm not certain he has. But I'll likely hear about it when he does."

"I don't know why you put up with him still," Leo said, shaking his head.

"Because, for now, it is my duty to put up with him. I am the head of the entire Thornfield family whether he likes that or not, and within that section of our family are innocent people who will be affected by my behavior. There will be a time for cutting ties with him, but there is no rush. Besides, I have a wedding to plan for."

AN UNEASY STALEMATE had emerged between Elodia and her father within the passing days. He didn't push her and she didn't mention her engagement. The plans went ahead, and Richard wrote letters every day as he'd promised, and she received them without any trouble. That lasted until the first of her banns were read. The Monday after had begun regularly enough, with them enjoying luncheon in a polite silence before he had left, presumably on business, and she had taken the opportunity to have tea with Ada and Isolde at Regina's home.

"Will you have a white wedding dress, Ellie?" Ada asked.

"Ivory, I think, with the blonde French lace."

"I think that would suit you better," Regina said. "White can be such a harsh color."

"I agree."

"Do you think you'll go on your honeymoon immediately?" Isolde asked.

"I'm less certain of that."

"Because of your father?" Regina asked.

"He plans to marry this year as well. If he does, then I wouldn't want to be out of town. In the event that he chooses to invite me."

"Will you invite him to yours?" Ada asked.

"Richard says we should, and I'm too angry to decide if it's what I want or not."

"Is he still against the marriage?" Isolde asked.

"He's been less defiant lately. I don't know what that means. I'm only grateful for the quiet."

"I never thought he would react so strongly to it," Regina said.

"Basil's family wasn't terribly pleased about me, and he has virtually no chance of inheriting anything," Ada said. "It's the idea of me being in the family at all, of their grandchildren not being of the best pedigree possible. The possibility of my children having a place somewhere previously forbidden. It's a loss of control."

Elodia shook her head. "Ada, he married my mother and she was a slave turned servant. He did so with the full intention of making her a viscountess. If my grandfather had died before her, she would have been a viscountess. What right does my father have to criticize Richard on the basis of rank? He is a hypocrite as well as a snob."

"Well then, let us discuss something more cheerful," Ada said, patting her hand.

"I agree," Isolde said.

"Your wedding night, what color will you choose?" Ada asked.

There was a question she hadn't considered at all. What color should she choose? Was there a correct answer? "What did you get for yours?" Elodia asked.

"I went with white," Ada said. "My wedding night was already done by the time I got my trousseau."

"Mine was green," Regina replied.

"How did you decide?" Elodia asked.

"Sometimes it's the color you prefer the most, the one you feel the most comfortable in."

Elodia wasn't certain she would feel comfortable in any color. While she was all too excited to marry Richard at long last, the idea of appearing in front of him in such a state of undress was terrifying. There would be nothing to hide behind then.

"If you need a suggestion," Ada began.

"Yes, please." Elodia turned to her and took her hand.

"Perhaps red."

"Why red?" Elodia asked.

"It is the traditional color for weddings in China, I believe. If it mattered enough to him that I receive some semblance of tradition, I can't imagine he wouldn't want the same for himself."

"Red is a bit scandalous, isn't it?" Isolde mused.

"Perhaps, but why be modest now?" Regina shrugged and Eloida laughed. It was true enough. If she had always stayed beholden to convention, she wouldn't be marrying Richard.

Convention was not something she and her father had even given much sway to.

On her way home a few hours later, she wondered if it was possible that she was holding too firm a line, and Richard was correct. If her marriage to Richard was certain then there would be nothing lost in extending the olive branch first. He was her father after all, and while he was staunchly against her marriage, there was a path back. There had to be. Her mother's heart would have been broken to see them lose each other.

Upon returning home, however, she was greeted by a veritable greenhouse full of flowers of every kind; at least fifty bouquets littered the entryway, spilling out of the sitting room. At first, she had wondered if Richard had decided upon spoiling her, but when she picked up the first card attached, then the second, it was made clear her fiancé had played no part in this demonstration. These were suitors.

Somehow, she now had men vying for her hand, despite the fact that her banns were being read. She didn't know how this was possible. She'd sat in the church between Regina and Aunt Theo and heard them read out only a day ago. Richard had been there.

Now, she looked around her in her father's house, seeing the results of someone's delusion. She picked up five calling cards. All were from sons of the nobility, including Mr. Lewis. What on earth had happened?

The front door opened and Elodia turned to see her father observing the floral display with a degree of satisfaction.

"What on earth is this, Papa?" she asked.

"I told you I would be taking steps to correct the record with respect to your status as my daughter. This is the result."

"This is more than that. There has been some misunderstanding. The first of the banns were read only yesterday."

"Yes, that is true. But as a lady, you are not beholden to anything until you sign your wedding certificate."

A horrifying realization fell over her. "You told them to keep making offers?"

"You have more options available to you than the one you are choosing to accept, Elodia. It is folly to throw them away for the sake of the first offer received."

"I refuse to discuss this any further."

"Where is the harm? If none of them suit you, then marry your merchant."

"I cannot believe you would do this. I cannot believe that you would humiliate him like this."

"You are worried about his humiliation?" he demanded, "What about mine? What about your own humiliation?"

In that moment, she knew she couldn't stay in that house any longer. She would say or do something horrific, something she couldn't take back. No, it was more than that. She couldn't stay in her father's house as long as he was determined to put an end to her engagement. She couldn't risk allowing Richard to be humiliated because of her father's petty pride.

Whatever came next, it would have to come somewhere else. Somewhere her father couldn't throw his weight or title around. She needed allies who couldn't be bent or bought. Thankfully, there was still one person available who met that description. Without another word, she turned and walked out the front door, ignoring her father's calls. She did not stop walking until she reached Harley House.

When she entered the salon of her aunt's city home, she found her there with Isolde. She lifted her head and frowned in her direction.

"Ellie, are you quite well?" Isolde said, rising to her feet.

Aunt Theo held out her hand to her. "My dear girl, what is the matter?"

"Aunt." She went to her and sat at her feet. "I need your help."

"Of course." She stroked one gnarled, wrinkled hand over her hair and Elodia very nearly burst into tears.

"I… Papa has done something horrible."

"What has happened?" Aunt Theo asked.

"He has been telling the ton that my engagement to Mr. Thornfield is somehow not a certain thing. That my mind can be altered if they present themselves as eligible suitors."

"But your banns—" Isolde began.

"They have been doing it regardless. There is a mountain of flowers at Melbroke House because of him. He is determined that I should marry a member of the nobility no matter what I say or do. I just know what he won't stop at this, he'll do something worse, something to make it truly impossible."

"What do you need from me then?"

"I cannot stay there. May I come here to live for the time being?"

"Until he agrees?" Isolde asked.

"Or until I marry. Whichever comes first."

"That is an extreme response, Ellie."

"It is the only way for him to understand that I mean what I say. Words have not been enough so now I must take action. Richard doesn't want to elope, and I will respect that, but I cannot plan my wedding there. He will try to sabotage it in any way he can. I cannot take the risk."

Aunt Theo watched her for a moment, her mouth pursed, her bright blue eyes sharp and steady. For a moment, Elodia feared she would send her back to her father with a few platitudes. Then the old woman let out a short sigh. "Isolde dear, ring the bell, will you?"

Isolde stood and followed the instructions, a pensive expression on her face. When the maid arrived, she curtsied to Aunt Theo who nodded. "Miss Elodia will be paying us an extensive visit; please prepare a room for her."

Elodia took her fragile hand in hers and kissed the back of it. "Thank you, Aunt. I am sorry for having to do this. I know that it is the last thing you need right now."

"Nonsense. I am happy to help you, don't worry. When my nephew comes, I shall handle him."

"I have to go now. I will pack my things and bring them tomorrow."

"I'll have the carriage sent to you around one pm. We can have tea together, it will be great fun."

Elodia stood, kissed her white hair and then left, returning to the home she would soon no longer share with her father.

The dark wood and black and amber marble floors had once been a sanctuary for her, a guarantee of safety. Now it only looked foreboding, the flowers still in the foyer a clear indication that this was no longer a place where she could find peace. She walked past them and up the stairs.

Her maid Béa looked up at her from her mending when she entered her room.

"What is it, miss?"

"We need to pack my things. I will be staying with my aunt for the time being."

"You are leaving home?" Béa asked in alarm.

"I am. Will you come with me?"

"You know I would never think of leaving you."

"Thank you, Béa." She hugged her tightly and Béa patted her back gently.

"When are we leaving?"

"Tomorrow."

"Tomorrow?" She yanked her away, looked at her in alarm again.

"It doesn't need to be everything, just enough to get me through to the wedding. I will help you."

"I'm not worried about that, girl. Does your father know you are leaving?"

"He will know when I am gone," Elodia replied, striding into her closet to begin pulling out dresses. She was tired of talking to no avail. Tired of being underestimated and ignored. Tired of waiting for something to happen, tired of being afraid. He'd made his move but two could play that game. She wasn't as trapped as he imagined her to be.

CHAPTER SEVENTEEN

*H*E IS MARRYING *her.*

The words kept circling in Rachel's mind as her hands fisted in her skirt under the table. Simon Thornfield sat across from her, utterly absorbed in his own private nightmare. She'd invited him to tea as the grubby little imbecile was her only real insight into Richard's life outside of rumor. Now she was tempted to flip the entire blasted table over and rage.

"Say it again, Mr. Thornfield."

"He is truly engaged to marry her. The banns have been posted."

"Your nephew is marrying Melbroke's bastard daughter?" He was truly marrying that little girl with the coloring of a field hand. He would rather marry that *thing* with the pedigree of chattel than be her lover. There was no greater insult.

He shook his head firmly. "Not his bastard. His true born daughter."

"Melbroke has another daughter?" She hadn't heard anything about a second daughter.

"No. Miss Elodia is his true born daughter."

No. "That is impossible."

"Sterling confirmed it. Melbroke married that girl's mother before she was born."

There was no greater insult to the social order. "That is inconceivable."

"Not to him, apparently."

She was a trueborn daughter of the nobility? If that was true then he would have a true and tangible connection, even if the chit was giving up the sphere in which she'd been raised. He'd found his golden goose after all, in *her*. How utterly ridiculous. It couldn't happen. If he wasn't willing to choose her then he would have to stay where he was, in the gutter. Richard was implacable; he would never listen to her… unless the girl could be persuaded. Unless his golden goose ran away. "What are you going to do about it?" she asked.

Simon blinked at her. "Me?"

"Yes. You do realize that if this comes to pass, you will never be able to get the better of him. Richard will always have more power than you unless you can find some blind, desperate fool to take one of your girls off your hands. Stranger things have officially happened. Although you don't have nearly as much money as Captain Mason and his heathen wife."

"What on earth do you suppose I can do about it?"

"Drive a wedge. Damage her in some way, or him so that they are no longer a viable prospect."

"Melbroke would destroy me."

"No, you would be protected. By them and by me. There are enough members of the ton who would thank you for finally putting an end to this rash of lunacy sweeping our ranks. Our best families have been infiltrated, Mr. Thornfield. First Sterling, then a Barony gone to a black commoner and his mongrel wife, and now Melbroke's first grandchild will be an abomination. He is your nephew; you must stop it and defend the social order. The nobility is meant for us, not them. If anyone can simply marry into it then where will we be?"

"You are right, of course,"

"If they are truly engaged, there will be a party. A ball or a soiree."

"But I have no invitation. I cannot simply attend a private function."

"Thornfield's uncle not invited to his engagement party? That is an oversight that must be rectified. Perhaps I shall mention it to Lady Sterling. No doubt she is educating that oriental girl on the finer points of entertaining."

"Can you do that?"

"Of course. But if I can get her on side, if I can get you there, can you handle your nephew?"

"Leave it to me, my lady," he said before standing, bowing and leaving the room.

Leave it to him? She scoffed. Not a chance. Idiot. He could blunder forth and give her the opening she needed. When whatever lunacy he proposed backfired then she had her own plan. Young girls in love were all the same: impressionable, desperate to please. All the better to manipulate.

CHAPTER EIGHTEEN

I T TOOK TWO days for her father to arrive. The first day she'd unpacked and waited with shaking hands for his arrival. She knew he would be angry, and when he eventually came, she would need to be ready. She'd written to Richard and informed him of her father's actions and her response. She'd half expected him to scold her, to suggest that she should have found a middle ground. Instead, he had shown only concern for her emotional well-being. She'd been coming in for tea when she heard his voice in the hallway.

Her first instinct was to hide herself. So she did. She hid by the garden door until she heard him speaking to Aunt Theo. Then she crept forward near the parlor door to listen to what was being said. If Aunt Theo didn't need her, she would stay where she was. If he grew belligerent, she would face him down. She just needed more time to steel herself for him.

"What are you doing?" she heard him say.

"I'm working with my great-great niece on her wedding."

"She is not engaged," he insisted.

"It would appear she is."

"No. I have not given my permission."

"My dear nephew, your permission is a formality at this point."

"So I should just let her do what she wants?"

"Your mistake is thinking you can stop her. Oh, come now, as far as choices go, she could do much worse."

"She could do better."

"She could do better than a respectable, handsome gentle-man—"

"—merchant,"

"—of good family and reputation with impeccable prospects who is clearly in love with her?"

"She's been at you, has she? Now you are all ganging up on me as if I am the one being unreasonable."

"You are."

There was a long pause.

"You have finally gone senile."

"It is a plain fact."

"He is not her equal."

"He is more her equal than any of the sons of the nobility you would have her marry. And, more to the point, she loves him."

Elodia heard his heavy sigh, footsteps. The creak of a chair.

"Does he love her? Truly?"

"I believe he does. He treats her with such respect and ten-derness."

"That is hardly proof of anything. Of course he would," he scoffed. "No doubt he wants her dowry."

"That boy doesn't need that dowry."

"Merchants always need money."

"Do you have any idea how wealthy he is?"

She had heard enough. "Father." She stepped into the room.

He turned to her from his seat on the couch. "Are you still listening at doors at your age, Elodia?"

She would not back down or apologize. "When it concerns me."

He turned to Aunt Theo. "I cannot believe you are encourag-ing this mutiny."

She shrugged. "If I didn't offer her shelter, she would have gone elsewhere."

Elodia sat near her aunt on the chaise and clasped her hands in her lap. "I would have us be married now. I would have gone with him to Gretna Green, but he refused."

"Did he?"

"What reason did he give for this sudden attack of conscience?" he asked.

"He said he wasn't a thief."

"I beg to differ." One of his eyebrows lifted in arrogant disbelief.

Her temper spiked and her hand clenched in her lap. "I am not property; I cannot be stolen. I don't understand you. I have no idea who you are or how you became *this*. All your judgements are inaccurate. Richard wants you and I to be on good terms because he doesn't want me to lose my last living parent due to stubbornness. Because he lost both of his parents in an instant and he doesn't want me to face the same pain."

"Whereas you can take or leave me, is that it?" he asked. There was something in his eyes, in his tone, that made her bite her tongue. Was he afraid? Was that what all this was? Did he truly believe that she was doing this to throw him aside?

"*You* are the one deciding that, Father. Not I. And incidentally, I did not accept Richard because he was the only man who'd have me. I always wanted to marry him. I have wanted to marry him since I was a girl."

"You were a naïve child, and you developed a fixation on him, like a swan imprinting on a duck. It does not make them a match. You should be old enough now to see the folly of maintaining such a position. It would diminish you. How could you expect me to agree to that?"

"If you think I will give up what I have with him for the sake of social standing then you are only proving my point. You look at him and only see that he is not a nobleman. I look at him and see everything else. He is kind and loving, intelligent and honorable and beautiful. You could show me a hundred other men and none of them would compare."

"You are very certain."

"I am. Not because of any fixation when I was fifteen, but because he saw me even when everyone else thought I was nothing. When these weak hearted cowards were content to leave me behind, he never did. I could walk away from every one of them without a second thought and never regret it because he is worth it to me. Because I am worth it to him."

"He said you would choose him over me. I didn't want to believe such a thing could be possible. I see I was incorrect."

Her eyes were burning. He *did* believe she was the faithless one, the one putting him aside. "*You* are the one making the choice, Father. You would choose the nobility over me and you want me to follow your lead no matter the cost to myself. Richard would never make me choose. If your love is so conditional, then I can and will do without it no matter how much it pains me."

There was a long silence in which she feared he would truly disown her. She was braced for it even as she forced herself to meet his eyes and not look away no matter how excruciating it was. They were almost frightening, stark and bright and full of too much emotion. Would he hate her forever? Was he really enough like his father to turn her away because she refused to do what he wanted? In that moment, she realized how right Richard had been. For all her anger, there was too much love there. She didn't want to lose her father.

Eventually, he broke first, lowering his eyes and nodding slowly. "Very well," he said.

"Very well what?"

"Never let it be said that a son of the nobility was less gracious than the son of a tradesman." He looked up at her but he didn't smile.

It sounded like a concession, but what did that mean? "So you consent to our match?"

"For what it's worth. Which is apparently nothing." He rose to his feet and tugged his waistcoat into place, letting out a short sigh.

Had he heard nothing she had said? Was blind obedience really all he cared about? She wanted to build bridges but he was clearly determined to remain at odds. She opened her mouth to demand an explanation, but Aunt Theo cleared her throat. Elodia glanced at her and she shook her silver head in silent warning.

"I will leave you to your plans. Good day, Aunt. Good day, Elodia." Without another word or a backwards glance, he left the room.

Tears of frustration burned Elodia's eyes but in the end, she followed her aunt's warning and said nothing. Perhaps in the end, this would be the best she could hope for from him. Perhaps she didn't have the right to demand more.

"Congratulations," Aunt Theo said, watching her with a small smile.

"Am I to be congratulated for that?" she asked quietly. If it was a victory then why did she feel hollowed out inside?

"It is more than you had before."

Yes. But why did it feel like less? As if he had simply renounced her, rather than any right to dictate her choices. She nodded and sat down, folding her arms around her torso. "What now, then?"

"Now we plan your engagement party and continue planning your wedding." She gave her cane a decisive thump on the ground. "Onward."

RICHARD HAD TO admit his sister threw one hell of a party. He loved the touches of evergreen garlands and the flowers. He didn't know how she had managed to find a soprano to serenade the assembled guests with romantic arias, but listening to her voice reverberate off the walls with Elodia's hand in his, he didn't care. She was perfect tonight, with tiger lilies in her dark curls and a dress of golden striped, lemon yellow organza silk.

He loved when he caught her mouthing along to the words, delighted tears glittering in her eyes. He especially enjoyed when she stopped in the middle of their turn during a game of charades to clap enthusiastically after one song in particular. Had he lost that round? Yes. Had it mattered? Absolutely not. He wanted to keep her that happy every day for the rest of their lives. He knew it was impossible, he knew that no one was so happy every day of their lives, but it couldn't be a bad goal, could it?

In fact, the whole evening was perfect save for one aspect. Or perhaps two.

The guest list.

Somehow, despite all Ada's efforts, their uncle had not only been invited, but he had also taken it upon himself to attend. Perhaps he thought it better to be present than seen to reject the daughter of a viscount or her fiancé on the basis of her race. It could have been a good sign. With so many members of the ton present, he couldn't possibly think to cause trouble. He'd smiled and greeted both Richard and Elodia with politeness.

Leo and Ada had watched him in visible surprise while Basil smirked behind his glass. Richard wanted desperately to believe that this was a call for neutral ground. He wanted to ignore the warning in the back of his mind, but he couldn't manage it. No matter what, he couldn't believe that his uncle had given up just like that. But he wasn't about to make a scene and ruin the night for Elodia.

Now, everything seemed to have settled down for the moment with the exception of Elodia's occasional glance towards the door. The first time he noticed it, his heart ached for her. She was such a brave little thing, but every time she glanced towards the entrance, he knew that standing his ground on leaving the bridge between her and her father was the correct one. She talked a good talk but she wanted that man to show up and prove her wrong more than anything else in her life.

The fifth time he saw her glance over, he set down his glass and crossed over to where she sat with Miss Walsh and Regina.

Her attention shifted over to him as soon as she saw him approaching, and she smiled a little too brightly.

"How are we doing?" he asked, laying his hand on her bare shoulder.

"So far so good," she replied, laying her hand over his.

"Elodia was telling me about her wedding preparations," Regina commented.

"I trust they are going well."

"I—" Elodia's eyes shifted and widened, her hand convulsing slightly on his. A faint lull in the conversation gave him a clue as to what had happened. When he turned, he was gratified and then horrified at what he saw. Lord Melbroke had finally arrived to be sure, but with him was the absolute last person Richard had ever expected to see.

Rachel.

His mouth went dry, and for a moment he couldn't hear anything at all.

What the *fuck* was she doing here? He noted the way her arm was linked with Lord Melbroke's and a horrible notion took root. She wouldn't. There was no way she would do such a thing. Elodia's small hand tightened convulsively on his arm and he looked down to see her apprehensive expression. Her father was here, which anyone would take as an endorsement, albeit a lukewarm one. He had to focus on her.

"Lord Melbroke, you're here," she said as her father came to a stop in front of them with his guest.

"I received an invitation," he replied.

"So you did. You've missed the first round of entertainment, but you are in time for the second half of the evening."

"Good."

She shifted her attention to the woman on her father's arm. "Lady Tremaine, what an unexpected delight."

"Am I?" She glanced at Lord Melbroke.

"Yes, I brought her as my guest. I've been meaning to inform you of it, but now is as good a time as any. If you have a moment."

Elodia glanced at him and he nodded even as his stomach sank to his shoes. She took her father's arm and followed him to a more remote corner of the room. It was childish, but part of him hoped that when he turned around, she would be gone.

She wasn't.

"Aren't you going to lead me in?"

"What are you doing here, Rachel?" he murmured.

"Lord Melbroke and I are courting."

His jaw locked against a torrent of angry words. She knew what she was doing. While Elodia's father was certainly still considered in his prime, and was by all accounts the most eligible gentleman on the market, he doubted her intentions were honorable. This was her making good on her promise to make him miserable.

"Are you going to congratulate me?"

He shot her a scathing glance. "I'll hold off on that."

"You think I'm not up to the task of securing him?"

"I don't think anything is beyond you." *Or beneath you.*

"Should I take that as a compliment?"

She was so unbearably smug, he didn't know whether to be angry or terrified. What was her ultimate intention? Would Lord Melbroke be enough? "He is a good man. If you are playing a game, you have no right to play it with him."

"On the contrary. I am very serious about this match."

For some reason, in some way, he believed her. "Are you indeed? Here I was thinking you had some demented idea of maintaining access to me through my father-in-law."

"Now that you mention it, once more for the road couldn't hurt."

He pulled his arm away from her. "I'm going to find you something to drink." *Something with arsenic.*

"Oh, don't be such a prude. Don't you think it could be fun?"

"What exactly?"

"You and me, behind the backs of the little miss and dear papa."

The idea of her touch made the hair on the back of his neck stand up, to say nothing of the idea of sleeping with her. He'd rather seduce a rabid bear. "You and I differ on the definition of 'fun'. Either way, I don't believe we have anything further to discuss."

"I did warn you. I am not a woman who can be cast aside on a whim. You owe me. You owe me this."

Owed her? He owed her nothing but discretion and he had managed that despite her best efforts. "I owe you nothing. What exactly do you imagine you could do? If you think my silence is for my benefit alone, you are sorely mistaken."

She smirked and tilted her head. "We'll see. She's pretty, for what she is. I'll grant you that. But she won't be able to satisfy you as I can. You may be able to lie to yourself now, but in time, you'll see I was right. I give you a month. Two at most."

Before he could respond, Leo arrived with Regina on his arm.

"I see we have a last minute arrival," Leo said, clasping Richard's tense shoulder and shocking him out of his livid trance.

"Yes, Lady Tremaine arrived with Lord Melbroke." He glanced at Leo who nodded and patted his shoulder roughly enough to send a message. *Calm down.*

"How interesting." Regina's eyes flicked from Richard's face to where Rachel still had a hold on his arm. "Where is Miss Hawthorne?"

"With her father," Richard replied.

"Ah, well then." Regina's smile was almost predatory. "Mr. Thornfield, your sister was looking for you. Let me introduce Lady Tremaine to our guests on your behalf."

"You are too kind, Lady Starkley," Richard replied, taking the clear exit she was providing. Leo raised his eyebrows and Richard shook his head slightly before walking away in search of Elodia. Whatever Rachel was here for, it couldn't be good, but whatever it was, Richard wasn't going to let Elodia face it without him.

ELODIA FOLLOWED HER father into the sitting room and seated herself across from him, her hands folded in her lap. She had no idea what to say. Seeing him arrive with another white noble on his arm, as if it had all been decided already. He cleared his throat and adjusted his jacket. It looked new; she'd never seen it before.

"So you are to marry this season after all," she said.

He nodded but didn't meet her eyes. "I told you that was the plan."

"I remember. I suppose I'm surprised, that's all."

He scoffed. "Not pleasant, is it?"

Elodia shook her head and looked away briefly, trying to get a handle on her temper. "It's not the same thing."

"How exactly, pray tell?"

"You've known Richard for years in one capacity or another. He has dined at our home. I've only just met Lady Tremaine and so have you."

"Not quite," he replied, again glancing away from her. "I have known her before this."

"You mean before she was a widow."

"Yes."

Well, that was something she supposed, although the fact that he refused to meet her eyes was making her doubt that report. "I didn't realize you liked her quite so much."

"I do not like her very much at all," he replied with an insincere smile. "But she suits my purpose."

She didn't know if she was happy to know he hadn't fallen in love with someone else, or sad that he was so resigned to spending his life with someone he disliked. For the sake of money. "Does she love you?"

"Not that I can tell," he replied, his tone light and nonchalant.

"Why is she marrying you then?" she asked. It made no sense at all. Her father needed to marry but as far as Elodia was aware,

Lady Tremaine did not.

"Not everyone finds my company so disagreeable," he replied, shooting her a glare.

Elodia let out a frustrated sigh and squeezed her hands in her lap to keep from slamming her fist down on the table beside her. "It is not that," she gritted through her teeth. "I understand why you have to marry but I do not understand why a woman of means and status, who has already been married once before, would seek to do so again without any real inducement."

"Some women want children."

"Yes. And they don't tend to wait until they are nearly forty to pursue that goal. It would be dangerous for her to try to have children now. Why take the risk if there is nothing to be gained from it?"

He stared at her for a long moment, his expression unreadable. He could have been amused or contemptuous. "It seems that you have decided to follow in my footsteps after all."

"What?" What on earth was he talking about?

"Either way, I did not seek or require your blessing."

Ah. Again, she took a deep breath to calm herself. Was there no age limit on the childishness of men? "Why would you? You are an adult after all."

"I only accepted your no doubt begrudging invitation to give you the news before you found out from others."

That hurt more than she'd expected. It hadn't been begrudging. But she'd be damned if she said it now. "Suit yourself."

He nodded then stood, turned sharply on his heel and left. She sank back into the sofa and buried her face into her hands. What a mess. Was every conversation between the two of them going to be like this for the rest of their lives?

The footsteps in the hallway didn't draw her attention but the clicking of the lock did. She didn't recognize the footsteps. She lifted her head and found herself alone in the salon with none other than Simon Thornfield, Richard's devious uncle. Cool shock poured over her as she straightened her spine.

"What are you doing here?" The words burst past her lips before she could think of a more polite way to state the question.

"I was invited," he replied evenly.

She shot to her feet as he walked further into the room. "No, I mean in here with me. You need to leave."

"Oh, I don't think so."

What on earth was he playing at? "This room is occupied, sir." She shifted to stand behind the sofa as he ambled forward, his hands in his pockets.

"This was my late brother's house. I do not need your permission to be anywhere in it," he replied with an arrogant sneer.

She moved towards the door but he shifted as well. She gauged the distance. There was no way she would get to the door in time, not in this dress. She needed to find a way to slow him down. How? How had she ended up here? Twenty minutes with her father, barely five minutes in which she was alone and this ingrate had managed to corner her. "I cannot decide whether you are bold or stupid to attempt this," she said.

"Attempt what?" he asked.

"Are you trying to imply that your intentions are innocent?"

He nodded in consideration. "Noble perhaps. I cannot allow this marriage to take place."

She couldn't stop the derisive laugh that escaped her. "And you imagine you can stop it? How amusing."

"It wouldn't take much. I will keep you here, an unmarried woman alone with a gentleman. When you are missed, people will come looking and find us. There are enough witnesses to spread the gossip all the way to Wales."

"And you think that will stop me from marrying Richard?"

"He still has a business to run, my dear. A union with a daughter of the nobility is one thing, but an alliance with a slut is something else."

She glanced at the door again. "No one will believe that I would choose to frolic with you, an old, ugly, stupid man, when I am a fortnight away from having your nephew as my husband."

"Your kind is capable of anything." He started towards her and she moved behind the sofa. It was a matter of time now. She just needed to keep him far enough away and she could escape unscathed.

"I'm sure you'd like to believe that," she said.

"Believe me, I will not enjoy it. It is sickening to think the person who will finally link my family to the nobility is something like you."

"Like me?"

"A half-breed,"

"Better that than a fool," she snapped.

"What is it about you that draws them?" he mused out loud. The disgust was mixing with something else. Fascination.

"I beg your pardon?"

"My brother, Basil Thompson, even your father… they all strayed and became mired in whatever trickery you all played. Ruining otherwise pure and correct bloodlines. And now my family's line will be even further polluted with your addition, producing even more unnatural looking offspring."

"I wouldn't worry about that, Mr. Thornfield. Based on the look of you, I could hardly do worse."

He darted forward, hideously fast despite his size. She jumped back and started to run but her dress was caught fast. A glance backwards showed what it was. He had grabbed the fabric of her skirts in his fist. He pulled her forward and her arms came out to brace against his shoulders, struggling to break his hold on her.

"Perhaps there is some skill you all have,"

"Get away from me," she hissed before stomping her heel on his foot. He cried out in pain but his hold didn't lessen. Instead, he pinned her roughly to the wall, and she went still. This man wasn't going to take anything from her. All her life, her governess had told her that her lack of a figure would protect her from exactly this sort of attention. But something darker than desire was driving Simon Thornfield.

"I'm only curious."

"Ellie?"

She heard Richard on the other side of the door. She only needed to get to him.

"There he is." Simon's eyes gleamed in triumph. "Not much longer now."

The doorknob rattled and Richard knocked again. "Ellie?"

Had he locked it as well?

"Ellie!"

"Richard!" She kicked away from the wall, trying to gain enough space to wriggle free but instead he leaned into her, pressing revoltingly closer.

"Oh no, you don't, you little harlot."

She brought up her leg between his as hard as she could and watched with grim satisfaction as he doubled over, howling in pain. She wriggled away but his grip on her wrist remained. There was a loud thudding sound, as if something heavy was ramming against the painted door over and over. *Richard.* She needed to get free.

"You fucking bitch!" he screamed, rounding on her. His hand closed around her throat, holding her in place. She cast her eye around for something, anything to use and saw the vase of flowers on the side table. That was it.

She worked her fingers under his until she could grab hold of his thumb. With as much force as she could manage, she wrenched it back. He howled again but his grip on her neck was broken. She darted to the side just as he grabbed for her gown, ripping the delicate bodice. She didn't have time to worry about that, however. She took hold of the obliging vase with both hands and swung it up at his head with all her strength. The porcelain shattered, sending water and florals everywhere.

Then she turned and raced to the door, not bothering to look back to see where Simon was. As she neared the wall beside it, the door burst open, sending shards of wood skittering across the floor and Richard was there along with her father and Lady Tremaine.

"Ellie." Richard entered first, his head swinging back and forth looking for her. She rushed towards him, throwing herself into his arms, burying her face in his chest as he hugged her tightly.

"Thornfield, what on earth do you mean by this?"

She lifted her head and Richard took her face into her hands.

"Are you alright?"

She nodded. Now that he was here, now that he had his arms around her, she was perfect.

"Did he hurt you?"

"I didn't let him."

"What happened?" he demanded.

"He came in after Papa left me. He wouldn't let me leave the room."

His dark eyes swept over her, lingering on her ripped bodice, then he looked over to where his uncle stood, half drenched and still clutching his head. He eased her away from him, and his hand slid down her arms to her wrists. She flinched, even under his light touch. His uncle's grip on her had been merciless, and there was sure to be a bruise. At the sight of her flinch, his face went flat, his body almost impossibly still.

"Richard." She had never seen such an expression on his face before. If she thought his harshness was frightening, he was utterly terrifying now. With steady, even strides, he started across the room.

"Thornfield," her father called out, but if Richard heard him, he didn't respond.

"You would dare," Richard growled, taking his uncle by the jacket. Elodia winced at the first punch, the sound of bone hitting bone echoing throughout the room. The force of that first strike drove Simon to his knees, and had him spitting blood, but Richard didn't stop there. He dragged his uncle up to his feet, ready to strike him again. Simon grabbed his arm, alarm in his face.

"She's lying," he cried. There was a low growl and then he

was in the air before Richard slammed him down onto the side table, shattering it in the process. The speed of it was shocking, the cacophony of noise alarming.

"Oh, Christ," Basil murmured. Elodia glanced over to see him arrive with Ada and Isolde close behind.

Ada took Elodia's hand and squeezed it tightly. "Are you alright?" she asked.

"I'm fine." She turned back to Richard who had followed his uncle down to the floor and was now straddling his waist, his left hand pinning his uncle down by his neck and his right swinging down in a repetitive, steady cadence that never seemed to lose any of its vigor.

"Gēgē," Ada murmured sadly, one hand covering her mouth.

Ellie watched in horrified fascination as a lifetime of pain and hatred was brought to bear. She couldn't see what damage he was inflicting behind the couch, but the garbled cries from her former attacker and the wet crunch of what she assumed was a shattered jaw was enough.

"He's going to kill him," her father murmured before starting forward.

"That man has had it coming," Leo replied, holding out an arm to stop him.

"He cannot kill him," her father snapped. "He's meant to be marrying my daughter within a week."

"True," Leo rolled his eyes and started forward. "Thornfield, that's enough." He grabbed Richard's arm mid swing, then went flying backwards when Richard turned to shove him away. She caught sight of the enraged expression on his face, the wide eyes, flared nostrils, the sneer of his soft mouth, baring his teeth. He was terrifying but he had never seemed more magnificent to her than in that moment.

Basil followed Leo into the room. "Don't kill him, Richard. He's not worth the trouble it would bring."

His wild, irate eyes fell on her for a moment, ensnaring her from across the room in his blood splattered face. She didn't know what her expression was, but he turned back to his uncle and rose to his feet slowly. She saw his bloody fists at his sides, the measured rise and fall of his chest.

"Get him out of here," he growled before walking back over to her. She ran into his arms and flung her arms around his waist, burying her face in his chest as she shivered. He held her tightly, his heart hammering in his chest, his body hot with his exertion.

"Goodness, what an exhibition." Lady Tremaine commented.

"Elodia, what happened?" Isolde asked.

"He was trying to ruin me so Richard wouldn't marry me."

"What a moronic idea," Lady Tremaine commented.

"I'm sorry," Elodia said.

"Don't," Richard grumbled, glaring down at her, his dark hair falling every which way. "Don't you dare apologize. You did nothing wrong."

She nodded.

"What do you mean to do with him?" Basil asked.

"Surely we must call the constabulary," her father remarked.

"No," Richard said, his voice gruff and menacing. "I have a better plan for him."

CHAPTER NINETEEN

Melbroke House, London,
The next day

IT WAS STRANGE knocking on the door to the residence she used to share with her father. The aftermath of the encounter with Richard's uncle had been disconcerting. She had gone back early to Aunt Theo's with Isolde. After a long, hot bath, she'd crawled into bed and managed to snatch some sleep. She didn't have nightmares exactly, but she kept waking up with an uneasy feeling in the pit of her stomach and then trying to ignore it long enough to fall asleep again.

In the morning, as she dressed, she kept thinking of Richard. It was thrilling to be defended in that way, but she couldn't pretend it hadn't also frightened her to see him like that. He was always so controlled, even when expressing his anger or frustration. He had been in some kind of berserker rage fueled by years of insult and pain.

She wanted to comfort him but she wasn't sure she could be in his presence when he was like that. So instead, she went to her father to deliver his wedding invitation. It was the same inside the house and yet, somehow, it felt entirely different. Perhaps it was her that was different. Perhaps she'd grown used to the light décor at Aunt Theo's.

"Elodia."

She looked over and saw him coming out of the salon. "Hello, Father."

"From the lack of baggage, I can take it that you are not coming home."

"No."

He nodded. Was he disappointed? She couldn't tell anymore. "Then what can I do for you?"

"I am here to deliver this in person." She handed him the wedding invitation, watching his face as he read the front of the envelope.

"Ah, very good." He paused awkwardly. "How are you doing?"

"You mean because of the incident last night?"

He lifted his eyebrows and blinked. "Yes."

"I'm well, all things considered. He barely left a scratch."

"That is good. I cannot imagine what possessed him to try something like that."

"Nor I." For all his disgusting diatribes, Simon Thornfield hadn't given a clue as to why he imagined he would be able to come for her. Did he really think that he would be able to assault her or ruin her reputation without repercussions?

Her father had said nothing further. Was it so far beyond him to invite her in to sit down? "I suppose I will leave then,"

"Oh, Melbroke, is that your darling daughter?" Lady Tremaine came out of the salon with exaggerated curiosity, as if she were already holding court in his house. The utter presumption.

"You have company, I see," she said.

"I do."

"Am I still company at this point?" she trilled, hooking her arm with his.

"For the sake of your reputation, I certainly hope so," Elodia replied with a tight smile.

"Elodia was delivering a wedding invitation to me personally," he announced.

"Did you need one?" Lady Tremaine asked.

"No," Elodia said.

"Yes."

Elodia and her father met each other's eyes, their simultaneous responses lingering in the air.

"He didn't need one," Elodia said, "but I thought it was better to make the invitation explicit rather than risk further misunderstandings."

Lady Tremaine smiled. It reminded Elodia of a snake she'd seen at the London Zoo when she was sixteen. "Very wise. You aren't leaving, of course?"

"I do not wish to disturb you both." And she had no interest in witnessing whatever nonsense they were engaging in.

"Oh, your father was about to leave on some business when you arrived. Stay and keep me company, won't you? I haven't had any time with you at all."

Oh, Christ, the last thing Elodia wanted was to deal with that woman. Her gaze slid to her father who raised his eyebrows, as if daring her to decline the offer.

"Of course, if it would please you."

"I will leave you both to it then," he said, bowing to them and walking away briskly.

Then Elodia's arm was taken hostage by Lady Tremaine, leaving her with no choice but to follow her into the salon. She didn't fully dislike her father's prospective fiancée. It was only that the woman was odd. She was certainly beautiful, with the womanly figure Elodia had always hoped for. Something about her seemed more artificial than most. As if she had an agenda. She smiled far too much and her smile was tense, almost angry.

"It was so kind of you to join me today, Miss Hawthorne. I must admit I was desperate to meet you properly at long last."

Elodia took a seat and bit her tongue against the instinct to remind the presumptuous bitch that this was her father's house. *Her* house. "It wasn't a hardship."

"I hope you are recovering well after that situation at your engagement party."

Something told Elodia she wasn't nearly as concerned as she wanted to appear. She'd leave her gloves on. She wasn't staying here longer than was absolutely necessary. "I haven't really given it a moment's thought, to be frank. There was barely anything for me to recover from."

"Yes. What a dashing fiancé you have, to thrash a man so soundly for a moment of indiscretion."

A moment of bloody indiscretion? "It was rather more than that."

"Oh, of course. I also meant to extend my apologies for you to find out about such an important life event so publicly."

"You mean your pending marriage with my father?" Elodia clarified.

"Of course. I had no idea you and he had been at such odds."

"It wasn't anyone's business, really."

"I quite agree. And now you are both on the path of reconciliation just before you are meant to leave him behind forever." Her smile was almost smug.

No doubt she'd been praying on it. "I don't believe it will be as bad as that."

"I'm sorry you already picked out your wedding dress all alone. A wedding dress is such an important affair. Almost the centerpiece of a wedding, honestly."

"Yes, well, I wasn't alone, was I?" Elodia replied.

"No?"

"No. Mrs. Thompson, Lady Starkley, my Aunt Theo and Miss Walsh assisted me."

"Yes, but that's not the same as having the benefit of proper guidance in your formative years. I suppose if you had been raised in England, you would have appreciated the difference. It's hardly your fault."

She was repulsive. "Yes, well, I've managed well enough despite it."

"I suppose your poor mother wouldn't have been able to give much advice."

It took everything in Elodia to keep from slapping her across the face. "Meaning?"

"Well, she was a slave, wasn't she?"

As if it had been her entire identity. "She was formerly en-slaved. But every woman has her preferences, regardless of her status."

"I suppose that is true enough. Have you picked out your trousseau as well?"

"I have."

"Oh? My goodness, you are in a hurry. No particular reason, I'm sure."

How many times was this woman going to insult her? "One. I want to be married to the man I love as soon as possible."

"How romantic."

"I see it rather as a practicality."

"Well, I'm sure they guided you well, but a word of advice, my dear, if you'll allow me."

"If you insist."

"You can never be too secure of a man's affections; you'll do well to keep his attention fixed on you. All of them have wandering eyes."

"Rich—" Elodia caught herself. "Mr. Thornfield is a man of honor and integrity; he would never dream of betraying me in such a manner."

"Oh, I never doubted it. However, loyalty should not become a hardship."

"What are you implying?"

"No disparagement to you, my dear, but unless I miss my guess, your Mr. Thornfield is a man of the world. He's travelled widely and tried more than most, so his appetites may be more varied than you can fulfill."

"He chose me."

"And a fine choice you are. Men used to variety can grow bored with it after a while, but it is in their nature to want more. You must make sure to keep his eyes on you at all times, lest they wander off and never return."

He wouldn't do it. She knew that. But she couldn't pretend there was no truth to what she was saying. "What do you suggest?"

"It's the small things, really; flattering hairstyles and fashion, of course. One can be such a slave to what is au courant, but not every fashion is a friend." Her eyes flicked down to Ellie's chest. "You would do well to make the most of what you have, even if it is less than ideal. Your face is pretty enough, but your figure, my dear, is not what is sought after. You must be aware of this."

Yes. Only too aware. "Thank you for that input, Lady Tremaine,"

"Not at all. I had to do it myself when I was younger, to ensure that I was always presented in the best light. For example, as a true Englishwoman, I wouldn't be caught dead in that color you have on."

"Oh?"

"Oh no, my dear, it would have made my skin look positively sallow."

"Ah."

"Whereas your darker complexion suits it quite well."

"And by that I take it you do not see me as an Englishwoman. Is that it?"

"Well, let's not get too bogged down in the semantics. Either way, when I am your father's new wife, I will rely on you to return this little favor."

"Oh?"

"Yes, to enlighten me as to his preferences. His passions I can discover on my own."

Bloody hell. She gritted her teeth and stood. "I will, of course, offer as much help as I can." From as far away as possible.

"As will I."

So this was the woman who was to replace her mother. How repulsive. "Good day, Lady Tremaine."

"Good day to you, Miss Hawthorne."

CHAPTER TWENTY

Harley House, Mayfair, London
Two weeks later

ELODIA HAD LONG considered the wedding she would have. It had manifested a thousand different ways over the years but one thing had always held constant: The groom. Now that it was her wedding day, after the years of waiting and the latest issue with her father more or less resolved, she found herself a bit surprised to see herself in a wedding dress.

It was made of an elegant ivory brocade silk trimmed with blonde lace. Her jewelry of choice were her signature baroque pearl earrings and necklace, while a tiara of baby's breath and myrtle held her gauze silk and lace veil in place. She looked like a bride but she wasn't sure she felt like a bride quite yet. It was strange. She expected to feel nervous, unable to settle anywhere. But instead, she felt… settled. Not numb, or unaffected, just calm. As if she knew in her bones she was doing what she was meant to do.

Her gaze kept drifting to the mirror and lingering, taking in every aspect of her clothing and hair. The gleam of her pearls in the sunlight, the curls of her hair, the curve of her bare shoulders. There was something there that was new somehow, a certainty she couldn't place.

"Don't be nervous, Ellie," Ada said while she finished tying off her bouquet of orange lilies and myrtle.

"I'm not nervous, Ada."

"Aren't you?"

Elodia shook her head. "I've been waiting for this. The only thing that matters is him becoming my husband. The skies could fall and it wouldn't matter as long as we both get to say 'I do'."

"Well, let's not tempt fate either way," Regina said, walking over to her, one hand on her stomach.

"You should be in bed."

"I will be after this. I compromised with Leo. He'll let me go to the wedding itself so long as I sit out the reception."

"I agree entirely."

"But I had to be here. We were both at Ada's and you and Ada were at mine. How could I not be at your wedding?"

"That is true."

"You look so beautiful, Ellie."

She was rather happy with her dress from the flounces and the blonde lace to the silk flowers decorating the wide bertha collared bodice and puffed sleeves. "Thank you, Gigi."

"And I must toast, while we are here." She handed them both champagne glasses.

"Indeed," Ada said, taking her glass.

"To all of us. The ton didn't want us, we thought we would have to trade love for supposed security, or position. We were told that we could only belong if we became something other than what we are. But I think it is fair to report all of that to be absolute nonsense."

"Here here!" Elodia said, lifting her glass, "To eating our cake and having it too."

"To eating our cake and having it too!" Ada and Regina chorused.

"Well, let's go get you married to my brother."

Elodia laughed. "Yes, let's."

They headed out of the room and down the corridor to the stairs. It was a shock to see her father standing at the foot of the stairs in a grey morning coat. He looked up at their arrival, and his eyes widened.

"If I may have a moment with my daughter, Mrs. Thompson,

Lady Starkley."

They glanced at Elodia and she nodded, giving them permission to leave her.

"My goodness," he commented when they were alone.

"Yes. Do you suppose I shall pass muster?"

"Just about," he replied. "You look beautiful, Miss Hawthorne."

"Thank you, Father."

"This dress is very like something your mother would have picked."

"Truly?" Her father rarely mentioned her unprompted.

He smiled and nodded. "Truly."

It had to mean something, didn't it? "I didn't think you'd come," she admitted.

"I was invited," he replied.

Her smile faltered and her gaze fell to their feet. Her eyes stung again. Was that it? Was he only here due to good manners? "Yes,"

He took her hand in his and she looked up at him. "I would have come even if you hadn't invited me. You are my precious child. Whatever odds we have arrived at, I would never have given up the chance to walk you down the aisle. God willing, I will only have to do it once."

Richard had been correct again. In the end, when given the option, her father had chosen her. He'd chosen to be her father and come to walk her down the aisle. She smiled and nodded, her throat aching and her heart unexpectedly full. Was this what she had been missing before? "Thank you."

"Thank *you*, Elodia." He placed his free hand on her shoulder, his eyes glistening with tears. "Thank you for being my daughter."

"Even when I vex you?"

He chuckled and tapped her cheek with one finger. "If you didn't vex me, you wouldn't be mine," he said, tucking her hand into the crook of his elbow and leading her out to the carriage.

Christ Church, Spitalfields, London

THE DAY OF Richard's wedding had dawned brightly, against all his expectations of life in England. He couldn't complain, however. He'd slept unexpectedly well considering the anticipation crackling under his skin. He'd dressed himself and arrived at the church, St. Bartholomew the Great, nearly an hour ahead of time to sit in the furthest back pew and wait.

It had been a good idea at the time. He didn't want to risk anything ridiculous happening. Like Rachel trying to set the vestments on fire or something. His uncle was recovering from the thrashing Richard had given him, and he had fallen entirely out of favor with not only Melbroke but Lady Sterling as well. Richard's hands still hadn't fully healed from the beating he'd given his uncle. Word of the event had spread to be sure but not the news he had been hoping for. He wasn't likely to make a nuisance of himself.

But now his mind kept drifting to his parents, wondering how different things would be if they were here. Would his mother have insisted on red banners or flowers? Would she have given some of her bracelets to Elodia? He liked to think his parents would have loved her as Ada and he did. That they would have seen her loving heart and fiery spirit.

His eyes stung as he sat and waited alone, watching the last of the flower garlands be hung on the pews, the last of bows positioned. He couldn't stop his hands from fidgeting with his signet ring, but he drew the line at pacing. He closed his eyes and took a few deep centering breaths. No one wanted a blubbering groom or a man unable to control himself.

"Alright there, Richard?" Basil's voice came and Richard felt a hand pat his shoulder.

"Yes," he replied, opening his eyes and looking up to see Basil and Leo watching him with some sympathy.

"You wouldn't be nervous about your impending marriage, would you?"

He shook his head. "I am not nervous, I am impatient."

"Ah."

"I want it done with."

"A word of advice, old friend," Leo said, "you only marry once, and you'll want to remember it after the fact. Take it all in, especially your bride."

So he endeavored to do just that. He looked at the flowers, the way the sunlight filled the church and brightened the stained-glass windows.

When Elodia appeared in her ivory silk and lace gown, her soft curls adorned with flowers, the sun glinting off her smooth brown skin, he didn't try to stem the wave of awe and joy he felt. She was here just as she had promised to be. It didn't matter that her father hadn't quite given his blessing, or that she would be giving up the protection of the viscount's rank in marrying Richard. It didn't matter to her that in the eyes of many she was sinking back to her natural level. All she saw was him, the man she loved.

So in the end, it didn't matter what anyone else saw, or if they ended up commenting on the besotted grin on his face. All that mattered was the way her smile widened when she noticed his, the way his love for her was reflected in her eyes as her father walked her down the aisle.

Her father placed her hand in Richard's then took his seat. Ellie handed her bouquet to Isolde and turned back to him with the brightest grin. Richard knew he was meant to hold her hand only when prompted, but he couldn't let go. Some irrational fear had taken hold of him at the idea of her leaving him, or of someone taking her away. The pastor began the service and Richard's grip on her only tightened. When her fingers curled around his in response, something in his chest relaxed. No, Elodia was with him.

When the time came, he gave his vows with a fervor that

equaled his grip and burned into his mind the memory of her tearful, delighted face.

When they exchanged their rings, her care in sliding the golden band onto his finger filled his heart with so much affection he couldn't stop himself from kissing the golden band engraved with flowers on hers.

When the vicar announced them husband and wife, he wasted no time gathering her face in his hands and kissing her firmly on the mouth, drawing her bottom lip between his, swallowing her gasp. Her fingers curled around his wrist and she kissed him back, reducing the applause in the church to a dull hum.

There were a few coughs when he drew away from her at last. The vicar wouldn't meet his eyes and Leo and Basil were far too pleased but he didn't care. There was no room for shame in him anymore. He was married to a woman he adored. The most brilliant, beautiful creature in the world, and she was watching him with an infinite amount of love in her eyes.

CHAPTER TWENTY-ONE

Thornfield House, Mayfair, London

S HE'D MARRIED HIM. After all the years of waiting and hoping and admiring him from afar, she was Richard Thornfield's wife. Her wedding had been everything she had hoped it would be since she was old enough to want one. She had never seen Richard smile so much, could never have imagined he would be so openly affectionate with her, from kissing her wedding ring to kissing her so passionately in front of the entire congregation.

Now, as she waited in a room she'd never seen before in a house that was almost as familiar to her as her own, she was left to imagine what the rest would be like. She'd already had a taste of his ardor, and the memory had left her distracted on more than one occasion. But tonight she would experience the rest and while she was excited to finally have all of him, a part of her wondered if she was ready for him.

Upon Ada's advice, the room had been decorated with red silken banners and bows. Vases of red and white roses with mint and lime blossoms held sentry on tables while larger vases filled with blood red peonies, orchids and ivy were placed on the floor. Even the curtains on the bed were red and the coverlet was a rich red brocade. A side table held two cups next to a decanter of wine and a platter of pomegranates and dried persimmons.

Under her green night robe, she wore the crimson night rail. It wrapped around her fastening at her hip with a single silk ribbon. It was beautiful, but there was nothing to hide how small her breasts truly were, how square her body was, how cumbersome and disproportionate her bottom and thighs were. Would he mind? She knew he would be kind, as was his way, but Lady Tremaine's words kept materializing in her mind. Did this show her to her best advantage? Was it possible to show her body to the best advantage when it was so uncovered?

Suddenly, she was terrified of him seeing her naked. Her nightgown didn't hide much but at least it hid something. The switch from the exhilaration she'd felt during the wedding was disconcerting. She'd pushed for this wedding and now that it was over, she wanted nothing more than for Richard to appear so they could get past this moment of ignorance and uncertainty.

She looked up at the decorations in the room. She had relied on Ada's imperfect knowledge of Chinese customs but now she wondered if she should have left it alone. What if he was offended by this caricature? Would he think they were pretty and thoughtful or would he see them as a mockery of the family he missed and culture he prized? Surely it was better to do nothing if she couldn't get it right.

Footsteps sounded in the adjoining room and she sprang up in a panic. He was nearby. Where could she hide all of this in a short period of time? Perhaps if she went to his room instead, they could do everything there. She ran to the door and flung it open, only to come face to face with his chest. A chest covered only by his robe from all appearances.

Her head tilted back to meet his eyes and saw him watching her with amusement.

"Was I taking too long?"

"No, I only…" How on earth was she meant to explain this? "I thought we could do it in your room instead."

"What's wrong with your room?" he asked, his eyes flicking up over her head. His face went blank and Elodia's panic grew.

"It's um—"

His hands closed around her shoulders firmly and she fell silent as he moved her out of his way. He'd seen it. She'd waited too long. There was no way around it now. Silently, he entered her room and closed the door behind him. She watched, wringing her hands while he took it all in, his eyes drifting over the rend silks, the fruit, the yellow paper cut out in characters that spelt 'happiness'.

His eyes fell on the table with the wine, the glasses and the red candles. "This is…"

She walked over to him, still too worried to reach out to him. "Ada said they drink wine as part of the ceremony in China. She said it was out of a gourd but I couldn't find anything like that. I'm sorry, I know it's not correct. I wanted to give you something like what you would have had if…"

"If my parents were still alive?"

"Yes, and Ada wanted to help me. I know it's not the same but so much of the wedding was about me, and I just wanted to give you something as well."

He turned and pulled her into a firm embrace, his arms almost uncomfortably tight around her, his cheek pressed against her forehead. She could feel his uneven breaths, the slight tremor running through his body as he held her close. He wasn't angry, but was he upset? Had she ruined the mood for the night?

"Richard?" she murmured, stroking his back tentatively. "Are you alright?"

He drew back and she was finally able to see his face and the faint gleam of tears in his eyes.

"Oh God," she reached up to touch his face. "What's the matter?"

He chuckled and shook his head in response.

"I told you we needed to go to your room," she fretted. Before she could move, his mouth was on hers, firm but gentle, kissing her deeply until her toes curled into the rug under her feet. His hand closed around the back of her neck, drawing her closer to him. Her hands clenched unconsciously in his robe and a moan drifted up from her throat. He'd kissed her before, but tonight felt different and it wasn't entirely due to her lack of clothing.

When he pulled away at last, Elodia was weak and breathless, clinging to him, barely able to open her eyes. He pressed his forehead to hers, panting softly.

"Ellie," he murmured.

"Yes," she nuzzled his nose softly, wanting to soothe him somehow.

"Thank you."

He was thanking her? Her eyes opened. He was happy? "For what?"

"For this." He pulled back further and nodded to the room.

Oh yes, the decorations. She'd forgotten them entirely.

"Do you like them? Even though it's all wrong?"

He smiled, "Not all wrong. Red is the correct color."

"The candles aren't right."

"The candles are perfect."

"You're being kind again."

"The fact that you would even think to do this for me, that you would think to do anything for me at all is… overwhelming."

"I was worried you'd hate it."

"It is impossible for me to hate anything you give me."

"It wasn't just me. Ada helped me."

"Mmm, and I will thank her in good time. Right now, however, we have business to attend to."

She swallowed hard as her eyes widened.

"Oh?"

He brushed his hand over her hair, trailing it down her arm to take her hand before leading her over to the bed. He lifted her by her waist and set her on the mattress with one swift movement. She froze, her eyes widening slightly, her heart pounding, wondering how they were going to proceed. Was he simply going to… begin like this?

Then he turned and walked over to the table with the wine and poured two glasses before returning with them in hand. "The wedding wine was traditionally drunk from two halves of a hollow gourd tied by a red cord; it's drinking from the same vessel, sharing all things, two halves of one whole."

"Oh."

"However, cups have been used for some time as well." He winked and handed her a glass.

"We don't have a cord to tie it."

"That's alright, there is one thing we can do." He sat down beside her, "We put our arms like this," and hooked the arm with the cup around hers, "and we drink." He brought the cup to his lips, and she followed suit, although she barely tasted anything with his eyes burning into hers. She couldn't tell if the flush of heat flowing through her body was from the wine or his fathomless dark eyes.

He was too gorgeous, and now he was her husband. She'd wanted to be his for so long, had wondered and dreamt about this night in the abstract and now... now she was too anxious to feel anything. He plucked the glass from her numb fingers and returned it to the side table with his.

All she could think was that soon he would take off her robe and it would be the closest thing to being nude she'd ever been with another human being. Why did the room feel so chilly all of a sudden? She kept her eyes down, unsure of what to expect from him. The bed shifted as he sat beside her on the bed again and carefully took her hand in his. She focused on that warm, large, elegant hand with its smooth, olive toned skin.

Soon. Very soon.

"Why are your hands so cold?" he asked, his voice soft.

She shook her head. "I don't know,"

"Are you nervous?"

"A little," she admitted.

"Do you need more time?"

Her head snapped up. His concern was visible, his patience. "No. I don't... I want to do this."

"But do you want to do it tonight?"

"I do, only... can we," How could she explain? She glanced at the door.

"Go slowly?" he asked.

She met his eyes. "Is that all right?"

He cupped her cheek, his thumb brushing over her skin gently. "Of course àirén,"

The relief she felt left her weak. "Thank you."

"What did you think I was going to do?" he teased.

"I don't know. I was so focused on all of this, I forgot to ask Ada about… that."

"Don't worry, I'm going to look after you."

She nodded, unsure of what to say. He leant forward and kissed her softly, his hand lingering on her face. Yes, he would take care of her, of course he would. He'd always looked out for her. Why would he stop now when there was no one there to limit him? She leaned in, allowing herself to relax and let him lead her.

His hand drifted down her neck to her shoulder, his fingertips drifting over her collarbone and cool air on her skin. *He's removing my robe.*

She pulled back and looked at him. His face wore that strange expression again. "Ada said—"

He nodded silently, his eyes fixed on her crimson shift.

"Is it alright?"

"It's perfect. You are perfect."

Untrue, of course, but it was a nice thing to hear from him regardless. He released her hand and removed her robe fully, sliding it off her body, his eyes moving over her scantily clad body. Then he kissed her again, his fingers tangling in her hair, pulling her closer to him until she was in his lap. His mouth was pulling and caressing hers, his warm hands stroking over her body with greedy certainty. Her hands fluttered awkwardly before settling on his shoulders. It was more comfortable than sitting beside him, but she had never been more aware of how little she was wearing.

His mouth drifted over her cheek to her neck, sucking on her skin. His touch drifted from her hip to her stomach, over her rib cage to close around her breast. A startled moan floated out of her mouth at the contact. He'd touched her before but without her stays and the padding, it was entirely different. His fingertips against her nipples felt so exquisite it was almost painful, then the gentle pressure as he squeezed stole the air from her lungs. She couldn't find the strength to lift her arms or open her eyes.

Then she felt the strap of her nightgown slide down her arm, and within seconds the spell was shattered. Her hand came up to close around his and she crossed her arms over her chest.

He pulled away, noticing the change in her. "Ellie?"

"Can I… can we leave this on?"

"What's wrong?"

Fear was chasing away every shimmering sensation he'd evoked, leaving her chilled and awkward. "Nothing, I just… I don't want to take it off."

"You don't," he paused, watching her with a worried frown, his hands softly stroking her arms. "Are you sure you don't want to wait?"

She shook her head forcefully. "I don't want to wait,"

"But you are uncomfortable,"

"Only because I don't want you to see me."

That didn't seem to appease him. His frown had deepened. "Sweetheart, there is no reason for you to hide from me."

"It's ugly," she whispered in humiliation.

"What?"

"My body, it's ugly."

He shook his head. "There is nothing ugly about you."

A mild panic began within her. The only thing she wanted more than for Richard to make love to her was to stay as covered as possible. How could she explain? She didn't want to talk about it; she wanted him to go back to touching and kissing her. Instead, he was watching her and her wedding night was going to be ruined. All because she couldn't just close her eyes and let him do what he wanted.

"Ellie, àirén, we have time. You're probably tired, let's just go to bed now."

"No, I—" she pressed her lips together as her eyes stung with frustrated disappointment. "I don't want to stop. Is… is that the only way we can do it?"

He let out a sigh and removed his hand from under hers and she closed her eyes in defeat. Then he slipped her strap back onto her shoulder and kissed her cheek softly. He slid his arms under her, lifting her up long enough to turn and rest her on the bed. Then he stood and walked around the room, dousing the candles except the two red ones beside the empty wine glasses.

"Richard?" she murmured, wrapping her arms around her legs.

He glanced back at her. "Lie down, sweetheart," his voice came from the growing shadows.

"I'm sorry," she whispered as the light in the room drew dimmer and dimmer. She'd wanted it to be special but now that was gone. And it was all her fault. Then she heard the rustling of fabric.

"I take it you have no objections if I remove my clothing?" he asked.

Her lips parted in shock before she shook her head. He wasn't putting her to bed? He wasn't leaving?

She watched in stunned silence as he untied his robe and shrugged it off, leaving him utterly, gloriously naked from his broad shoulders and chest to his flat ridged stomach and powerful thighs, hanging heavily between them was his penis. She didn't move, didn't breathe, just stared greedily at every angle, every ridge of muscle under that smooth skin. She watched him walk around the bed to the other side and climb up onto the bed, a moon kissed god of love.

Like Eros coming to Psyche.

Her husband.

CHAPTER TWENTY-TWO

H E DIDN'T KNOW who had made her so self-conscious about her body but if he found them, he would make them regret it. Nothing could have prepared him for the disconsolate anxiety in her eyes. It was more than maidenly modesty. He'd almost made the decision for them both to wait, but the tears in her eyes had stopped him. It was the moment he realized it wasn't fear of sex that had her anxious, it was the idea of being naked. As it was, he wasn't going to push the issue, or complain. The sight of her in that flimsy, crimson night shift with her dark curls set loose was the stuff of dreams, even if he would have preferred to feel her bare skin against his the first time they made love.

His focus now had to be on pulling her out of her thoughts and fears. If she needed a layer of silk between them to be comfortable then it would stay there until she didn't need it anymore. He wanted her attention on what they were about to do, not whatever jackass had hurt her with cruel, thoughtless words. He would go slowly and show her exactly how sacred, how exquisite she was to him.

He touched her shoulder and pressed her backwards until she was laying on her back beside him, her wide brown eyes finally fixed on his. He took the elegant hand wearing her wedding ring in his and brought it to his lips, watching her eyelids flutter in response. Interesting. He turned her hand over and pressed a kiss to her palm, dragging his lips down to the sensitive skin of her inner wrist. She gasped audibly, her eyes now focused on his mouth and the path it was tracing down the inside of her arm.

He kissed along her shoulder and up the graceful column of her neck, as he lowered himself next to her, listening to the soft, almost bashful moans she uttered as she squirmed against him. Her hands rested lightly on his chest, eager to touch but still unsure. He'd fix that soon enough. He wanted her hands on him, everywhere. He took her mouth again, his hand curling under her neck to hold her in place, tasting their wedding wine.

She whimpered and broke away, panting hard. Her fingers curled over his bare shoulders and he nuzzled her soft cheek, breathing her in.

"Richard," she murmured, gasping when his hand closed over her silk-covered breast, her nipple hard against his palm. She tensed for a moment then her hand covered his lightly. He paused, waiting to see if she wanted to move it. Her eyes fluttered open to look at him then her grip tightened, pressing his palm against her. "Don't stop."

"Àirén," He moved back down her neck and she arched back into the pillow under her head. He continued down, sucking on her skin, nibbling on her collarbones, dragging his mouth over her other breast. He exhaled, allowing his warm breath to waft over her flesh and she gasped until his mouth closed over her nipple through the thin silk. Her moan echoed throughout the room, her fingers tightening on his shoulder and his hand.

He moved further down, mouthing her stomach over her nightgown as his hands moved down her body, to pull the fabric up her legs. She writhed, her stomach tensing and flexing under his lips and breath. Once it was high enough, he parted her legs with one hand on her thigh and settled between them. She breathed in sharply, her eyes fixed on him, and he wondered if she had the same reservations about him seeing her legs. "Is this alright?" he asked, and she swallowed nervously and nodded.

He ran his hands down her outer thighs, feeling the muscles in them flex at his touch. They were thick and just firm enough.

Powerful. Her equestrian skill seemed more inevitable now. One day, he promised himself, she would ride him with those gorgeous legs. He kissed the inside of her knee, moving further down her firm, smooth thigh. She cried out when he nipped at her skin, arching up closer, her eyes fixed on him in the near darkness.

He slid his hand up her leg, watching her eyes widen as he drew closer to her sex. At the first touch of his mouth against her, she gasped, her legs tensing under his hand. He parted her folds and licked deeply, tasting salt and musk, smelling her perfume and the sweetness she leaked out with every brush of his tongue against her clit. Her hands tangled in his hair and he pulled her closer, sucking her into his mouth with voracious delight as her thighs trembled around him.

Yes. She called out, her body squirming, her skin growing hotter as she clenched down around his tongue. Soon, she'd be there soon. He slid a finger inside her pulsating depths, brushed against her slick walls and she shattered with a scream, undulating against his tongue. She wasn't thinking about her fears now. He wanted to keep tasting her, to make her fall apart again. He could spend hours there until she was weak, until she was begging for mercy.

Her fingertips brushed his jaw, her hands straining desperately for contact. Later, he promised himself. He'd slake his thirst later. He moved up her body, bracing himself over her, with his elbow on the bed beside her as his hand played with the curls covering her vagina. She lifted her head to kiss him, pulling him close as his fingers explored her hot wet center. He kissed her back hard, pressing her head backwards, swallowing her moans. Her hips bucked against his hand when he brushed her clit, her fingers tightening in his hair.

He stroked against it in a steady circular rhythm and she cried out against his mouth, her legs twitching against his hips. When he felt her grow wetter, he sank a finger inside her, maintaining the pressure against her clit with his thumb. Her hips arched into him and her head fell back, her eyes squeezing shut as tightly as her depths around his thrusting finger. She was stunning, giving herself over to her pleasure. He pressed his lips under her jaw, feeling her pulse beating through her skin until her scent and her heat drove him to taste more of her skin, sending him back to those small dark breasts he was still dying to taste.

He sucked her nipple into his mouth and she jerked against him again with a desperate cry before she shuddered against him, her depths clenching down hard as more moisture flooded his palm. A thrill flowed through him. She'd come for him so easily and openly. Perfect. She was perfect.

All he wanted now was to see it again, as many times as possible before the night was over. He slipped in a second finger beside the first, curling them up towards his palm to drag inside her. She bucked against him, her hands clutching at his shoulders. She pressed her forehead against his, her hips churning against his palm as she chased a second peak.

"Richard," she gasped.

"Come for me again, àirén," he whispered, pressing a fraction harder on her clit. She whimpered, her mouth falling open.

"Please," she gasped, pulling him closer, her thighs pressing hard against his hips. He felt her ripple around his fingers before she cried out again, trembling and curling up against him. He kept moving his hand, encouraging her to keep going until her hand curled weakly around his wrist. He slid his hand free, his heart pounding in his chest as she went still.

Now. He had to be inside her right now. He lifted her legs over his, spreading them wider and took his cock in hand, stroking the swollen length with his slick hand. Carefully, he positioned himself at Elodia's opening before leaning over her once again. Her hand brushed his cheek and he looked up to see her watching him with those beautiful dark eyes. He drove himself in until the resistance from her muscles was too great. She winced slightly, and he brushed his hand over her head, stroking her hair.

"Are you well?" he asked. She nodded and pressed her lips together, wrapping her hand around his arm to brace herself. He withdrew then reinserted himself, deeper this time, almost halfway in. She closed her eyes and inhaled sharply. "Ellie, can you take more?"

"I don't know,"

He lowered her hips to the bed and withdrew partially. Then, he pushed deep until most of him was buried within her. She arched back with a groan, her grip on his arms tightening. His hand fisted in the sheets, as she flexed and clenched around him.

He lowered himself over her, bracing himself on his elbows, pushing her hair back from her forehead. Clenching his jaw, he pulled out and thrust again, feeling her body give way to him further with each drive even as it held him in a vice-like grip. She opened her eyes, panting as her hands clutched at the pillow. She lifted her head, her eyes fixed on his mouth, her intention clear. He kissed her hungrily, following her down.

He'd waited so long to have this, to be with someone who cared for him. All he wanted was to feel her hands on him. She'd touched him a little, a graze of his cheek, a grip on his bare arm, but he was desperate for more. He wanted to feel her everywhere, be claimed with all her love and passion.

"Ellie," he pulled back a fraction and her eyes opened. "Put your hands on me."

One of her hands lifted from the pillow to tangle in his hair, her fingertips trailing along his scalp. "Like this?" she asked.

He shivered and pressed his brow to hers. "More," he groaned, "please, more."

Her second hand touched his face, drifting down his neck to his shoulder then over his chest. His mouth crashed down on hers, startling a moan from her as her hand moved to his waist. Then he began to move in earnest, rolling his hips and thrusting deep. He could have pounded himself into oblivion at that moment but she felt so small in his arms. He couldn't bear to hurt her. Her legs came up around him and the mental image had his breath catching in his throat.

He buried his face in her hair, listening to her gasp and moans sound in his ear. He squeezed his eyes tight, fighting against the encroaching orgasm with every fiber of his being. Then he felt her kissing his neck down to his shoulder, her mouth sucking at his skin. The grasp on his self-control slipped and his hips snapped against hers with more force than he intended. She cried out and he froze in alarm before lifting his head to check her.

Her face was frozen in a mask of rapture, her eyes shut tight, her mouth still forming around the cry. All his experience told him she was fine, everything was fine, but still the fear lingered.

"Ellie?" he called her name roughly, and her eyes drifted open. "Baby, are you alright?"

She nodded weakly, her hand shifting to caress his back. "Don't stop."

She was going to be the death of him. He thrust again, deep and hard, allowing himself to let go more than he had before. Her eyes fell shut with a moan, her fingertips digging into his back, encouraging him to go deeper, to take more. He hiked her right leg up higher on his hip and buried his face in her neck, tasting her damp sensitive skin. Her scent was clouding his senses, her voice ringing in his ears, her breath flowing over his skin. He could feel her tightening greedily around him, her cries growing louder.

He wanted to see it, the moment she gave over to the pleasure he gave her. He lifted his head to watch her eyes fly open and widen in surprise, her mouth falling open in a wordless cry until the tension in her body shattered, clutching him close with her arms and legs, her entire body shaking with tremors beneath his. He'd wanted to see it again, wanted to spend the rest of the night driving her up that peak again and again.

But then everything caught up to him, the joy of loving her, the relief of no longer being alone and the bone splintering pleasure tearing the breath from his lungs. He cried out, pressing his forehead to hers, closing his stinging eyes as rapture ravaged his body. Her hands brushed his cheeks, holding his face between her palms with the same tender care with which she carried his heart.

ELODIA WOKE THE next morning feeling thoroughly cuddled and sore. The source of the cuddling was obvious and wonderfully novel. Her face was pressed to Richard's bare chest and his arms and leg were wrapped around her. As far as ways to wake up, she had to admit, this wasn't unpleasant. She ran her hand up and down his back, taking the time to appreciate the firm muscles under his warm smooth skin.

Last night had been everything she could have hoped for, and she had spent years hoping and imagining. He hadn't forced her into removing her nightgown as she'd feared. He hadn't seemed to mind at all. The things she'd done to her, the feel of him inside her for the first time, the way he'd looked at her the entire time like a hungry wolf would stay in her mind forever. She didn't think she'd ever be comfortable being naked with him, but she had to admit she enjoyed feeling his bare skin.

Did he always sleep naked, she wondered, or was it only for last night? If he showed up in nightclothes, she would be disappointed. Perhaps he wouldn't mind if she made a small request. He shifted and let out a sigh before adjusting his hold and kissing her hair. Goodness, her hair must be a sight. She hadn't wrapped it the night before as she normally did.

"Good morning," he grumbled, and she smiled.

"Good morning husband."

"How long have you been awake for?"

"Sometime. Did you sleep well?"

"Like the dead. You?"

"Mmm," she squeezed his waist and kissed the skin under her cheek. "I think I like being held all night."

"That's convenient," he replied. "Where should we go for our honeymoon?"

"Hmmm, Provence? I haven't been there in so long."

"France." His brow furrowed again, his mouth twisting in thought.

"Is that a problem?"

He certainly didn't look enthused about the idea. "No. I'll make arrangements."

"If possible, could we wait until my father is married? I don't like his choice of wife but I wouldn't want to miss his wedding."

He smiled at her. "Of course, àirén, whatever you like."

"What shall we do today?"

"I didn't plan on doing much else," he replied, rolling to face her, shifting her head to his arm.

"We can't just stay here."

"Why not?"

Why not indeed? "We'll need food for one thing."

"We have fruits thanks to your planning."

She fought past an onslaught of giggles as he dropped soft kisses on her face and neck. "I'll need more than that to keep up with you."

"Are you implying that I'm demanding?" He pulled back and peered down at her.

"I'm not *implying* anything," she replied, sliding her leg between his, feeling his manhood heavy against her thigh. He lifted one eyebrow, then in one smooth movement, he rolled her over, pinning her to the bed on her back. Was it normal to enjoy the weight of him pressing her into the mattress?

"Why do I get the impression that you aren't exactly complaining?" he murmured against her neck.

"Because I have no complaints at the moment," she replied, giddy delight rising in her chest as she took in his lustful eyes and silken dark hair, "but you are going to have to feed me at some point."

"Fair enough," he murmured before capturing her mouth in a

searing kiss. She had been hungry moments ago for breakfast. She was certain of it. And no doubt when he finished driving her wild, she would be even more so. But in this moment, all she could focus on was him. His tongue stroking into her mouth, his hand in her hair, that wonderfully strong lithe body of his and the length hardening against her.

He pulled away and she whimpered, chasing his mouth. "Àirén, are you alright for this?"

"What?"

"Are you sore?"

She hesitated too long before opening her mouth to reply. He shook his head and kissed her once more before rolling onto his back. "I'm going to have to keep an eye on you."

"What do you mean?"

"You are too greedy for your own good."

"Well, if I am, it's your fault," she complained, curling into his side. "You were the one who made the act so..." Enticing? Incredible?

"So?"

She made a face at him. "Who's the greedy one now?"

"Me," he replied, kissing her temple and cuddling her closer. "I'm very, very greedy."

She grinned, looking away from the bold intent in his eyes. "Silly,"

"Greedy," he corrected with a devilish gleam in his eyes. "Engrossed. Insatiable."

She giggled and buried her burning face and aching cheeks into his chest.

Then a sobering thought occurred to her. What if Lady Tremaine was correct and his greed surpassed her ability to sate it? What if she never could sate him and he was left unsatisfied for the rest of their marriage? What if he needed more than she could give?

"Ellie," he asked after they'd lain there quietly for a moment.

"Hmm?"

"Why don't you want me to see your body?" he asked, his hand running over her hip.

"I told you before, it's ugly."

"Why do you think it's ugly?"

"Because… I have virtually no bosom, my hips are too narrow. My bottom and my legs are too large."

"Who told you that?" His voice was deceptively even.

"It doesn't matter."

"It matters if you've been made to feel like you are unsightly when you are anything but."

"You don't know that."

"Yes, I do."

"It wasn't anyone in particular. My nanny in Trinidad said it was a good thing my face was pretty but my body wasn't too distracting. She said it would protect me from unwanted attention."

"Did she?"

"She meant well. When Papa and I left Trinidad, we stopped in France for a new wardrobe. I heard the modiste talking. She called me *La centauresse.*"

"The centaur," he translated the word.

Yes. It had been shocking to hear herself described that way, embarrassing, but by that time, she'd already been aware of how unattractive she was. It had been a fact of her life for years, but in his arms, with his sympathy so apparent, the memory stung more than usual. "They laughed. I don't know if she knew I understood her."

"That is disgusting behavior."

"It was unkind, perhaps, but I do look like a centaur." She shrugged. "A male one anyway."

His hand stilled. "I beg to differ." His tone brooked no argument.

She really didn't want to discuss it any further. "You know what I mean, though, I'm not curvy or womanly like Regina, or Ada."

"Would it shock you to know that I haven't seen either of them in their undergarments?"

"That's not true. Ada said she used to sneak into your room when she was younger."

"Firstly, if we must discuss my sister, she was in her night clothes, not her undergarments. Secondly, the last time Ada did that, she was maybe fourteen years old and even then I was almost always barely half awake. Sometimes I didn't wake up at all when she'd scamper in. I'd roll over in the morning to the sight of this adorable little interloper."

Elodia laughed and shook her head. "She is such a strange thing. Half strategist, half coward."

He chuckled. "When she was a baby, it was shadows on the wall. Then it was nightmares whenever our parents were gone. They weren't always traveling for long periods of time but if they went to China, she was always in my bed come morning."

"You didn't look happy to go to Provence. Would you prefer to go somewhere else?"

"I don't like the sea,"

She stared at him. "You live on an island."

"I'm aware. It's why I don't usually stay at our property in Brighton. Do you know my parents died at sea?"

"I think I did."

"I'd traveled ahead of them. I was home with Ada. They had sent the goods from my grandmother ahead of them. Lotus seeds, persimmons, soap, spices, silks, wine, ink, paper and new brushes. Two months later, I got notice that their ship had gone down."

"I'm so sorry."

"After that, I kept wondering when and how it had happened. I'd done that journey. I kept thinking of what it would have been like to be there. I had nightmares about a ship sinking and leaving Ada alone in the world. After a while, I just hated it, hated the way it made me feel, hated that it reminded me of their deaths."

"We don't have to go to France."

"I'm not afraid of it, Ellie, I just don't like it. If there was a way to get there without involving the ocean, I'd take it. But there isn't, so we shall sail."

"Are you certain?"

"It's not even a day of sailing. I'll manage." He frowned at her. "I know you distracted me by the way."

"Do you?" she blinked up at him with wide eyes as she pressed her lips together against a smile.

"Alright, I'll leave it for now."

"While we are on less palatable subjects, what are you going to do with your uncle?"

"I'm going to repay him in kind."

"You won't have him arrested?"

"I don't actually have anything to arrest him for. He put his hands on you, which is unforgivable, but he hasn't actually committed a crime. Not a crime I have evidence for anyway."

"I thought Leo was—"

"He was. The trail never fully connected to Uncle Simon. The connection would have been Trent himself. When he died, it was over."

"So what can you do?"

"His finances are under my control."

Her eyes widened. "You mean,"

"He put me in a debtor's prison two years ago. I will return the favor."

That would be almost diabolical. To allow his uncle to die in poverty, knowing he had the means to save him. Could he do that? "How long will that take?"

"Not long. He already has debts I'm meant to settle. They will take him."

"What about his family?"

"That will depend on them."

"When will you go?"

"Within a day or two." He looked at her and flipped her onto her back, nuzzling her neck as she squealed in delight. "I have some important business to see to first."

CHAPTER TWENTY-THREE

L EAVING ELLIE BEHIND was a tactical error. Richard discovered that the moment he'd tried to get comfortable in the carriage as he left the train station. He'd already decided to stop off by his uncle's country home to speak to his aunt before he acted. He'd decided even before his wedding that he was ready to cut his uncle off. He didn't care about what happened to him and he was only too willing to throw him to the wolves. Now that he had incurred the wrath of no less than three noble families, he knew his time had come. But before he did, he needed to know how far he should go when it came to his aunt and his nieces.

After he finished his business at Durant Mills and made sure the accounts and staff were in order, he headed down to Redfern Hall. He'd seen it a few times before when his father was alive, but since then he hadn't felt a need to return to see it. He'd barely recognize his aunt as it was. He vaguely remembered a brown-haired woman with a serious face but the distinct features of that face were elusive at best.

He handed his card to the butler who blinked once and nodded.

"I'll get the mistress, sir."

"Thank you." He turned in a small circle as the man walked away and took in the foyer as he waited for his aunt to arrive. It seemed a bit worn. The wallpaper was faded and the wood paneling was in desperate need of revarnishing. What had his uncle been spending his money on if he had so many debts to cover?

"Who are you?" a small voice called. He turned to see a small girl of no more than five with straight brown hair much like his father and uncle.

"I'm your cousin," he replied.

"You're too big to be my cousin," she reasoned.

"Are you Bethany?" He knew his uncle had managed to have a second child. No doubt he'd been disappointed that it was a girl.

"I am."

"Betty, who are you—oh." An older girl closer to fourteen stared at him. "Who are you?"

"He's our cousin." Bethany went to her sister and took her hand.

"Winifred?" He hadn't seen her since her baptism when she was a squirming red-faced newborn.

"How do you know that?" she asked.

"I make it my business to know," he replied.

"Are you a Chinese?" Bethany asked.

He turned to her. Not quite the way to ask that question but her big blue eyes were so earnest, he knew she couldn't mean anything by it. Better for her to be curious instead of suspicious. Richard crouched down to her level. "You are about half right in that assessment."

She rubbed the side of her nose. "I think you look Chinese."

"My mother was Chinese."

"Oh."

"Richard?" An older woman's voice announced the arrival of his aunt. He looked up to see a middle-aged woman with dark blonde hair, brown eyes and a thinner face than he remembered. Was that due to time or care?

"Aunt Cordelia," he replied, rising to his full height.

"What are you doing here?" She glanced at her two girls and then back to him. There was no outrage on her face, only well-hidden concern.

"I am here to speak with you about a matter of reasonable importance to you."

She blinked and took a deep breath. "Oh. Then I suppose you'd better come into the salon." She crouched down near her daughters. "Go outside and play, darlings, while I speak to Cousin Richard."

"Yes, Mama. Come, Betty." Winifred took her little sister's hand and walked down the hallway, sending a worried glance over her shoulder.

Cordelia glanced over at him and gestured for him to follow her.

"They are growing well," he commented, for lack of anything else to say.

"Yes. I don't know if you've ever met them before."

"I may have met Winifred when she was a baby. Your husband was never keen on my sister and I meeting your family, especially after Father died."

"Yes. The last time I saw you might have been your parents' funeral."

He didn't respond to that. Based on his calculations, Winifred had been born well after his parents passed, but it made sense that she didn't quite remember that. In the salon, she invited him to take a seat before settling in an armchair that needed to be reupholstered. In fact, all the furniture needed new covers. Like the foyer, the room was clean but worn.

"Simon told me that your sister Adelaide married two years ago."

Adelaide. Not 'that girl'. It was promising. "Yes. Did he tell you why my sister was forced to marry so suddenly?"

"I…" She swallowed hard, her gaze shifting away from his for a moment. "He has been under a significant amount of pressure lately."

"Did you know that he had me kidnapped two years ago?" he asked.

Her gaze slid down to the floor, her hands clenching in her lap.

Interesting. It was just as well, at least he wouldn't have to expend any energy convincing her of anything. "So you did. Good. He's never liked me, that much has been clear, but that dislike has now escalated in a way that has caused real harm to me and those I care for. I have had enough."

"What did he do?"

"In my defense, I've given him multiple warnings. But his most recent infraction was to assault my fiancée at our engagement party."

Her head came up to meet his eyes now. "You're engaged?"

"Married now," he clarified.

"Oh. Congratulations." She seemed dazed. How much had Simon kept her in the dark?

"Thank you."

"What are you going to do?" she asked.

"I've cut him off financially."

She gasped, her eyes widening. "You haven't… you can't do that."

"Yes, I can. He is recovering from the thrashing I gave him, but soon the creditors will arrive."

"Richard, they will take everything."

"Yes. I imagine they will. Everything in his name at least, but it won't be enough to cover his debts."

"I knew he'd had troubles," she mumbled, rubbing her forehead. "He told me that you weren't giving him enough, that—"

"He has received roughly ten thousand pounds a year as was determined by my father before he died."

"Ten thousand?" She stared at him in bewilderment. "But we never had… he always said we had no money because of you. I don't understand."

He supposed in his uncle's mind he was poorer than he would have been because of Richard's existence. Although he wondered if he would have been quite so bitter if he had been white.

"They will take him to debtor's prison now," Aunt Cordelia continued.

"Yes. They will."

"How long will you leave him there?" she asked.

"As long as it takes," he replied.

"Does he know?"

It was interesting. He half expected her to plead his case for him, but she seemed uninterested in that. Considering his lies and neglect, he couldn't blame her. "No. But he will find out soon enough."

"What will become of me and the girls?" she finally asked.

"That rather depends on you. It is said that the clever learn from their own mistakes but the wise learn from the mistakes of others."

She swallowed hard and stared at him.

"What kind of person are you, Aunt? Are you wise?"

For a moment, her face didn't move, then she gave a slow nod. "I am."

He smiled. "I am glad to hear it. In that case, you and your daughters will be provided for. The annuity I provided to your husband will come to you instead until your death. No doubt you will make better use of it than he did. You will be placed in a comfortable home and your daughters will have dowries provided. Any questions?"

She shook her head.

"Good. Now I have another question for you. What do you think of Bath?"

"Bath?"

"When they take this house, then you will need another at least for the time being. I have a property there you and the girls may use until we find a more permanent place for you. It's healthier than town, but not so far from society for at least part of the season. Does that suit you?"

For the first time since he'd arrived, she smiled at him. "I like Bath."

He nodded. "Good, I shall make the arrangements. My aim is for you to be out of this house before they take it."

"What about the staff here?"

Better and better. "You will still need them when you find your house. They will be provided for until they can join you. Or if they do not want to leave the county, we will find a new position for them."

She let out a relieved sigh. "Thank you."

He nodded and rose to his feet.

"Will you stay to dinner?" she asked.

She wanted him to stay? It was a novel experience but not an unpleasant one. For a moment, he wondered if it had truly only been his uncle all along. "No, thank you. I have to get back to town. I simply wanted you to receive the news from me so you could prepare."

She let out a short chuckle and shook her head. "Yes, that would have been quite a shock."

How had his uncle managed to find a woman like this to marry? She was levelheaded, responsible, kind and pretty. She'd given him two adorable children. Perhaps his neglect had served them in the end. No doubt his daughters would have been nightmares if he had been allowed to influence them.

Cordelia walked him out to his carriage in a comfortable silence that he couldn't have imagined he would have with his uncle's wife.

"Tell your daughters I said goodbye."

"I will. I hope that this means we will see more of you. It was never my will or intention for you and your sister to be strangers."

"I would like that," he replied, surprised to find that he meant it. He climbed into his carriage, and she pushed the door closed.

"Richard, thank you for not holding his behavior against me."

He stared at her for a moment, wondering what their marriage had been and what other lies he'd told her to make her think that he would see her and her girls in a poor house due to his actions. "I am not him. Continue to raise your daughters well, and you will have nothing to fear from me."

She nodded and he knocked on the carriage ceiling, signaling he was ready to depart.

WHEN ELODIA HAD opted to visit Aunt Theo, the last person she'd expected to be there was her father. The last time she'd visited her father, the female he was currently courting had been there and Elodia was not interested in spending more time with her. Not solely because she was effectively replacing her mother, or because she would unquestionably make her father unhappy, but because she actively disliked her as a person.

She disliked the way she spoke about Richard and the assumptions she made about Elodia and her mother. She was wildly prejudicial if not outright bigoted and she hid it all behind a mask of propriety and politeness. Even Lady Sterling wasn't that unseemly. Not knowing if she was lurking made her father's house off limits, but she could still visit her aunt.

She was so old with more bad days than good, and when she and Richard left for their honeymoon, there was no telling if she would still be alive when they got back. With Richard out of town on business, staying in their home made her too morose. So instead, she decided to bring her aunt fresh flowers as a way to thank you for all the help she'd given both of them. She'd driven over in her phaeton with a variety of flowers she bought from the market. With her collection of hydrangeas, violets, irises and daffodils, she climbed down from her vehicle and walked in. The first footman she passed nodded to her.

"Hello, Miss Elodia," he greeted her then stopped short, shaking his head. "No, it's Thornfield now, isn't it?"

She smiled widely. She would never tire of hearing herself called that. "Yes, it is."

"Congratulations, ma'am."

"Thank you."

"Are those flowers for the missus?"

"Yes, I shall need around two large vases full of water brought to the garden salon, please. And a pair of shears,"

"Very good, ma'am."

She strolled into the salon and stopped short when she saw her father reading his paper in his shirt sleeves and spectacles. "Lord Melbroke,"

He looked up and blinked at her and then at the flowers in her arms. "Mrs. Thornfield."

"Where is Aunt Theo?"

"Resting. She wasn't herself today."

"Oh,"

"She'll appreciate those flowers you brought her."

"I didn't know you would be here."

"Were you avoiding me?" he asked.

"No, I was bringing Aunt some flowers. What are you doing here?" She set down the flowers on the side table and took a seat on the sofa.

"My fiancée has a habit of calling unexpectedly. And the conversation at my club is… tiring."

"Oh, I'm sorry."

"How is married life?" he asked with a small smile.

"I am enjoying it. Richard had some business at Durant Mills but he is returning soon."

Her father frowned. "He is already back to work?"

"Not exactly. He just needed a few days. We are preparing for our honeymoon and we could be gone for some time."

"Of course."

She fiddled with her wedding band, wondering if he would be willing to answer the rest of her questions about his relationship. He was here, and he seemed to be in a good mood. After he married Lady Tremaine, who knew how much time she'd have to ask him about her mother?

"There is one matter I wanted to discuss with you, if you can spare the time."

He closed the paper, folded it and set it beside him on the sofa.

"It's about mama. I remember you behaving as if you loved her. I believed that you loved her, but I cannot remember ever hearing you say it."

He took a deep breath and his mouth tightened. "Is this about—"

"It's not about anything." She rushed to confirm. "I... I only want to have a better understanding. I have an image in my mind of the both of you but I don't know if it's true, and after all of this, I need to know. For myself."

"I have journals I kept during my time there. I can give them to you to read."

"Thank you, but... can you not simply speak to me?"

He looked as though he was about to argue but instead he nodded. "Alright."

"How did you meet her?"

He shifted in discomfort and began to fiddle with his hands. "She was given to me by your grandfather the first time I visited the sugar plantation in Trinidad with him at eighteen. I had only just finished my studies."

Elodia frowned. "Given?"

"Yes. She was meant to be a 'comfort to me', I believe was his phrasing."

Elodia frowned and her stomach turned. "A comfort?"

"A bed slave. That was a formative part of my understanding of the truth of slavery. Before then I believe the lies circulated by the men in my father's circle. What they told their wives. But when I arrived, it was impossible to avoid the truth anymore."

"What did you do?" she asked, breathing through her nose as her gut churned. Her grandfather had simply given her to be *used*? Like a shirt or a chamber pot?

He pursed his lips again. "Well, I certainly didn't touch her, if that's your question. But I freed her the first chance I got. Her and the other members of my staff my father had given me at the time. Needless to say, your grandfather wasn't at all pleased."

"Was that when you began courting her?"

He shook his head. "No. I had no idea of courting her at the time and I am positive she only stayed with me because being my servant meant protection. I wanted them to learn a trade to have a way to support themselves if or when they decided to leave. She learned to read and write like the others did and they devoured the books I had. She decided on being a maid. There was another freedman who was interested in her, I believe."

"When did you fall in love with her?" she asked.

"That was sometime later for me, further again for her. She loved to read. She learned in no time at all. I fancied myself a scholar before I got to know your mother, but she truly was one. She wanted to learn everything, questioned everything and I appreciated that about her. The more she became of herself, the more I admired her. But I didn't pursue her,"

"Why not?"

"Because I didn't think she would sincerely want to be with someone like me. I thought she would agree out of gratitude or some nonsense and I didn't want to put her in that position."

"Because you were white?"

"Partly. Mostly because of who I was. Not only a white man but the son of the man who owned her and treated her and her family and her people so inhumanely. You couldn't understand Ellie, my father treated his horses better than his slaves. I didn't believe that she could or would be able to separate me from him."

"But she did."

"Somehow. I was also too nervous to approach her. I was never a ladies' man, you see. I was always with my nose in a book or the clouds. She was so clever and brave and resilient, and I was so ashamed of my own limitations. Compared to her, I felt so small and silly. I spent half my time trying to measure up to her. Not in an envious kind of way but... she made me want to be better than I was."

She could just see it. Her father the shy, bookish young man and her mother the brilliant, bold beauty. "When did she fall in love with you?" Elodia asked.

"I don't know, I never asked her that. I was too grateful that she was willing to be with me at all."

"Grateful?"

He smiled. "There were times where I believed that the only impressive thing about me was the fact that she wanted me. That she loved me. I still feel that way, honestly."

"When the courtship began, how long did it last?"

"A year, I believe. She didn't want anyone to know. We wrote letters, sometimes took walks."

Yes, she'd read those letters. "And the wedding?"

"It was at The Trinity Church in Port of Spain. It was raining that day, she wore a simple white dress and flowers in her hair. We had two witnesses. I sent a man to retrieve those records by the way, of our wedding and your birth."

"Thank you. How did Grandfather take it?"

"Apoplectic," he replied with a sly smile. "He had already returned to England at the time. When he got word, he came back. He threatened to sell all of the people I'd freed back into slavery, especially her. He tried to take them to America. That was the last time I saw my father."

"What did you do?"

"I fought him, then I picked up a cutlass. I told him that if anyone ever tried to enslave them again, I'd kill them. Even if it was him."

"What did he do?"

"He left. He threatened to disown me."

"Why didn't he?"

He shrugged. "Honestly, I thought he had for the longest time. But I suppose in the end he didn't have another heir. He could have done it. Who knows why he didn't. Some years later, we had you."

The sound of footsteps brought two maids with a cart carrying two porcelain vases and a pair of shears.

He nodded toward them. "I believe that is for you."

She stood taking the flowers with her and set them down on the cart. She waited until the maids had left before she asked her next question.

"How old was she when she had me?" she asked, picking up a hydrangea and snipping the end at an angle.

"She was around your age, I think. I was twenty-five, not much older."

"What was she like then?"

She heard footsteps and then her father was there. He picked up a shear and watched what she did before he began trimming the ends of the irises. "Don't you remember her?"

"I can't remember her as you do."

"You take after her more than you realize. She was bold and clever like you. She loved color and music and learning. Marrying her was… it made me happy, we were happy, but it made it difficult for us to do more for those on the plantation. We did what we could. Stopped some of the whippings, most of the sales, but we didn't own them, so we couldn't free them. We couldn't stop it. It took parliament for that in eighteen thirty-three, and even then the actual emancipation was delayed for another six years. They wanted them to serve as apprentices in the interim. In Trinidad, there were protests at the government buildings the next year and we went with them."

"We?" she asked, dropping a trimmed daffodil into the vase.

"Yes, we took you and all, you were strapped to her front. We went to every one. They still ended up waiting, but in the end, they managed to expedite the abolition of the apprenticeship ruling by two years. Your mother was part of that. She was free, but she never forgot the truth of her life and she fought until every last one of them were free. It was my privilege to stand by her side and use everything at my disposal to help her and make sure they got everything they were owed."

Elodia smiled at the recollection, thinking of the sketches of her mother she'd found. Yes, that sounded like the woman he'd drawn. "She sounds wonderful."

"She was. Her stubbornness could be heartwarming or terrifying, just like yours. Her moral compass was implacable just like yours. You are a credit to her in so many ways. When she died with your brother, I nearly didn't survive it. She had been the center of my entire world for so many years at that point and the space she left behind… I didn't know how to fill it."

"I remember when she died, I didn't see you for two weeks." She paused in her task as bitter memories came to mind.

He set down the garden shears and watched her with somber eyes. "I'm sorry for that. My grief was like a dark pit pulling me in deeper. I couldn't pull myself out. Then your grandfather died and there was something to do. Finally it was all mine. I could finally run that estate the way I'd always wanted, the way she wanted. When that was done, there was you. I didn't want to leave our home there. I wanted to stay in the land that gave me your mother, that gave me you. In the end, your grandfather got the last word." His smile was wry and lacking humor. "Perhaps that was why I found it so difficult to agree to you marrying Thornfield. I saw what it was like with your mother. They couldn't attack her exactly when she was my wife, but no one accepted her. I was her only protection for so long, just as I was yours. The idea of you living without it is terrifying."

She put down the shears and began arranging the flowers into the two vases. "Was it difficult for her?"

"Not exactly. She didn't care to be around the society groups, knowing what they were. It drove them mad that she wouldn't bend over backwards to fit in with them, that she wouldn't attend their parties even if they invited her. But it bothered me. It bothered me that I couldn't make them treat her with respect."

"You did it for me."

"Did I? You were correct in everything you said about me. I failed you and her. I was so certain of myself that I forgot who I was. Or rather the sinister side of what I am. I am a white member of the peerage, which meant that I could offer you more protection than anyone else. But it is precisely that which made me blind to what was so obvious to you and your Mr. Thornfield. I am ashamed of myself, Ellie."

"Father," she reached out and took his hand.

"I am so sorry that I didn't do better protecting you and her memory. I should have come with the papers proving your legitimacy and hers. I should have known that they would assume the worst. I should have known that my father would do everything to protect his reputation. I should have done better. I'm sorry that I made you think you couldn't stay in your own home."

She nodded in acceptance, squeezing his hand before releasing it. "You are forgiven,"

"The idea of you being whisked away so quickly and to someone without that protection for you… I thought it was taking you away from me and my name just as your grandfather wanted. It felt like he was winning, and I couldn't handle it."

"Richard protects my heart."

"I know. He's a good man. A formidable man."

It meant more than she could express to hear him admit it to her face. "Do you love Lady Tremaine?"

"No." The answer was swift and uncompromising. "I could never love someone like her."

"Do you at least like her?"

He shook his head. "Not particularly."

"Why are you marrying her then?"

He gave her an impatient look over his spectacles and sighed. "I already explained this to you. I need to marry this year and she is the most eager candidate. She's within a reasonable age range, she is the correct race and nationality to suit your grandfather's terms."

"I don't want you giving up your happiness to give me something I don't even need."

"It is not just about you, darling. I have a duty to my staff and my tenants. The same duty your Mr. Thornfield has to his tenants and his workers. Your mother was my first love and my only love."

"But that was years ago, Father,"

"It was, but most don't even get that. I already had my happy ending. Now I need to make certain you have yours, and that those still under my protection are secure."

It made sense, but she still didn't approve of it. "I don't like the idea of you being unhappy."

He chuckled, but there was a weariness there. "How could I be unhappy with you in my life?"

"How could that be enough?"

"How could it not? You and that gentleman will give me grandchildren to dote upon; I will have a son, God willing. Worst case, I shall see about leaving things to your first born. That would really send the old man spinning in his grave."

She couldn't help but laugh. "You're just as troublesome as I am."

He laughed and shook his head. "As your mother used to say, 'dogs don't make cats'."

CHAPTER TWENTY-FOUR

Thornfield House, London

HE WAS FINALLY home. Two days away from his bride had been far too long. But it was done, and now, as he strolled through the doors of his home, Richard flattered himself that he wouldn't have to leave her side again for the foreseeable future.

"Ellie?" Richard called out as he laid his coat on the banister.

No response. Where on earth was she?

"Richard?" he heard footsteps on the second floor and looked up to see her appear near the stairs. The minute she saw him, her face brightened and she flew down the stairs, launching herself into his arms with a delighted cry. "You're home,"

He closed his eyes, wrapping her in a tight embrace. Christ alive, he'd missed her. "Yes, at last. Did you miss me?"

"Not a bit. I wasn't sad at all having the bed all to myself."

"Wicked little sprite," he teased, and she giggled.

"Did you miss me?"

"Desperately," he replied, giving her a squeeze as he walked them to the salon. How on earth had he gotten anything done without her nearby? He was sure that anything he needed to do could be done with her in his lap. Or at the very least with her hand in his. He wouldn't do without her again.

"What did you have to go away for?"

"Business concerns. My signature was needed on a few things."

"They couldn't simply send them?"

"In time they will, but not for this."

"Why not?"

If he didn't know better, he would think he was being interrogated. Something had happened and she was doubting him. He sat on the chaise and pulled her into his lap.

"It was a change in process, Ellie. After Trent, I don't want bigger things approved without my signature. Money doesn't go out without my signature and I don't give it unless the books are reviewed."

"Oh." She laid her head on his shoulder and sighed. "I'd forgotten about him."

"I trusted him with too much and the cost is still felt. I'm not making that mistake again."

"I understand."

He paused, wondering if he should say the rest. "I also took the opportunity to visit my aunt."

"Your aunt?"

"Uncle Simon's wife."

"Oh!" Elodia lifted her head and looked at him with wide curious eyes. "What is she like?"

"She's alright, I hadn't seen her in years because of my uncle. You'll meet her eventually, once I'm more certain of her."

"Alright."

"I have another matter I've made a decision on which I hope you'll agree with."

"What?"

"No more trips alone, business or otherwise. I'm going to keep you close at all times."

"What about when we have children?"

"We will bring them along as well. We'll be a caravan across the country at all times."

She giggled and snuggled her face into his neck. "I'm glad. I missed you so much."

"What were you up to when I was away?"

"Oh, nothing much, still repairing things with Papa. We had a good long talk about Mama to clarify things."

"That is good. I'm glad you are on better terms with him."

"So am I."

"Is he still marrying Lady Tremaine?" Richard asked, dreading the answer.

Elodia rolled her eyes. "Yes. And she is determined to be involved in far too much. Papa said he's already had his love match with Mama and that he's marrying Lady Tremaine for the estate. And for me. He said he didn't want anyone too young because he'd be uncomfortable."

"I can imagine. I had reservations on the matter for you and myself."

She shook her head. "Ridiculous."

"It is ten years of difference, Ellie."

"I like your age. You will just have to make do in any event. I have no intention of allowing you to have anyone else."

"I appreciate that, darling."

"Papa invited us to dine with him in a week. He wants to offer his support to us publicly."

"That is good for you."

"It's good for both of us. Shall I accept?"

"I thought it was a foregone conclusion."

She flicked his shoulder. "I didn't want to make assumptions about your time."

"I thought that was your right as my wife."

She rolled her eyes but she smiled. "Good, because I have tickets to the opera tomorrow night. Father is allowing us to use his box."

"Which opera?"

"The Marriage of Figaro."

The Lyceum, London

ELODIA WAS ALWAYS happy to attend the opera, but tonight she was particularly excited because it was her first outing in society with Richard as his wife. She could hang on his arm, whisper secrets in his ear and no one could say a thing about it.

The only thing that made it better was the opera they were about to watch. She had always enjoyed The Marriage of Figaro from the first time she'd seen it with her father.

"You look very happy," Richard commented as they sat in her father's box. It was a subtle gesture, but one that others wouldn't be able to miss. No matter who she married, she was still The Viscount Melbroke's daughter.

"I love this opera." She replied.

"What about the play?"

"Hmmm… I like the music most."

He didn't reply. She looked over at him after a moment to see him watching her with frank admiration. His head was tilted, his dark eyes trailed over her from head to toe and a soft smile curved his mouth.

"What is it?"

"You are very beautiful tonight."

"What was I last night?" she asked cheekily, despite the fluttering of her heart.

He smirked and leaned in, nuzzling her ear and the soft curls framing it. "A vision from heaven," he murmured.

"You are a menace."

"You are perfect."

She turned to him, meaning to scold him again but he stole a kiss instead. She pulled away with wide eyes, fighting against a smile. "Richard, we are in a public theater!"

"You are correct, what do you suppose the penalty will be if we are seen?" He glanced down at her body, looking at her skin, the low neckline of her dress.

"People will talk,"

"Very true, but what do you suppose they will do?"

"I suppose they cannot make us marry a second time."

"Mmm, I'd marry you again."

"Really?"

"I'd marry you a thousand times in a thousand lifetimes,"

"It sounds expensive."

"Mmm," he trailed his fingertips along her collarbone, up her neck, under the edge of her jaw, his eyes following their trail. "I'd make sure you never had to wait for me ever again."

Her eyes fell to his mouth.

"Your skin is so soft àirén,"

"What does that mean?" she breathed, her eyelids fluttering closed as he brushed over her bare shoulder with the back of his hand.

"What, 'àirén'?"

"Yes."

"It means, 'beloved'"

She waited with tingling lips, watching as his came closer. Just as he was close enough for contact, he tilted his head and brushed his mouth over her cheek, to her ear. His warm breath wafted over her hair, teasing her with its ghost like touch. "Richard,"

"How many times have you seen this opera?"

Applause sounded, startling her out of the seductive bubble he'd entrapped her with. She turned to face the stage, one hand pressing against her pounding heart. Her eyes roved over the audience, checking to see if anyone had seen them.

Then she felt his hand close around her thigh. She pressed her lips together and fought back a gasp. If she looked at him, she would dissolve on the spot, so instead she kept her eyes forward even though it was impossible to focus on anything with every nerve focused on his touch.

He pressed her against the wall, tucking them both behind the curtain and yanked her up against him, kissing her hungrily. She moaned, her entire body feverish with desire and gripped his head in her hands, tangling her gloved fingers in his silken hair. All too soon he pulled away, breathing hard.

"Tell me we can leave,"

"Yes, take me home." She could practically recite the damn

opera from memory, but her husband's body was another story. She slid her hand around his arm and followed him past the curtain to the sitting room and out to the hall. Ten minutes and they would be able to enjoy the relative privacy of their carriage and she could get her hands on him again.

"Ah, well, if it isn't the happy couple."

Elodia bit back a curse and glanced at Richard. His jaw was tight with annoyance. They had to stop; people had noticed her calling out to them.

She turned with a smile. "Lady Tremaine, good evening."

"So formal, we are practically family, are we not?" She brushed a kiss over the air on Elodia's cheeks then turned to Richard. She saw him stiffen slightly as the older woman leaned in, her hands practically caressing his arms. Elodia watched, her hands curling into fists. What the hell was she doing touching him like that?

"How are you enjoying Mr. Mozart this evening?" she asked, turning to Elodia with a small smirk, her hand still lingering on his arm. She wanted to rip it off and Béat her with the bloody limb.

"Very much," she replied.

"Yes, you seemed quite… enraptured."

"Mozart has that effect."

"I'm sure he would, for you. I prefer the newer composers myself. There's something so invigorating about the young and novel, wouldn't you agree, Mr. Thornfield?"

He gave her a small tight smile before turning to Elodia, "Are you ready?"

"Extremely."

"You're not leaving, are you?" the older woman's voice came. Sweet and dark like poison.

"Is that a problem?" Elodia asked.

"It's only surprising. I thought you'd want to watch the rest of the performance."

"I've seen enough," she replied, sweeping her eyes up her

body before fixing on hers defiantly. "Good evening."

"I'll see you for dinner with your father, yes?"

"Good night."

IN THE CARRIAGE, she sat opposite him, folded her arms and turned her head towards the window. She had rarely been this angry in her whole life. In fact, she was almost certain that she'd never been this livid. He hadn't done anything wrong, but there was a strange energy in her looking for a fight. All she could see was that pale hand touching him and him not shaking her off. She knew he couldn't reasonably do it without drawing unwanted attention, that waiting her out was the best and most dignified approach. But another part of her wanted him to shove the impudent hussy away.

"Are you not going to sit beside me?" he asked. She didn't reply but she didn't move either. She didn't want to be too close to him. He was too magnetic, too attractive, too skillful. He'd bewitched her into allowing him to seduce her in a public place with hundreds of witnesses. She didn't know what she would allow him to do in the relative privacy of a carriage. "Are you cross with me?"

"I don't like her."

"Yes, that much was obvious,"

She glared at him.

"I don't like her either if that matters."

It didn't. "She is far too familiar with you."

"Yes. It wasn't a pleasant experience."

She glared at him again. "You didn't seem overly opposed."

"I wasn't sure how it would look if I did what I wanted to do."

"You—" she cut herself off and looked away from him again.

"Why are you cross with me?"

"I am not cross with you exactly."

The carriage came to a stop. She waited until they were inside their home, walking up the stairs to their rooms before she asked the question she wasn't sure she wanted the answer to.

"Do you know her?

He blinked in silence for a moment. "I don't understand the question."

"My father said that he'd known her before this. That he'd met her before she was a wealthy widow."

"Ah."

"Did you?"

"Not exactly." He glanced at Béa, "I'll finish. You can come back in the morning for the rest."

She glanced at Elodia for confirmation before nodding and taking her dress and petticoats with her.

"She behaves as though she's known you for a long time," Elodia commented.

"Do you think I've encouraged her?" he asked as he began unlacing her stays.

"No, but do you find her attractive?" She unhooked the front of her stays once they were loose enough and he laid them on a chair before removing his waistcoat.

"Why are you asking me this?"

"I don't know." She sat down at her vanity in her undergarments and began removing her jewelry. "She looks like every woman should look. For a moment, when you were standing there with her, it seemed almost natural."

"More natural than us?" he asked, watching her closely with his hands in his pockets, one broad shoulder leaning against the bedpost.

She would be damned if she admitted to him that she was, in fact, jealous. Her eyes drifted to her reflection in the mirror before her. Lady Tremaine had said Richard had no doubt been with women built more like her. It placed her own underdeveloped body in harsh perspective. Unlike her father's future bride, she was flat and square with skinny arms and a bottom that was far out of proportion. Easy enough to disguise in clothing, but looking at herself now, in only her chemise and stockings, there was no way to ignore it.

"Come here," he said, his voice low and firm. She met his eyes for a moment then looked away. The anger had melted away, leaving her feeling small and cold. There was an unease in the back of her mind that she wanted to go away. His touch would chase it away surely enough, but she wasn't sure she wanted it just yet. Too much of her wanted to follow him anywhere no matter what it meant. What if he wasn't being honest about his attraction?

"Would you rather I not touch you now?" he asked.

She stood and walked over to him. He slid his arm around her waist and pulled her to his chest, pressing her back against him and turned her to face the full length mirror opposite the bed.

"What are you afraid of?"

"Nothing."

His elegant hand came up to take hold of her jaw and lifted her head. "Look at yourself."

"No,"

"Àirén, look," he murmured. His fingers were firm but careful, always careful with her. Her tear glazed eyes met his in the mirror. "Tell me what you are seeing."

She shook her head, refusing to speak or meet his eyes. But she didn't want to move, didn't want to give up his touch or the feel of his strong lithe body at her back.

"Shall I tell you what I see?" he asked. She didn't speak, but her head fell back against his shoulder. "Your hands," he relinquished his hold on her jaw to bring one of her limp hands to his lips.

"Skinny," she murmured.

"Slender, with the softest palms. I love watching them play the piano. I'm always jealous of your mouth when you lick your fingers. I'm especially fond of the way they feel on me, in my hair, on my skin." He lowered her hand to her side and then moved his over her hips.

"Too narrow,"

"For?"

"Children,"

"Nonsense, they are perfectly serviceable for children." His hands drifted up to her ribs to cup her miniscule breasts, cupping them gently in his palms. "These here,"

"Nonexistent,"

He squeezed and a shiver ran through her. "I beg to differ, but do you know what is particularly charming about them?"

She shook her head. His thumb brushed her nipple over her chemise and her knees buckled.

"They are so delightfully sensitive," he murmured, nuzzling her neck, rubbing his thumb back and forth as she arched into his touch. His breath skittered over her skin and she shivered. "All of you is so sensitive, your breasts, your mouth, this wonderous silken skin."

She could hardly catch her breath, could barely keep her eyes open as she watched him touch her with masterful tenderness, with delicious intent. He moved them backward towards the chaise at the foot of the bed and sat, resting her on his thigh. She could feel him hard and insistent against her hip and moved her hand back to touch him. He snatched her hand and moved both of hers into his.

"So impatient, I'm not finished as yet."

"Richard," she whined.

"Shhh, let me show you what a treasure, what a wonder you are."

She wanted to argue, but the idea of moving from where she was or stopping him was debilitating. With every word, every touch, that knot in her chest was unfurling. No doubt it would return tomorrow, but right now, in this moment, she wanted to believe she was the woman in the mirror. She wanted to be the brown skinned beauty in Richard's arms, sprawled wantonly in his lap, breathless and ravenous, receiving her worshipful due.

"Are you watching?"

"Yes," she replied breathlessly.

"Good girl." He ran his hand down her thigh to her calf. "These legs here,"

"They are too big."

"I love how strong they are. I love how tightly they wrap around me, how they grip me when you ride me."

For a moment, she closed her eyes as a tear slipped through her lashes, rolling down her cheek.

"This bottom here." His hand slid over it, giving the lush curve a daring squeeze. She wriggled into his touch wishing, for the first time, she had removed all her clothing so she could feel his hands all over.

"Tell me," she whispered, nuzzling his cheek with hers.

He smiled; his reflection wickedly amused. "I love how round it is."

"It's too big."

"Not when it's pressed against my cock."

She shivered. That word.

"It feels just right. When you were drunk that one night and you sat in my lap, I thought I would die on the spot."

"Served you right."

"Such a cruel mistress," he murmured against her neck.

"What else?"

"Fishing for compliments now?"

"Tell me,"

"I saved the best for last."

His hand slipped under her chemise, then slid high on her bare leg, curving towards her inner thigh until he cupped her sex. The sound that escaped her was almost feral, half gasp, half moan. His fingers slid between her sodden folds, brushing her clit as he'd called it, and she gripped his leg, shuddering.

"This part of you here is so perfect, not many women have it."

"A vagina?"

He snickered against her neck then slid two fingers inside her, his thumb braced against her clit to drive her mad. "Not quite. There's a delightful little spot inside you just here," his fingers flexed inside her and stroked an area of such sensitivity she forgot how to breathe.

"Oh God." Yes, she loved when he did that with his fingers.

"Mmm," he murmured, "I love that you have this àirén, it means I can please you so much more." His fingers began to move in and out, his thumb brushing softly against the side of her clit. She went rigid, her hold on his thigh tightening. She clutched at the wrist of the hand between her legs as her breath shuddered past her lips. "Look at me." The soft command came again from him.

She hadn't even realized her eyes were closing. It took more effort than she'd thought herself capable of, but she met his gaze in the mirror again. His lips were parted slightly, his eyes moving from where his hand was hidden by her shift to her face and back again. He seemed enraptured by her, by them, by what he was doing to her. Had he always looked at her like that or was it because he was watching them together?

"Every inch of you is beautiful, every inch was made for love, made to be loved and cherished. Nothing is wanting."

She nodded weakly. She wanted it to be true. Wanted to believe the woman she was watching was her. That woman was sultry with perfectly even skin that seemed to glow with golden light. Her eyes were wide and fathomless, her hair a wild mane of shining dark curls. *She* was exquisite, especially as she was in his arms, reveling in his touch as he stroked her to tumultuous completion, her heart racing so hard it was uncomfortable. He kept going, following every squirm of her body until there was nothing left, until she covered his hand with hers, a silent, desperate plea for mercy.

His hand stilled, resting against her. He pressed his face into her hair, breathing her in while his eyes burned into hers in the mirror, pitch-black and mesmerizing.

"Ellie," he murmured, his hand fisting in her shift over her stomach.

"Yes," she breathed.

"Yes what?"

"Yes, more. Make love to me. Do it here."

His forehead dropped heavily onto her back for a moment, his breath branding her skin through her shift. His hand retreated from between her legs to unfasten his breeches and pulled her shift up higher until she could feel his trousers against her bare bottom. He pulled her closer to him with one arm, lifting her high against his chest. She felt him against her hard and hot, sliding into her slick eager sex from behind.

She arched backwards, her hips squirming as she slid slowly down his length, feeling it stretch and make room within her until she was flush against his hips. She leaned against him again, feeling his body behind her, inside her, tense, breathless and hard as granite. She felt dizzy and weak. He felt deeper than before, as if he'd never been this far inside her previously. She wanted to move but moving her hips produced a sensation that was too overwhelming.

His hands settled on her hips and helped her to rock them back and forth in a steady rolling motion that rubbed him against that spot inside he'd shown her with his fingers. It felt so perfect. Everything he did to her, everything he made her feel, was like heaven. She didn't know how he was able to make her feverish with desire every time. It made her want to rock her hips harder, to feel that shimmering cascade of sensation over and over, while his wandering hands chased its path over her stomach to her breasts, pulling her closer, caressing her body with wonderous intelligence.

And his midnight eyes followed every undulation of her hips, every gasp that parted her lips, every shudder. She reached behind her to hold his cheek and press his face to hers, anything to keep her grounded while he drove her towards another peak.

She couldn't stop herself from clenching down harder on him when his hand once again dipped between her legs, under her shift where her sex enveloped his. His fingers caught her clit between them, the desperate churning of her hips giving her the extra friction she needed to send them both over the edge.

A voice cried out, thin and desperate with rapture. He pulled her squirming body hard against him, his hips thrusting up into her. She heard the groans he buried into her hair and against her neck, the moans she pulled from his chest, the harder she rolled her bottom against his groin, that additional force sending her spiraling into ecstasy. Her head fell back as she cried out, her eyes barely open but unable to look away, hypnotized by the sight of them together.

All the while, he observed her with that hungry, focused, worshipful gaze, one hand buried between their legs, the other curling lightly around her throat, tender and palpable, holding her in place. All she could feel was him, and even when her eyes finally rolled back as vicious delight dragged her under, all she could see in her mind was his face as he watched her.

CHAPTER TWENTY-FIVE

Melbroke House, London

RICHARD WAS MORE than grateful to attend Lord Melbroke's dinner, especially for Elodia's sake, but he would have been lying if he'd said he was enjoying it. If he did marry Rachel, Richard would have to find a way to keep her away from himself and then his family without excluding his new father-in-law. The only thing keeping Richard from saying or doing something regrettable was Elodia. He'd spent most of the season hiding his connection to Rachel for both of their sakes. But she seemed determined to reveal their sordid past to the world.

He knew Elodia loved him, or rather loved the version of him that she was familiar with. The man without fault. It was flattering but he would be lying if he said it didn't make him uneasy at times. Uneasy that if he fell off his white horse, she would see him as something not worth keeping or loving.

Basil leaned over to Richard and murmured under his breath. "Am I wrong in thinking you have a particular dislike for your future mother-in-law?"

He glared at him. "What gave me away?"

"Your face. What's the matter with her?" Basil asked, "Other than her condescending bigotry?"

"I am familiar with her from before."

"Before when?"

He stared at Basil hard. *"Before."*

It took a moment for Basil to understand him. "You mean…" his head whipped around to Lady Tremaine, and Richard took a gulp of his wine, trying to hide his exasperation. "Richard."

"What?"

Basil's eyes looked set to pop out of his head. "She was your…"

"Yes." He grumbled.

"Do your wife and father-in-law know?"

"What do you think?" he hissed back.

"I think that I wish Leo were here."

Richard looked up at the ceiling, praying for patience. Of course that would be the one thing he had to say.

"What on earth is she doing here?" he asked.

"She's punishing me for leaving her behind."

"You have to tell Elodia at least." Basil reasoned.

"How exactly?"

"The devil if I know. But she must know regardless."

"Gentlemen do not, as a rule, speak of such matters with their in laws and especially to their wives."

"Yes, but typically they are not in danger of having to call them belle mere." Basil hissed. "Think of how much worse it will be if they actually marry."

His head was pounding. Basil was right, of course, he had to speak up, but what on earth could he say to salvage the situation? Would Lord Melbroke even believe him? "I am aware."

"Richard,"

"If you have nothing useful to add then I beg of you to hold your tongue."

"As you wish."

He was being a coward, he knew that. But he didn't want to risk his life with Elodia. She held nothing but contempt for the woman. If she found out that she had been his mistress, she would never be able to look at him the same way again. There was nothing he could do to change the past. It wasn't as if he'd done anything wrong. He'd merely taken a despicable woman as his lover for a few years. He hadn't spread any rumors or taken advantage of anyone. He'd done the honorable thing and made a clean clear break when he'd decided to marry. How could he have known that his mistress would end up trying to be his mother-in-law?

His eyes caught Elodia's and she winked at him. For the first time, it didn't loosen the knot in his chest. He smiled and nodded, taking a sip of wine. His eyes dropped to the plate in front of him. He didn't want to keep secrets or lie to her, and it would be impossible to keep this a secret. If Rachel wanted to play this game, he would have to meet the challenge with more than silence. The only way for him to truly move forward was to break free of her entirely. He had been willing to leave her her dignity, but if she was willing to put it at stake then why did he have to bend himself into shapes to protect it? Was it more his responsibility than hers?

The only person he wanted ignorant of all of it was Elodia, and she was arguably the person who needed to know the most. He needed to tell her the truth and he couldn't wait until he wasn't about to throw up. The moment he thought about it, the feeling returned.

With dinner nearly over, he didn't have much more time to wait. He'd tell her when they got home, and she could tell her father. She would be angry with him, but at the very least, it would be over one way or the other.

"Sir,"

Richard looked over to see a servant leaning over his shoulder with a silver platter.

"What is it, Marks?" Elodia asked.

"A message for Mr. Thornfield, it just arrived," Marks said.

"Thank you," Richard snatched up the ivory envelope and stood, glancing at Lord Melbroke.

"The reading room on the first floor is free for you, Thornfield," he said with a nod.

"Must you see to it right now?" Elodia asked.

"I must. It shouldn't take long," he replied with a wink.

"Let the man see to his business, Ellie," her father said.

"Thank you, my lord, I will rejoin you all shortly."

"We'll be in the sitting room,"

He stood and followed Marks out to the reading room. The note was from his lawyer. The magistrate had given the injunction. His uncle was being sent to debtor's prison. It had taken less time than he had anticipated. The creditors must have been after him for some time. Now, he only needed to wait for him to be picked up. He would have to expedite the arrangements for Aunt Cordelia and her daughters.

When he got back, he'd write to her with the news. Would they want to stay in Bath, or should he offer to house them with himself and Elodia for the time being? He'd have to see what humor Elodia was in before he decided on that. He could end up in Bath by himself in very short order as it was.

He wasn't in the habit of courting messes. This one was likely to upend his life entirely.

"Hello, lover," he heard her voice over his shoulder and his whole body tightened in alarm.

Rachel.

Here.

For fucks sake, even *here* she wouldn't control herself.

"What are you doing?" he demanded.

"I see you still imagine yourself to be suited for marriage, how droll," she said and he heard the door close.

He turned around to see that she was unfortunately still in the room. "I see you are still laboring under the delusion that you know me at all."

She gave him a smug look. "Oh, I know you, lover, you may convince yourself otherwise but I know you better than you realize."

"This is a pointless conversation." He started to walk past her.

Her hand whipped out to grab his arm. "I will not be cast aside, damn you."

He jerked his arm away, balling his hand into an angry fist. He didn't want to use it, but by God, she was testing his patience.

"Then see it as the inverse. I do not care overmuch."

"Because you are too good for me?"

"I thought it was the other way around."

"What if I changed my mind?" she insisted.

"You haven't."

"And you know that because you know me so well?"

"You aren't that unique. I've faced you a thousand times. You like to play games, you are good at them. But my life is not a game. You do not love me, you do not want me—"

"—yes, I do." She slid her hand up his arm and his skin began to crawl. The last thing he wanted was her anywhere around him.

He shoved her hand away and started towards the door. "No. You just don't like that I ended it first. I am telling you one last time to leave me be. If you disregard me on this, don't blame me for being ruthless."

"You think that little girl has what you need?" she snarled, the switch from cloying seduction to rage swift and disconcerting, but he was already at the door.

"She is more than you ever were. More than you could ever be." He turned the handle or at least tried to. It wouldn't budge. Fucking hell, had someone locked the damn door?

"Having trouble?" her voice came from behind him.

His body went cold as he turned to face her. "What did you do?"

"I've explained my position before this, but you seem to think it wasn't anything you needed to be concerned with."

"And you thought this would get you your way?"

"There's only one way out of this room and I have it." She held up a key then dropped it down her bodice. "Give me what I want, and I'll let you leave. Otherwise, I cannot promise you won't be missed. That child will be so heartbroken to find out that her shining knight still has a taste for the finer things. What will happen to the wedded bliss then?"

"I don't suppose you've considered the danger you might be

in."

"Me? I've had two bad husbands, but they left me money." She strolled up to him again and his hands curled into fists at his sides. "My worst case scenario means I go to Italy until the scandal dies down." She pressed her body against his, straining upwards to bring her face closer to his. "Yours involves the love of your life, that simpleton, realizing just how soiled her new goods are." He snapped into motion and shoved her back into the wall. She staggered backwards and laughed.

He turned to face the door and started banging on it. "Is anyone there?"

"Too overdressed? Shall I get started for you?" she asked.

"Stay away from me."

"I'd stay away from that door, darling, unless you plan on using it. You don't want her finding us alone, do you?" He glanced over his shoulder and saw her dress half undone. *Fucking hell.*

He pounded on the door again, harder and harder until the door frame began to shudder. "Hello?"

"Richard?"

"Basil?"

"What are you doing in there?"

"Can you open this door?"

Hands slid around him from behind and he shoved them away.

"Give me a minute," Basil called back.

"Hurry."

There were voices on the other side of the door while he fought against Rachel's tentacle-like arms.

"Get the fuck off me." He snarled.

"Don't you remember how it was before?"

"Rachel, I swear to Christ if you put your hands on me one more time, I will rip them off."

She smirked, reached for him and the door swung open. Richard turned to see Elodia standing there, her eyes wide with confusion. "What is happening?" she asked. Behind her stood Leo, Regina and Lord Melbroke.

Richard couldn't speak. It was like a nightmare. Mouth agape, Elodia's eyes slid from Richard to Rachel, half undressed and widened in outrage.

"You—" she stalked forward, nostrils flaring and slapped Rachel to the ground. It was incredible to see the power she housed in that petite body. He'd heard about it from Ada, but he'd never witnessed what she was truly like in a rage.

"You impudent little slut, what the hell are you doing here with my husband?" she growled.

Rachel looked up, wide eyed with shock, before turning to her fiancé. "Melbroke, are you going to do something about this?"

"Not yet," he replied coolly. "What do you mean, Lady Tremaine, by getting locked in this room half undressed with my son-in-law?"

Her eyes widened. "Aren't you going to ask why he's in here with me?"

Richard looked at her in shock. Was she really going to try and turn this around on him and play the victim?

"No," Lord Melbroke replied, "because I sent him here with a message he received in front of all of us. I know why he's here, but why are you?"

"And why are you undressed, ma'am?" Ada asked.

"Isn't it obvious?" she shrieked, scrambling to her feet and turning to Elodia. "Your husband attacked—"

"Before you slide further into your web of lies," Basil began, "I feel that it's important to point out that the door was locked. The likelihood that you entered a room already occupied by someone and they managed to lock you in with them as well, is low at best."

"He attacked me!" She insisted.

"Did he attack you because you were trying to molest him?" Elodia asked.

Rachel gasped again, her eyes flooding with tears. Her theatrics were impressive, if ineffective. "Why on earth would I even bother—"

"Why was the door locked?" Lord Melbroke asked.

Rachel blinked rapidly. "How would I know? Perhaps he arranged for it to happen, just as his repulsive uncle."

Melbroke's eyes narrowed as though he was about to lose his temper. "For that to be true, he would have needed to ask you to meet him in this room and close the door. If he was here first, then you would have seen the room was occupied, entered it regardless and you closed it."

"Are you accusing me of something, my lord?"

"*Accuse?* It is clear as day what you did and how shameless you are," Elodia railed.

Rachel's mouth hung open, her flushed face now bearing a visible handprint. "I am shameless? You were parading yourself in front of the ton with your—"

Something silvery fell onto the carpet from her chest and she fell silent. Richard took one step forward, bent over and picked up the key before showing it to his father-in-law and dropping it into his open palm.

Melbroke stared at her. "I don't suppose you have an explanation for this, do you?"

She burst into tears, garbling on about her innocence and her hurt dignity. Richard looked away, unable to watch any longer. He wasn't in danger of being deemed a rapist, but he was tired. So fucking tired of all of it.

"That is quite enough." Lord Melbroke said, his voice low and resonant, his face implacable. "Mr. Thornfield, will you take my daughter home, please?"

"Yes, my lord,"

"I believe it's time we all left," Basil replied.

Elodia finally took her furious gaze from Rachel, only to grab Richard's wrist and drag him out the door behind her.

Once they were in the carriage, he finally brought himself to look at her. She was curled up in a furious ball, her eyes fixed on the window of the carriage seat. He couldn't speak. He felt nauseous, a sickly sweat covering his body at the idea of Elodia knowing the full truth. He would have to tell her, there was no way around it, but he still hated it.

"What was that?" she said finally, still refusing to look at him.

"Ellie,"

"I knew she was far too forward with you. I knew something was wrong with her. Who is she to you?"

"Can we discuss this at home?" he pleaded.

"No." She turned her head to face him and tears glinted in her eyes.

"For a time she was… my lover," he replied, as he grew sicker with shame.

She stared at him for a long moment, so long he wondered if she had heard him over the horses. "Your what?"

"My lover. We had a sort of arrangement for some years."

She blinked again. "How many years?"

"Does it matter?" He needed fresh air.

"Yes, it bloody well does," she snapped.

He'd always wanted her to treat him as a mere mortal. Had wanted her to know that she could be angry with him without consequence. Now he was about to experience the feeling for the first time and he was not enjoying it. "I was around nineteen when I first met her." He couldn't look at her anymore.

"And when did this arrangement end?"

"Earlier this year."

Her eyes narrowed dangerously. "How much earlier?"

"A few months ago." He nearly left it there, but with every half answer, he could feel her ire increasing. Her ire and her distrust. She deserved his honesty. "At the beginning of the season. When I decided to marry, I broke it off. It was before you confessed to me before any of that."

"Is she aware of the fact that your arrangement is broken off?"

"Yes. But she refused to accept it no matter what I said or did."

"Why didn't you tell me this before?" she asked, turning her body to face him.

"Because it's not exactly the sort of thing one mentions to a fiancée, let alone a wife. It's not the sort of information a gentleman spreads around at all."

"But when my father began to court her. How could you stand by and allow my father to court and marry your former lover, knowing that she refused to accept the end of your relationship?"

"Because I didn't know how to. There are rules of engagement for this sort of thing and frankly, I never truly imagined she would take it so far. It was going to hurt her more than me in any event."

"That remains to be seen," she grumbled.

The carriage came to a stop and he bolted out, pausing to help her down before they entered their home. She marched ahead of him, a furious little thing, holding herself tightly. He didn't know if it was to comfort herself or to keep herself from slapping him as well. He followed her to her room where Béa was waiting.

"Béa, can we have the room for a moment?" he asked, and she nodded before leaving, closing the door behind her.

The minute it clicked shut, she whirled on him. "You had to be aware that she was trying to do something with you."

"I was. You have to believe me, Ellie, I kept turning her down. I didn't want to be with her. Especially after I knew my feelings for you."

"She even had the audacity to lock herself in a room with you, undress as if preparing for a dalliance and attempt to pin her actions on you."

"I know," he said, closing his eyes to block out her angry, disappointed face.

"Did she think that would be enough encouragement or did she know it would be?"

His eyes opened again, as disbelief flooded his mind. Tears

were streaming down her cheeks now. He hated to see her cry. "What are you saying?"

"After nearly a decade, she must know you very well indeed. Far better than I do."

He shook his head in denial. "That is not true."

"It must be. Because I cannot fathom how the man I love and admire could be entangled with such a woman. A crude, selfish, common bigot."

"It wasn't exactly my preference to be with her." He started towards her but she held up a hand to stop him.

"I find it hard to believe that you would stay in a relationship with a person for over a decade because of what, convenience?"

He didn't have an answer. The fact of the matter was it had been exactly that, but she wouldn't understand it.

"Did you love her?" she asked.

"No."

"Did you like her?"

"No."

She scoffed. "You must have felt something for her. Was it attraction?"

"In part."

Her face grew more incredulous by the second. "*In part?* It had to be significant for you to overlook so much. For you to allow her access to your person so intimately and for so long."

He didn't know what to say. She was too romantic, too sheltered to believe the truth without it affecting the way she viewed him in the worst way. "Are you expecting me to answer that?"

"Do you expect me to believe that there is truly nothing between the two of you when you only ended a decade long relationship a few months ago?"

"There was no relationship between her and I," he insisted.

"She clearly feels something for you."

He scraped his hands through his hair. "All she feels, if you can call it that, is a sense of ownership. She sees me as a plaything she owns and cannot fathom the idea that I can make choices of my own volition. There is no feeling on either of our parts."

"Then how could you give yourself to someone like that? How could you bear to have her touch you? Was it so easy to ignore that because of the way she looks?"

"What are you talking about?"

"She's beautiful and has the sort of body men like. Clearly you were not an exception to that."

Was this jealousy? Did she think that he was in some way still attracted to her? "Elodia,"

"And it is so disappointing because I thought you were a person who would see past those things. I never imagined that you would debase yourself with such a person for the sake of something so immaterial."

"Immaterial?" Did she think it was easy to go through life being undesired and unwanted? Being seen as an oddity?

"Yes."

"Elodia." His throat tightened uncomfortably. "You couldn't understand."

"I understand well enough. But there is nothing that could induce me to give what I've given to you to someone like that." With that, she turned her back and began angrily removing her jewelry and the flowers in her hair.

He'd known she would see him like this, that she would be repulsed by him, but he hadn't been prepared for how much it would hurt. His mouth was dry and the room was spinning. All over. He couldn't bear it. He needed her to understand. "I was young and lonely. My parents had just passed away. I had spent my entire life at that point as a curiosity."

"I know what that's like." She snapped.

He shook his head. "No, you don't. Your status is the curiosity, not your entire being. There are places in this country where you can blend in even if it isn't within your natural sphere. There is *nowhere* for me here. I might as well be from another planet. In the eyes of others, I am either an effeminate clown or an unnatural deviant."

"That is not true."

"Yes, it is. If you go back to Trinidad, you have a culture you recognize, a place to belong. I do not have that anywhere, not here or in my mother's country. My existence is alien. Do you know what that is like?"

She stared at him in silence, her eyes wide.

"Why was I with Lady Tremaine? Because I felt half dead and I wanted to be touched and she was the only one who would do so without being paid. Not everyone has the luxury of options. When you are hungry enough, you eat what's in front of you."

The words were ugly and crude, but they had been the truth at last. And now the one person who had loved him enough to touch him the way he'd ached for was looking at him as if he was some kind of filthy mongrel. He ran his hand over his face, a bitter taste in his mouth and turned to go to his room. He didn't need her to tell him she didn't want him in her bed tonight, or any other night. Not after this. He paused in the doorway. "I'm sorry if that makes me disgusting in your eyes. And I'm sorry to have disappointed you. I never wanted to hurt you or embarrass your father."

CHAPTER TWENTY-SIX

H E WAS DREAMING. He knew he was. Elodia was there in red silk, her eyes laughing, running just ahead of him. He chased after her, reaching for her hands, her loose hair, the hem of her dress but to no avail. She darted and jumped like a hummingbird, forever out of grasp, forever too high above him no matter how high he climbed after her. There was that sickening feeling in his stomach as his body grew more exhausted that he would lose her, that she was slipping away and he couldn't stop it.

He strained above his head, his fingertips brushed hers… just a little further. Orange blossoms filled his nostrils and arms wrapped around his waist from behind.

"Hello, lover," Rachel's voice came.

Elodia's eyes flooded with tears as she pulled her hand away. He struggled to free himself but Rachel's arms grew tighter and tighter until he couldn't breathe. He called for Elodia over and over but no sound came out. His foot slipped. Then he was falling. Falling away from Elodia, falling from grace, falling back into Rachel's unkind embrace.

When he hit the floor, his eyes flew open. He was in his bedroom, his sheets tangled around his legs, even as he lay on the hard wood. His body was covered in sweat and his stomach… Christ, he felt ill. Gingerly he rolled over, pulling his leg free and pushing himself up to his feet.

He was fine. Elodia was likely in her bedroom and Rachel was nowhere near him. But the shirt he was wearing still smelled like her. He ripped it off and threw it across the room. He wouldn't be easy until he'd washed her scent off of him for good. Then he had to go to Lord Melbroke and apologize for the travesty that had taken place under his roof.

The door to his room opened and Morris entered.

"Good morning, sir," he greeted him, his gaze falling to the bed that Richard hadn't used since he and Elodia were married.

"I need a bath, Morris, please."

"Very good, sir," he said, picking up the discarded shirt off the floor.

"Burn that shirt."

"Sir?" Morris blinked at him, clearly wondering if he'd lost his mind.

"The shirt, burn it. And the jacket I wore last night as well. I don't want to see them again."

Morris stared at him for a second longer than usual then nodded. "Very good, sir."

After bathing, Richard dressed and wrote a short note for Elodia before handing it to Morris. "Give this to Mrs. Thornfield when she wakes up."

"Very good, sir. Will you be taking breakfast, sir?"

His appetite was nonexistent. "No."

It was cowardly, but he couldn't face her that morning. The note would suffice until he had the words to face her. The night before had left him raw and sickly. He'd shared a side of himself with her that he'd never shared with anyone and the result had been disappointingly predictable. She hated him, and there was nothing he could do to fix it now.

He opted to walk to Melbroke House. It would take a half hour at most and he didn't have the wherewithal to ride in an enclosed space just then. He needed fresh air and exercise to walk off the anxiety and nausea that had been plaguing him since before he'd gone to bed. He'd tossed and turned half sick all night with dread that his marriage was over after barely a fortnight. That no matter what he did, his affair with Rachel was going to cost him everything and leave him forever alone. After a taste of Elodia's love, he couldn't bear the thought of it.

When he arrived at Melbroke House, the butler let him in and directed him to the breakfast room where he found his father-in-law in his house robe, enjoying what seemed to be the last of his breakfast.

"Mister Thornfield, my lord," he announced.

Melbroke glanced up and caught sight of Richard. They stared at each other for a moment, the older man taking in Richard's appearance before nodding.

"More coffee, I think, Ingsley," he said.

"Very good, my lord," the man said before leaving the room.

"Have a seat," Melbroke gestured to the empty chair with an almost friendly smile.

"I didn't mean to interrupt your breakfast, my lord," Richard began, before sitting across from him.

"Not at all, Thornfield. You look rather bright eyes this morning." His smile was annoyingly amused.

Richard almost groaned. "I came to apologize for the scene that transpired last night."

"Ah, yes, what was that about?" He actually seemed curious.

"Lady Tremaine and I were involved for some years before this and I broke it off at the beginning of this season," Richard explained.

Melbroke nodded as if he had suspected something of the kind. "And she didn't take well to her puppet cutting its own strings?"

"Essentially."

He nodded again. "That makes sense. I imagine you didn't mention this earlier because of some notion of gentlemanly discretion?"

"Yes."

He nodded again and bit off a corner of his toast. "You will be pleased to know that Lady Tremaine has taken off for the continent, permanently this time. She's unlikely to trouble you again."

"That is good to know." Although he still had no idea what was happening. Of all the reactions he'd expected from Lord Melbroke, this wasn't one of them.

"Good riddance, I say," Melbroke said.

"I thought you would be angrier with me, Lord Melbroke."

"Oh?"

"Yes. She may not have been the love of your life, but my actions have disrupted your plans significantly."

Melbroke sighed and leaned back in his chair. "I want to be annoyed or displeased with you, but frankly, I can't manage it. I was beginning to dread the rest of my life as her husband; I could not really stand that woman at all. The second issue is, of course, that for all your bad judgement, I can't imagine that I would have done anything differently to what you did if the shoe were on the other foot."

"Ah." He didn't know what to say to that.

Melbroke smirked. "Yes. Considering my earlier bouts of stupidity, you may take that statement as you will."

Richard didn't know what to say to that. Was the man joking with him? Did he really not care?

"How is my daughter?"

He sighed and rubbed his forehead as a headache began to throb behind his eyes. "Livid and possibly disgusted,"

"Yes, you look like she's taken a few swipes at you. I know what that's like. Cheer up, the nausea fades after a few weeks."

"Weeks?"

"Mmm," He pushed the rack of toast towards him. "Have some."

"Do you think she will forgive me?" Richard picked one up for want of something else to do, and bit off a piece. He wasn't hungry, but surely toast couldn't hurt.

"God, yes," Melbroke scoffed, sipping his coffee. "With how

much she loves you, it is a matter of when, not if."

He swallowed the dried bread and spoke the words that terrified him the most. "She didn't know me when she said she loved me. What if this new information makes her rethink that?"

"Because she is stubborn. She loves stubbornly as well. Your judgement was impaired, but she will not give up her love for you over that harlot. The truth is no one truly knows the person they fall in love with, you merely know enough." He paused for a moment then sighed. "You gave me some very good advice a few weeks ago, so I shall return the favor.

"Yes?"

"Give her time and space but don't go far. She's angry, but she's like her mother, so she doesn't want to feel alone. Stay close by until she comes to you."

Richard shook his head. "She doesn't want me anywhere near her at the moment."

He nodded. "I understand, but she doesn't want to be alone either. Did you have any business ventures you were planning to see to?"

He thought of Aunt Cordelia. "Not long one's, I'd only be gone a day,"

"Cancel them," Melbroke said, shaking his head. "Show up for a kicking now and then and take it willingly. She'll run out of energy soon enough and that is when you apologize profusely. Grovel." He tapped the table with a finger.

"Grovel?"

"Like your life depends on it."

He nodded. He had his marching orders. Stay nearby and grovel the moment the opportunity presented itself.

THE NEXT FEW days were exhausting. Elodia could barely sleep without Richard and they only spoke to each other when there was no other option. She spent her days in her sitting room, or the garden. Occasionally taking rides out on her horse alone. They should have been doing those things together, planning for their honeymoon in France. They should have been happy. Instead, they were at an impasse where she didn't want to be around him in case he was able to placate her and he clearly didn't want to force his presence on her.

She kept waking up wondering if he would leave but invariably she found him at home, either in his study or on the grounds. If he went out, he always left a note behind, giving her patience and remorse instead of defensive impatience. She knew her anger with him was perhaps a bit unfair but she couldn't see her way out of it. He had withheld vital information, and his inaction had embarrassed her and her poor father.

The simple fact was she didn't know how to face him, knowing he and Lady Tremaine had been lovers. Had they done all the things she had done with him? Had she pleased him more than Elodia had? Every passing aside, implying her knowledge of Richard or men like him kept ringing in her ears. Of course she knew all about Richard; she'd been intimate with him for years. All she could see was him with that woman. That cheap slattern.

She had been so smug every time she caught Elodia and Richard together, so revoltingly presumptuous. At the opera house, he had clearly been uncomfortable. Was it because of his alleged distaste for her, or for the revolting spectacle of her behavior while he was with his wife? He'd said his reason for keeping silent was respect for Elodia as his wife and discretion. It was true that gentlemen of the ton didn't inflict their mistresses on their wives, not even to speak their names. It was considered the polite and gallant thing, to keep a lady's secrets to the grave, but surely there was a point when that ignorance no longer served.

Once again, she had been left in the dark while members of the ton were privy to information about her life. How many of them had known that she was his mistress? If it had been another open secret, she would be ill. How could he let her be humiliated like that?

"Ellie," Richard's voice came from the doorway and she looked up from her angry, tangled embroidery to see him standing there, wearing his jacket and holding his hat and gloves. Was he going out or had he only just arrived? "Are you taking visitors?" he asked.

"Why?"

"Your father," he said, "he is downstairs for you."

Papa... Yes, he would have answers for her. "I will see him."

He nodded and turned to leave.

"Will you be receiving him with me?"

He turned back to her and shook his head. "I have business in town. I will likely be gone most of today."

She nodded, turning her gaze down to her needlepoint. He lingered there for a moment then let out a sigh and walked away. The next time she heard footsteps, her father was there, watching her with an almost amused expression. Before she could stop herself, she stood and ran to him, wrapping her arms tightly around his waist.

"Papa," she murmured.

"Ellie, my sweetheart." He squeezed her tightly with his free arm and kissed her hair.

"I am so sorry for what happened."

"What on earth do you mean?" He rubbed her back briskly.

She leaned back to look up at him. "That business with Lady Tremaine and—"

"Richard."

"Yes."

He let out a deep breath and rubbed her arm before leading her to the sofa for them to sit down. "Thank you for that, although it is hardly necessary." She snuggled beside him, still wanting to be in his arms.

"I can't imagine why not. I am very cross with him, Papa. I would not blame you if you were cross with him as well."

"He has already come to see me. He told me what had happened."

"You mean that he and she were lovers at one time."

"Yes. Suffice to say, Lady Tremaine is no longer in the picture." He glanced down at her with a small smile. "Don't feel the need to pretend to be disappointed."

"I won't. She was a common shrew and I wish us all to be well rid of her."

"Yes. I believe she means to go abroad."

"Good. She should stay there, or I'll give her another walloping."

He chuckled. "Of course this now places the issue of your dowry in real jeopardy."

She was so sick to death of hearing about that money. "I do not care about that blasted dowry, Papa. I meant it then and I mean it now. What I wish for is your happiness."

"Either way, I am sorry for it." They sat there in companionable silence for a moment before he spoke again. "I don't mean to interfere, but why exactly are you cross with your husband?"

Elodia glanced up at him. "Are you not angry with him?"

"Whatever for?" he asked.

"For withholding the true nature of his relationship with Lady Tremaine."

"Well, I'm assuming their relationship did not overlap with your own?"

"No, of course not. But he should have said something."

"It is not something that a gentleman would discuss. Not with another man and certainly not with his wife. You cannot hold that against him."

"Even to the point of letting you marry her?"

"Ostensibly, her relationship with him shouldn't preclude her having one with me. If it were anyone else, his withholding of the truth would be a mark of respect for her agency as an adult to live her life as she sees fit. Discretion is something to be admired, Eloida."

She rolled her eyes. "No accounting for taste, I suppose."

He laughed again.

"What? She is a monster. I confess to being disappointed in him."

"Have you forgotten that I was also involved with her. I would have married her, Ellie."

"That is different, you didn't like her."

"I don't believe he did either."

I was lonely. His words echoed back. His stricken face was visible as he confessed the darkest truth of his life. "It is still different."

"Why? Because I'd already fallen from grace?"

"What?"

He looked down at her, a patient smile on his face. "Darling Ellie, do you think part of your reaction to his past is based on your unrealistic expectations of him?"

"Unrealistic?"

"I think you see him as flawless."

"He—" Damn, she'd nearly confirmed it. "Regardless, I cannot pretend that this hasn't changed the way I see him."

"Mmm, a little less perfect?"

"Yes." Was it her?

"My darling girl, he was never perfect. The things you admired about him are still there. He is a good, loyal, honorable man who loves you deeply."

"Why are you defending him? His silence resulted in your humiliation. I had to listen to her shameful nonsense not knowing that it was based on firsthand knowledge instead of cruel conjecture."

"From what little I know of her, she would have said those things out of malice, not out of a need to be helpful. Cruel conjecture would still apply."

"It was still embarrassing. He should have told me."

"Yes, he should have."

"And he could have told you."

"Well, yes, but it's not as if we were close and I'm not certain I would have believed him if he did."

She glared at him.

He rolled his eyes. "Alright, you little bully. He should have told me. But I will say that as a gentleman, I can understand why he did not."

"Am I wrong to feel this way then?" she asked.

"No. You cannot be wrong to feel anything, but just because you feel it doesn't mean you should discredit everything else. Do you still love him?"

What a ridiculous question. "Of course I still love him."

"Do not let that all go because of someone who, by your own decree, is not worthy of your confidence or your notice."

She sighed and closed her eyes, trying not to pout. It was true. She wouldn't trust Lady Rachel Tremaine as far as she could throw her. She wasn't a woman that Elodia would take advice from. She was so tired, and she hated being angry. But most of all, she hated the idea of allowing someone like Lady Tremaine to ruin her marriage with Richard, a man she'd loved. A man who defended the defenseless but rarely had anyone to defend him.

If he had been lonely enough to turn to her, hungry enough to eat poison, as he'd suggested, didn't that deserve her sympathy instead of her judgement? Her father was correct, of course; she did see him as perfect. Before, it had been a compliment, but now she wondered if she hadn't treated him unfairly.

Giltspur Compter, London

IT WAS THE final victory, or very near to it. This place of hopelessness where he'd been sent via conspiracy lived only in his nightmares. Now he was here again, for what he promised himself would be the last time, finishing a task that he hadn't relished. Even if he was well within his rights. As Richard walked through the dismal little courtyard, he recognized some of the men but not all of them.

Finally he reached the room where his uncle would be staying. Where he would likely spend the rest of his life. He was sitting at a roughhewn table in a dim room just below ground level. A far sight from where he'd lived most of his life but still not as bad as the small supply closet Trent had thrown Richard in only two years ago.

When Richard entered, he squinted up at him, a fading yellow bruise on his thinly bearded jaw. He'd lost weight as well. He was pitiful, his inner lack of strength now fully on display.

"Hello uncle," he greeted him, closing the door behind him.

"You," Simon hissed as he finally recognized him, "You little—"

"Yes. Let's skip over all that. I have no interest in staying here longer than I must. I promised you some time ago that if you continued to cross me, I would return the favor you paid me."

He slammed his fist on the table and rose to his feet. "You have no proof that I was involved with that."

"I do, in fact, just not enough for a judge."

"That is impossible. I never directed Trent to send you here."

Richard smiled and tilted his head. "It's interesting. I never mentioned Trent."

Simon blinked, his face going grey. "Yes, you did."

"No, I didn't. I mentioned a debtor's prison. There are quite a few in London. But I never mentioned Mr. Trent." Satisfaction at last, but it left him even colder. "Thank you for confirming. I didn't have the evidence before, and even this won't be enough to press charges but I like knowing for certain. You could have gotten away with it, you know, but you had to keep pushing, and now you have destroyed yourself."

"You are the one who destroyed me. It is your duty to settle my debts, damn you. Your father—"

"—It was," Richard agreed, "when I still felt an obligation to you and your wellbeing. Thanks to your behavior, I no longer feel such an obligation."

"You would throw me and my family into ruin?"

"Not your family uncle, just you. Not that you would have done that for me. You would have disappeared me off the face of the earth and disposed of my sister at the earliest convenience without a thought to her happiness or dignity. You've been lying to more than yourself, it seems. Aunt Cordelia, Bethany and Winifred will be well looked after by me, if that gives you comfort."

"I should have been able to inherit, not you. You are an unworthy child. You do not deserve to bear my family's name."

"That is your opinion. Not that it matters."

"I'll get out, you know. I still have friends. People of influence who won't allow me to be here long. It's a paltry hundred pounds I have left to pay."

"You attacked the daughter of a viscount. Who do you know that would be willing to cross a peer of the realm for someone like you?"

"You don't even know how many enemies you've made with your arrogance. Lady Tr—"

"Lady Tremaine is gone, sir," Richard interrupted. So they had been in league as well. "Her reputation is lost. She will not be in England for a good long time. She no doubt used you for her own ends and left you twisting in the wind when it suited her." He watched the horrified realization settle onto his uncle's face. He staggered backward until he collapsed into the empty chair. "There will be no help for you, from me or anyone, you made sure of that. You will rot here as long as it takes for the world to be rid of you. It is a rare thing indeed to be the kind of person who improves this cruel world by leaving it."

"Richard." He grasped at Richard's hand, his face growing paler by the minute. "You cannot mean to leave me here. I am your uncle. I am the last link to your dear father."

"Don't." Richard snapped, jerking his hand away, his eyes burning with angry tears that he refused to let fall. How dare he invoke his father's name? "Did you ever try to be family to me? Did you ever think that I would have wanted someone to help me when my parents died? I was twenty-three years old. Ada was fourteen. Did you ever think we needed someone to fill that space for us? Did you ever think that we would have traded that fortune you coveted so badly for another day with my father and mother?"

The tears in the man's eyes only filled him with disgust. He could cry and plead now for himself but he never imagined what it felt like to be attacked when one already felt like they'd lost everything that mattered.

"You are right. We are family. We can still have each other, Richard—"

"Did you think of those things in the last thirty years? The past decade? The past month? Think on them now, as you have the time. I have my own family now, and you, you are already dead. Goodbye uncle."

He turned and left him behind in the nightmare, walking into the light.

CHAPTER TWENTY-SEVEN

Thornfield House, London

H E HADN'T RETURNED yet. Part of her was terrified that her behavior was the reason. She was still annoyed even if she wasn't quite as angry. What if he was tired of placating her? The more she thought of it, the more she understood her father's reasoning. Richard had made a foolish error in judgement but he hadn't done anything out of malice. He deserved a chance to make amends. She still wanted to be his wife. Even now, there was no one else in the world she would rather spend her life with, no one she would trust more than him.

Now she simply needed to tell him that and hope that he felt the same. After all, she had treated him as though he was diseased. She'd treated him just as she'd feared he would treat her, believing that she was illegitimate, but he had never considered it. No matter what she did, he met her with affection and kindness. Could she say the same? She heard his footsteps in his bedroom. He was home. Of course he was home. He wasn't the sort of person to make others worry.

The door was still open. She padded across the room in her bare feet towards the half opened door. When the door creaked open further, he paused in removing his waistcoat and turned towards her.

"Yes? What is it?"

"Are you back for the night?"

He nodded. "I am."

She nodded and stared at the floor, fiddling with the sleeves of her nightrobe.

"How was it with your father?"

"It was good. He's single again."

He nodded. "I went to speak to my uncle, to close the door on that."

He didn't walk towards her but he didn't seem willing to walk away either. Perhaps he was waiting for her to come forward. It was such a stark difference from the last time they had spoken. As if he was waiting for her to begin shouting at him again.

"Did you need to speak with me, Ellie?" he asked.

That name. He wouldn't call her that if he was angry with her. Maybe he wasn't opposed to hearing what she had to say.

She shuffled forward to stand in the middle of his room. She sneaked a glance up at him and saw him watching her with curiosity and perhaps… yearning? Had he missed her as well?

His words were echoing in her mind. He'd trusted her with his loneliness and she hadn't listened. All she could see was that woman's hands on him, all she could imagine was the two of them doing what she had done with Richard. All she'd focused on was the idea that while she was pining for him and loving him so ardently, he had been messing with that harlot who didn't even care about him.

But it was wasted effort to dwell on such a thing, wasn't it? He loved her and he'd shown that over and over again. She still loved him.

She crossed the room and slid her arms around his waist, burying her face in the center of his chest. His arms came around her instantaneously, holding her close. She felt his face press into her hair, breathing her in. "I'm sorry." She mumbled.

"No, I'm the one who should apologize."

"Well, I did it first," she replied.

He chuckled and scooped her up into his arms, before settling into a chair with her in his lap. "With your permission, àirén, I would like to go first."

"Very well," she agreed, wrapping her arms around his waist and laying her head on his shoulder as his hands stroked over her shoulder and back, down to her legs, pulling her closer.

"You are right that I should have told you the truth of my association with Lady Tremaine once I understood she was likely to become your stepmother. I want you to know that I didn't stay silent out of any need to protect her or embarrass your father."

"Why did you stay silent?"

He sighed heavily. "The truth was I was ashamed."

"Because you had a mistress?"

"No, that *she* was my mistress. I knew that she was a small, bigoted, hateful woman. My arrangement with her wasn't anything based in friendship or even human decency. She wanted an exotic boy toy, and I wanted sex that wouldn't expose me to disease. There weren't many interested in me for the kind of thing you would condone."

"There was me."

"Yes, but àirén you were a child."

"You really never thought about marrying me at all?"

"Ellie, I didn't even think you were an option for someone like me. When you kissed me that first time…" he trailed off, shaking his head. "No one had touched me like that before in my whole life. It made me realize for the first time what I wouldn't have and what I wanted more than anything. It felt as though my heart, my whole body, came awake for you."

She cuddled closer.

"After knowing what that felt like, I hated that I'd ever allowed her to touch me. I was embarrassed that I'd let it happen for so long."

"I understand."

"That is why I could never want her or consider her again. It's why making love to you, being your husband, is the most rewarding thing I've ever experienced. What we have feels like the most precious unexpected gift, Ellie."

"You were lonely. I never imagined you could be. No, to that extent at least. To me, you were this paragon of a man, brave, kind, loving, intelligent, disciplined. Beautiful. Successful. I couldn't fathom you making a bad choice or feeling insecure. I never imagined that you would see yourself as anything other than those things. The way I found out about her made me wonder what kind of base simpleton would turn to someone like that. That thing you said, the bit about 'eating what is before you', I thought it was disgusting."

"Yes, I could tell."

"But you are correct that I've never felt like how you described. I saw you as perfect but I lost sight of you as a person first. I haven't truly seen you as a human being and that is unfair. I should love you as you are instead of as some idol."

"It's alright."

"It is most certainly not alright. I want you to know that I love you as you are, for all that you are. Even when you are stupid."

He brushed her cheek with the back of his fingers.

"I know you do."

"I'm sorry that you were so lonely. I'm going to make sure you never feel that way again."

He chuckled. "And I'm going to make sure you time you spent waiting for me is worth it."

She kissed him, softly at first and then with growing ardor. It had barely been twenty-four hours but it felt as though it had been an age since she'd last kissed him. He pulled her into his lap, wrapping his arms around as much of her as he could before picking her up in his arms and carrying her over to the bed. He set her down and removed the last of his clothing before joining her on the mattress.

She straddled his lap, her shift riding higher on her thighs as her legs spread to accommodate him, but she didn't care. She slid her hands around the back of his neck and kissed him harder, allowing herself to sink into him in a way she hadn't before. She had never felt more certain of him, of them, than in this moment.

She had never believed that, like her, he had set her apart in his mind and heart as something precious and glorious, meant to be not only protected but exalted.

His touch had always brought untold pleasure but even that felt different tonight. Was he touching her in a new way or was she finally able to feel what he'd been saying from the very beginning? His hands were stroking her legs up to cup her bare bottom in his hands. For a moment, she tensed, that old fear flashing in her mind, but then she felt him squeeze it, pulling her closer, and she remembered what he'd said before. How specific he'd been about what he liked about her body, and that part of her body in particular. She wanted to feel his hands on her skin everywhere. There was only one way to give them both what they wanted.

She released his neck and began lifting her shift up her torso. The last thing she expected when his mouth left hers was to feel his hands close around hers, stopping her. Her eyes opened to see him watching her with concern.

"Ellie?"

She shook her head and smiled. "It's alright, I'm not afraid anymore." In one motion she pulled the thin fabric up and over her head and dropped it onto the floor, before she could think herself out of it. His gaze dropped, taking her bare body with rapt interest. She wanted to avoid his expression but she forced herself to look at it. His touch trailed up her arms to her shoulders, lingering there for a moment before closing around her breasts.

She had been waiting for it to happen, but the contact still drew a soft gasp from her. Then his mouth was at her throat, pressing kisses along the line of it as her head fell back. He slipped his arms around her waist, pulling her closer so their bare bodies touched. She pushed against his shoulders, leaning him backwards onto the bed. His hand curled around the back of her neck as he kissed her back harder, his mouth opening wider beneath hers.

Then he flipped her onto her back, his fingers blazing a trail down her body with his mouth following close behind. He teased and coaxed gasp after moan from her, following every undulation of her body until his mouth closed over her sex. Her hips bucked against his mouth in shock, her eyes flying open before the feel of his mouth on her had them falling shut again. She couldn't hold still in the wake of the sensations he compelled from her most sensitive flesh.

His hand pressed down on her stomach, holding her in place, taking his fill until he'd chased her up a peak that left her shuddering helplessly, her hand curled around his. He rained kisses on her thighs as she lay there replete, her muscles twitching occasionally. He moved up her body again, pausing to kiss her stomach and mouth, her breasts, sucking on her nipples, stoking the fire within her yet again.

She reached for him again, pulling his mouth to hers so she could kiss him. He pulled her legs up around his waist and rolled onto his back again, sliding himself inside her fully with one stroke. She braced her hands on the bed and pulled away. Did he mean for them to make love like this? She met his eyes and saw them gazing at her with desire and affection.

"Like this?" she whispered.

"Just like this. Ride me àirén,"

She rolled her hips forward, half braced against his chest, and felt him slide out of her partway, rubbing against every nerve ending within her. Then she rocked forward and he filled her again, hitting that spot inside her that made her nipples furl tighter, as liquid heat flowed through her veins, pooling between her legs. She met his eyes again and he nodded in encouragement.

"Go on and do it, let me see you," He rasped. He wanted this from her; he wanted her to take him. She took a deep breath and continued to move, working her hips, bracing herself on his chest when he began to arch up into her. She clenched down on him involuntarily as she struggled to maintain her balance. She watched his eyes fall shut and his lips part as he moaned, a frown of rapture on his face.

More, she wanted more of that. She wanted to ruin him ever more than she already had, claim him as he had done to her so many years ago with one smile. His hands gripped her thighs, then caressed her bottom, urging her to move faster, to take him deeper, to grind against him harder even as his back arched up. She leaned down and kissed him, the angle shifting his length within her to rub even harder against the spot that sent her wild every time. He clung to her, stroking her body in long sweeps of his hands as they gasped and groaned against their mouths.

The pressure was building inside her, promising and elusive at first but then more urgent, driving her further as rapture overtook her mind and body. Felt his hands at her hips hard and uncompromising as his hips bucked up into her, his shuddering groan echoing after her cry in the candlelit room.

EPILOGUE

Lodge Hall, Cumbria,
Late April, 1860

"T HEO, GO GET jiùfù!"

That sounded like Thomas, Basil and Ada's eldest son.

"No! You go get him, Ellie."

"Umm," the uncertainty in the voice of Basil and Ada's eldest told Elodia what was coming next. "Gigi, go get your diē."

"Ok!" Giselle said before the door to the bedroom opened wider.

Elodia turned her face into Richard's chest, fighting back a smile. Their youngest daughter was a fearless little thing. Half of that was her personality and the other half was how effectively she'd placed her father under her tiny thumb.

She and Richard were hosting a full house this spring. Regina and Leo were in London, using the season to push more legislative change through parliament along with her father, but their four children and Naomi were staying at Lodge Hall with them. Basil and Ada were also staying with their two children. Of course, this meant that there were five adults to manage around ten children, three of which were notorious for showing up in their parents' bedrooms before dawn. Just like their Aunt Ada.

There was a soft patter of feet before Giselle began tugging on Richard's arm.

"Diē," her little voice came. Richard's body jerked back and forth but he didn't move. Elodia kept her eyes closed and her face down. If she didn't move, she could likely get away with not having to leave her warm bed and her soft covers.

Richard grumbled and sighed. Then Elodia heard a muffled squeak and a small body ended up wedged between her and her husband. Giselle squirmed, trying to get her father's attention.

"Diē," she whispered.

"What is it, Zhenlin?" he mumbled. He only ever referred to her by her Chinese name, especially at home.

"Come look!" she insisted.

"No."

"Come!" she whined.

"Where am I going?"

"The garden."

He groaned. "Absolutely not."

"Diē, the tree."

The tree?

"Which tree?"

"The pes-mon tree."

"What's wrong with it?" He sounded more awake now.

"It's spotted."

Richard untangled his limbs from Elodia and sat up. "What do you mean by that?"

"Flowers, diē, there are hundreds of them," their eldest, Alexander, spoke up.

Elodia sat up at that, her eyes wide. They had waited years for a sign that the trees would be more than decorative. A failed experiment. Richard shot her a playful glare. "Oh, you're awake now, are you?"

She rolled her eyes and slid out of the bed in her nightgown. "Go on out, children, we'll join you in a moment." She watched the two eldest, Alexander and Emmeline, usher the younger ones out to the hall before closing the door behind them.

"Trust Basil and Ada to leave them all to us," he grumbled, sliding out of the bed in his loose linen drawers.

"You don't know that they aren't awake."

He gave her a pointed look, "Believe me, if they are, we wouldn't know it."

She turned to her husband. "Are you alright?"

"I don't know," he replied.

"Do you think they are mistaken?" she asked, pulling on her heavy house robe and sliding her feet into her slippers.

"I don't think so, flowers are flowers after all." He pulled on his trousers and a shirt before reaching for his own robe.

He didn't look at her even when he was finished dressing. If she knew her husband as well as she believed she did, he was trying desperately to keep his emotions under control. He paused at the door and held out his hand for her. She strode forward and took it, meeting his silent request for support. His hands were cold, which was unusual for him. He closed his eyes and took a few deep breaths, before lifting his head, opening his eyes and leaving their bedroom hand in hand. They were greeted by a crowd of children, all within the ages of eight and four dressed in their nightwear.

"All right, let's go," Richard said. Their youngest, Gigi, held up her hands in the universal request to be picked up and he automatically bent over to scoop her up into his arms.

It was a wonder the girl ever learned to walk at all.

That was when Elodia noticed her dirty feet. Except there wasn't just dirt there, there were dried leaves as well.

"Miss Gigi, where are your shoes?" she asked. Richard looked down and his hand closed around her tiny, no doubt ice cold foot.

"Did you go outside without your shoes again?" he asked. She blinked up at him with her wide brown eyes, no doubt considering the merits of lying. She wasn't malicious, but she was proving to be an 'act first and see if forgiveness is strictly necessary' sort of person.

"They were leaving me behind," she whined. Elodia twisted her mouth against a smile. Whenever her little girl knew her answer was not going to do her any favors, she answered with the justification.

"That is not what I asked."

"They wouldn't wait for me."

"Irrelevant. You do not leave your room without your house slippers, let alone the house, am I understood?"

She frowned, her little cupid bow mouth twisting in frustration.

"Dearest, what if you caught a chill?" Elodia asked, stroking her small back. She grumbled and laid her head on Richard's shoulder.

"What if you were bitten by a snake or a rat?" Richard asked, a scheming glint in his eyes. "What if you stepped on a rusty nail and we had to cut off this adorable little foot?"

Her head came up and her eyes were wide with alarm. "Chop off my foot?" She didn't like the sound of that at all.

"Oh yes."

"Then you'd need a peg leg, Gigi," Alexander joked with a glint in his eye too much like his father.

"You'll sound like the La diablesse when you walk," Emmeline added.

She whimpered and buried her face in his shoulder again, and Elodia frowned at her eldest. He opened his mouth to defend himself, but in the end pursed his lips and faced forward as they continued the trek down to the garden.

"I don't want to be like the la diabesse," she mumbled, fumbling the name of the mythological creature.

Richard fought back a smile and nodded. "Neither do I, that is why the rule is in place, my love."

"But...but—"

"Your brother will wait for you from now on, won't you, Ningkai?" Richard asked.

Elodia saw Alex roll his eyes, "Yes fùqīn," he replied. "Brat,"

Giselle's head came up, her eyes flashing with outrage. "Di—"

"You scored your point, Gigi. Let it go now."

The little girl pouted again, but she pressed her face into her father's neck while Richard fought valiantly against a laugh. The children were always either inseparable or at each other's throats. Alex had adored his baby sister from the moment she was born, but the little girl was at her core a bossy bit of business who ultimately knew exactly how adorable she was.

"Diē, am I a brat?" her little voice came, clearly attempting a different tactic.

"Yes," Richard replied flatly.

"Really?"

"Yes. But we still love you. You are our brat."

That seemed to placate her for the time being. Elodia pulled him towards her and slid her arms around his shoulders as they finally reached the back door to the gardens.

It was cold in the garden. Spring was still lingering in the damp morning air. Beside the greenhouse, there were a patch of trees. They started forward, the children close behind, and Elodia saw it. Hundreds of yellow flowers dotted the branches of two rows of trees, three rows deep. On the right they were short and close to the branch shaped like stars, but on the left they were forming clusters like upside down pots.

Proof of life. Proof that five years of consistent and deliberate care hadn't gone to waste. Life had taken root despite all odds and would continue a tradition.

Elodia glanced at Richard and saw the water glistening in the corner of his eyes. She hooked her arms around his and he let out a shuddering breath. "Ellie," he whispered.

"I see them," she replied, pressing a kiss to his arm.

"Jiùfù, mŭ qīn says that it takes these trees five years to flower," Emmeline said.

"That's true."

"Does this mean we get persimmons this year?" Theo, Regina and Leo's first son asked. He and his twin brother Galen were peering up at the trees in fascination.

Richard shook his head, "No, Theo. They have to bloom twice before they give fruit. Five to flower, seven to bear fruit."

"So we have to wait another seven years?" Theodosia asked.

"No, silly, it'll be the year after next. Right fùqīn?" Alex asked.

"Yes, that's correct."

"That's still a long time to wait," Galen mumbled.

"Diē, I'm cold," Gigi whimpered.

"Ningkai, will you take your mèimei inside?"

"Yes fùqīn," he said, accepting the sleepy bundle into his arms while she curled around him with perfect trust.

"All of you should go in now. Don't catch a cold."

"Yes, go wake up your parents, Zhenfu," Richard called out. Emmeline, as she was otherwise known, grinned and ran back to the house.

"Still a little prankster," Elodia commented, sliding her arm around his waist.

"Mmmm,"

"Well done." She gave him a small squeeze. "You waited a long time for this confirmation."

"We aren't there yet. As Alex said, it will take two more years before we know for certain."

"True, but I have yet to see you fail at something you set your mind to," she replied.

"Likewise," he replied, giving her a sidelong glance.

"Are you implying something about me?" she asked.

"What's the use of implying?" he teased. "I got my orchard, I got my family at long last."

"Mmmm, and I got you."

"We got each other." He gestured to the male and female trees, planted side by side to pollinate the other. "Like these, one doesn't work without the other."

Et Fin

About the Author

Born in the tropical paradise of Trinidad and Tobago, Addy Du Lac moved to the US with her mother at the age of twelve. She began writing historical romance while she received a double major in History and Creative Writing from the University of South Florida. She enjoys writing books with diverse characters and steamy happy endings. When she isn't plotting her next series, she enjoys watching movies and Asian Dramas, traveling, and tempting her fate with new recipes.

Addy Du Lac lives in Florida with an eclectic library of books and a carefully curated wall of beautiful men.